The Strong Weet Society

Also by DH Parsons

THE 60S
Life ain't Nothin' but a Slow Jazz Dance

1967 San Francisco:
      My Romance with the Summer of Love

The Muse: Coming of Age in 1968

LIFESTYLE AND INSPIRATIONAL
Eat Yoga!

Book of Din

All available on Amazon

The Diary

of **Mary Bliss Parsons**

Volume 1

The
Strong Weet Society

D H Parsons

BLISS-PARSON'S

BP

PUBLISHING

The Strong Weet Society

This book was originally published in 2011 as *The Strong Witch Society*. This edition contains considerably more material and deeper insights than the previous version and more acuratly expresses the author's views and intent.

Bliss-Parsons Institute, founded by DH Parsons, is devoted to the exploration and expression of Truth, with the intent to guide as many people as possible toward Right Living and the healing of spirit, soul, and body.

ISBN: 978-1-948553-12-4
Library of Congress Control Number: 2020911052

Contents

Introduction

My Grandmother, the Witch?

On March 2, 1675, not long before the infamous Salem Witch frenzy of 1692, Mary Bliss Parsons was formally indicted in Boston, Massachusetts, for crimes of witchcraft. Mary's subsequent trial, her incarceration, and her experiences with not only the criminal justice system at the time but with her family and her peers were a collective ordeal far beyond anything the contemporary mind can conjure.

Eventually, Mary was acquitted of all charges and released to the custody of her husband, Joseph, who was a prominent citizen of Northampton, Massachusetts. Some said that it was her husband's prominence and wealth that bought Mary's freedom. In actuality, very few believed in her innocence. To further complicate things, even though her trial records state that she denied being a witch, in fact, she never did. She never professed to be a witch, either. When questioned, she merely smiled and said to the court, "Because I am not of this world, does not make me a witch. Do not make such a simple assumption." All pleas for leniency and/or innocence were entered into court records by Joseph, not by Mary herself.

Following her acquittal, the Parsons family prospered in the community, bouncing back and forth between Springfield and Northampton, Massachusetts. Rumors of Mary's involvement in witchcraft persisted throughout the years — not because of anything Mary was doing, but because of the simple minds of those who wished for her to be something they could find fault with. After Joseph died in 1683, Mary isolated herself in her home, fearing that any interaction with the townsfolk would bring about more accusation, incarceration, and even execution.

1

Regardless of what some accounts claim, Mary lived for years in virtual exile from the "normal" citizens of the community. During those years, there developed around her the false reputation of a person to be avoided at all costs. Any mysterious occurrence in town, any mishap on any farm, any illness or death was attributed to Mary Bliss Parsons, the "Witch Woman" at the edge of town. And so she lived out the remainder of her life until her own death in 1712, at the age of eighty-five.

Bits and pieces of Mary's story appear throughout the pages of history books — a paragraph here, a chapter there — but only now, with the release of *The Strong Weet Society: The Diary of Mary Bliss Parsons*, have the intimate and incredible truths been allowed presentation in their entirety. Mary's own experiences would never have come to light were it not for a freak of Nature, which opened a channel of communication between Mary and her ninth great-grandson.

My name is DH (Bliss) Parsons. I am a former school administrator, an author, a church pastor, an artist, a history teacher, and the founder of The Bliss-Parsons Institute. Mary Bliss Parsons is my ninth great-grandmother. The entries that follow, as fantastic as they may seem, are true. Anyone interested in the life and times of Mary Bliss-Parsons can look up her name on the internet and find many entries. If you do, please remember that a great deal of the information you will find is incomplete, much having been lost over time. However, this book will not only fill in the blanks, but it will also bring you into close proximity with the woman herself. Mary Bliss Parsons has an essential message for this world at this time, and it is all revealed in the following pages. We must all take Mary seriously.

22 June

How It Began

On June 22, while lounging in my living room, I glanced out the front window at just the right moment, and BAM—I was blinded by a globe of light the size of a Volkswagen, hovering in the air about twenty feet above the street. The light appeared to be spherical, with the intensity of a bolt of lightning, but it wasn't a "bolt," it was perfectly round like a giant silver beach ball. Oddly enough, just two days earlier, I'd been reading an article in a science journal about a rare phenomenon called ball lightning. I thought at the time what a treat it would be to see such a thing, but I never thought I ever would. Synchronicity?

I didn't just see it; I *felt* it! It was more than just "out there" over the street. The bright flash didn't merely illuminate the surrounding landscape; it *became* a part of everything around it, momentarily fusing trees and pavement, rocks and flowers, all together in one blazing display of pure, explosive light.

It was an astonishing moment, being in just the right place at just the right time. What are the odds of witnessing such a spectacle in one's lifetime? And how interesting that it would happen just a couple of days after I'd been reading about it. The coincidence added to my excitement, but that wasn't the end of the story. I didn't know it then, of course, but the ball lightning was the catalyst for an extraordinary journey I was about to begin—a journey that would test the limits of my imagination.

I should have suspected something unusual at the time, because even after my vision recovered from the brightness of the flash, I just sat there on the couch staring out the window, spacing out. Ordinarily, I would never have done that, but there I sat, motionless, for the longest time. I couldn't move my arms, I couldn't blink my eyes. In fact, even though my eyes were wide open, it was as if they were closed, and my mind was drifting somewhere far out into deep space. I was totally unaware of anything in the room.

I don't know how long I sat there staring into nothingness, but I do remember that a parade of memories rushed through my head almost faster than I could sort them all out. Images of past experiences paraded through my mind—like the old cliché of seeing your entire life flash before your eyes. Strangely, they all had something to do with Nature, like the first time I saw a bald Eagle in flight, my trip to the California Redwoods, the tornado whirling over my childhood home in Tulsa, my first ice storm in Missouri, and wild Buffalo grazing on the Oklahoma plains. But none of those could compare to the ball lightning. That wasn't just another experience.

I now know, of course, the real reason why the ball lightning appeared to me as it did. While most folks thought it was just another typical storm on another regular day, it was far more than that. And while everyone else in town was sitting around reading the newspaper wishing the thunder would just go away, I was literally interacting with the storm. Even now as I write these words, I can feel the intense heat bursting outward from that incredible ball of energy, passing through my closed window as if the glass wasn't there, entering my chest, traveling right through me, exiting my body in the back, and leaving me feeling somehow changed on a deeper level, as if my own molecular structure had been rearranged at the subatomic level.

A cleansing had occurred within me, something Spiritual had happened. While I didn't know it, I was being initiated by a supernatural fire, installed, if you will, by that fire, as the leader of a long-forgotten, incredibly powerful society of … but this will all be clarified in the pages of this Diary.

All in all, it was a morning to remember. What followed only a few hours later, though, was even further beyond belief. The wonderment continued into the evening when I came face to face with another phenomenon far more inexplicable, something I'd never dreamed possible.

***

Later that evening, as I lay in my bed reading a book, I thought I heard a voice. It seemed to come from about two or three feet in front of me, from out of nowhere.

Of course, it startled me. I'd assumed that I was alone in the house except for my little black poodle, Natalie, so my first thought was that it wasn't a voice I had heard, but Natalie getting into something. But a quick glance to my left revealed Natalie, sound asleep on the floor by my bed.

If it wasn't Natalie, and it wasn't me, there had to be some other logical explanation for this voice out of nowhere. I'd probably heard a dinner plate or a piece of silverware shifting around in the dish drainer. The kitchen is just down the hall from my bed, and it wouldn't have been the first time I'd washed dishes and left them perched precariously. So, I shrugged my shoulders and went back to my book, dismissing the voice as having a perfectly mundane explanation.

But then I heard the voice again, as clear as a bell.

I would speak with you.

I'm sure that's what it said. I couldn't believe it! It was one of those times everyone's had when we hear something, but know it's impossible to have heard it, so we just chalk it up to the wind or anything that would make more sense.

But I heard it twice.

I would speak with you.

I couldn't ignore it. Someone was in my room!

I leaped out of bed, sending Natalie scurrying out of the room as if she were being chased by a freight train. Looking for something to defend myself with, I reached down under the bed where I keep my shoes. All I could think to do was to throw a shoe at the intruder. So, I grabbed the closest shoe, took a defensive stance, and stood quivering in my bare feet, not failing to take note of the fact that Natalie was nowhere to be found. So much for man's best friend.

"Who's there?" I stuttered.

Silence.

"Who's there?" I demanded.

More silence.

"Who's there?" I asked politely, not knowing who or what I was dealing with.

And this is where the story begins. Please remember that what you are about to read is true. The following transcript of Diary entries is very nearly word for word as I originally wrote them during my actual experiences with Mary.

23 June

Her Diary Begins

Here I sit under the Linden tree in my back yard, writing, writing, writing, dripping sweat down onto the paper, and smearing the words altogether. I wish I had a dollar for every sweaty word I've smeared down onto the pages of my personal journal over the past forty years. Geez, have I been writing in this thing for forty years? Good grief.

Man, it's hot! I really ought to be inside with the air conditioner blasting full in my face, but I can't be in there right now. Not after last night. I need to be out here under this beautiful tree because this is where I always come when my mind is troubled or when my world is spinning just a little off tilt due to some silly thing I've gotten myself into. This is where I always end up when something slams me hard in my gut, something out of the norm — for my little universe, that is. Sitting under this tree always clears my head. But I don't know how I'm going to find any words to write about what happened last night. Still, I feel like that's why I came out here — like I'm being compelled to make a record of the crazy night I just experienced.

So, here it goes. I heard a voice. I swear it. I heard a very distinct, very feminine, melodious voice. And it came out of nowhere. I guess I heard it two times:

I would speak with you. I would speak with you.

That's all the voice said. But there was nobody there! I was lying in my bed reading a book, minding my own business when the voice came, but there was nobody in the room with me — well, the poodle, but she can't talk. It really shook me; I didn't know what to do about it. I tried talking with her — the voice — this woman. I asked her who she was, but she wouldn't answer back. I knew

7

I hadn't imagined it, so I began a frantic search of the room to see if somebody was hiding under the bed or in the closet. I even looked behind the door. Zilch.

I didn't know what else to do, so I lay back down on the bed and finally drifted off into a nervous, sweaty sleep. Then I started dreaming. There was a strangely familiar woman who popped in and out of my mind all night long. She was standing in a primeval forest area, and I was there with her. I mean, I was really there! It didn't seem like a dream at all.

I was standing in a woodland space filled with large, deep green trees. I remember actually wondering to myself if they were Oaks or Elms or even Lindens, like the one I'm sitting under right now. For some reason, it seemed to be important that I identify their particular species, but I didn't have a clue which tree was which. Even in my dreams, the sum total of everything I know about trees wouldn't amount to much.

But it was a lovely sight. A little brook ran by just a few feet away from the trees. The sound of trickling water was distinct and pleasant. In fact, it surprised me at first because I couldn't recall having heard the sound of anything in my dreams before. Occasionally as I surveyed this dreamy landscape, I'd catch a glimpse of sunlight reflected off the surface of the little stream.

Each moment of the dream was like a single frame in a reel of film, or like some forgotten moment somewhere in time. So colorful, so idyllic. I was enchanted. I can scarcely find the words to describe the sensation. It was all so perfect as if it had fallen off the canvas of a Maxfield Parrish painting.

The woman was walking on a grassy slope that led down from the trees to the water's edge. She seemed familiar to me, and I felt that I should know her by name.

Her long, pale blue dress floated about her like a soft mist, and she walked so gracefully that it was evident that her feet were not touching the ground. She glided down the slope in slow motion, more like a butterfly than a human, her feet only a few inches from the ground.

When she came to the edge of the brook, the woman glanced up at me. It was as if I were there with her, in that place, standing on the opposite side of the brook. It was all so real. She was looking straight into my eyes. In fact, my eyes were so locked on hers that I couldn't have moved my gaze away if my life depended upon it.

We stood there motionless, her face turning slowly in my direction like I was zooming in on her through the lens of a camera. Then her lips began to move, and words came floating toward me. Not just the sound of her voice, but the visual imprint of letters coming toward me on some wavy line with single-file letters that grouped into words and flowed through my head one at a time until the sentence was complete.

I would speak with you.

I would speak with you.

I would speak with you.

The dream was repeated all night long, and the familiar-looking woman appeared and disappeared over and over again. It was the most vivid dream I have ever ha . . . 'e. I felt as if I was awake, but I knew I was his morning, I knew I had been sleeping. I earness of that woman's face. I could sense om her skin. I could feel the warmth of ifted toward me and gently made con- ace. I could feel every word she spoke to me. We were that close.

I was paralyzed, captivated by the intensity of her deep, gray-blue eyes. They seemed to pull me to her as if I were caught in a whirlpool.

I believe I was sensing her more than I was actually seeing her. She was beautiful. No, not merely beautiful — she was stunning. Everything about her was breathtakingly beautiful. Her dark hair was almost black at first glance, but when she turned her head a bit, the sun's rays revealed a deep red glow that highlighted the beauty of her pale, rose-tinted, almost white skin.

Then the voice came again, awakening me from my dream!

I would speak with you.

***

At one point during the night, after thoroughly searching my room and coming up with nothing, I went into the bathroom, where I splashed cold water onto my face. I stood in front of the mirror, examining the odd emotions welling up inside of me. I wasn't afraid, but I was disturbed. What was happening to me? Was it something I ate for dinner, or was I losing my mind?

Once again, I went back to bed, and within moments, I was asleep. But wait a minute. That doesn't make sense. As I look back from the comfort of this garden chair, feeling the hot wind striking against my cheeks in the here and the now, it seems odd that I would be able to fall asleep so quickly after such an encounter with whatever she — or it — was.

What the heck went on last night? How do I write about it? I'm trying to think of words that might come close to describing something that is far beyond my ability to express. Was this really a dream? How can I even be if I went to sleep—or if I was transported somewhere else? Like some form of astral travel. That's what it seems like now. Did I really wake up and get out of bed? Did I really go into the bathroom and splash my face with water? The entire night seems to both exist and not exist at the same time. Should I be afraid? I'm not. In fact, I'm entirely at ease. Something deep within me tells me this isn't a thing to fear. No, it's a familiar thing. Just like the woman is familiar to me.

And then there's the promise she gave me just before I finally did wake up this morning—more words that came drifting out of her mouth and into my mind.

Do not fear. Never fear me, for I am part of you.

What in the world does that mean?

***

I remember every word she spoke to me last night as if I'd been fully awake and having a conversation with some long-lost friend I hadn't seen in years. I can even see those words forming in my mind as I sit here now. It's as if they have been indelibly burned into my Spirit.

Do not fear... Do not fear...

My hand is writing them automatically as—But wait! Something's happening inside my head! New words are forming, and I feel compelled to write them. My hand is tightening its grip on the pen and I... can't... control...

I am here, Din. I am with you.

These aren't the words from last night. Am I still asleep? These are new words. But how is that possible? I'm not asleep. Or am I? Am I just dreaming that I'm sitting in my garden, or am I really here? Here? Am I really writing, or am I just dreaming that I'm writing?

I am Mary Bliss Parsons, your great grandmother many times removed, and I would speak with you.

I'm awake. I know I am. This can't be happening! I can see her words appear in my mind as if on a computer screen. I can see them now as I sit here in the garden with my eyes wide open. Or at least I think my eyes are wide open. How is this happening?

You are the one I have awakened in. You are the one who has accepted me. You must hear me, and you must respond.

I must be delirious. The garden is hot. The sun is reflecting brightly off the orange marigolds next to the cucumber vines. It's blinding me. My head is spinning. The colors are so vivid. I'm sweating profusely, and my sweat is trickling down into my eyes, stinging them sharply. Does this pain prove I'm really awake?

But how can I be awake? How can I be writing down a conversation between my own thoughts and … Mary Bliss Parsons? Yes, I did have a great grandmother named Mary Bliss Parsons. Several years ago, I traced my genealogy back a few hundred years. Mary appears in those records during the 1600s. But that's at least nine or ten generations ago. I remember her name distinctly because the record states she was tried for witchcraft before the infamous Salem Witch Trial era. That fact always impressed me, but why is her name popping up now? I haven't thought about her in years. And where are these words coming from?

I will come to you often and in many forms. I will be a word, a thought, a sound, a smell. You will feel my presence at all times, for I cannot be separated from you.

Sometimes it takes a while to really wake up from a dream. Is that what's going on here? But her words aren't going away.

I will speak to you in your mind, and you will know the difference between your thoughts and mine. You will know.

Mary? Are you really here? Mary? Okay, I'll play along. Talk to me. Either make me believe this or wake me up!

I am here. I can be nowhere else but here, and I will be speaking with you often. It is your task to become more aware of my presence within you.

If you really are here, Mary, I have no idea what you're talking about. And I really don't think you are here. I think I'm crazy! I think something happened in my sleep last night, and I went off the deep end.

Please, concentrate on my words.

Incredible, her voice is crystal clear. She's here somewhere in this garden, but I'm looking around, and I can't find her. There has to be an explanation for this. My neighbors have their TV up too loud or—what's the alternative? A ghost? Some ethereal specter floating around somewhere? Baloney.

I am with you, My Dear.

This is uncanny. Is there truly someone here? How is this possible? Are you really . . . Mary? And why am I writing this? Are you controlling my hand? Do you want me to write all this down? What—?

You must write everything, for there must be a record of what transpires between us. That is my purpose in revealing myself. You must record as much as you can. Our eternity depends upon you being my hands, for I cannot hold pen to paper. You are to be my witness.

No way! Have I been taken over by some dark spirit? Is this what they call *possession*? Am I possessed? Am I experiencing some sort of automatic writing command at the whim of some poor, disembodied soul? What's going on here?

You are not possessed, and I am not a demon. I am in truth, Mary, your great-grandmother, and I have been with you for these many years. It was only last night after the ball lightning thinned the veil that my mental essence was able to join with your own. We have been allowed to awaken within each other to become one.

This is very difficult for me to believe, but I can see my own hand holding the pen that writes these words that are not coming from me.

Fear not, Grandson, for it was destined that it be we two who would make this one that we now are. Others have come before you, but I could not join with them.

What others? What are you talking about? Good grief, I'm talking to myself!

Your father and his father and his father before him, all the way back through the years until we reach my own dear husband, Joseph. One wonderful night when Joseph and I came together in love, our coupling produced a son. With that son, a human lineage began. Your lineage, Sweet One. I have tried to awaken my Spirit within the Spirits of your fathers before you, but have failed until now.

I still don't have a clue what you're talking about or what I'm sensing you're talking about if you're talking at all … or if I'm sensing at all …

It is all about sensing. You carry within you all of the memories of all your ancestors, as did your fathers in the past. I have tried to bring life to those memories in every father from Joseph down to you, but the veil was too dark and too thick. My power was too weak at the time. But the lightning has awakened the memories!

You'll forgive me if I tell you this is just a little bit unsettling, and I'm more than just a little bit confused.

Your mind contains all of the memories of everyone who has come before you in your family line. As time passes, you will be able to sense these memories in your heart as if they were your very own.

Are you talking about genetic memory? Genes, DNA, and all that?

Those are the labels your culture uses to describe something

*far more complicated than you can understand at this time,
but they will serve us for the moment.*

I'm not sure I——

*All your life, you have carried me inside you. I have been a
silent witness to everything you have ever experienced from
your birth to this day.*

You're kidding.

*I am incapable of speaking anything but Truth. I have been
everywhere with you. I have seen everything you have seen.*

But you're dead!

*My physical body died centuries ago, but my Spirit has
been alive forever. A small part of me has been present in all
your fathers throughout the ages. But in you, Grandson, I
have found completion. The higher energies, which activate
and sustain all things, have had their way with us.*

Higher energies?

*God's ways are mysterious, His energies are numerous,
and far more varied than humans know them to be. You
will learn more as we go forward.*

And you were always there? You've been everywhere
I've been? You've seen everything I've seen?

*Somewhere within me, I carry all the knowledge you have
collected throughout the years. Every book you have ever
read, every problem you have solved, every notion you have
entertained, all of these are mine as well, but they will be
slow in their revelation.*

What do you mean?

*The more we commune with each other, the sooner and
more complete will be your awakening. It is the commu-
nion that stimulates the shared memories. In the beginning,
however, there must be an occasional separation. My consciousness, which is housed within your subconscious, must
draw back from time to time. In these early stages of communication, the waves of energy, which unite us in our thought,*

will ebb and flow like the ocean tides ebb and flow.

My dear grandmother, you seem to know far more than I do about whatever it is that's going on.

May I suggest you call me Mary, and I will call you Din, for it is the name I have known you by since you were born.

My mother calls me Din!

I have already determined the goodness of your mother. She has a loving heart for all creatures, especially the little birds.

Why, yes, she does. My mother is a very special woman.

How very like her you are, Dear Din. I learned much about her as I was contained within her womb during the time she carried you.

You mean ... even in my mother's womb?

I have experienced many wombs throughout the centuries.

This is incredible.

It is not incredible at all. It is only that your contemporaries have not yet achieved this state of understanding. One day they will, and such concepts as these will be entirely credible. But we will touch on that later. Now my frequency is growing weak. I am afraid the tide is ebbing, and I must take time for rest. Do not be concerned when I leave you, for I will not travel far.

But, Mary, I have so many questions!

I must go. It is a law. All of your questions will be answered in time.

***

And she's gone. Just like that. I think. Mary? Are you gone, Mary? But where does she go? Wait a minute. This is crazy. I'm going to wake up in a minute and find myself back in bed, and this whole Mary Bliss Parsons thing is gonna disappear! I'll wake up knowing it's all been one big dream ... or nightmare.

But what if it's true? I'm still sitting here in the garden.

I'm still writing. Why is that? I feel compelled to write, even now, after she's gone to wherever it is she needed to go. Ebbing? Flowing? What did she mean by all that? What kind of energy are we talking about here that can bring back to life a person who has been dead for over three hundred years? And just exactly where is it that Mary goes when she ebbs? And, more importantly, how will I know when she's going to flow back into my head?

Hello? Mary? Hello? Hello, me! Hello, Din! Din? How odd that she would choose that name. It's such a personal, family name. None of my friends have ever called me that. I've always just been *DH*. But what am I talking about? This whole thing is odd. And where do I go from here? Do I pinch myself and wake up, or do I just go with the flow ... and the ebb?

For cryin' out loud! There's really no reason to believe I'm asleep. I don't feel like I'm asleep. And everything looks like it should if I were awake. The garden seems real enough. My chair feels real. And if this is a dream, it isn't like any other dream I've ever had. Look at all that color out there. Bright yellow crookneck squash, purple eggplants you can see your reflection in — I don't usually have such vivid dreams. My dreams are generally short, sweet, and to the point, then I wake up and forget about them. This Mary thing is way too real, but —

Okay, there's one way to find out if I'm awake. I'll slowly put down my paper and pen, I'll rise up out of this chair, and I'll walk around in the heat of the sun for a few minutes. Then I'll go inside the house and get me a big glass of iced tea and pour it all over the top of my head! That ought to do it. Proof positive that I'm fully awake. But if I don't wake up, if I just get wet, it will also prove that Mary is everything she claims to be. Then what? What if Mary's on the level? I'm not sure I want to find out.

25 June

What Really Happened—Then and Now

It's been four days since the ball lightning incident and my encounter with Mary, and I'm a nervous wreck. I can't think of anyone or anything else but her. Could it be that Mary really was a witch? A *real* witch? Could it be that she's everything she presented herself as being—some sort of genetic energy source lying dormant inside her grandkids for so many years, then, *poof*, here she is?

If that's the case, then somehow she's been able to find a way to tap into the supernatural time continuum that governs both life and death. She's cast a spell or something, and she's come back to life, or at least her mind is fully functional. But what the heck's going on here? Is it magic? It's gotta be magic! What other explanation is there? Good grief, is she really living up there in my head, or in my genes, playing around with my DNA?

I've spent a lot of time with my books, looking for information on witchcraft and the supernatural, trying to find anything that might offer some explanation about how Mary and I are able to do whatever it is that we're doing. I've always been interested in amazing and fascinating things. It's been a lifelong pursuit, and I've collected quite a library on those subjects—even the Bible is filled with such things. I've managed to read enough of those books to know that there is such a thing as extraordinary knowledge that lies beneath the surface of the daily mundane stuff of life and that it is not easily recognized or understood. If this Mary stuff doesn't fall into that category, I don't know what does.

I did find several books addressing various forms of ancestral communication and the like, so there appears to be some valid research in this area. Several times in the Bible, we find this or that prophet or apostle speaking to someone from the past, or someone who was speaking from the "Other Side." I even found a couple of authors who mentioned the possibility that a person's DNA holds genetic memory. Big problem, though—these guys didn't explain how an ancestor could wake up inside someone's head and begin a relationship.

Even so, I can't deny what is happening to me. I feel a difference within me since Mary made herself known to me. I can't put my finger on what it is, but something's changed. I have thoughts and compulsions that I've never had before. Even now, I feel like I *need* to be writing in this diary. It's more than just an urge of the moment; it's something I know I need to be doing. I don't just *want* to write, I *have* to write. I don't think I have a choice. It's as if something is coming alive inside me. Some sweet energy ... yes, sweet. Sweet is the right word for it. A comforting, warm, sweet feeling that fills my head and my chest and radiates out into my arms and hands. And when the feeling gets into my hands, my brain seems to connect with it, and I feel the compulsion to write. Is this Mary's doing? Is this how I'll know when Mary wishes to communicate with me? Is it this sweet tingle I'm feeling right now? Does she just, sort of, take over my head and my hands, and there you have it? Then what? Is this what they call possession? Do I just start writing down her words instead of my own? Am I to become the ghostwriter for her diary instead of my own? The Diary of Mary Bliss Parsons—it has a nice ring to it. But possession? I don't like that word.

Here's another good question: how do I know these thoughts, and these words are from her? Why not some specter or some demon? Isn't that what possession is all about? Look at *Rosemary's Baby* or *The Exorcist*. Yipes! But those weren't witch things, those were Satan things. And from everything I've read, the consensus seems to be that witches don't even believe in the existence of Satan. So, if Mary is a true witch, she can't be hooked up with him. Can she? I'd probably know that, wouldn't I? I think I'd know if a satanic witch had been running around in my head all these years. I'd have some sort of clue, wouldn't I? I mean, I am a pastor. I study the Bible and try to do what I can do to be right with God. I'm not even sure what to believe about the old Devil guy myself.

I do believe that there's some sort of malevolent force at play on this planet—at least where human beings are concerned—because we get ourselves into so much trouble all the time. But I have to admit that I'm pretty confused about the Satan thing. The Bible isn't really clear about it. He's a fallen Angel, and he's against everything Jesus says and does, and even though he's already defeated, he's still very active in this world. But then Jesus is going to toss him into the pit in the end—whenever that is. It's all a bit complicated. All I know for sure is that if Jesus is against him, so am I.

Hmm ... I wonder if Mary believed in Satan, the Devil, old Beelzebub during her time? Apparently, her contemporaries did. That's what the whole Salem debacle was all about, wasn't it? Witches were hung from trees because of their alleged association with Satan. But was Mary in cahoots with him? Somehow, I don't think that she was. I sense that she was a *good* person with great strength of character—an independent thinker who wouldn't buy into something just because everyone else was buying into it. In fact, I'll bet it's her independent thinking that got her into hot water in the first place.

But enough of that. Something else even more bizarre than fuzzy warm feelings and compulsions to worry about the devil has been moving around inside me. Over the past few days, Mary has also been allowing me to witness brief glimpses into her own Being. At least, that's what I believe to be happening. I keep getting these little scrapbook photos from Mary's life without warning. I'll be sitting in a restaurant, or driving my car, or walking down the street, and these split-second freeze-frame moments in time that are not of my time appear in my head. They aren't there long enough to cause me to trip over anything or slam my car into anything, but they happen. They just happen. Quick — then they're gone.

Subliminal advertising — that's what it reminds me of. Like you're watching *I Love Lucy* or something, and without your knowledge, the sponsor is flashing those dastardly subliminal messages during the program. BUY A BUICK! That's how these Mary moments pop into my mind. But they aren't like anything I've ever seen before. They don't seem natural or contemporary in any way. They're different. More like photographs from another era — before photography was invented!

Each image is accompanied by emotion. Mary seems to be allowing me to feel what she felt during the very moment she's showing me. It's as if I'm standing right there beside her, or I may even *be* her! That's it! I think I *become* Mary for the time it takes to experience one of these subliminal impressions.

So far, the images have been quite pleasant: a flower meadow and the side yard of a small, crudely built, but comfy house. A line of rough, brown rope strung with freshly washed clothes and a black kettle suspended over crackling flames occupied the yard. I swear I could smell the simmering contents of the pot — some sort of stew. The most intriguing of all the images was also the one that froze my mind for the longest time, possibly for a full minute. It was an outdoor scene, sometime around dusk, just after the sun had gone down. Although it was getting dark, I could make out the details as vividly as if it were in full sunlight.

I'll try to describe it as best as I can. I feel that's what Mary wants me to do, but it won't be easy. How can I describe something so intensely wonderful? And I use the word, wonderful, on purpose because this entire experience goes way beyond the mundane, falling about halfway between the fantastic and amazing. I suppose that's just about where wonderful ought to be.

So here goes. I saw a circular clearing, thirty feet or so in diameter, in a wooded area not too far behind the same rough-hewn house that had appeared in the other images. I sensed this to be Mary's house — it had to be — and these had to be Mary's woods. I could feel her presence in everything around me. It all seemed so familiar as if I had been with her in that same setting before. But I wasn't just casually viewing a photo in a scrapbook; I *was* there. I could smell the scent of dusty Pine as the gentle breeze sifted through the branches of the trees, and I could feel that same breeze brushing against my face as I stood staring into the center of the clearing.

I could hear the woodland creatures begin their evening serenade to the full moon, which was visible in the twilight sky just over the top of the woods. Crickets, cicadas, and birds of every kind chirped loudly as they flittered among the tall trees silhouetted by the darkening sky.

This particular image was even more unusual than the others because it wasn't a mere moment frozen in time. This was a moving picture, and I was there, physically transported 300 years. I was witnessing, first hand, one full minute of ancient time, just as if it were taking place in the here and now.

Mary was there beside me ... or in me ... or I was inside her mind. I knew we were sharing this moment together. I caught periodic glimpses of a woman's hand rising and falling beside me. She appeared to be pointing out various trees. No, more like she was introducing me to each tree and calling them by name. It became apparent that the trees were not all Pines, as I had first assumed. The surrounding forest was predominately Pine, but the trees bordering the clearing were all different. I could hear Mary's voice speak softly:

There are thirteen stands of three trees, each comprising Her addition to this world. Three of Ash, three of Holly, three of Oak...

She went on to recite the names of all thirteen species of trees, speaking in reverential tones as if she, herself, were in awe at being there among them.

What did she mean when she referred to *Her?* She distinctly said, *"comprising Her addition to this world."* "Addition to this world." What the heck is that all about? Was I wrong to assume that this land belonged to Mary? In previous images, it seemed that this section of the woods was not too far from her house. In fact, I remember another scene of the garden directly behind the house. It was magnificent. The flowers and vegetables looked as if they were advertisements for a seed company catalog. The images jumped from one to another so quickly that it was difficult to relate one location to another. I assumed that the circle of trees was directly behind Mary's house and garden. But was it? And if it wasn't, where was it? What was the purpose of this special place surrounded and hidden by this beautiful forest? *Thirteen stands of three trees each...* thirty-nine trees growing in a perfect circle.

As I write these words, I'm sitting in my own garden under the giant Linden tree, and despite my mind jumping back and forth like a ping-pong ball, I feel at peace. I think that's why I come here—to sort things out. Every day I'm drawn to this spot as if by an invisible magnet. I am compelled to be here. Over the past several years, I've become a part of the outside world far more than the inside. I love my house, but everything in there has become uncomfortable; mainly the appliances, the man-made stuff—the radios and the TVs and the depressing, negative news that comes out of those nasty, awful things. For some reason I can't identify, I haven't been able to turn on my TV to watch the news since my visit with Mary. I used to watch cable news every day, but something inside me is now repulsed by the silly goings-on of the culture in which I was raised. There's a voice ever so remote—is it Mary's? A resonance that rises up within me, like some primal tutor. It's trying to rearrange everything I've ever learned. The voice is teaching me new things. It's teaching me that everything that I've been made to believe to be significant or worthwhile is not. It's teaching me that there's a whole lot more to this earthly existence than meets the eye and that what meets the eye is rarely what it seems to be.

I can't explain this yet. This is all too new for me. I confess I don't have a clue what's happening. Over the past few days, I've even questioned my own sanity, but it all seems so real. These brain photos I've been receiving are far too lifelike to dismiss as mere daydreams. But I have so many questions.

And they shall all be answered.

Mary! Are you there? Is that you? Are you back with me, or was that the wind?

I am here, Dear One. My energy has returned.

You're sure it's really you? This isn't my mind playing tricks on me, is it?

Your mind is well. I am with you.

I've been going crazy since you left me. What's the deal, anyway, just picking up your bags and ebbing out on me like that? You sure left me in a pickle. Not sure if you were a dream, or I was crazy.

I'm sorry, Din, but there are things I must do that I have very little control over at this time. And I assure you I do not really leave you at all. I recede into you.

This really is too much, you know. I'm not sure I'm going to be able to handle this. I've been going into these fanciful vision-like sessions, not knowing if I'm here or there or where the heck I'm at, remembering things I know I've never experienced before. And I never know when this is going to happen. What if I'm driving my car and I start this daydreaming stuff? I'll run over somebody!

I have introduced all the visions you have been experiencing. I am in complete control of when the images appear and for how long they remain active in your mind. I assure you that I will never interrupt the ordinary course of your daily activities with my revelations to you. It is, however, necessary that I share with you in detail the highlights of the life I once lived as a human in the mundane world. The knowledge you glean from these images will be crucial in solving my own considerable problem.

What problem?

I will explain my problem in due time. It involves a Great Plan, but there is much to be done first.

Like answering a billion questions from your great-grandson?

Perhaps I can answer some urgent questions a few at a time. I must be careful not to expend too much energy during each session with you — this is what causes the ebbing times. If the output of power is not controlled, my time with you will be short. If I carefully manage the energy flow, I can remain active for several minutes, perhaps even hours.

So, how many questions can I ask?

Let's take them one at a time, Dear Heart.

Well, let's start with the most obvious. Are you really…a witch?

Of course not. Just know that we are all more than we appear to be. We are more than our images in mirrors and more than what scientists view under microscopes. We are more than merely physical. We are even more than what great spiritual visionaries have conjectured over the centuries. We are more than Spirit—for that brings to mind vapor and smoke. We are more than spinning molecules of light and energy. We are more than what is defined by every theory that has ever been conceived about us. We are nothing, nothing at all, and yet we are everything. And amid this nothing and this everything, resides the Self that we truly are. The physical bodies that we assign labels to are merely the machines that transport our true Selves from point A to point B. The true Self within us is who we really are. And that Self is always watched over by God, THE ALL of THE ALL.

Okay. I'm not sure if you answered my question or not.

Be patient, Dear One. The answer is within you already, but I shall make it clear. You see, in my time, some called themselves witches but were not, and there were some whom others called witches but also were not. I was called a witch by one and all, and by their definition, a witch I truly was. In actuality, I was and continue to be far more than what the world would describe as a mere witch. My gifts and abilities are not from the darker side but from the realms of Heaven.

Mary, I've done enough reading to suspect that our understanding of witchcraft today may be different from how your contemporaries viewed it. I know very little about what a seventeenth-century witch really was like, and I don't know anything about *you.* All I have is a brief genealogy of the Parsons family that goes back to the fifteenth or sixteenth centuries. You have about five lines in the record. Something about you being accused of being a witch in Springfield, Massachusetts. But you were acquitted, weren't you?

I was acquitted, but I will get to that later. Again, I must clarify for you. In my time, there were only two kinds of so-called witches — those who were murdered and those who were not.

You mean the hangings?

Not only hangings. When a so-called witch was dangled from a tree, that was a legal murder. But countless illegal murders occurred that were never recorded in history books. Your books tell only a small part of the larger story. The times of persecution were far more horrendous than you can ever imagine. If you did not live them, you could not understand. For instance, your books do not detail the random and unrecorded examinations of innocent people. These examinations often ended in the deaths of both men and women who were falsely accused of witchcraft.

Examinations?

I will relate a few terrifying instances. I once saw a woman walking in the town square on her way to Church. As she neared the Church building, someone cried out, "Witch!" All who were around fell dead silent. The cry of witch was always a prelude to torture or death, and everyone knew it. That word would freeze even the strongest of men in his tracks. Then a crowd would form, as it did in this woman's case, and from their midst, a large man stained with soot and filth grabbed the poor woman, pulled her from the square, and dragged her screaming down an alleyway. I witnessed this myself. Later, I learned that the man had given her his own "examination" without the sanction or participation of the court, and in his eyes, she was found to be entirely a witch. The poor woman was never seen again.

There was no trial? The woman just disappeared?

Some women who disappeared were later found in the deep woods, their bodies naked, and terribly misused.

I've never read that before.

There is much you have never read. Men who were obviously not witches, but who were disliked by other men for other reasons, disappeared as well, only to be found later with knife wounds to their bellies, or with cords wrapped tightly around their necks. Most had crudely written signs pinned to their chests, reading only, witch. And their murders were never questioned.

Nobody asked questions?

The death of a witch was good riddance. Everyone was terrified of how those in authority had portrayed the evils connected with witchcraft. In their eyes, to be a witch was to be possessed of Satan. The unwritten penalty for possession by Satan was death by any means, not just hanging. To even question these unrighteous murders, was to risk suspicion of having sympathy for an accused witch.

Forgive me, Mary, but questions are popping into my head like crazy. Why were you accused of being a witch? What did you do? And how did you get off so easy? I mean, these people don't sound too rational to me. Why did they let you go?

Again, there is far more to the story. I was accused many times throughout my life, but only twice was I brought to trial. In both of those cases, my dear husband, Joseph, purchased my freedom. This is another detail of the times the history books don't mention. History books give the impression that everyone accused of witchcraft was imprisoned and/ or put to death. The fact is that some were able to buy their freedom. Many who were hanged on Gallows Hill were guilty only of not being able to add to the magistrate's purse.

I was fortunate enough to be married to a man who had been successful in his business dealings. There were those at the time who wished me dead for reasons other than witchcraft, and it was only my husband's money that kept my neck from a sure noose.

Other reasons?

Jealousy! All to do with jealousy. I don't want you to think that I am filled with my own glamour, sweet Din, but I turned many heads in my own time. It was a fact that every man in town wished me for his own pleasure, and it was also a fact that every man's wife wished ill of me for that very reason. It was Sarah Bridgman who first cried, "Witch!" She hated me because she had seen her husband, James, cast side-glances at me in Church. It may have been so. I do not know; I never saw him do it. But Sarah swore he did and threatened him in some way, and James, being the weaker vessel of the two, admitted to a wandering eye in my direction.

It might have stopped with that, except for the fact that James began feeling prideful at having been accused of false relations with the most beautiful woman in town. He commenced to brag and embellish the truth to his male friends. He told them he had been with me in more than just casual glances. Distorted and exaggerated with each telling, the tale took on a life of its own. The story soon spread throughout the town and into the surrounding country. My own good name was shamed by accusation after accusation until the court took note and was forced to act against me.

You're telling me that you were brought to trial for your beauty and not for being a witch?

My face and my hair were what nearly got me hung.

But how could you have been tried for that?

I was tried because Sarah Bridgman was jealous of my beauty and made up stories about me — terrible stories that

*put the whole community in an uproar. But it wasn't just
my beauty; Sarah was terrified of losing her man. A single
woman led a terrible life in the seventeenth century. The work
was hard, and every day was fraught with risk. A man was
more of a necessity then. To lose a husband back then was to
court poverty, danger or even death.*

*And I wasn't the only woman Sarah hated, either.
Everyone in the village knew of her mad jealousy, but I
was the one she chose to attack. To hear her tell it, I was the
Devil himself, come to the surface of the Earth for the sole
purpose of tormenting her. After James had done his damage,
Sarah knew, at last, that she had the upper hand with me.
She pushed things further by approaching my own friends
with the sad tale of how I had tried to steal her man from
her, but my friends did not receive her well. They questioned
all that she said and accused her of lying. Out of fear of losing
her own reputation, Sarah began spreading even greater
lies about me.*

*"Mary Parsons has this or that demon in her head! Mary
Parsons mutters to herself! Mary Parsons has an evil eye
against children!" All of these things she said of me.*

And none of these things were true?

*Of course, they were not true, but still, some thought I
was possessed of a demon. There were times when, against
my own will, I would fall down, my body shaking, and my
eyes rolling back. Even I was terrified, but I couldn't help
any of it. I would just collapse. I know now from coming
alive in your own head, Din, that I had an illness that, at
that time, was thought to be a form of possession.*

Epilepsy. You were epileptic?

*At that time, no one knew what brought on my convul-
sions. What they did not know, they feared.*

Good grief.

During my fits, I could not speak. I could only make odd

sounds as my head bobbed back and forth, and my eyes rolled upward. During these times, if children happened to be near, they would begin to cry and run away as if they were afraid for their lives at just the sight of me. I did not blame them. I must have terrified them so. Each of these ordeals left me weak and humiliated. I could not stand up from the ground without help, and if Joseph were not there with me, I was left alone to fend for myself.

But these aren't the actions of a witch!

Times were different then, my Sweet. Your time has answers for such things as this, but 300 years ago, my symptoms were the wild gyrations of a witch whose soul had been taken over by evil.

So, you weren't really a witch.

I was not, but there is more than meets the eye in the full answer you seek.

What do you mean?

I will tell you, but not at this time. I must recede from your thoughts once again. I feel the energy becoming less effective with every word I portray to you. I must go away for a while, but I will not be gone for very long, and each time away will be shorter than the time before. Soon, I will not have to leave at all.

But, Mary... Mary!

Good grief, she's gone. Just when we were getting somewhere.

***

Anyway, I guess that pretty well puts the doubts to bed. I'm not dreaming now, and this isn't witchy stuff at all. This is real. Mary really is here, inside my head, but she's ebbed again. And what the heck does that mean? What does she do when she recedes? Does she go to sleep? Is that how she gets rested up for the next contact, or is she

entirely awake and watching everything I do? She must
be awake. That's how she learned all the things she knows
about the current century. Maybe she has access to some
sort of enormous memory bank. Maybe she's able to tap
into all of the memories throughout history. She must
be able to view events simultaneously as they happen all
around the world.

You don't suppose there's something to that theory of
universal energy, a web-of-life type thing? Good grief,
Mary! You told me that you're in there watching everything I do. Talk about an Angel in your pocket. That's
how my childhood Sunday school teacher used to scare
the heck out of me. He told me that God had assigned
a personal angel to watch everything I did—*everything*!
And If I did *anything wrong,* the Angel would report back
to God, and my *sin* would be written down in a big black
book, to be forever used against me. Unless, of course, I
repented of my sin, and then God took a big eraser and
erased it out of the book.

So, Mary … Mary? Are you following my thoughts here?
Are you *really* in there watching *everything* I do? Do you
hear *everything* I say? This could become a real problem.

So now, what do I do? I guess I just try to live my life as
usual until the next time you decide to pop in for a visit.
Wait a minute. Should I be writing this in the first person?
Should I write "until the next time *Mary* pops in" or
"until the next time *you* pop in?" Is she—are you—like
one of those imaginary friends little kids have? Should
I talk to you or think about you or write about you as if
you're always there with me? Kinda like talking to myself,
sort of. Or, in the off times, can I just go about my daily
business and forget you're there?

Ha! Fat chance I'll forget you're there. This kind of
thing doesn't just happen to people every day. Mary! Help

me out here! I'm screaming this at you for a reason! I'm going crazy out here! Look! I'm writing an exclamation mark after every sentence! Here! Take some extras!!!!!!!

Okay, so you're there, but you're not. I think I'll just assume that you're awake, and you'll be like one of those imaginary friends. I'll get used to it. I used to have a little purple alien hand puppet when I was a kid. I called him, Marty, the Martian. Real original, huh? Marty was alive to me. I talked to him all the time, and it didn't seem to hurt anything, so I guess I can do that with you. But I don't know if I like the idea of you watching everything I do. Still, if you've been doing that since I was born, you've already seen the worst of it. My life's pretty dull right now.

But where do I go with this? What if you want to talk to me while I'm down at the bookstore or buying gas for the car? Or can you even do that? So far, the only time you've ever spoken to me—except for that first night in bed—has been under my Linden tree. Do I have to be under that tree for all this fantastic mumbo-jumbo to work, or can I be anywhere? Maybe I ought to buy one of those little pocket-recorders. That's a good idea! Then you can talk to me anytime and anywhere you want, and I won't have to write it. I can just dictate it into the recorder. Is that okay? Remind me to ask you the next time you come around.

27 June

Mary Explains Her Presence

I'm back in the garden under the Linden tree. I miss Mary. I want to talk with her, and it seems like I need to be under this tree to do so. Maybe if I sit under here long enough, she'll pop in on me. I don't mind; it's beautiful out here. Just look at those flowers! If I had the power to make it summer all year long just so I could enjoy the color of these flowers, I think I would. No, I wouldn't. I'd miss the changing of the seasons—the way a hard winter explodes into green spring almost overnight, or the rattling and crackling of autumn leaves blowing in the wind, never really coming to rest anywhere, just blowing here and blowing there, and then they're gone. Some get raked up and burned. Others just go somewhere else. Like the hummingbirds that migrate down to Mexico, leaves migrate from one yard to the next until there aren't any yards left. They just disappear. Or they get covered by the first snowfall. And when the last snow melts away, the leaves are nowhere to be seen. It's crazy.

Speaking of the Diary, I have that same feeling that I felt before when Mary wanted me to jot down some thoughts. I just don't know what thoughts she wants me to jot. It's been two days since Mary broke contact with me, but I've been able to feel her presence in many ways. I think I may have discovered the source of the phenomena we call intuition—it's this Mary thing. Maybe everyone has a little Mary running around inside his or her head. Everyone has ancestors. Why isn't it possible for everyone to have at least one ancestor who has been able to jump over from the Other Side, so to speak, and do a little subconscious nudging now and then? This could explain a lot. Schizophrenia? Déjà vu? Past Life Regression? Why not? Even ghosts. What someone sees as a ghost could be someone's ancestor trying hard to communicate with that person. That desire becoming so intense that the ancestor is brought into existence, at least for a little while. Just long enough for someone to see them. Does that make sense? Could be. My guess is as good as anyone else's.

At any rate, what now? What do I do with all of this? If I took this to the media, I could have my fifteen minutes of fame, but how could I prove any of it? And would Mary want that?

I know you're in there, Mary, but you still haven't told me *why* you've decided to contact me. What, exactly, do you want from me? You said something about how our eternity depends on it. What does that mean? You told me I was to be your witness. What does that mean? What does any of this mean?

Whoa! What the heck was that? Mary, I just got this flash...of you...I think...in my head. Mary? Was that you? Wow, the color! How did you do that? How do I write that down? It was you, wasn't it? Good grief, you're beautiful. I want to enter this into the Diary while the vision is fresh in my mind. Vision. Yes, that's the word. You are a vision! And it was like you were right here in front of me. As if you were alive and made of real substance.

In time, I will be able to materialize for you.

Mary!

I am here.

Did I just see you in my head? Is that what you really look like?

It was I. I am now able to bring more substantial images to your mind. I attempted this earlier but was unable to hold the image for long.

That night when you first spoke to me while I was in bed, I caught a brief glimpse of you, didn't I?

You did.

But you're so young. In the visions, you look like you're about thirty years old.

Because you are cooperating, my powers are becoming more energetic, and they are far more efficient. I am now able to manifest any image of myself that I choose and place it into your mind's eye, but only in your mind for now. It will be some time before I can materialize before you.

You mean to tell me that one day you'll be able to stand in front of me and I'll be able to reach out and touch you?

You have much to believe first, Dear One.

What do you mean?

I mean that you have read much that is true concerning the powers of that which is beyond this world's shallow reasoning, but you have failed to place faith in what you have read.

I'm not following you.

There are Laws that govern this universe. I have access to your mind, Din, and I know that you have studied these Laws, but you do not believe in them.

For instance?

Have you not read that the entire universe was created by pure thought energy?

You mean, as if some Higher Power thought up ideas and the ideas became realities? I know that's what most religions believe these days. That's God, right?

It matters not what religions believe. Some religions are highly flawed, Din, but God is real, and His Laws are immutable. And each one of us has the ability to tap into His Universal Laws and adapt them for our own use.

I'm afraid I don't understand.

Everything in the universe was created by the pure thought energy from GOD, THE ALL. Our people, yours and mine, called it, "The Glow." It is the Life Force that sustains all things.

Does that mean you really do believe in God? I mean, I wasn't too sure because of that old Puritan Pilgrim thing you belonged to. Those guys could be a bit odd at times.

Of course I believe in God, and I would not be here now if He had not sanctioned my being here. It is for His Purpose that I am here.

Wow, you're kind of like proof that there is a Creator. I mean, you know the Guy!

There is a Creator God, but the word "God" can mean many things in your society, Din. In my day, the concept of God had come to conjure only one thing in the minds of ordinary people: an immortal, tyrannical old man from a realm called Heaven, whose primary purpose was to instill fear in human hearts. Very few people of my time had an awareness of the true God.

Before journeying to America in that lifetime, our family held a different belief — the belief of our ancestors. They never referred to the Creator as God. They spoke only of THE ALL, Who was The One Beyond. They would whisper their requests in reverential tones to THE ALL, and they believed firmly that He answered each and every one. Their visions and dealings with our Creator were merry ones, filled with laughter and dance, not with guilt and shame. But THE ALL of that day is the same God today. God is God, regardless of how mankind attempts to change Him or give him bizarre names.

Tell me more about this Life Force, this Glow. What does it have to do with your being able to materialize before me?

In your studies, you have read about the manifesting of things, have you not?

Yes, as in positive affirmations and all that?

I speak of more than just affirmation. When one manifests something, as I am using the term —

You mean in Heaven-person talk?

If you wish to put it that way, you may, but it is best to use the term, "one of higher awareness." When one of higher awareness manifests something, she or he brings it into being from out of the depths of her or his imagination. The imagined becomes the actuality.

You mean like THE ALL created the universe out of nothing? One minute you have open space, and the next minute you have Mount Shasta?

That is precisely what I mean.

So, just to put this witch thing to bed, you are not a witch and all those so-called witches back there weren't witches either? You are one of those people of higher awareness, right?

In my era, those of higher awareness were the ones that society inaccurately named as witches. And even though the word, witch, holds a dark meaning for your day—and, quite frankly, it should—witch, was all they knew back then. In Truth, there was another word that better describes many of the higher ones of that time. That word is Weet, and it comes directly from Heaven.

Okay. If I've got this straight—forgive me for belaboring this—what you are telling me is that none of this stuff has anything to do with witches or witchcraft. From this point forward, I am supposed to start substituting the word Weet for "witch" in this Diary I'm writing for you?

That is correct, Din, and the word must be capitalized for its meaning is substantial. I am sure that "Weet" is a new word for you, as it will be for those who will one day read this Diary. But it is the correct label to be used for those higher ones I will be discussing with you soon.

Okay. Your wish is my command.

You will understand as the Diary flows forward.

I'll take your word for it. When are you going to give

me some more details? I'm kind of hanging here.

Very soon, but first, let us finish the thoughts we began with, or you will lose the context for all that is to follow.

I'm all ears.

When a Weet manifests, in essence, a Weet creates. Out of the nothing comes the something. Out of the void comes physical form.

Do you mean that a Weet has the power to simply think things into becoming physical?

A Strong Weet can do this, but only God has the power to place within every created thing its own Glow. No human in all of history has been able to animate an object with the Glow.

I think I'm getting this, Mary. You're telling me that you can create something out of nothing, but you can't bring it to life. In today's terms, the Glow is what we would call the Spirit within a person.

That is correct. The Spirit, or Glow, of every individual is connected directly to the Original Life Force, which both emanates from and is THE ALL.

So, you can't create this Life Force, but you can tap into it, borrow from it.

I can borrow from it, and I can use it in the ancient ways that have been forgotten in your time except by only a few. You can do this as well, as can anyone, if only they reawaken to the power within them.

Even me, huh?

Especially you, Dear One, for you are descended not only from me. There are many powerful Weet in your line.

Do you mean you're not the only one?

My mother and her mother before were both Strong Weet.

And because I'm descended from all of you, that makes me one of these Weet?

You are.

But…I don't feel like a Weet.

You don't? Are there not experiences you have had through-
out your life you are unable to explain? Emotions you have
felt, or intuitions you have sensed so strongly that they nearly
overpowered you?

Well, I suppose…

If you think hard enough, many things will come to mind.

I guess there are a few rather bizarre things I've had
trouble understanding. When I was a kid, I used to do
some pretty odd things with my body. Like always feeling
the need to turn to the right instead of the left. I'd be
walking down the street or going up a stairway at school,
and I'd get this urge to turn around in a complete circle,
and always to the right. I could never turn to the left
without feeling awkward.

And sometimes when I was walking, I'd feel an urge
to lift my leg up. I know that sounds weird, but I would
take a few steps and hike my right leg up in the back like
I was kicking backward at something. Or I would stand
in line at the lunch counter, and that right leg would go
up like it was spring-loaded, and I'd just stand there, balanced on my left leg like a flamingo or something. Really
strange. But I couldn't help it. My mother thought I had
a nervous tic. She finally took me to a child psychologist,
but he couldn't find anything wrong with me.

You are describing physical actions that were exhibited by
your long-gone ancestors, the Weet, and Priests of our lineage.

Priests?

Druid Priests. The ones who stood on one leg with one
eye closed while they interpreted the mist within the clouds.

You're kidding! I used to squint my left eye shut all the
time while looking up at the clouds. My parents thought
that it was a tic!

The Priests would then turn three times to the right —

I used to do everything in threes. I still do. I can't eat two pieces of fried chicken; I have to have three. I always have to carry three one-dollar bills in my wallet. When I'm asked to pick a number, I always pick the number three.

The number three is sacred to our people.

I just remembered the time when I was seven years old, my mother bought me this short-sleeved, plaid cotton shirt. Every time I wore that shirt, it would rain! This is no exaggeration. I could wake up on a bright, sunny day, not a cloud in the sky, and if I put on that shirt, it would be raining within two hours. It was uncanny. Since I was a kid, I didn't think much about it then. I got to where I just expected it to happen. In fact, it was so accurate that I used to purposely not wear it on days I wanted to play outside.

It was a red, yellow, blue, and green plaid shirt, the tartan of the Clan MacPherson, your own family from olden times.

You know about the shirt?

Do you not recall that I have total access to your memories?

Of course. I've known for some time that the Parsons family is linked to the MacPherson Clan, but I sure didn't know it when I was seven years old. Isn't it a bit odd that my mother would have accidentally purchased a shirt resembling the ancient family tartan?

Not in a Spiritual universe, Dearest.

So you're saying the whole shirt thing was magic?

You can call it that if you wish, but it was only one magical experience out of thousands during your lifetime. We need to talk about that word, magic. It is widely misused in your culture, especially since there is really no such thing. Magic is nothing more than science that has not been discovered yet. You will hear me remind you of that often.

Okay, okay. We're getting way off track here. We can come back to this magic stuff later, and believe me, we will, but I think my original question was about how you were going to be able to materialize in front of me one of these days.

That, too, would be magic to you, but it is difficult for me to explain it to you in terms you can understand. Suffice it say that in due time I will be able to recreate a corporeal image of myself for you to interact with. It will be as solid as you are yourself. It will move its lips and words will come out of its mouth. It will walk and stand and do all of the things any living human can do, but my Glow will still be inside of you. I will control the solid image from within you, but it will appear as if I am without you. You will then no longer hear my words within your mind, you will converse with me as if I were a physical being.

Good Lord—

You are speaking of THE ALL?

I mean, you can actually pull that off? This is very difficult for me to buy into. It's like something out of Star Trek—holograms or holodecks or *"Beam me up, Scottie."*

The principle is similar to that of holographic imaging but far more complicated than current theories. There is much knowledge existent in my realm that has yet to be revealed to your time. I am afraid that the details of such things are beyond your understanding. When my power builds enough to bring this to fruition, I will attempt to explain it in more detail. Until then, I have much to share with you that is of far greater significance.

Mary?

Yes, Dear One?

Before you share whatever it is you wish to share, will you show yourself to me just once more?

I will, then I must leave you for a while.

Mary…

1 July

Mary Explains the Old Gods and Goddesses

It's almost noon, and I'm sitting on a lawn chair in the hottest part of my garden — smack dab in the middle of a large patch of orange marigolds. The sun is beating down on my forehead, my hair is matted down with sweat, and this Diary page is so white from the reflected sunlight that it blinds me to look directly at it.

I don't know where Mary is. I've been contemplating her last visit, which is still very fresh in my mind. Especially vivid is the vision of her own Being that she gave when she ebbed out on me. I don't believe I've ever seen a more stunningly beautiful woman. It's no wonder all the men back in her day were after her. And she looked so familiar to me — at least her face did. Where have I seen her? That hair! Hair like that doesn't exist anymore. That color doesn't exist. How can a color be both black and red at the same time? And how can hair be so thick? Maybe I'm just used to seeing contemporary hairstyles. Women don't wear their hair like that anymore. They cut it, and shape it, and dye it, and hang beads and things from it.

But it's her eyes that are burned into my mind, even as I write these words. I know this is a cliché, but Mary's eyes are hypnotic. When I looked into them, I couldn't look away. She literally held me captive with her gaze. No, not in captivity, but in the willing imprisonment of my Spirit inside hers. For a split second, it seemed that I *became* Mary. I felt an emotion pour over me like a warm, wet mist, And the thought came to me that this is what it must be like to really be in love. Not as the world defines love today, but complete infatuation — enchantment.

To be totally taken with a woman, so much so that you could be content for the rest of your days to place her on a marble pedestal and just stare at her until you starved to death because you couldn't leave her presence even to eat. That's what I felt for Mary when she pulled me into herself like that. And that's precisely what it was like — being in love. Pure love.

There's no doubt in my mind that this whole Mary experience is beyond human understanding. But am I really a Weet like her? She used the term *Strong Weet*. What does that mean? Am I a Strong Weet? Or, in more precise terms, some sort of higher being? Things have been popping into my head all morning. I don't know if Mary is doing this on purpose. Is she planting ideas in my mind, or am I just remembering all of the odd moments that punctuated my childhood?

I was a weird kid. Some of the behaviors I exhibited actually embarrassed me, even at the time. But looking back through the eyes of an adult, I now see that those behaviors weren't just embarrassing. They were abnormal. While other little boys were content playing war games or tackle football, I was out in my backyard sitting up in a tree. My father had placed a large wooden plank up in the branches of an old Pepper tree, and every day after I got home from school, I climbed that tree and sat on that board. It's all I wanted to do.

I'd sit in that Pepper tree for hours staring deep into the depths of its branches. And every time the wind blew, I imagined faces popping in and out of its leaves — dozens of faces of different shapes and sizes, all of them smiling down at me as if they were beckoning me to climb up higher into the tree to be with them.

One face was more prominent than all the others. I called that face the Leaf King because he lived near the top of the tree and seemed to dominate all of the others. Even though he was much larger than the rest, and a bit menacing at times — especially when the wind blew — he was always friendly to me. Other kids might have run from such an image, but I felt more as if he were some sort of Guardian, and as long as I sat in that tree under the protective gaze of the Leaf King, no one or no thing could ever harm me. I felt secure among these leaf people, and I was far more desirous of being with them than I was of being with my human playmates, who, I have to admit, never held my interest.

I have always had this thing for trees. Two venerable Pine trees stood in the front yard of our house in California, towering over it. I used to climb those trees, hopping from branch to branch, like climbing up a ladder, and my physical grandmother, who looked after me while my parents were at work, would get so upset with me when she saw me at the top of one of those trees. She'd yell up at me, "Are you tryin' to kill yourself? Get down from there!"

Then my granddad would saunter over to the bottom of the tree, wondering what all the commotion was about. "Throw me one of those Pine cones while you're up there, Boy," he'd say calmly.

Then my grandmother would walk off in an affected Scots fit, muttering something under her breath like, "Just wait 'til yer mother gets home, young man."

I had the sweetest grandparents in the world. They're both gone now, but when they were alive, I never did see them get really mad or have cross words with me or with each other. My granddad was a carpenter and spent most of his time in his little wood shop making furniture, while my grandmother — I called her Nana — busied herself in the house drying herbs, baking pies, or canning the produce she had raised in her garden.

My grandparents' garden was the eighth wonder of the world. It must have covered at least half an acre, and to this day, I can see my granddad hand tilling manure and mulch deep into the Earth, with Nana coming along behind him sprinkling seeds into the rows he had made with his wood-handled hoe. I wasn't much help during the planting process, but Nana and Granddad always let me pick the vegetables as they ripened in the summer. Everything I know about gardening I learned from my grandparents.

At least, I think I learned it from them. Tuning in and out of Mary's world over the past few weeks has made me aware that she was a gardener, as well. That's putting it mildly. Mary didn't just grow things, she communed with them. And they weren't just "things" to her; they were more like people. Mary treated all living things as if she were related to them.

Mary sent me one of those brief mental movies last night while I was lying on the couch, resting my eyes. These visions are her own memories, so I see things from her point of view, as if as I'm looking through her eyes. In this particular scene, I saw her forearm and hand reaching forward into a patch of brilliant, yellow daisies. She picked one of the flowers and brought it up to her face, where she spoke to it. "Hello, little one," she said as she twirled the flower around in her fingers like a little spinning top. "May I take you home with me and use you this night?"

But that isn't the strange part, Mary talking to the flower. The weird part is that I heard the flower answer back! "Thank you for choosing me. I am ready," the flower said. And what's more, as the clear voice of the Daisy came into my mind, the flower itself began to glow with a bright halo about it, and I swear I saw a little face in the middle of the flower. I saw tiny little lips speaking those words to Mary. I swear it!

Before I could comprehend what was going on, the movie ended. That was it. One minute I'm lying there on the couch minding my own business, thinking about getting up and going to bed, and then I'm transported back into Mary's world as if I'm caught up in some supernatural time warp just for the time it takes to confuse the heck out of me. And then she simply ends it. The movie's over. And I'm flying back home to my couch faster than the speed of light — even though I think I remember reading somewhere that Einstein claimed it's impossible to travel faster than the speed of light.

So, how does a guy deal with this? Dead grandmothers popping in and out of my head, talking Daisies ... I mean, what the heck's a guy to do —

You use far too much profanity, Din.

Mary! Heck?

What you will never read about me in books is that after Joseph died and I was living in exile on the outskirts of town, my garden became my most prized possession. The townspeople even called me the Garden Woman. They ceased referring to me as Mary after the exile.

What exile?

As a single woman who had been accused of being a witch, even though I was acquitted, it became increasingly difficult for me to walk freely among the people. Many still suspected me, many hated me, and some wanted me dead. Since I had children, I feared for their lives as well, so I exiled myself as far from the town center as possible. I felt that the more distance I placed between myself and the everyday world of the town, the safer I would be. My husband had built a small cottage out in the wooded area. He kept it as a place of retreat, and we would go there often just to get away from the business of our little town. We used it as a kind of second home, and after he died and the children were grown, I chose to reside there more than in our family home in the town.

Out of sight, out of mind?

Exactly.

But you were acquitted. You were innocent.

Justice was different in those days, Dear Din. Please remember that I am not a witch, but a Weet, one of higher awareness, but I was suspected of being a witch. At any rate, the Strong Weet were not the ones who were hung. We were far too clever. We knew the evils of the time, and we were able to predict the likely behaviors of those who meant us harm, so we were able to stay one step ahead of them. That is how we survived.

Can you tell me some of the differences between a Strong Weet and a regular witch?

There are many self-professed witches in this world, even in your time. Supposedly, a witch is one who merely follows the original Nature ways of the pagan ancestors, but a Strong Weet is one who stands above the rest. A Strong Weet is one who has the knowledge and wisdom of generations of Higher Beings flowing through his or her veins. Down the ages, their extraordinary abilities have multiplied and strengthened. They have become so powerful that even the elements bend and shape themselves at their will.

Is that how you're going to be able to pull off the Mary hologram one of these days? Does that mean you will actually be made of substance? You told me before that you would have a solid form, but I didn't think you meant it literally. Will I actually be able to touch you without losing my hand in a glob of ectoplasm or something?

My flesh will be as real as your own, but that will take some time.

Mary, this is all very difficult for me to imagine. I can understand the logic and the science behind it all, but you're proposing something here that seems way beyond human technology.

That it is, Din. That it is. But you are not dealing with human technology. You are dealing with me.

I have a feeling that you are far more than mere genetic memory, far more than you're willing to reveal at this time. Am I right?

We will discuss that at a later time as well. But you were also wondering about the Daisy vision I sent you.

Yes. What's with the talking Daisy? Did I see that right?

You did. I placed the image within your mind for the purpose of a lesson. I will be instructing you in this fashion over the next several months, even years. You must be able to rightfully practice the true talents of the Strong Weet. It is essential, a responsibility like no other. For you, too, have the power within you to shape the elements.

You've got to be kidding!

I have a wonderful sense of humor that I will one day test on you, Din, but in this, I assure you I am quite serious.

You mean I'll be able to manufacture these hologram things?

You already have the power within you, but you must learn to produce it correctly. One does not decide one day to simply move the elements. A Strong Weet will be very considerate as to the wishes of the elements themselves before he or she alters them in any way. Elements should only be moved or shaped after they have first given their permission to do so. You must remember that elements have their own Glows within them just as we do. For instance, a Strong Weet would never attempt to conjure a storm from a cloudless sky without first seeking permission from all the elements involved. Deliberate overpowering of the natural elements without their consent or without good reason is contrary to the will of Nature, and the direction of THE ALL. It can be done, but it is not advisable, and it is usually only attempted by those who have chosen to walk the Dark Road.

You mean bad guys?

There is both bad and good in this world, and very little can be done about it until the end of The Great Plan. In the meantime, it is often necessary to maintain a balance on this planet.

Slow down, Mary, you're losing me again. What do you mean by *this* planet? Are there other inhabited planets out there? And what's the difference between darkness and evil?

You must not concern yourself with questions of life forms on other planets. You must first learn to interact with life forms on this planet. There is life on other planets, but your culture will be shocked and, perhaps, delighted when the details are revealed.

Are you teasing me?

You have no need for this knowledge as yet. But you do need to know the difference between evil and dark. Both evil and good are matters of intent. That is the Law. If one's intention is pure, then one is working with the good. If one's intention is not pure, then one is working with evil. But darkness is an essence unto itself. It is a substance. These distinctions will become evident to you as you progress in your lessons.

You must never forget that magic is not witchcraft, and it is not a thing of the devil; it is merely the act of manipulating various frequencies of energy found within Nature. Scientists and medical practitioners have been working magic throughout all time, they just don't call it that. Contemporary physicists are playing with magic nearly every day now. Remember, what is called magic one day, may become truth the next.

You have heard of Mother Nature?

Of course, I have. Isn't she like a pagan goddess?

Yes, she is, but she is not what they think she is. Many so-called pagans misinterpret the historical figure, Mother Nature, for a dark, and often evil goddess of the forest or the moon, even of death. Actually, Mother Nature has little to do with the images that humans have warped her into over the centuries. She is neither a witch nor a goddess. She is merely the personification of the powerful, sentient energy frequency God used to create and sustain this world and all other worlds found throughout the universe. Mother Nature is not a person and never was, but she is very much alive and sentient and can take physical form at will. You would be wise to research the principles of energy frequency, for they shall become dear to you as we move along.

Here is another lesson for you, Din. All of the so-called gods and goddesses, who have been worshiped, regardless of era, culture, or country, are not flesh and blood people with heads and legs and arms like human beings. Like Mother Nature, they are the energy forces that animate all things in the universe. Cultures throughout time have personified them with social titles and names. In reality, they are more like Angelic Beings, who can, if they so desire, appear to us in any form they wish—as men and women, yes, but also as plants and boulders or the air itself.

Because the ancients did not understand these forces and were often even afraid of them, in their ignorance, they worshiped the power they had called Mother Nature as one of their goddesses. And, yes, "she" has been referred to by many names in various different cultures—in fact, by thousands of names—but that is irrelevant because there is only one Creative Force coming from God. Regardless of which name a culture uses, it all comes back to the fact that it isn't from a manufactured deity; it is from God. The original name that God gave His Creative Force would be unpronounceable to humans, but can be more closely interpreted as the Mother of Humankind. That is also the name she prefers because it was given to her by God.

Never forget that EVERYTHING *is alive and has some form of sentience. Imagine how a powerful, sentient* FORCE *such as the Mother of Humankind might have seemed to an ancient culture. Are not the Angels of God sentient? Do they not have names, and are they not referred to with pronouns such as he and she? It is merely a matter of respect given to the most powerful Energy Force brought forth by God to bring life and sustenance to this world. In effect, it is Mother H, as she is called by a chosen few, who manufactures the* GLOW *that we spoke of earlier—the force that animates and sustains all life after it is created and given the first Spark of life by the Holy Spirit that is God.*

Makes sense to me.

Mother H is also the one who controls the energy which can be tapped into by those of Higher awareness to manifest harmony upon the Earth. This has nothing to do with the concepts of evil or goodness but is necessary to correspond with the Laws and principles that govern the universe on all levels. Your modern scientists are only beginning to discover these as they are just now delving into the mysterious world of quantum physics. Din, they have only turned the first page in an incredible book that will one day lead them into new sciences not yet known in this world.

Is this something I will understand as I continue in my lessons?

This is very difficult to grasp because you are attempting to understand extraordinary principles with the natural mind. It can never really be understood in that fashion. That is why ancient humanity invented such things as gods and goddesses in the first place. They simply could not understand the complexities of Nature. It must be felt rather than understood. And, yes, it will all be made apparent to you in time, but the important thing for you to remember at this point in your learning is that things are not always the way they appear to be. Nor are things the way you may have been taught that they should be. Honey may not always be sweet and nourishing. It can be laced with arsenic. And death is not always a condition to be feared. Sometimes death can be a cleansing as well.

So, does that mean that Aphrodite doesn't look like Marilyn Monroe?

Even though I live within your mind, Din, I find it challenging at times to understand your train of thought. The energy that is Aphrodite, as the ancients named their goddess of Love and Beauty and Romance, can take any form she wishes. If she wants to appear as Marilyn Monroe, she is perfectly capable of doing so, but she is far more likely to appear as a beautiful yellow flower on a summer's day.

The Daisy! You were going to tell me about the yellow Daisy with a voice.

The Daisy vision was to illustrate the fact that all living things have life and Spirit, not just human beings. Every flower that grows has its own Glow, its own Being. And every flower is capable of experiencing emotions, such as joy, and even physical feelings, such as pain. That is why every living thing must be approached with sensitivity and respect.

You mean, when I pick a flower, it feels pain?

Everything in the natural world is relative to the Law of Intent that I spoke of earlier. For instance, if a little girl goes into a meadow and picks a small flower because she thinks it's pretty and she wants to take it home to her mother, the flower will feel only the intent of the love of that child. However, if a greedy man plows up a meadow of wildflowers to clear the way for a shopping mall, every flower in that meadow will feel the pain of violent death. In the natural world, this would be an act of mass murder, not of progress.

I mentioned to you earlier that my garden became my prized possession after my self-imposed exile from the town. That is because when I left the world of people, I joined more deeply with the world of Nature. In effect, all of Nature became my garden, and all plants, being of Nature, became my new friends and family. I knew I could never trust human beings again, but I also sensed that I had powerful new allies in the trees and the animals and wild streams.

But the flower spoke to you.

One day soon, the flowers will speak to you as well, sweet Din. All in due time. Now I must ebb from your conscious mind, for I have much that needs to be done.

Before you go, I need to ask you one more question.

You may ask.

When you gave me that vision of yourself during your last visit … well … it was so real. I felt as if you were right there with me. And you were so beautiful, Mary. I've never seen a more beautiful woman. But—

You felt as if you were inside my mind. You felt great love for me.

Yes! I felt great love for you!

We will discuss that at a later time, Sweet One. But now I must ebb.

And she's gone.

7 July

Mary Talks About the One God and Reveals the Guardians of Nature

It's dumping rain outside. I'm sitting at my desk and gazing out the window toward a small stand of trees across the street. There are at least three deer grazing peacefully on the lush green plants that seem to be flourishing under those trees. The serenity of the scene punctuates a thought I awakened to this morning. It seems that no matter what mankind does to destroy this beautiful Earth, there's no way they're ever gonna really destroy it. At worst, they can only temporarily deface it and use up its resources, but they can't kill Mother Nature. Even if they blow everything up with nuclear warheads and the Earth lies dormant for centuries under the poisons unleashed upon her, one day in the far distant future, one little seed will sprout, push itself up through the diminishing nuclear waste, and one tiny, bright green leaf will appear. Yes, human beings will be dead and gone, but they aren't really all that necessary in the scope of all things natural. Plants can come back without the help of people. In fact, the more help people offer, the more damage they seem they do.

The damage isn't irreversible, though. A friend called me on the phone this morning to chitchat. Somehow, we got off onto the subject of clear-cutting the forestlands of America; not so much the vast swaths shaved off by the logging companies each year, but the smaller areas that go unnoticed. Environmentalists choose not to see some of the worst of the land rapes in this country. Like bulldozing natural woodland, a few acres here and a few acres there, without a thought of the multitude of life forms that call those acres home. Why? So that college football stadiums, or sports arenas, can be built, along with all the outlying buildings, parking lots, and support centers it takes to keep such operations functioning.

I've never been a sports fan. It just seems such a waste of time, money, energy — everything. Recently though, the thought occurred to me that the national passion for sports has become environmentally unsound. Here in my own town, *sports* is spelled with a capital *S*. Even though the local university has a mediocre, at best, football team, the stadium is packed for every game. On the mornings following each event, the streets, parking lots, and open areas around the stadium for several miles in all directions are littered knee-deep with beer bottles, styrofoam cups, paper plates and towels, cigarette butts, pieces of clothing, and food wrappers.

It's not just in my town, either. This scene is repeated around the millions of other stadiums not only in America but around the world, creating one heck of an environmental concern. Still, many of my acquaintances who consider themselves to be environmentalists have bragged to me on many a Monday morning about the really great game they attended over the weekend, not failing to mention all the beer they drank and all the food they ate. Why is this not hypocrisy? How can anyone who professes to be concerned about the environment or ecology or the wellbeing of Mother Nature, Mother H, in general, ever set foot in one of these stadiums, let alone pay money to do so? Then, to sit there and participate in all the silly yelling and hoopla that goes on during one of these events — how childish, how un-evolved. Hypocrisy doesn't seem to be a strong enough word.

Even before I met you, Mary, I knew that Mother Nature was far more than just a lady in a margarine commercial and was not to be taken lightly. I sensed a power there, and I felt an inbred disgust for anyone who purposely and frivolously defaced or abused the Earth in any way. I always felt that Nature, although wounded at times, could never be killed entirely. She was going to win in the end.

I was only half-joking when I told my phone friend that the soil here in Missouri is so fertile that I can spit a tomato seed onto the ground Thursday night, and on Friday, I'd find a full-grown plant. He laughed, but we both knew that my statement wasn't far from the truth. The Earth is so fertile, the growing process is so vigorous, and the mysterious energies within the Earth are so beyond the grasp of human understanding. The *all of it all* just can't be stopped. Wow! That's got to be God's full name—THE ALL of THE ALL. Mary? Are you here? I know you must be close by, or I wouldn't be writing so fervently about this environmental stuff. If you are here, how do you feel about sports? Hmm, that brings up another question. How do you feel? Can you feel at all? I mean, like emotions and—

Genuine emotions are generated within the soul. They are not really felt at all as one physically feels other things. They are experienced at a deeper level.

I knew you were there. This is the first time you've popped in on me that you haven't startled me.

I would never startle you intentionally.

I know that. I don't mind any more anyway. I'm beginning to look forward to our times together.

As am I, Dear One.

I actually thought you'd be back sooner this time. You've been away for almost a week. I was beginning to worry about you.

Although you are sweet for doing so, I assure you there is no reason for worry. No harm can come to me.

I guess you're right. It would have to come to both of us. That's not a happy thought.

Fear not. I will not allow harm to come to you.

That's comforting. But I have about three hundred questions I've saved up for you. I guess the first one is, why were you away for so long? I thought this ebbing and flowing thing was supposed to speed up or go away as you got stronger.

The ebbing and flowing are no longer necessary. I am quite strong now. But I will still ebb from you regularly for your sake. As a human being still housed within the physical vehicle, you will need periods of rest. You cannot rest if you are always in communication with me.

I guess you're right. So, what kept you?

I chose not to leave the sanctity of the realm in which I now primarily reside due to a large number of explosions occurring throughout your domain. I understand the celebratory nature of the day you call Independence Day. However, I wanted to be sure that the combined nature of the explosive devices could not reverse what the ball lightning has given to us both.

You mean the fireworks?

I now know that the effects of these devices are infinitesimally small in comparison to even one bolt of ordinary lightning and can do no harm to either of us. The noises are, however, a bit annoying, and I cannot understand why your people still practice such childish outbursts in this current age. What purpose does this serve?

I don't know, Mary. I suppose it was once a time for genuine celebration, but now it's just another excuse for people to get drunk and act stupid. It goes along with what I was just thinking about sporting events—all the noise and the hoopla. Did you catch any of that?

If you mean, did I experience your thoughts regarding the rape of the land due to the obsession of the current society with sporting events, the answer is, yes. It is an immature and selfish act for anyone to commit. I am sure you know already that those who involve themselves in such things are not only antagonistic to THE ALL, whether consciously or not, but are, in the scope of all things eternal, far behind in their spiritual development.

I've always thought these people were missing a few brain cells.

They have much to experience before they reach full understanding.

You are so tactful.

It has nothing to do with tact. It has only to do with Truth.

And the Truth is, you still haven't told me about your emotions and feelings. Maybe I should be more specific. When you speak of Truth, how do you know it really is the Truth? How do you know it isn't just your opinion about something?

Sweet One, there is no need for mere opinion in the place where I now reside. Truth is evident in all matters. All matters are Truth. Answers are no longer needed, for there are no longer questions. Opinions are nonexistent, for the width and breadth of all knowledge is readily attainable to any Being at any moment. While there are a few pieces of information here and there that THE ALL chooses not to reveal, for the most part, we are ignorant of nothing. Opinion can only exist where there is ignorance. There can be no ignorance in the presence of Truth.

I guess that was another stupid question.

You have no choice but to ask such questions, for you still dwell in the physical. Only by that means can you continue to learn so that you may grow toward your ultimate destiny.

Which is?

*Which is to be where I am. It is the destiny of every phys-
ical Being to become as I am and to reside where I reside.*

Can you give me a little more detail? What's it like
where you reside?

*I cannot place such images within your mind at this time,
for you are not capable of processing them. I will tell you only
this, that I reside in a state of such high vibration that no
human can see me, yet, it is the True vibratory state for all
Beings that are not encased in human, physical form. It is
not really another dimension; it is the essence of all Higher
Beings. It is the essence of Heaven. You will, however, be
allowed to visit my residence one day. Then you may bring
the memory of your experiences back with you.*

I've read about astral travel and out of body experiences. Is that what you're talking about?

*Not really. It is far more complex than what you have
read. It will be a merging.*

A merging?

*Please do not concern yourself with such things as yet.
When it is time, I will guide you into them.*

Is this all part of being a Strong Weet?

It is.

I guess I really need to know more about this Strong
Weet stuff. You seem to be using it as a label of sorts, but
I don't recall having ever heard the term before you told
me about it.

*You have never heard the term before because it has not yet
surfaced in your time. The title of Strong Weet was used only
among a very select group of Beings during my own era and
in eras past. It is not a term that was ever used outside the
secret world of those Beings who possess real power. When
two Strong Weet would meet face to face, each was readily
recognized by the other. I first heard the term from my own
physical mother of that day who, when I was five years old,*

said to me, *"One day, my child, you shall suffer much for who you are, but you shall never die, for you are a Strong Weet. It is in your line to be such, for your mother and your mother's mother are both Strong Weet. It is your destiny."*

And you're telling me that it's my destiny, too?

I am.

Are there other Strong Weet out there? Or am I the only one?

There are others, Din. It will be your responsibility to seek them out and band together with them. Together you will generate a preferred complementary power to do what you one day will be required to do.

I beg your pardon?

Why do you beg my pardon?

I meant, what's this responsibility thing? What am I going to be required to do?

As a Strong Weet, you will be required to do many things that others are not. You are already meeting one of the critical requirements by simply recording my words in this Diary.

Sometimes I don't think I have much choice about that.

But you do have a choice. You can always choose not to. I can ebb from your conscious mind permanently if you wish.

Don't do that!

It is not my desire to do so, Din, but I would if you were unhappy with my presence in any way.

No! Mary, I never meant that I was unhappy because you're here with me. In fact, I don't think I can remember being any happier. It's just that all of this is so weird—if that's even the right word—but I really am glad you're here.

And that's another thing I can't explain. I feel so comfortable with this. I've only been aware of you for a few weeks, but I feel as if I've known you all my life. I know—you tell me I have known you all my life because you've been inside my head since I popped out of the womb. But I didn't know you were inside me. Does that make sense?

Why am I so happy about this? This thing going on here is not normal, but it feels normal. It would be abnormal if things were to go back to the way they were before I met you.

A flower is most beautiful when it is in full bloom.

I'm not following you.

You speak of being normal or abnormal. But you cannot use those classifications when describing yourself, as you are neither the one nor the other.

I'm still not following you.

As a Strong Weet, you can never be held to the same standards as those you walk among in the physical. There are no standards for you here because you are not fully here.

Mary—

Many things will be difficult for you to understand because of the false information already housed within your mind, but there is one thing you must learn from the beginning—you do not belong to this time or to this space. You are present in this world and absent from the other, but you can pass through the veil that separates the two whenever you so desire. You only have to awaken to that desire.

Within the parameters of your current era, you cannot be labeled as normal, for there are no others like you. Others who are even close to being like you have remained in the shadows all their lives. A large part of your responsibility will be to seek out and unite these others to support The Great Plan.

When will you tell me what this Great Plan is?

When it becomes necessary.

And where do I find these other Strong Weet? Is there someplace they hang out? A Strong Weet bar or something?

They will seek you out when they have read this Diary. That is one of its purposes.

How will I be able to tell a genuine Strong Weet from a phony?

You will be able to ascertain those who are genuine and those who are not. There will be many who will profess to be Strong Weet, but the difference between the authentic and those who are merely playing at being so-called witches will be evident to you.

Well, okay. When is this going to happen?

You have much to learn yet. But rest assured that it will be manifested sooner than you expect. It must, for it has already been initiated in the place where I reside.

I don't have a clue as to what you mean by that, but I do have one concern here, Mary. How are people going to react to all of this—to me?

Those who aid you will become a part of something extraordinary and will be rewarded beyond their dreams. Those who mock you or impede The Great Plan in any way will be going against a massive current set into motion by THE ALL. To ignore or to fight against that current will mean for the weaker ones to be swept away by it. This is not a desirable fate.

Well, that sounds pretty darned dramatic. I guess we'll just leave it at that for now. But could you clarify one thing for me? You mentioned that bringing Strong Weet out of the woodwork was only one of the purposes of this Diary. What did you mean by that?

The Diary has many purposes, but it is principally meant to be a revelation. Not only will it reveal to you your future Society, but also it will speak many new Truths to those of your time who need to hear these Truths. If the Truths are honored, it will alter the destructive course of this planet's history. If the Truths are ignored, all human life forms upon

this planet will perish quickly, never again to reappear.
God.
He will not help them.

Mary, my head is spinning. I don't even know what to write. This is really serious stuff you're coming out with here. All this impending doom stuff—

No one needs to experience these things. The course of history can be changed for the better, and those who are responsible for that change will not only be rewarded in this lifetime but in the next life as well, and they will leave behind them a legacy that transcends any that has come before.

What do you mean by "future Society" capitalized? What kind of Society?

The association of Weet was kept secret in my day, and only a few knew of its existence. The genesis of this association is so ancient and so mysterious that no one has ever determined its origin. Some believe it to be as old as humanity itself, with roots on some faraway island in the distant sea. But its beginnings have been as well concealed as the span of its life.

I was a member of this hidden, yet honored, alliance, and when I came to America, I brought its beliefs with me in the hopes that I would be able to continue its practices here. But during my long existence in America, only one Strong Weet was ever revealed to me. Toward the end of my life, I had a vision in which Mother H appeared as a great White Horse with a flowing silver mane. She spoke to me and told me that with my death, the association would also meet its end. She also promised that it would be revived in the distant future, "by one of your very own, who will become dearer to you than any you have ever known." You, my precious Din, are that Dear One.

I'm going to revive this association? What association are we talking about here?

I speak of the Strong Weet Society. But you must swear

never to utter its name until this Diary is laid open to the public eye.

Strong Weet Society? I didn't know they had societies in those days. I thought that was a more modern thing.

There have been many societies throughout history, both famous and infamous.

But if the Strong Weet Society died out with you, how can there be any more Strong Weet to restart it?

Those Strong Weet who produced children, not only in America but also in Scotland, Ireland, England, Wales, Norway, Israel, Sweden, India, and a few other countries, have offspring who are alive today. When they read this diary, they will come to you.

Do you mean there are others out there who have grandmothers or grandfathers talking in their heads?

You are the only one who has been given this great gift, but those who really are Strong Weet will know that they are. They will be able to FEEL their heritage, and once felt, their power will begin to grow within them.

But I'm the only one with the grandma?

You were the most receptive. We have all been trying for some time to awaken within one of our own. I was the first to awaken within you because our line is the strongest.

But why has it taken centuries for one of you to make contact with a grandkid? What about all of that great power you people wield from wherever it is you reside? I'd think it would be a simple thing for you guys to jiggle around a few genes and turn the movies on in just about anybody's head.

It is neither the power nor the magic that is at issue here, Din, it is the receptivity of the one who is to be awakened. For such a great work of magic as this to be successful, the human being who is to be affected by it must be one who is entirely receptive to the consequences, regardless of what those may be. Yes, I have tried for many years to awaken within my own lineage, but those who came before you were simply not as receptive. If the magic is to work, there must be an exchange between the two worlds, and the free will of those who still reside in the physical must be considered, as well.

But how did you know that I was finally the one who would work with you on this?

I did not know. The final decision was not mine but belonged to Mother H, herself. This is one of the few secrets she chose to keep from us. But when her ball lightning was released near your home, we all knew who she had chosen.

I was chosen by this Energy Being?

You were.

And was this in her persona as Mother H, the personified, or in some other manifestation? I'm still kind of confused about this. What about all these goddesses and gods running around, all of the mythologies and pantheons? We've got to go into this a little deeper, Mary. I'm not a complete dum-dum on this stuff. I've read enough to know that every culture has had its own group of goddesses and gods, and they are all just conceptual like we talked about earlier, but how does this relate to the concept of a Creator Being? Is Mother H the Creator?

I will try to clarify it for you. There is only ONE God. Mother H is not God, but God does produce many different forms to wield the energy needed for the creation and maintenance of Earth. As I mentioned once before, the configuration THE ALL employs depends upon what kind of energy is required to produce exact results in any particular instance. In ancient times, for the most part, the magic worked in the daylight was called "of the god," and any magic worked at night was "of the goddess." It must be understood that THE ALL contains no genders. THE ALL is a Spirit without personification, even though "He" has been given a personality throughout all of human history. Mother H has been called "she" for much the same reason. Humans must also be made to understand that all of the little fusses and spats they have with each other over gender titles for God are nonsense in the eyes of God. When God has found it necessary to manifest human form for a specific purpose in this world, "He" chose the masculine rather than the feminine, simply because of the physical strength that a male image portrays over that of a female.

Can you give me some examples?

It is foolish for the human mind to try to grasp the true and total nature of God. Several verses in the Bible speak of this. Humans can never know the Mind or the Ways of God. They can never know His Name, or what He looks like. Yet, they continue to devise thousands of religions and denominations within those religions professing to know all those things. God is the one Mystery that humanity will never solve. It is not necessary to define this great Mystery. What is important is to join with it and come to know it as a relationship of Spirit. The totality of this joining, however, is experienced only after a human being separates from the physical realm and seeks the Will of God.

It is a difficult task, but I will attempt to provide clarification as best as I can. To translate Heavenly Truths into mental images that can be understood by the natural mind is similar to the process of translating one language into another. There are many differences, some subtle and some not so subtle.

The nature of THE ALL, and the nature of my True life, goes far beyond this discussion, but I will try to inform you in a way that you can understand.

There is only ONE God over ALL universes. The name for God, again, is merely a description of the energy issuing forth from God as needed for specific acts of creation or sustenance within the universes. In all manifestations and under all names, it is always still God. Excepting a few violent, abominable religions on this world, when a human prays to or worships any of his or her made-up names for God, they are in reality praying to and worshiping the same God as everyone else. God is not confused about this. It is really so simple, but humans have manufactured this confusion all by themselves. Do you understand?

It's all about bringing God down to their own level so they could understand Him and not be afraid of Him, but in the process, they made up all kinds of gods and goddesses that don't really exist. I get that.

Since the beginning, human beings have grown in number. Tribes and clans became separated from each other by thousands of miles or by vast oceans. Each tribe or clan came up with its own name for God independent of the others. There are millions of names here on this tiny planet for God. But does that mean humanity has the right or the power to manufacture millions of different gods out of thin air, just because they feel the urge to do so? Of course not. There is only ONE Creator God.

The major problem that humans have always had is their insistent addition of false attributes to God. Those attributes then become part of their culture and belief in them seen as a sign of faith. As participation in religion increased, unnecessary rituals, costumes, and dogma were added to everything else. The denominations differentiated from each other and moved away from the fundamental Truths of God. Countries do not fight wars over the differing names for THE ALL. They fight over false doctrines that have nothing to do with the real Creator. That is why this world is in such a terrible state of danger today. Humanity is fighting a religious war that is based on false doctrines and dogma. That is not God's fault. It is the fault of human beings playing at being little gods, putting words into God's mouth, and professing those words to be truths when they are not, making up rules for judgment and condemnation, becoming the sole authority on what is sin and what is not sin. They are very wrong, and they will be sorry for this.

So, where does that leave me? What do I do now?

You must go out into our garden, for you have much to learn that can only be discovered in the wild.

But it's dumping rain out there!

You must do as I say, Dear One.

If you insist. But I don't know how I'm gonna write your Diary in the middle of a downpour.

You underestimate my Power.

In the Garden latter the same day

I stepped out from the kitchen onto the back lawn. The very second my foot touched the ground, the rain stopped! Not only did the rain stop, but within moments the dark clouds that had filled the entire sky from horizon to horizon totally evaporated. Poof! Just like that! They didn't blow away or gradually disperse; they just vanished.

How did she do that? It has to be that Strong Weet stuff. Mary is in control of the elements, but how can that be? This whole thing is getting bigger and bigger by the hour. I know I've said this before, but I really don't know what to think anymore. I mean, look at me, I'm sitting out here in my back yard, on the ground in the middle of a mud puddle. I'm writing a Diary that is being dictated to me by a long-dead woman who informs me that she's here to teach me lessons that will, quite possibly, save this planet from some mysterious future demise. What the heck am I supposed to think?

What is it she wants me to learn out here? I didn't want to sit in the mud like this; I felt compelled by that odd feeling I get when Mary wants me to do something. When I get that feeling, I know some sort of important message is on the way. This is her doing. She wants me to sit here in the mud, but what can she possibly —

Will you please be quiet?

Mary! What's the meaning of this? Why do you have me sitting in this puddle?

I just thought it would be funny.

Funny? You mean there isn't some deep and mysterious lesson I'm supposed to learn from this? This is just a joke?

I told you I have a sense of humor. I thought I would prove it to you.

Good grief.

Please relax. I do have a serious lesson for you to learn this day, but first, you must get up out of the puddle and then go over and sit down under the Redbud tree next to the fence.

Your wish is my command. Hold on a minute … okay, now what? I'm sitting under the Redbud tree. What am I supposed to do?

It is not what you are supposed to do. It is what you are supposed to see and to hear.

What I see is the tangle of weeds and dead limbs I haven't gotten around to cleaning out of the garden, and what I hear are the horses in the back pasture snorting at each other.

You must use your other senses. You must close your eyes to truly see, and you must shut out the dominant sounds of life so that the delicate voices of those who are smaller than you can be heard.

Those who are smaller than me?

Close your eyes and be very still.

What was that?

Keep your eyes closed.

But I heard something!

Speak very softly and tell me what you heard.

It sounded like…the laughter of children. No, not children, really. It was more like tiny voices. Or the trickling of water. Like a little waterfall trickling over round pebbles. I'm not sure. I'm just not sure.

Listen again.

There, I hear it again. It's the laughter of tiny voices! Like the Munchkins in the Wizard of Oz, only much smaller. Ha! It's delightful! What is it, Mary?

It is the song of purity. The last remaining sound of innocence to be found upon this globe. Now open your eyes.

What was that? I saw something right there in front of that rock! Wow, what was it?

Close your eyes again and listen.

There's a sound…like a song. It's so beautiful.

Now, open your eyes again and speak very softly when you see them.

See whom? Who am I supposed to…Wait a minute. Good grief! I can see—holy cow, I don't believe it.

They are not born with names, but I have named the pink one, Rose, and the yellow one, Daisy.

They're like tiny little women, and they're glowing.

They choose to have you see them as little women, but I assure you they are not. And what you have heard is not laughter, but the sound of their Glow. It is the life energy they share with those they have been given the responsibility to care for.

This is like something out of a movie. This can't be real. You're not going to tell me these little cuties are Faeries—

That is one of their titles, but they are more than simple cuties. They are the Guardians of Nature. Every living Being has its own Guardian Energy.

Even humans?

You are familiar with Guardian Angels.

You mean to tell me that Guardian Angels are nothing more than giant Faeries?

Faeries are nothing less than Guardian Angels.

So these things both exist? Faeries and Angels?

They more than just exist, they are responsible for existence. Guardian Angels are protective entities assigned to every individual Being from the moment each Being is conceived until the moment each Being passes from your world into my own. THE ALL places His Glow into each seed when it is planted in the ground or in a woman's womb. From that moment on, a Guardian is assigned to each seed. It is then the responsibility of the Guardian to keep watch over her charge.

And what I saw—

What you saw were the Guardians of your garden.

But they looked like little people.

In your mind's eye, they can appear as anything they wish, depending upon the reason for their appearance. They were directed to appear to you as little people because you have been conditioned to imagine Faeries in that way. If you were to see their true nature, it would not only blind you, it would burn a hole clear through you, for their true nature is a form of energy far purer and far more intense than any energy source known in your time.

So, they aren't little people at all.

They are not. But you may refer to them as Little People. They have gone by many titles throughout the ages, and Little People is one of the oldest of those titles.

This all just seems too fantastic to believe. Of course, I've heard of Faeries and Elves and Little People and all the other Nature folk, but I always thought they were only make-believe. Now you're telling me that they not only exist, but they're some sort of Guardian Angel energy form that's been around for hundreds of years. You know, if I hadn't seen these Little People myself, I would never have believed they existed.

Please do not forget that the world you see with physical eyes is not the only world there is. There are other levels of frequency and other worlds that occupy the same space and time as your own, but you cannot see them in conventional ways. There are other Beings from other planes, but they will not come out and perform for the human population at whim. They must have a specified reason for their interaction with humanity, and they must be chosen by THE ALL to be seen. You must remember that, unlike human culture, there is a Divine order to the Mystery world. Everything that occurs within it has both organization and purpose. Because of the Truth that resides there, it can not be otherwise.

What did you mean when you said these Guardians are responsible for existence?

The purpose of the Guardian is to ensure the survival of its charge from birth to death.

But I don't get it. If every human being has a Guardian Angel to keep them safe, why is it we have problems anyway? Why is it we're even able to die?

First of all, Faeries are not the same as the Guardian Angels mentioned in the Bible, those are reserved solely for the specific task of guarding their charges. God has total command of them. Faeries are independent creatures that may or may not choose to be Guardians. That being said, a human being does not die because his Guardians failed to protect it, but because of unwise decisions made by that human during his lifespan. Guardian Spirits can only protect against outside influences. They cannot help humans who are bent on destroying themselves from the inside.

So we do have the power to chart our own life's course?

For the bad or for the good, human beings must make their own decisions. The problem is that some decisions are irreversible, and the Guardians are helpless in those instances.

Like if an emotionally distraught person decides to throw himself out of a fifteen-story building, an Angel isn't gonna catch him on the way down?

That is correct.

And all of these people who claim to have seen their Guardian Angels? Those aren't just made-up stories?

Many have seen their Guardians. Mostly, these have been the Strong Weet throughout time. However, others who claim to have seen their Guardians are not telling the Truth. It is unfortunate for them. Because of their dishonesty, the very thing they so desire to experience will be denied them. Because of their lies, the Guardians will never appear to them while they live in their physical form.

Are you implying that if a person is honest about it, he can see his Guardian?

A person can. But, as I have already said, a Guardian will only appear if it is necessary, and in most cases, the person never knows he is seeing his own Guardian. Guardians can take the form of human friends, relatives, teachers, ministers, anyone, or anything they wish.

You mean someone may think they're having lunch with their girlfriend, but she's really a Guardian?

It is entirely possible, and highly probable, for it happens frequently.

This is incredible.

Guardians may also choose to appear as a tree or a rock or a cactus. Every problematic human situation is highly complex, so Guardians are instructed to do what they must do, and take whatever form they must to achieve success in each instance.

My mind is boggled. If what you're telling me is real, and every blade of grass, every insect, every tree, every weed, every worm has a Guardian, then there must be millions of Guardians in this back yard!

I am capable of speaking only Truth.

I know that. Go along with me for a minute. You have to understand this is all new to me. I don't think I ever doubted that we have Guardian Angels, and I always kinda believed in Faeries anyway, but am I right? Is my garden teeming with Faeries and Angels? I just can't see them?

If you were able to see your garden through my eyes, you would be astounded.

Will I ever be able to see what you see, Mary?

I can only give you brief glimpses of such magnificent sights while you are in your present physical state. If I were to reveal such energy to you for more than just a moment, its intensity would be unbearable.

But where does all this energy come from? And why can't I feel it? Why can't I hear it buzzing, or humming, or something?

It comes from everywhere. It comes from the north, the south, the east, and the west. It comes from up and down. It comes from herbs and rocks and fields of flowers. It comes from horses in that field. It comes from the clouds, and from the very air you breathe. It comes from the moon, and it comes from the sun, and it comes from every star that shines in the night sky. It comes from the sky itself and from the firmament beyond. It comes from God. The reason you do not feel or hear it is that it is a part of you, and you are a part of it. You cannot hear the energy rushing through the mundane forms of trees and horses and mice any more than you can hear the blood rushing through your own veins.

You asked me earlier if there is life on other planets. The answer is, yes, there is life on every planet in the universe. What is more, every world is connected by its own essence to the essence of every other world. From planet to planet, star to star, galaxy to galaxy, all energy touches itself. Life touches life. THE ALL, who operates the entirety of the universe, is aware of every touch. Do you understand this?

Sort of. It's the old web of life idea.

That is exactly right. You may liken THE ALL to the spider at the center of her web. Whenever even the tiniest of insects becomes trapped in the web, the spider can feel the vibrations of that insect as it struggles to free itself. The difference between the spider and THE ALL, however, is that THE ALL does not sit at the center of the web of life. There is no center to something of infinite size. God is omnipresent, everywhere in Creation all the time. There is nothing in any of the farthest corners of this universe that is beyond the awareness of God. Every breath from every Being teases His web.

Truly amazing. I suppose, indirectly, you're also telling me that there is human-type life on other planets as well?

I will tell you that there are many worlds in this galaxy alone that are inhabited by creatures similar to humans. The nearest, however, is nearly five light-years distant, and impossible to reach using conventional methods of space travel. It will not, however, be necessary for Earthlings to be the first to make contact with others of their kind in deep space. If The Great Plan ends well, one day, travelers from a distant world will arrive, bringing with them information and knowledge that will forever alter the course of this planet.

Are aliens from another planet on their way to Earth at this very moment?

They are not.

Well, if they haven't even left home yet, they aren't gonna be here any time soon. Even at the speed of light, it takes years to travel that kind of distance.

You have much to learn, Dear One. They will travel from their world to ours within a matter of moments.

How is that possible?

It is not "possible," Din. It is beyond the realm of what is possible. It is Truth.

Now I know I don't understand.

You cannot. But you will.

It seems like this is going far beyond the capabilities of a Strong Weet.

Not as far as you might think.

And why do you say that?

Because the Strong Weet are the ones who are open to the Truth. It is they who have the ability to recognize natural signs and wonders, impending omens, and the subtle vibrations of the universe beyond.

Are you implying that most people wouldn't recognize the Truth if it bit them on the butt?

I am saying that your current society is the result of its own limited process of conditioning. What your leaders, from politicians to priests, are advocating today are the same beliefs that were implanted within them by those who immediately preceded them. As a consequence, the recognition of universal Truth is buried by the banality of the status quo. It does not make it wrong, but it does retard the development of the human species. It must, therefore, fall to those who are outside and above the established authority to transform the collective societal mind of your generation into the purified state it must reach before it is capable of working the magic it must work to properly maintain this world.

I understand what you're proposing here, Mary, but I just don't see how it's possible that a handful of Weet—I don't care how Strong they are—are going to be able to do much good. Most people today think witches are a bunch of kooks! Or they're afraid of them. And I know the Weet aren't witches but ...

You must trust in God, Dear One. It will all come to pass just as it is meant to do. None on Earth can stand in the way of universal Truth. Its Essence is far greater than any power generated upon this minute planet, in this tiny solar system, in this small galaxy among billions of galaxies, within this single universe which occupies an immeasurably small corner of the larger universe that surrounds it.

I believe *wow* is an appropriate word to throw into the Diary right about now.

It is as good as any.

So, what's the main lesson I'm supposed to learn from our meeting today? You've given me a lot to chew on here.

The lesson you are to learn concerns the energy that empowers the Beings of this planet. That is why I summoned the Guardians, Rose, and Daisy. I wish only that you begin to sense the enormity of the strength that is contained in even the smallest of Beings who inhabit this planet. I want you to gain an appreciation for the true nature of all life. Remember, THE ALL is The Life, and The Life is THE ALL. Every Being, no matter how small, is connected directly into the same power source that feeds a trillion suns. If physicists were to discover how to properly utilize the power contained within one tiny flower, they could provide enough energy to light every city in America for a thousand years.

Holy cow, how is that possible?

Once again, you think in terms of what is possible and what is not. These limited concepts are of no use in my realm.

But, Mary, one flower running the entire planet? If you could teach me how to do that ...

It is not something anyone does. It is something that is shared.

I don't understand.

I am afraid this, too, must remain hidden for now. In due time, all will be revealed.

So my main lesson is to be aware of the inherent power within all living things.

To be more than merely aware. You must respect the life energy of every Being. A weed must no longer be a mere weed to you. You must greet each plant as you would an old friend. You must speak with the rocks you are so used to treading upon with your feet. You must wave to the hawks when they soar over your head. You must question your Linden tree as you would a forest saint whose wisdom far surpasses that of any mortal man who has ever walked this Earth. Finally, be always aware that everything — every leaf on every limb, every blade of grass, every feather on every bird, every tiny grain of sand, even the smallest children of God — all contain more power than the combined force of every nuclear bomb ever manufactured.

But how can that be so? How can anything be more powerful than a nuclear explosion?

My dear Din, here is a part of the answer for you, but only a taste. The energy produced in a nuclear bomb is an energy that has been forced by the will of man. How much more would it be if the atom were not forced to split, but did so of its own choice?

Oh my.

Indeed.

But, Mary —

I am going to leave you with your thoughts for a while. You have been given much to contemplate, and my desire is that you understand well what I reveal to you in small portions. There is no need for you to learn everything at once.

But, Mary —

You must trust me. I must leave you alone to consider how you will use this new information, for this is the foundation of all that is to come. It must become as natural to you as taking a breath.

Will I be able to see those little Guardians again?

Oh, yes, Dear One, and much more.

But, Mary…

8 July

My First "Touch" and What it Means

I will attempt to describe what happened — what I saw — after Mary left me yesterday. The moment she spoke her last thought, just as I felt her receding to somewhere deep inside me, I was given the most beautiful vision anyone could ever receive.

It was subtle at first. I remained seated under the Redbud tree, somewhat dazed. As I looked around the garden, I noticed the gradual appearance of a glow. It was faint at first and started with the grass. It's been hot this summer, and most of my grass appeared to be dead, but the crinkly Brown and Yellow blades had begun to glow with a pale Blue, almost imperceptible light. The light soon intensified, and the Blue shifted and split into multiple colors all at once, like a rainbow. No, more like a waterfall of color, or one of those handheld sparklers on the Fourth of July. Every blade of grass flowed with a fountain of crystalline color. Little droplets of colored light streamed from each tip and rained down upon the ground to join the pulsating energy beginning to well up from beneath the lawn and garden.

The light spread from the grass into the plants in the garden. Then it flowed from the stems into the leaves, and from the leaves into the fruits and the vegetables. Tomatoes and cucumbers and eggplants began to throb with vibrant color and light. A surge of Gold and Silver traveled upward through the trunks of the trees and into the branches and the leaves, causing them to sparkle like Christmas trees. But my Linden tree! The energy moved through it with such force and speed that it exploded forth from every twig and leaf in a spray of light like little stars, shooting off in all directions to go spinning across the sky at a million miles per hour.

The light that flowed down into the ground now had such force and brilliance that it shook my body and illuminated the Earth beneath me for hundreds of feet. The roots of every tree in my yard and garden were visible to me, as were the rocks and boulders beneath them. I could see tiny creatures burrowing below me. I could even make out a small stream of water on its subterranean course from east to west. It was as if the dirt was transparent, made of clear crystalline gold, glassy and see-through, all the way to the center of the planet. It was beautiful.

The vision—if that's what it was—lasted for only a few moments—perhaps less than half a minute. The brilliance faded to just the slightest incandescence, leaving everything with a subtle halo. I'd read about seeing auras, but I'd never been able to see them before this. Now, everywhere I looked, everything had an aura, even the so-called man-made objects. My shovel had an aura! I knew the reason was that my shovel isn't a man-made object at all, but consists of millions of tiny molecules of energy and life all working together to manifest the shape of a shovel just so I can dig holes in the ground.

The wonder of this vision is that it isn't going away. Even today, I seem to be able to turn it on and off at will—not the wild, dramatic, sparkling part, but the subtle aura part. All I have to do is want the auras to appear, and immediately, there they are. I don't even have to try, I just have to wish it, and it is so.

This is so strange to me. I remember reading several books that claimed to be able to teach people to read the auras of others. Each book was a little different. One author instructed the reader to stare directly at the subject and squint the eyes ever so slightly. By this method, the aura should become visible just to the side of the subject's head. The other book told you not to squint, but to dim the lights, close your eyes about halfway, and concentrate hard on seeing the aura form around the subject's entire body.

I really wanted to be able to see auras, but even after reading the books and trying the techniques, I could never pull it off. I thought I was doomed to failure in the aura department. Maybe I didn't have the squint down right. Maybe I wasn't grunting enough. I was getting a headache, though, so I gave up.

It seems so simple now. I just think about seeing the aura of that horse in the field, and there it is. No grunting, no squinting, no concentration. I just want it to be so, and, like flipping on a light switch, there it is.

The thing I'm looking at doesn't have to be alive, like animals or people or plants. I can see the auras of coffee cups; I can even see the aura around my Dodge Dakota, It is the most fantastic thing I have ever experienced, but it also scares me just a little. What more does Mary have in store for me? If she's done nothing else, she's instilled within me an awareness of, and deep respect for, the massive power contained within this universe.

✳✳✳

It's late afternoon now, and I'm sitting in my office staring at a photographic collage of the NASA space shuttle program. I've always been fascinated by the possibility of space travel. My stepfather was an aerospace engineer, and even though he was a man of few words, every once in awhile, I could squeeze some pretty interesting stuff out of him. What fascinated me most were the little things. He once told me about his role in designing a bolt that would eventually be used in one of the space shuttle orbiters. It was just a simple little bolt, but each one cost thousands of dollars to produce. I remember asking him if he could bring a few of them home so they could be used to put me through college. He said, "Sure, but you'll have to come visit me in the State Pen after you graduate." It seems that, even back then, nobody left the design facility without being both thoroughly searched and passing through a metal detector. I would imagine it's even more challenging to lift a bolt or two now, given the fear and paranoia of our current culture.

I was always delighted whenever I got a chance to converse with my stepfather. He was a brilliant man, and he was much closer to me than my real father. My mother divorced my real father when I was about one-and-a-half years old. I guess he was pretty much a dreamer and a bit of a drunk, but he wasn't a bad guy; he just couldn't get his act together. I suppose I'll have to learn more about him one of these days. He must have had some redeeming qualities. I am a bit curious. He is, after all, the last link in the long genetic chain leading back to Mary, and the only thing I really know about him is his name. That and, judging from the three photos I have of him, the fact that I look just like him. Maybe Mary can give me some more info.

Anyway, recently I discovered the NASA photo collage at a local antique market. It had a $65.00 price tag on it, but it was well worth it. It's got some really cool photos: the Houston Space Center; a Cape Kennedy shuttle launch; the Challenger orbiter in flight—obviously predating the Challenger disaster in 1986. And, coolest of all, it is signed by the entire Houston ground crew. Personally, I always thought the collage was worth much more than what I paid for it. From a purely historical aspect, you'd think this thing would bring in some big bucks from the right kind of collector, but to me, it really is priceless.

I don't think I'd sell it even if I had the chance.

This morning, the thought popped into my mind that the wall where the NASA collage is hanging would make the perfect backdrop for an altar. Ever since Mary allowed me to see the atoms in my backyard come to life in the form of small Beings of energy, I've felt the urge to construct some sort of special place to honor God; a place I can go every day and be alone with my thoughts about the world beyond.

So, this morning after my shower, in a wild burst of energy, I began shuffling and shoving things around, rearranging pictures, sweeping, and cleaning. My newly-constructed shrine is dedicated to what I call The Great Mystery of The All Who Manifests in Many Forms. What a title, huh? But that's the only way I can relate to God at this moment in my life. Mary has really done a number on my spiritual beliefs. Because of her, I now know that God isn't just what I've always been taught God is. God truly is a Mystery, as the Bible professes. I now know that it doesn't make any difference what denomination one belongs to. The important thing is to admit that there is a God, and then to follow the Laws that God placed on this world—including laws of physics and other sciences that help to explain the more bizarre Mysteries that confront mankind every day. I also know that I will be learning more about God as these little lessons from Mary continue. And I'm also discovering that I really like calling God, THE ALL. Considering the Mystery of God and of how He created ALL things out of NO things, it just seems the right thing to do. If God doesn't have a name like humans have names, then THE ALL certainly is a perfect title for the only GOD of ALL.

So, there are the reasons for my altar, and there it is in front of me. I've been working on it all day, and it really is lovely.

How lovely is it? Glad you asked, because I'm sensing that Mary, for some reason, wants me to describe the altar on the pages of this Diary, so here goes. I brought in a piece of an old kitchen cabinet I'd stored in my garage and set it in front of the wall. The cabinet is about three feet high, two feet wide, and three feet deep. It's an odd shape, but it makes a perfect altar table. I covered the top with some black cotton towels I had in the linen closet, and then said a little prayer of dedication that all objects placed on the altar would be lovingly devoted to the True Creator Being.

Here's the odd thing. I've picked up various odds and ends from antique stores all over the United States. Oddly, many of the items I've acquired are perfect for placement on an altar. I can't explain this, either, because these are not things I would typically collect; they just seemed right at the time I came across them, so I had to have them. I never actually ever used any of these objects for anything. In fact, they all just got packed away somewhere and forgotten. I wonder now if maybe Mary had something to do with it.

At the very back of the altar, I've placed a beautiful crystal Christmas tree that I bought from a mail-order catalog a few years ago. It had been sitting in my garage for some time, and I stumbled upon it this morning while looking for a light bulb. I knew immediately that it would be perfect for representing the energetic Spirit of God. The tree has tiny colored lights that alternate their colors when the tree is plugged in and turned on. It is not garish or kitschy as one might expect but looks quite delicate and lovely when all the other lights in my office are turned off. It is indeed a most peaceful sight to study when contemplating all of this new information I am receiving. The tree now sits at the back of the altar, and to the right of a photograph of the Helix Nebula I had hung on the wall at the center. The Helix Nebula looks so much like a human eye staring down at the Earth from the deep Cosmos that I thought it would be a perfect representation of the Essence of God—a simple visual image to focus the intentions of my thoughts during my time in front of the altar.

A few years ago, I bought a small wooden figure of an Angel. I've placed that on the left side of the Helix Nebula photo. It seems to be in perfect balance with the crystalline Christmas tree.

Several smaller objects grace the remainder of the altar top: an abalone shell I picked up on the beach at Monterey; California; a pine cone, some acorns, and several small stones with intriguing shapes—one has a hole clean through it. I'm not quite sure why I felt I needed such a sacred surface, but I felt it very strongly, so I imagine Mary was urging me on from within.

My office walls are hung with dozens of photos that I have grown to love over my lifetime. Taken from calendars I have collected, most of the images are of various deep space constellations, galaxies, and a few planets. The pictures are colorful and compelling representations of the Greater Essence of THE ALL that can never truly be known by man, at least not while walking this planet in the physical form.

I'm confident that as I progress in Mary's teachings, I'll be moving things on and off my altar appropriately, depending on the lesson I need to learn, or how I am being led to honor THE ALL at specified times throughout the year. At least, that's what I sense I will be doing. For now, I haven't a clue as to what some of this means. Even so, it all seems familiar to me in a distant sort of way.

My office now feels quite comfortable. Thank you, Mary. I used to dread coming into this room because it felt so lifeless and sterile, but now the place is alive. It's as if my office has a heartbeat all its own, and the beat of its heart is merging with mine. Together we are growing stronger and more ... powerful. My mind is no longer limited to the boxed-in, superficiality of the humdrum contemporary world — my mind is free to roam the entire universe at will.

Something is happening in this room. An incredible force is being generated as I sit here, synchronizing my pulse to the pulse of this room. It feels as if the two of us — me and the office — are becoming one, a single, living organism ... merging ...

For the first time since Mary revealed herself within me, I am aware of the fact that I am no longer who I used to be — or who I thought I was. I have become something new and yet something very, very old. I am no longer just *me*, I have become both her and me. Now, together with Mary and this room, I feel such incredible strength.

Good grief! What's going on? The walls are beginning to move. They're spinning slowly from left to right, in a circle. Just the walls. The chair beneath me is rooted firmly to the floor, and my altar is unmoving in front of me, but the walls are slowly turning around me. I want to close my eyes to keep from becoming dizzy. Spinning around is not something I do very well. It usually only takes about one rotation, and I'm on the floor. I'm not getting dizzy at all now. I should be, but I'm not. The walls are speeding up, spinning faster and faster. This has to be an illusion.

I know you're there. Mary. I know this is you. You're up to your tricks again, but couldn't you slow it down a bit?

Wow, that's really fast. I can't continue to write if this keeps up. In fact, how am I able to write at all? This is incredible, Mary. I can see little bolts of lightning flashing in the air around me. It's as if I've been strapped inside one of those old-fashioned spinning tops I used to play with when I was a kid, the kind that made sparks as it spun around.

Mary? I'm afraid to move, Mary! The walls are only a blur now. The heat is becoming intense. Why is that? And I really can't write anymore. What if I drop my pen? Will it fall to the floor? Where is the floor? Will my pen hit the floor, or will it go spinning wildly off into space?

What if my pen gets sucked into the spinning wall? What kind of damage would that do? Will it go through to the other side? What's on the other side? Or will it cause an explosion so massive that the shock wave will destroy the entire surface of the planet?

Mary. Mary, I can't do this any longer. Help me! I can't hold on. I think I'm going to destroy the world! I can't go on writing!

Don't be silly, Din.

Mary!

Keep writing, Dear. The lesson is complete.

Lesson? Hey, the walls have stopped.

Of course they have.

Everything's back to … normal?

Of course it is.

Mary, you wanna tell me what the heck just went on there?

You have just experienced your first Touch as a Strong Weet. And please stop using foul language.

What the heck is wrong with heck? And what does that mean? What's a *Touch*?

A Touch is a truly magical moment in time when a person experiences a supernatural joining together with his or her immediate surroundings. It is when time, for all intents and

purposes, stands completely still. In fact, this kind of aware-
ness is often referred to by the Weet as a Still Point. Since
you are no mere human, but a Strong Weet, and since your
powers are increasing rapidly because you are now aware
of who you are, your little moment in time was a bit more
dramatic than most.

That's putting it lightly. Time certainly wasn't standing
still. Nothing was!

Think back, Din. You have had these moments before on
a smaller scale. I have sensed them with you. Remember
those times when you were sitting in your garden, and all
of a sudden, everything seemed to grind to a halt. Not a leaf
vibrated. There wasn't a sound to be heard. The birds seemed
to stop their flight and freeze in midair. Every color became
more vivid. You were there, and yet not there. It was as if
you were an impartial observer who had been placed awk-
wardly into a world where he didn't quite fit.

I do remember moments like that. One in particular
when the wind was blowing, but nothing was moving, and
everything had a kind of golden tint to it.

I remember, as well. That was a Touch.

But why the word, Touch?

It means you were able to Touch a little bit of the creative
resonance of Mother H.

What?

In everyone's life, there are times when this occurs, but most
do not even notice it. Often these are the pensive times we
all experience when our Spirits are most at ease with their
surroundings and when we are peaceful in our actions and
gentle in our thoughts. When we are in our most meek, least
threatening state of Being, sometimes, just for a moment, our
Spirits are Touched briefly by the eternal resonance of the
Energy of THE ALL. This universe was created with that
Energy when THE ALL unleashed the power of Mother

H and allowed her to use it on the empty void of space. These moments can be gentle and pensive, as you saw in the Garden, or dramatic, as you have just experienced. And time did stand still while you were spinning. But if one blinks at any time during the experience, the moment and the sensation are gone.

I know exactly what you're talking about. It happens all the time, especially when I'm outside.

Human beings are far more at peace when they are outside the confines of their houses. Their houses contain a glut of man-made objects that were made to be servants of mankind and are contrary to the ways of THE ALL. Just being in the presence of these objects will short circuit any chance of ever experiencing the Touch.

But houses are made of wood, and wood comes from trees. Aren't all objects a part of all of THE ALL? I can see an aura around every item in my house.

Do you not recall the Law of Intent? Yes, a television set is made up of spinning molecules of light and energy, and all of these molecules are joined with the Spirit of God via the Creative Energy Essence. In that sense, what humans profess to be nothing more than an ordinary television is, in reality, nothing less than an innocent, living entity in and of itself. Yes, it is the pure intent of that entity to exist as an innocent Being in and of itself; however, since a television is used primarily for base purposes — due to the intent in the heart of the human who controls it — it will become for that human a symbol of negativity. Few humans experience the Touch inside their houses because there are too many negative symbols that prevent it from occurring. Symbolism is a potent force.

But how is it that I can see auras on everything, even my TV?

Because of who you are.

A Strong Weet.

Exactly. The innocence within any entity, no matter how deeply its human controller has buried it, will always be evident to you. You will always be able to experience the Touch regardless of where you might be. You are a favored child of God.

I'm sure all of that will become clearer in time, but getting back to the spinning around bit—

It was not the room that was out of control, it was you.

I beg your pardon?

You had just completed your devotional altar, and the positioning of the objects upon the altar created a powerful Touch. Your Glow immediately sensed the Touch and began to merge with it. Your mind became confused and even fearful about what was happening because it was such a new and powerful sensation. The fear caused what you were sensing to be magnified out of proportion. Because you are a Strong Weet, the Weet energy within you was activated, enhancing the entire experience. These things are automatic. You must learn to control them.

Great.

But your altar is beautiful, I must say, and THE ALL is pleased.

I assume that you will one day teach me how to control my own outbursts of energy? I mean, before I hurt myself?

You will learn to control it yourself. It is much like riding a bicycle. You will fall over a few times, but in time it will become easy.

So, I did good with the altar, huh?

Yes, Dear One. It is very nice.

I wasn't really sure what to put on it.

You chose well.

I don't suppose you had something to do with it.

I might have nudged you a bit here and there. Not so much

in the choice of objects themselves, but where to place them.
Is that important?
It is the most important part.
So, is this a good time for a more comprehensive lesson on altar building?
Perhaps.
I really would like for you to explain a few things because I'm a bit confused — go figure. When I was placing the objects on the altar, I seemed to know exactly where each object should go. For instance, when I first tried to put the Angel figure on the right side of the altar, it just didn't feel right. It looked okay, but the feeling was wrong, so I moved it to the left side.
As you approach your altar, you will be facing north, and all of your rituals will be oriented toward the north. The Angel figure should be on the Western side of your altar because Angels first came to this world from out of the Western skies.
Okay...
In the True Faith of this Earth since before the time of Abraham, altars have always been oriented toward the north. That is because after God had created the Earth when He first Touched the ground with His Life Energy to bring sentience to this world, His Spirit came out of the northern heavens. That Touch Point became the first Shrine to God in this world. In the beginning, the Shrine was visited only by those creatures of Nature that were the first to be seeded on Earth. Since then, humans have faced the north while observing their daily devotions.
That's another thing. I was going to put the altar in front of the south wall because I had an empty space there, but it just didn't do it for me.
You are sensing these ancient ways within you. You have situated your altar the way humans have been doing for centuries. The reason you decided to put the Christmas tree

on the right side of the shrine is that the Spirit of THE ALL come down from out of the eastern skies when He first created trees here on Earth.

I knew that. I really did. I read it in a book years ago when I was studying about the ancient Druids. I don't remember the name or who wrote it, but it explained that, to the Druids, the four directions of north, east, south, west, were all somehow related to the Creation of the world and all that is on it. The priests consulted these directions as if they were living Beings before working their rituals.

That is correct. The original Druids were a branch of the True Faith. They were aware of many of what the Bible calls the Mysteries of God. They worked very hard at trying to learn more about those Mysteries.

You know, Mary, somehow, I get the impression that you could blow the lid off every religion in the world if you wanted to. One of these days, I'd like to just sit down with you and ask questions about that.

I could correct the many misconceptions of your contemporary religions if I wished, but the result would be disastrous for this planet at this time. However, I have every intention of introducing bits and pieces of the Truth into your culture as I see fit to prepare the world for the re-introduction of the Strong Weet Society. This is a necessity. Soon you will understand, Sweet Din.

That's another thing. You still haven't told me much about this Strong Weet Society stuff.

I will. When it is time.

But back to the altar, right?

Yes. You have much to learn about your altar. You will be responsible for changing its appearance from time to time, as need be.

But I like it as it is!

For the most part, it will not change. You will, however, be replacing some objects with others, depending on the seasons and the intent of your work.

Don't you mean *our* work?

I do. I am afraid you are forever a part of me now, Dear One. We will be inseparable in all that we do. This is not a bad thing, as we will each provide for the other a dimension of life that was before impossible to achieve.

But what can I offer you, Mary?

So much, Sweet Din, and one day it will be made apparent to you. I only hope you will be pleased.

But you aren't going to tell me what that might be, are you?

Not at this time.

And in the meantime, back to the altar. Didn't I just say that?

Here are the basics you need to know about the placement of objects on your altar. I will teach you how to practice your devotions at a later time, for you will eventually be teaching humans how to Truly devote their lives to THE ALL. For now, you must know only the following: First of all, the altar is a sacred space. You must treat it with great respect for it is because of the altar that you will be able to not only commune with THE ALL but gain entrance into His World that is beyond this world. Second, you must never place anything upon the altar that does not belong there, and whenever you do place an object on the altar, you must perform the Rite of Consecration.

How do you do that?

It is simple. After placing an object on the altar, you recite the following words: My Creator, I thank you for your gift of this part of You. I will use it only in Your Name. Please bless me whenever I merge with it.

That's all?

*It is enough. And it will not be necessary for you to per-
form this rite for very long. Soon you will be able to drop
it. You are doing it only so that you may learn it by heart
and teach it to others. In fact, in time, the rituals I show you
now will no longer be necessary for your own devotions. At
some point, you will learn the simple Pure Devotions and
share those with this world. Rituals are used only as tools
to ease humans into Truth, but Truth, ultimately, does not
require ceremonies.*

Okay, that's something to look forward to. What's next?

*After you have performed the Rite of Consecration, the
object should only be used for specific, sacred purposes. When
it becomes necessary to remove the object from the altar, you
must recite the following words before placing the object
away in a secure, well-hidden place: Sweet Being, I thank
you for your service to The One Creator you belong. May you
rest well until we merge once more.*

Precisely what is it that is being consecrated? The
object, or me?

*Neither. You are both already an integral part of what
THE ALL has created to be your surroundings. As such,
you have no need for consecration. The ritual is for the blessing of the act itself. By reciting these words, you are merely
acknowledging the Law of Intent. You are expressing to THE
ALL the purity of your intent in any work you may perform
in partnership with the specified altar object. Remember, it is
not you doing the consecrating, it is THE ALL who makes all
acts sacred. This is why it is called the Rite of Consecration.*

So it's really all about recognition?

*That is the main problem with your contemporary reli-
gions, including the latest, so-called pagan faiths. They
have become rites only, without genuine recognition of the
Mysterious, awesome Deity the ceremonies are said to honor.*

You mean they go through all the motions and say all

the right words—

But they do not go through the proper motions, nor do they say the correct words. The formulas used in contemporary religious rituals are the result of centuries of impure additions to the True Faith. The phrases and motions I have revealed for use in your rites were set forth by THE ALL. They are the same words and movements that have been used by Strong Weet for thousands of years. There is no substitute for them. In fact, one of the duties of the Strong Weet is to preserve the purity of the True Faith. That being said, as we approach the final days of this planet, after the Pure Devotions to Earth have been introduced, no past rituals, rites, or devotions will be recognized by God. Humans must then choose either to remain with the practice of superficial ceremonies or move forward with Truth.

A lot of this is confusing to me. I have a feeling that I need a lot more info about the True Faith before I can pull off this Strong Weet stuff. It seems like I have some work ahead of me, and I think it's going to require some memorization that I may or may not be able to handle because I'm not as young as I used to be.

Yes, you have your work laid out before you, but it will not be as difficult as it might first appear. Remember that your chronological age is irrelevant in the scope of eternity. It does not matter how old your physical body is. I assure you that your Glow is far older. I am trying to awaken you gently, Din. Remember that your memory is tied to mine. The lessons I reveal to you are not so much a matter of memorization but of recall. Deep inside, you already know everything I will be discussing. I will merely be jogging our collective memory.

"Our collective memory." Do you know how weird that sounds, Mary?

You will learn much that might at first sound weird to you, Din, but it will become as natural to you as taking a breath as we progress.

I still can't get used to it.

You will, my Dearest. But you have experienced much this day, and you need to rest. I will leave you for a while.

You won't stay away long, will you, Mary?

I will only stay away from you for as long as is necessary. I never want to leave you. But I will also be with you in everything you do.

You know, I hate that—and I love it at the same time.

What is it that you hate?

The part about your being able to witness everything I do.

It has been quite an entertainment for me over the years.

Oh, great. That's what I needed to hear.

Believe me, my beloved, there is nothing you can ever think or do that I will find fault with. You are a human being, as I have been as well.

Still, I'm going to be a little self-conscious at times.

I know. But this is the way it will always be. If you like, I will close my eyes during those times.

Very funny.

Goodbye.

10 July

The Nature of Worship and the Origin of Religions

I'm seated at a small table in the corner of the Barnes & Noble bookstore in the mall. I'm not a big fan of shopping malls, so I'm glad that Barnes & Noble has a separate entrance so I can just pop in out of the parking lot and skip the mall entirely.

I spend a lot of time in this bookstore. Can there be a more pleasant place on Earth than a building filled with books? All that knowledge, all in one spot, with a cafe franchise inside to boot!

Today I was drawn to the so-called New Age section of the store. I'm not in any way enamored of that popular pseudo-philosophy, but that's where they stick the books dealing with esoteric topics. Since my initial encounter with Mary, I've been reading a lot of books on many arcane subjects. I'm not reading them because I believe in all that they profess, I am reading them to collect information.

I don't know if this would be considered synchronistic, but I've been studying comparative religion for most of my life. When I was a child, I couldn't keep my hands off those comic books-style *Classics Illustrated* mythologies. I devoured them. The textbooks for the art history classes I took in college were copiously illustrated with examples of paintings and statues of the gods and goddesses of every world mythology.

I also took classes in philosophy, history, and general world religions. When it came time to get a job, though, those kinds of courses didn't get me very far.

I eventually became an educator, winding up at a junior

high school. What a nightmare that was. I loved the kids, and I loved teaching, but the slanted politics of the system got to me pretty quickly. I knew it would only get worse, so I got out of education as soon as I could.

So, what does all that have to do with philosophy, spirituality, synchronicity, and the like? Simple. My bad experience with public education forced me to look inward. It demanded of me that I take a good hard look at my own values and philosophies concerning the deeper aspects of just about everything in the universe. This was the time in my life when I started to ask the old cliché questions with sincerity: What is the meaning of life? What is my purpose? What is anyone's or everyone's purpose? What follows life as we know it? Who's in charge of all that? Is there a God? Is there a *true* religion? On and on, my little mind went. I did a lot of soul-searching back then, which led me to read tons of books, mostly about — surprise — religion. I believed that if I started with the current mainline denominations, followed each back to its genesis, and then went back farther, I would eventually find the very first religion practiced by human beings here on Earth.

My thought was that the first religion should be the most authentic one. It would be the one that the Creator might have personally instilled into the hearts and minds of His creatures. It would be the pure religion, the innocent one. The one all humans were meant to have from the beginning. Therefore, it would be the correct one.

I truly believed that if I could figure out what that first religion was and if I could understand its tenets, I would have all of the answers I'd been seeking. So, I read, and I read, and I read. I went back through just about every religion you can think of. This elaborate study eventually culminated in my founding the Bliss-Parsons Institute.

It seems that when people undertake this type of "religion quest," they tend to get bogged down at the ancient Egyptians. That culture is one of, if not the, most popular among the hip, in, and groovy New Age crowd. I think it's because of the pyramids and the colors and the cool outfits, although they will deny that and say that it's all about the mysteries. There are dozens of these contemporary groups of Egyptian wannabes that claim to have traced their own beliefs back to the mysteries of ancient Egypt. Even though no living human on Earth has a clue about what those were, they will tell you that they do, and they have all the funny handshakes and the long, stern faces to prove it.

Well, here's a real clue—religion didn't start with the ancient Egyptians. Ancient Egypt was, if anything, a time and place in history when humans muddied the picture almost beyond recognition. What is touted today as great and powerful mysteries, were, at that time, nothing more than experiments and guesses by a group of people who were as confused in their age as we are in ours. They were just trying to find their own answers to those same questions I mentioned earlier. The one thing I do give the Egyptians—and all of the other ancient and/or primitive cultures—credit for is that they were closer to the Truth than modern humans are because they sought their Truth in the Natural world around them. They looked up into the night sky. They looked out into the blowing sands of the desert. They studied the forests and the oceans and the seasonal storms. They didn't have computers, or sacred books, or even traditions, to use as tools for fabricating meaning around whatever it was they were struggling with at the time.

Man's quest for God, and a formula for worshiping that God—religion—predates the ancient Egyptians by thousands of years. In fact, all of my studying led me to discover that religion really began when the first man and woman stepped out of their lowly cave, stared up at the stars, and grunted, "Uh … what the heck is all this about?"

Then the thought occurred to them, "If I didn't create all this—and I know I didn't—then somebody else must have done it."

The man and the woman knew it would take a really powerful Being to create a universe, so their immediate reaction was the urge to worship that Being—out of fear, or respect, or whatever—and worship they did.

As time passed, the simple rituals and emotions that were the essence of those innocent, original forms of Creator-adoration were lost. Mankind had to muck up the works by adding their own ideas to something that was already perfect. Isn't that just the way? We're never satisfied with the simple. We always feel the need to improve even a good thing—even a God thing! The result of all this human tampering is the mish-mash and hodge-podge of the variety of contemporary religions and philosophies we must now put up with.

Once a religion is invented and practiced within a culture, it is established forever. As absurd and as infantile as it may be, you will never be able to get rid of it, hence the reason for the thousands of religions, faiths, and beliefs being practiced all around the globe today. To further complicate matters, each and every one of them believes *theirs* to be the only true religion among all the others, thereby causing friction, hatred, and violence to erupt at any time. Most of the wars we have fought throughout time have religion at the bottom of them.

I guess there really can be only one *True* Faith. Surely, they can't all be right, despite those who would have you believe that all religions are similar paths leading to the same great Truth. That's nonsense. Many lead nowhere, and there are several that lead to violence and oppression. There are others still that are so ridiculous that one doesn't really care where they lead—regardless of the destination, you wouldn't want to go there if it's going to be populated by the wackos who produced it.

So, here I am on my own mission to discover the roots of the True Faith, as is being revealed to me in bits and pieces by Mary. A faith that I find myself not merely practicing, but living as an integral part of all that I am, and of all that Mary is within me. I can no longer separate myself from her, nor would I ever wish to.

Over the past many days, I have devoured dozens of books, and guess what? It appears that the love of Nature and Nature's connection to God form the foundation of the very first religious Faith in this world. In this regard, Nature outweighs all other considerations. There is no other belief system that comes close. Since the Nature religion was introduced by THE ALL eons ago, humans have managed to screw it up pretty good. Every religion under the Sun (including most of today's pagan practices) contains some sort of added doctrine or made-up mystery that disqualifies it from being a part of the *original* Nature religion. Nature-*based* maybe, but not *pure Nature.* It isn't as if the original Nature religion demanded that its members glorify Nature, the Creation of God—that is simply not the case. Only God was worshiped, but His Creation, all of Nature, was to be treated with respect and kindness. Nature is very special to God for some reason, and that is why Mother Nature is also the greatest, most potent Energy Force in all of the universes, and why God loves her so much. I guess it's kind of like God is an artist, and Nature is His painting, and He likes for all humans to honor Him for His great work of art. He also expects all humans to treat His work with great respect. But worship Nature? No. Worship is reserved only for God. I think it's also interesting to note that fully 85% of the Teachings of Jesus either use Nature as a subject or to illustrate a point. Something to think about.

That seems to be the gist of what I'm getting out of all this. I may be wrong, but I think I'm pretty much on the right track. I must be, or Mary would be popping in about now to pick on me.

Speaking of Mary, I'm finding a lot of intriguing stuff in the books I've been going through. From what I can gather by reading between the lines — especially in the more credible history books — witchcraft, as practiced several centuries ago, had little or nothing in common with the stylized and fanciful rituals observed by so-called witches today. Those considered to be witches way back then were not witches at all, but women — usually older — who grew gardens and were knowledgeable about herbs. Many of them had learned how to make medicines and foods that would help people stay healthy. They often took on a younger woman as an apprentice so that the knowledge would continue. They were just ordinary people. They got up off their straw mats in the morning, worked hard all day, and went to bed on their straw mats at night, without thinking much about it. They lived life daily, interacting with Nature. Period. Everything they did was either a byproduct of Nature or a giving back to Nature. They didn't have televisions, so they spent most of their time studying birds in flight, or the shapes the clouds made. They didn't have hobbies like we do today, but they used their extra time to experiment with the medicinal uses of forest plants. They couldn't go to the movies for entertainment, so they used their imaginations more than we do today. They were born with ways of looking at the world that we have forgotten entirely in our mad rush to become the technological clones we are today.

It was not only how they existed, but also how they co-existed with a Natural world that could easily destroy them if they didn't find ways to befriend it. And befriend it they did. Our long-distant Ancestors were as at-home with all the wild things of Nature as we are at home in our living rooms with our own Children.

These Nature people of old walked among the denizens of the forest and the field without fear or concern because they associated with them in ways we would consider crazy or impossible. We think it's really something if we go camping out in the wild and read a deer track in the dirt or happen onto a bird's nest lying in our path. Behold, the mighty woodsman!

Well, I guess that's a start. But the original Nature people could talk with the animals. They didn't need to read deer tracks; they were in constant intuitive communication with the deer themselves. They always knew where they were.

I've come to the conclusion that there can only be one *True* Faith. There are many New Age religions today that profess to be close to Nature, but they have little to do with the True Faith. Ever since Mary reawakened within me, I have made it a point to read everything I can possibly find on Nature, and that's why I'm sitting here today in Barnes & Noble.

As I said before, I'm on a mission to continue my research into the roots of the True Faith. I am endeavoring to conform to it and make it an integral part of all that I am—and of all that Mary is within me. I can no longer separate myself from her, nor would I ever wish to.

It really is not easy to sort out the truth from the fiction in all this stuff I've been reading. Most of it is interesting, and all of it is entertaining, but the bulk of the more recent religious stuff is kind of silly. None of today's religions or denominations can hold a candle to the simple ways of the original Nature religion. Who wants to sit inside a stuffy old building for a couple of hours on a Sunday morning listening to a bunch of insipid contemporary songs sung by teenagers who know nothing about God, Nature, or much of anything else having to do with True worship. I know I'd rather be—

Good morning.

Mary?

Were you expecting someone else?

No, it's just that you don't often reveal yourself to me outside the confines of my house and yard.

I am with you wherever you are.

Well, it's a lovely surprise.

Thank you.

So, how have you been?

I have been well, thank you.

I guess that was a silly question, huh?

It was a very polite question.

But I'll bet you're here for a reason.

I have been monitoring your thoughts this morning, and I would like to bring clarification if I may. It seems you are a bit confused.

That I am. Do you know how many books have been written recently on all this religious stuff? It's really hard to separate the serious works from those of fiction.

You must understand that most of them are fiction, Dear One. I have been reading along with you, and I have found much of the contents of the newer works to be highly romanticized, and that is putting it mildly. It is really more the way the author wishes it to have been than the way it actually was. You are also correct in your suspicion that a good portion of the modern ritual is fabricated and even unnecessary.

Unnecessary?

In most of the books you are reading, the authors go into great detail about needless ceremony and ritual. They do go on! It is all such elaborate silliness.

What do you mean?

They state that you must first go into deep meditation or take yourself through one of their "guided journeys" to prepare yourself to join with the "other world." That is just plain nonsense. Everyone is already joined to the other world at all times. To realize the joining, all one must do is appeal to THE ALL for that awareness, and it will occur. Meditation and the like are simply unnecessary. And the books on witches and the like — oh my, how embarrassing.

Yes, I've read some of those guided imagery thingies, and they all seem a bit corny to me. It looks to me like this stuff either works, or it doesn't, and if it does, then it should work in and of itself without all the foreplay. According to these guys — some who profess to be either New Age priests and/or witches — you have to have a different color candle for everything you do, and you have to say different words for this or that or the other. They call these triggers or catalysts for things in the so-called Astral Plane, and they claim you have to use all these correspondences and invoke all these energies — and everything has to be done in just the right order and in just the right way, or your "magic" won't work. Geez, it just seems so silly to me.

They also suggest that elaborate spell-work be written in rhymes and then recited with grand drama and gesture as if they were acting in a Broadway play.

I didn't know you knew about Broadway.

I am a Strong Weet, and my mother was a Strong Weet, and never once did either my mother nor I write a poem or a rhyme to accompany our work. If one is a true Weet, then one has only to intend for it to be. God's Law of Intent governs everything in our world. The desire and the intent of the Weet is the catalyst for the work he or she performs. Such overly dramatic, outward displays are simply not necessary and were not used in my time. One either has the FAITH, *or one does not. What is displayed today is all driven by ego.*

What about magic wands

I did not know what a magic wand was until the eighteenth century. We did not use them then, nor are they necessary now. All so-called magic has nothing to do with witchcraft — it is science. It is a matter of FAITH *and* BELIEF. *Remember, magic is nothing more than science that has not yet been discovered in this world. Real science is produced in the realm of God, by the Spirit of God Who recognizes the sincerity and intent of the one requesting it. It is an act of* FAITH. *Likewise, power is not conjured by a stream of energy coming from a witch's finger, nor are elements changed simply by pointing a little stick at things, even if the "witch" desires it with all his or her heart. This universe belongs only to God, and God must approve of any changes to it. If there is approval, then it is God that makes the change, not a human. Listen carefully to what I say. A person's abilities lie not only in one's intent but in one's relationship to God. That is the foundation of everything.*

I'm not sure I'm following you.

You must understand that not just anyone can go around altering the molecular structure of physical objects at will. Would there not be chaos if this were the case? This universe is a highly structured and orderly place. God created it so for everyone's own good. Would it not be foolish to allow the creatures to go about destroying a universe designed just for them? There are, however, those who have been entrusted with the ability to do these things. They have carried out their duties throughout time with no thought of personal gain or self-aggrandizement. These few have been personally selected by God to act as caretakers of creation. It is their task to make changes as needed to ensure the survival of all things. That is what I mean by it being necessary for a person to have a relationship with God. Without the original connection of having been chosen by God, that relationship is not there, and neither is the gift.

So, all of the elaborate rituals and formulas and spells for doing everything from finding a soul mate to becoming invisible, and all of the guided imagery stuff is just malarkey?

Have you tried to do these things using their methods?

Not yet.

Do not waste your time. Those methods do not work. Have you not noticed that every book contains a disclaimer that says something like, "It takes time to do this. If you have not succeeded in doing it, just keep trying harder, and one day you will."

I did notice that.

With sufficient effort, one might convince oneself of certain things, thereby producing fleeting images in one's mind. This is the nature of wishful thinking and positive affirmation, neither of which have any place in the True Faith. A person Truly in harmony with the Teachings of THE ALL has only to present their petition. If THE ALL deems it so, then the appeal is granted immediately. The petition of a Strong Weet is always blessed by God. There is never any need for silly spells.

And what about all these herbs and stones and such?

Of course, herbs can be used for physical health and for food, and stones are alive and filled with wisdom. Never forget that all things are sentient, even the stones. The secret is to treat all things with respect. Do not command them. Do not wear them around your neck and expect them to perform for you. Treat them with love and let them do as they will.

Come again?

I will teach you more about herbs and stones at a later time.

But the books here in this bookstore are filled with references to "Tools of the Craft" and resources and websites, where to buy products—

It appears that one can make an excellent living selling such wares as these, but they are not needed. Perhaps they are useful in that they would bolster the ego of the self-proclaimed witch while using them, but they have no inherent power other than their own Glow. The healing qualities of herbs, for instance, are an innate part of their own Being. Healing is gifted through them into the creature who ingests them, just as nourishment is gifted to anyone who eats any food source. Just as some stones have been used as conduits of energy by scientists, many stones are repositories of wisdom gathered over millennia by patient observation. Still, one must have the ability to correctly release and receive that wisdom from them, or the stones will continue as mere rocks. What New Age practitioners are missing is the fact all of this is moot without the input of God. God is behind everything in this universe. When it comes to power manipulation, healing, or any type of change within the laws of science, a human cannot do anything unless God desires it to be so.

Some things have been around for a long time, Mary. What about the circle? Witches have been making circles for centuries, haven't they?

The circle is, perhaps, the oldest of all the human-designed symbols, but its use today holds little actual significance. In my day, it was used as a secret symbol to identify Weet to Weet. If two Weet were to meet on the road, one of them would draw a circle on the ground. The second Weet would then draw an equal-armed cross in the circle, and the identity of both Weet would be validated. This was only necessary when confronting those you did not know. Strong Weet did not need to do this because they could feel the presence of another Strong Weet in their midst. Other than that, a circle is nothing more than a circle. Do you understand this, Dear One?

I believe I do. I watched a program on TV the other night about a so-called witch ceremony in Salem, Massachusetts. A couple of reporters were given permission to be witnesses, with cameras and the whole works. I just couldn't believe what I was watching. They filmed an entire ritual while this obese man who professed to be a "high witch" took them through every cliché in the book. I mean, this guy wore a long black robe and had long pointy fingernails that were painted black, and he had dark makeup under his eyes—to make him look a bit demonic for the proper effect, I suppose. He kept rolling his eyes back up in his head so that the camera was sure to see the whites, making him look even more bizarre. I was actually embarrassed for this guy, who was obviously more interested in how he looked on camera than in maintaining the integrity of what he might be presenting as authentic witchcraft.

The funniest thing was his line delivery. You could tell he was trying to come up with just the right words to make himself sound spooky and important, but it just wasn't working. He stumbled and paused over every line, and most of what he said was ludicrous. I couldn't help but laugh. I just wondered about the viewing public. What must they have thought? What kind of impression was this giving? It was one of the corniest things I've ever seen, like a parody of a stereotype. Am I off base with this?

I remember that program. I was watching it with you. The man was disgraceful. Any person who would perform for a camera in such a way is a charlatan. There is a sacred trust of silence placed upon those with the TRUE gift. To mock the ways of THE ALL through such a ridiculous portrayal is a grave offense. I must say, though, this is one way true Weet can always be distinguished from false witches. The true Weet draw no attention to themselves. You can pass them on the street and not know them. The false witches wish to be known for something they are not, and they are embarrassingly obvious.

Which brings to mind this whole idea of group ritual and covens. Am I wrong, or are these witchy groups just a little bit too showy for their own good?

They are. The Weet never did work in groups or in what witches today call covens. In my time, this was impossible. In the first place, there were not as many people professing to be witches in those days. It seems that in this present time, anyone who claims the label of "witch" is a witch in their own eyes, even though they are not. I laugh when I read in current books that a coven must consist of thirteen witches. I would have been hard-pressed to find one other true, self-professed witch in the entire county back in my own time. Strong Weet have always been few and far between. It would have taken, perhaps, a dozen lifetimes to locate thirteen of them. Also, those were dangerous times. Anyone coming close to thinking they were a witch worked alone for fear of drawing too much attention to themselves. As far as contemporary "witches" are concerned, there is one way to tell the difference between them and the Weet. Ask them to prove their power to you, and they will not be able to. Ask a Weet to prove it, and you'd better run.

God will never allow anyone but His True emissaries access to the secrets we possess as Strong Weet. It is His Law that those who mock the ways of God will never be granted any power. And the more one mocks, the less is the chance that he or she will ever be given any great responsibility found within the work of The Great Plan. The most powerful Being is a silent Being who loves God and respects the wishes and ways of God.

Can I ever be worthy of such an honor as you have thrown in my lap, Mary?

I did not throw anything in your lap, Din. It has been a part of you since the beginning of time, and no one can ever remove it from you. God has known you forever, and He also knows that you will never betray The Great Plan.

My, oh, my. As simple as that, huh?

As simple as that. The one who knits the sweater knows every stitch.

You know, I am deeply touched by this—how God has chosen me to do whatever it is that He has planned out in that Great Plan of His. It's kind of odd, but all my life I guess I've always known something big was planned for me. I've always wondered about there being a God or even a goddess of some sort. I never told you about the dream I had back in 1975.

Do you mean the one with the goddess sitting in the tree?

Yeah, that's the one. You had to dream it with me, didn't you?

I do not dream dreams with you, Din. I observe them in even greater detail than you, and some dreams you dream are gifts from God.

You mean like the one back in 1975?

I do.

I still remember that dream vividly, even after all these years. I had just become a Catholic at the time and didn't know much about goddesses, or even God, so I thought I was having one of those Blessed Virgin Mary apparitions. In the dream, there she was, sitting up in that dead tree in that desert wilderness area wearing that beautiful electric blue dress. It was easy to make the assumption it was Mary.

I must be careful how much information I give you about this so that you do not misinterpret the meaning.

Try me.

Mother H caused you to dream that dream. It had profound significance for you at the time because you were lost in your own search for the Truth. Mother H wanted you to believe that it was the Virgin Mary so that you would remain on your quest for spiritual meaning. Your life back then was without direction, and you were approaching a crossroads that could have been disastrous for your calling as a Strong Weet. You could have made a seriously wrong decision regarding which direction to take with your life, so Mother H placed the image of the Mother of God in your dream to keep you interested in the spiritual rather than the mundane. Had she not done so, you quite probably would have done something very foolish, and your calling would have been in great jeopardy.

But that's when I was getting involved in public education. What could be worse than that?

It is irrelevant at this time in your progression.

Which means you don't want to tell me.

I don't want to tell you.

So, the figure in the tree really was the Blessed Virgin Mary?

It was hoped that by giving you this dream, you would, in your subconscious, draw a connection between the Virgin Mary … and me, Mary.

You?

Other than the Blessed Virgin Mary, I am the only Mary of any significance housed within the deep recesses of your mind.

You are? I mean, you were? Even at that time?

Oh, yes, Dear One. Even at that time. You do not remember

it now, but if you search those hundreds of moldy old manila folders that you keep in your office, you will locate one labeled, Genealogy. In that folder, you will find the original genealogical record that you received from one of your cousins years ago. You mentioned this record earlier in this book. It is the record of the Parsons family tracing the family tree back to the time of King James I himself. It contains the first mention of Mary Bliss Parsons that ever met your eyes. When you first read the part that stated I was tried for witchcraft, you thought, "Hmm, that's really interesting. I have a witch in my family!"

I think I remember thinking just that.

You did. But that was several years before 1975. On the very day of the dream you had of the Virgin Mary in the tree, you had taken out that same genealogical record and read it again all the way through. You probably do not remember, but it made a stronger impression on you that day. As you reread the entry in the record about my being a witch, you paused for quite a few minutes in deep reflection, attempting to feel how I must have felt during that awful time of my life. I was with you then, and I could feel your emotion as you imagined my own anguish, the fear in my heart that I might be hung for being a witch. You then projected your thoughts into my jail cell as I sat awaiting my fate. Do you not remember a tear forming in your eye as you contemplated how I must have felt? Tears formed in my eyes as well as I watched you, Dear One.

I do. It's coming back to me. I do remember feeling an incredible sense of remorse ... and fear. Yes, fear. And I remember feeling anger. Deep anger at the false accusation against my own grandmother!

But it was not a false accusation. I was indeed a Being far above any those people had ever known—just not a witch.

I guess you're right. But I was angry with them for

locking you up and threatening to hang you.

Indeed, you were, my Sweet Din, and your own emotion made quite an imprint on your subconscious mind. In giving you the dream, it was hoped that you would draw a correlation between Mary in the tree and the name Mary, thereby triggering remembrance of me, also Mary, from your genealogy files. The purpose of that dream was to tweak a series of events that would have awakened you to me much earlier than the ball lightning event.

You mean if I'd recognized the significance of that dream back then, I would have had you with me for the past thirty years?

I was with you anyway.

But you know what I mean. I would have been aware of you, and we would have been having conversations and all that.

And more than you can ever imagine.

Darn!

Din…

Sorry, is darn a cuss word?

But this, too, is irrelevant. Now that we are once again together, our relationship will flourish, and our work will be made manifest.

What do you mean, *"once again together?"*

That is difficult to explain at this time. Rest assured that the knowledge will be revealed in proper time, and you will, no doubt, enjoy what it brings into existence for both of us.

Intriguing.

Now you must leave this place, for I wish us to drive your automobile to another location. There is a particular lesson you must learn, and you can only learn it from the source.

And what is the source of this lesson?

Nature.

So we're headed back to the house?

No, we are not. Take us to the car, and I will direct you as we drive.

Thirty Minutes Later

I figured out where Mary was taking me as we pulled off Providence Road and headed toward the large wetlands area southeast of my house. I'd visited the wetlands many times over the years. For the most part, though, my visits had been fairly unimpressive regarding any sort of spectacular bird migration, or woodchuck behavior, or whatever.

Are you finished yet?

Mary!

Are we ready to begin our lesson?

Just for the record, Mary has given me a few moments to enter into the Diary the fact that we have indeed arrived at the wetlands. I believe she is impatient to impart to me some of her timeless wisdom regarding something about this place.

I'm sorry, Mary.

Not only this place but all of Nature. And for the record, the concept of impatience does not apply to me. I have all eternity to teach you these things. However, this Earth cannot wait that long for you to learn them. You must learn as much as possible in very little time, for this is the knowledge of what you are required to employ at specific times and seasons over the next few years to accomplish what must be done.

And thereby save the world?

You should not be so frivolous in this matter, Din, for I assure you that the stakes are high. You must perform your specific tasks when the exact time comes, and perform each one in its proper sequence.

I don't mean to make light of it, Mary, but I still don't

know what the heck you're talking about half the time. You've barely hinted at this doomsday stuff and how it all turns out in the end.

On the Path of Life, whenever one comes upon a fork in the road there are three possible paths to take. Such is the way of pure logic. One is to turn back the way one came, which in this instance is impossible. The other two must then become the focus of a critical decision. Choose one road, and the destination is the correct one. It will lead to life, light, and abundant happiness. Choose the other, and it may lead to a terrible fate. What you must understand, Sweet One, is that you and I hold the key to the crossroads. To treat this lightly would be a terrible mistake.

I'm sorry. I wasn't treating it lightly. I was just running off at the mouth again.

I know your sarcastic sense of humor, Din, and I know you do not mean things the way they come out of your precious mouth. I do want you to realize the gravity of every lesson we discuss, however, so that when it comes time for us to do what must be done, there will be no question as to how effective our work will be.

You have my complete attention. You really do.

Then we shall begin immediately. It is not for any trivial reason that we have arrived at this place called the wetlands. I realize that you have been disappointed here upon occasion, but that was only because you were not sufficiently awakened at the time of those particular visits. You have now had the benefit of the degree of enlightenment that has been revealed to you by me.

You mean the talking flowers and the vision I had of my back yard exploding in color and light?

I do. And everything else you have learned from me up to this point.

I hope I can remember it all.

You do not have to depend entirely upon your memory, for I am here to guide you as we progress.

Thank THE ALL for that.

It is right for you to thank THE ALL for that. There is much to learn of His ways in this lesson, as He is present in all of Nature. I also have a surprise for you. It has been revealed to me that THE ALL will reveal Nature to you for a very brief moment in a more personified form. This is a rare blessing and not given often.

You have got to be kidding. THE ALL—*The* THE ALL—is going to show Mother Nature to me? This is going to come from God?

Remember, there is no such thing as Mother Nature as characterized in human stories, Din. It is merely one of Mother H's human, descriptive names. THE ALL is, indeed, going to present a visage of Nature to you in a form I doubt you will ever forget. It will be only for a moment—Not even a moment—and it will only be the slightest glimpse. If God were to reveal the True *makeup of Nature in all its splendor at this early stage in your Awakening, you would be vaporized into tiny energy particles and blown away into the farthest reaches of outer space.*

Vaporized…

Vaporized. And be aware that I am not sure as to what point during the lesson the form will appear. That is for THE ALL to decide.

Can I ask just what kind of lesson it is for it to be so important that the Creator Himself feels it necessary for this to happen?

You are to learn how to walk in Nature. This is one of the lessons that provide the foundation for much of what you must be able to achieve one day. It is the Mother of Humankind, herself, who will be appearing before you, not because she must, but because THE ALL has summoned her, and she has chosen to show herself out of her love for you.

What? What do you mean out of her love for me? And she isn't a goddess, right?

She is not. As we have discussed, she is the personification of the Energy the Spirit of THE ALL uses to get things done in this universe. Because she has taken that form for so long, THE ALL allows her to do mostly as she wishes. As we also mentioned before, Mother H is more like what humans would perceive to be as an Angelic Being of enormous Power than as a mere goddess. So, if you wish, you may imagine her like that, an Angel, only much more powerful.

I really don't know what to say.

You may say anything you wish, Din. You may ask any question.

So, where does the lesson begin?

It begins here. In this place, standing next to this small pond of water that is home to a myriad of wildfowl who come back to this site every year whether you are here to witness it or not.

Will I witness it today, Mary? I don't mean to be sarcastic, but I count only three birds on that pond.

You will see marvelous things this day, Dear One, for THE ALL has arranged for all of Nature to turn out for you. First, though, I must teach you a thing or two.

I'm ready.

Then let us begin. The more often you walk in Nature, the more you will come to resonate with Nature. You can observe this happening one small experience at a time. At first, you might notice only the nervous glances and fluttering wings of birds. You may be aware of insects buzzing through the air. You will probably assume that the trees and the flowers are planted firmly in their spaces and that their only sound and movement is caused by the gentle breeze. Nothing, in particular, would stand out to you. It would be just another mundane experience outside the confines of your home.

As you frequent a specific area, and as you walk in the quiet peace of that area, you will begin to see small changes. The insects fly a little closer to your head and land on flowers near to where you sit. The birds continue their activities and song as you approach, casting only an occasional glance your way. The trees and the flowers seem a little brighter in the sunlight, and you will become aware that their lively movement is independent of the wind.

After a while, all of Nature will open up to you. You will be able to sit amidst a bed of flowers as the bees, ladybugs, dragonflies, and hummingbirds go on about their business — even land upon your shoulder at times — and pay no attention to you at all. You will see faces appear and come alive in the leaves of trees just as you did when you were a child, and the birds will come even closer, perhaps landing on your knee as you read a book.

You will mingle with Nature unnoticed because you will have become an integral part of it. In fact, you have always been a fundamental part of Nature. This is merely a reawakening to the reality of who you are.

Are you following me?

Yes, I am. I think.

At this point, you will have become such a part of Nature that the living Beings within Nature no longer fear you or suspect your intentions. They now consider you one of them, and you can move about as freely as a bird would hop from limb to limb without any other Nature Being taking notice.

So if I were to sit here long enough beside this pond, the birds and the insects would all grow accustomed to me and accept me as one of their own?

It has to do not so much with the habit of your being here, or the creatures becoming accustomed to you, but rather with the trust you earn from them. As you take the time to learn their ways, they will take the time to understand you for who you really are — one of them — and not for who they assume you to be.

Who do they assume I am?

They naturally assume that every human is the same. Since you appear to be human, they will assume that you are aggressive to their species, that you are loud and volatile in your actions, and that you are abusive to their habitat. That is the way most humans act even when they attempt a personal wilderness experience.

You mean like some people who go on camping trips?

Exactly. Those people seek to experience something they lack in their hectic urban lives. They attempt to return to Nature, yet they bring their urban ways along with them, inflicting chaos on the serenity that is the heart of Nature.

That's why I don't go camping anymore. The last time I went, I had such a terrible experience that I never wanted to set foot in a campground again. Every space was filled. Unruly children were running around all over the place, yelling and screaming and fighting. Teenagers were playing boom boxes so loud that you couldn't have heard a bird chirp if you'd wanted to. Kids were sneaking out to the woods to smoke, leaving cigarette butts on the ground behind the trees, and the adults were drinking beer and carrying on even worse than their kids.

Nature's creatures are not impressed with human beings. Most have shown that they are not to be trusted or respected, and are to be feared for the damage they can cause to the wilderness that is home to so many of the Gentle Ones.

Can this ever be reversed? I mean, can we ever gain back the respect of Nature?

It is doubtful, for it must be a communal effort, and obtaining consensus among the majority of the human community is highly unlikely. The secret to being a true person of Nature is first to give God His due — admit that He is alive, that He exists, and that He not only has relevance to the human sphere of existence but that He CREATED it. Then one must honor God in thought, word, and deed and vow never to abuse or disgrace His Creation, but only love and bless Nature and protect the animals, herbs, and insects, Nature's innocent offspring. This planet is suffering from a disease more virulent than cancer. It is caused by those who refuse to give the most precious of all God's Creations, Nature, it's due, and who choose to ignore the sanctity of Nature and to wallow in the shallow ignorance of this present culture. You must join your will to that of God in the effort to heal this world.

Everyone from every culture must acknowledge The Glow, that inherent spark of sanctity within all things and the glimmer of immortality that brought mankind into existence and sustains all of life. An ordinary aura is simply a physical gauge of the energy within any body. The Glow, which emanates from THE ALL, is the spiritual indicator of a being's spirit.

Think of it in terms of fiber optics. Each point of light at the end of a fiber represents a soul. While their numbers are infinite, all the fibers transmit light from a single Source, the Glow. If a fiber tip is cut off, the light is not cut off with it. Instead, it retreats back into the Source. So it is with all living things — their Spirits are never extinguished. When humans die, their Spirits return to the Source. They are examined by THE ALL, given immortality, then sent on their final journey — for better or for worse. The amazing thing is not that the Source can do this, but that the unique identity of each one of the trillions of Spirits ebbing and flowing in and out of the Source is retained.

Like snowflakes, no two Spirits are alike. And each Spirit keeps the memories of all of its human experience. Only God

*knows how this truly works. It is far beyond human compre-
hension, and far beyond physics or any other science known
to humans. The Great Mind of THE ALL is never static,
never at rest, and is aware at all times of the activities and
endeavors of all humans. God's Mind has been growing
since the beginning of time. How foolish mortals are for
entertaining, even for a moment, the thought that they can
compete with God. The spark within a human identity is
vitally important, but it is not meant to lead people into a
false sense of self. It is intended to serve only as a light, a
beacon of Truth, to guide people gently through the eternity
that is time.*

But why are people here at all?

*To explore! Each Spirit is like a single brain cell in the
vast mind of God—a Mind that is continually searching for
knowledge. It is our nature to be curious, to be inquisitive, to
gather information, and to store knowledge. Every question
ever answered, every lesson ever learned, every theory ever
proposed, every thought ever conceived, every memory ever
made, every experience ever encountered all come back to
God. It all joins. It all is. It is why God is called THE ALL.
When it all comes back and merges together in the Mind of
God, it becomes ALL that there is.*

It sounds like God is nothing more than a giant computer.

*But so much more. Contemporary computers are so primi-
tive in comparison to one tiny cell of the entirety that is THE
ALL. Just look around you, Din. Every blade of grass, each
drop of water in this pond, and every gnat is more complex and more amazing than the most advanced computers
known to this day and age. The most astonishing thing of
all is that every cell in every blade of grass, drop of water,
or gnat has the memory of the entire universe built within.
If you were to break apart your home computer and separate it into individual molecules, the information found in*

just one would be more valuable than all the information that was stored in the memory of the original computer. Computers are limited to only what humans place within them. Individual cells and molecules are linked directly to the infinite knowledge of God.

You're right, this is all way beyond my understanding. I mean, I get it. I think I understand the main idea, but there's no one alive who can understand how God does all this—how God puts this all together into some sort of intelligent system that seems to function perfectly at all times. Every leaf on every tree is doing exactly what a leaf on that particular tree should be doing.

That is because of the total order of things built into the fabric of the universe. The scientists come close with their Big Bang theory for the creation of this universe. What they fail to realize—or refuse to admit—is that creation was an orderly process designed by the Mind of God. There is nothing haphazard about how the universe began or sustains its existence. They also refuse to admit the very reason for the event they call the Big Bang. The science community has all kinds of speculations and guesses, but their theories are far from the truth. The massive explosion that began this universe resulted from a single Thought from the Mind of THE ALL. It was the Thought that brought forth all form and substance. From out of nothing, God created what you see before you in the night sky. That single Original Thought was such that human beings will never comprehend it. The greatest minds in scientific research will never touch, even briefly, the vast creativity of that one single Thought.

This sounds like the story in the book of Genesis in the Bible, where God says, "Let there be light," and it came into being at that instant.

That description is as close as mankind can come to describing how God began all things. It was all done in a single moment too small to measure. God simply imagined the universe and everything in it—past, present, and future—became a reality with that one, creative Thought.

So what's all the fuss about? Why do scientists and religious people fight all the time? Why is it that they can't see the Truth?

It all has to do with ego. It is as simple as that. In addition, billions of dollars are spent each year to perpetuate the antagonism between the two. It is embarrassingly simple. Ego and greed fuel the fire that keeps religion and science from ever progressing enough for both sides to reach the point where they can work together.

But that is not why I brought you here. I brought you here so that you can interact with Mother H. What do you see, Sweet Din?

I see ... several ponds over there to my right ... the rocky bluffs to my left. There's a clump of Oak trees over there with one bird sitting in it. Holy cow! What the heck was that?

Tell me exactly what you saw.

I was looking at that big bird when it seemed like the lights went out for a second, then my head was filled with brilliant golden light. I almost fell to the ground. I'm not having a stroke, am I?

No, Dear One. Just watch and wait.

***

Wow! I mean, WOW!

Describe it for me. I see the same things you see, but you must understand what it is that you are experiencing and be able to put it into words.

That bird, the big one over there, suddenly became ten times larger than the tree it was sitting in and the tree just ... exploded. Then the bird grew even larger until it filled the entire sky, and the golden glow became so bright that I couldn't look at the bird. It was like an aura around the bird—intense, with golden crystalline rays shooting out in every direction. Then the bird raised its wings, and there was nothing left. The entire wetlands had disappeared. The whole Earth disappeared. Nothing was left! I almost blacked out. The glow became even brighter, and I thought it would make me blind. I remember crying out in my mind, *Save me!* Then a waterfall of something like warm liquid began to slowly pour down on me. As it began to engulf me, I heard … I swear I heard my mother crying out in her labor pains to give me birth. I know that was what it was I heard.

Then—and this is the most amazing thing—I saw a face. For a brief moment, the face of a beautiful young girl, maybe fifteen or so, appeared to me in the middle of all that glittering gold light, and I was slammed by a wave of gut-wrenching emotion. It grabbed me deep inside and made me begin to weep. Oh, man, I'm crying now. This … teenager smiled at me and brought me to tears. And I know that all of this happened in just one single moment, almost no time at all. What's going on here, Mary?

Listen to me very carefully, Sweet Din. You have just met the Mother of Humankind, and she has given you a blessing that I have never before seen her give. Though she is your Spiritual Mother, she has chosen to appear to you in the form of your daughter.

I don't have a daughter.

You do. She is the most beloved of all the children you have raised throughout all of the human lives you have chosen to experience, and her name is—

Annie!

Her name is Annie.

Where did that come from!? Where the heck did that come from? That name, Annie, just popped out of nowhere. Where the heck did that come from?

It came from your heart, Sweet One. Annie has long been with you. When you decided to jump back into this life, she chose to go with you but only in her Spirit Form. She watches over you to this day. Mother H has chosen to honor the love between you two by taking her face and form, and by reminding you of the great love you shared because Mother H is manifested by and comprised only of the purest love. Stand very still and watch and feel.

Oh, Mary, what is this? I can feel it. I don't want to write it down. It's so … it's … words … I can't describe this.

What you are feeling is the intensity of the purest form of Love there is. You and Annie were and still are closer than close can be. At one time in a past sojourn here on Earth, her physical mother, your wife, was taken from you by soldiers under the authority of the British King in the sixteenth century. You were a Scotsman who had moved from Scotland to Devonshire, England. Your wife and Annie were the most beautiful women in Devon. When the king's soldiers were marching through that day in October, they saw sweet Annie and took both her and your wife away. They did terrible things to both and then presented them to the king. They both became his wife by force, but before they were to bed the king, they — Annie and her mother — committed suicide. Such was their love for you. You eventually learned of this and attempted to kill the king. The guards apprehended you, and you were hung several days later.

My God.

And then Joseph was born.

Your Joseph?

My Joseph.

Uh, Mary, what are you implying here?

There is no implication, Dear. I must tell you this. It will be difficult for you, but it must be revealed. You are both the many-greats-grandson of Joseph Parsons, and you are also Joseph, himself.

What?

The explanation of such things is beyond your comprehension until the time when you Awaken fully. You must simply trust me. We Strong Weet choose to interact here on Earth by jumping into and sharing various lives. It is part of what we must do for THE ALL. You chose to be my husband, Joseph, and at a later time, you chose to come back and merge with who you are now and become my great-grandson. This is not what you think or what this world calls reincarnation. Nor is it some sort of incestuous relationship. The science behind this is far beyond the understanding of what is taught from the minds of human beings, but it will all be explained in full to you very soon.

Holy—

No, no, no! You must not use such language in front of your daughter or Mother H.

What?

They are both present.

You've got to be kidding. Good grief!

Enjoy this, Din.

Ten Minutes Later

Explain your experience, Sweet Din. I expected that it would make you cry, as I see that you are.

Of course, you did. I don't know if I can explain it. I just saw my whole life flash before my eyes. At least the life I lived when I was Annie's father. I saw her conception, her birth, every time she fell and scraped a knee. I saw everything. I even saw the king's guards when they took her and her mother away, and I ran after them on foot.

I ran until I couldn't run any longer. I fell to the ground weeping. And I felt this terrible emotion. I wanted to kill everyone and anyone I met. I didn't like that feeling.

That's because that is not a part of you. You are not a cruel Being, but you are a Being of Justice.

I ran back home and got my sword. Somehow, I knew that the king was near Devon, in the woods on some sort of an excursion. I went after him. But the guards seized me before I could do what I wanted to do.

I felt the strangulation of the rope around my neck when they hung me from a tree a few days later. They were laughing.

The strangest thing then came to my mind. Almost immediately, I seemed to fly forward in time, and I saw you, Mary. And I saw Annie. And I saw this moment, right here. And I felt this intense emotion—have I said that before? Geez. Like a family type thing. I don't understand genetics, or how this jumping around from life to life works, but I know now that, back in the 1500s, Annie was not just my daughter, she was also—

She was our daughter.

She was our daughter? How does that work? What's going on here, Mary?

You have one more vision you must experience, Din. Please brace yourself.

Whoa! Where did that come from?

Tell me what you felt.

A flow of brilliant gold liquid, like water, entered into my head from above. It worked its way down, flowing through me and filling my entire body. It seemed to be cleansing me in some way. More than that, though, I felt more of that intense, incredible love I had felt earlier.

It was all you and Annie. You looked so beautiful to me. You were...I don't want to write this. I don't understand this.

You don't have to write it down, my sweet. This is so different for you because, in this physical form, you have forgotten all your past life interactions and the previous choices you made in the Spirit World. You cannot possibly understand until you return Home once again. When you do that, you will understand everything.

So I have to die to get back my memory?

No, Dearest. Annie and I are going to attempt to speed the process.

My head is spinning.

Let us end this session so that you might rest. Thank Mother H for what she has done this night. As I mentioned earlier, I have never seen her do such a thing. You can see that she loves you very much.

It probably has more to do with you than with me.

No, it is you. You are very special to her. One day you will know just how special you are.

A bit ago you said something about Mother H being my Spiritual Mother, what—

Not now, Din. Later.

12 July

My Amazing Family

Two days ago, I received the shock of my life. Mary told me that not only do I have a daughter I didn't know I had, but that she, Mary, and I had been married. Annie is not just my daughter, but hers as well.

Mary gave me so much information that I had to write it down as quickly as I could. I'm just now trying to make sense out of it, but it goes something like this: I was married to my great-grandmother. It was a long time ago and has nothing to do with so-called reincarnation or me actually *being* Joseph. Apparently, there is some sort of life interaction between Joseph and me, created and orchestrated by THE ALL.

The experience of learning all that was overwhelming. I was filled with an all-encompassing feeling of love. I've never felt anything like it before. The images of Annie were so real. She was so beautiful, and I could feel the connection between us — really *feel* it.

I could also see the resemblance. Annie looked like a combination of Mary and me, except Mary's hair is dark auburn, almost black, and mine is blonde. Annie seems to have inherited something in between.

I am so excited about this. What an incredible thing it is to find that I have a daughter. She isn't dead, either; she's very much alive in some sort of high-vibrational realm or region that exists between here and what Mary has been calling *Back Home*. Does she mean Heaven? Regardless, Annie's waiting for me and has apparently been overseeing certain events in my life, watching over me like a little Guardian Angel.

Anyway, I will try to describe her. She's young. Fifteen? Brownish to blonde hair — kind of reddish, really. Sienna?

She wears it pulled straight back in a ponytail. Her eyes are big and bright, and I think they're a reddish-brown color. Her nose is more like Mary's—a bit wide but beautiful with cute little freckles all over. And that smile! I just can't describe it here. I need to experience it more. This is all so new to me.

I can also sense the beauty of Annie's Spirit. For some reason, I know that she is what is called an *old soul*, one that has been around for a long time. And—

Din?

Mary!

I am so happy that you are beginning to interact with the images that have confronted you. We have a most beautiful and wonderful daughter.

I know. It's so odd. I can smell her hair. I can taste her breath. All of these sensations—

And that is the way it should be. She is a part of us, and she will be interacting with us from this point forward.

What do you mean by "interacting with us"?

She will be popping in and out of our interactions.

Incredible!

Indeed. But now you must experience something else.

What's that?

Just watch. Do you see that tennis ball in the basket by the door?

That's one of Natalie's toys.

Your Poodle is very precious. Watch this and record it well.

Five Minutes Later

I had to stop writing while Mary worked her magic. I just couldn't believe it— I know, I've written that before. When Mary told me to "watch this," my toy Poodle, Natalie, entered the room. She walked over to the door and looked up to where I assumed Mary was standing in some invisible Spirit form. Natalie barked, then looked over to the basket where the ball was. At that exact moment, the tennis ball flew out of the basket, and Natalie caught it in her mouth. And then—get this—Natalie carried the ball over to the place where Mary must have been standing, dropped it on the floor, and looked up expectantly. The ball flew up again and hurtled down the hallway. Natalie chased after it, brought it back and dropped again at the feet of Mary, who tossed it a third time. They were playing fetch.

Just when I was getting used to the fact that my dog was playing fetch with my dead grandmother/long-ago wife, something truly amazing happened. Mary tossed the ball toward the kitchen, but before the ball had a chance to go through the kitchen door, it stopped, right there in mid-flight, and flew back toward Mary. Then a flash of brilliant white and gold light nearly blinded me, and when my vision cleared, I saw Annie.

There she was, all bright and beautiful, in the doorway between the living room and the kitchen playing keep-away with Mary and Natalie. My heart melted. She was so sweet. She smiled at me and flipped her ponytail back, and then she ... she winked at me. My vision blurred again so that I could barely see her, this time with tears.

I wish I could describe my emotions. I wish I could tell you how beautiful Annie appeared. Oddly, she was wearing clothing more like that of the late nineteenth century rather than of the sixteenth century, as I had expected. I watched as Annie dissolved into a million twinkling lights of all colors, and I heard her speak to me for the first time, "You will see me again, and often. I love you, Daddy."

I couldn't hold back my tears as the experience came to an end.

MARY: *Do you see what a lovely daughter we have?*

Mary!

She is the one we have chosen to be ours for eternity.

I can see why. She's so beautiful, and I can feel her beauty and her life. Mary, I don't know what to say. I don't know how to react. This is beyond anything that a human being can ever wish to experience. But I'm getting used to it. I guess.

Yes, you are Sweet One.

Mary, can I ask you a question?

Yes, Dear.

What is the purpose of all this? Why is it that all of a sudden this is happening to me? I mean, one minute I'm lying in my bed, and I hear this voice, and then the next minute — or so it seems — I find out about you and my daughter and all that stuff. I can't make sense out of it. No, that isn't true; it's beginning to make sense. Man, oh, man. I know this is all true now. I know it because you two are such a part of me that I can never ever ... I just can't dismiss this. I don't want to. I feel such love for you. I feel such love for Annie. We were a team back then. We were three, but we were also one.

You are ready now for the next phase. You asked me what the purpose of all this is, and I must remind you that it all relates to your ability to find the Strong Weet Society.

I'd forgotten about that.

I know, but you must now remember. You must now become serious about the task before you.

You haven't really told me what that task is.

That is because you were not ready, but now you are. With the help of our combined energies, you and I and Annie and the Strong Weet Society will be able to do what must be done.

And what exactly is that?

As I have said before — we must save this world from destruction. It will take all of us, but if we can find the others, it can be done.

The others?

There are only a few ancestral members of the Strong Weet Society remaining on Earth, counting you. You are their leader. When you find them, they will recognize you, and you will know them.

Mary, two things here. Number one, I really don't know how to find these folks. I mean, where do I look? What do I do? Do I put an ad in the paper? And number two, if you have been so close to me throughout the eons—geez, I just wish there was some way we could…touch…on some level, some way we could—

You want to hold me.

It's just that I've seen you, and you are the most beautiful woman I have ever seen. And I have felt your love for me. This is all still very confusing to me, but Mary—

You must have patience. I cannot find the energy to interact in that way as yet, and there is a much more profound mystery that simply should not be revealed at this time. Please, have patience.

Mary, I don't know what to say. Do I need a psychiatrist? I'm having this bizarre interaction with a ghost—no, make that two ghosts.

Rest assured, you do not need a psychiatrist. What you are experiencing is real. Keep in mind that the physical world you see around you is the illusion. The real world in which you have existed for eternity is the Spirit World. I do so want to return you to it, as that is where you truly belong. First, though, we have a task to do, and it is to face the most significant challenge this planet has ever faced.

I can give you this, however. Close your eyes and think of me.

***

Wow! Thank you, Mary. I felt that. Please tell me you just kissed me on my left cheek.

I did.

How can I say this? How can I write these words? I think I love you, Grandma.

Indeed, you should, Din. I've put up with your antics for centuries. I deserve to be loved.

Very funny.

Just don't call me Grandma again. That's not the way it works.

I know, you aren't really my grandma, Mary, you just jumped into Mary back then. But ... wait a minute ... if you aren't Mary, then what's your real name?

A measure of your Awakening is that you will come to know my real name without my help. For now, though, you can call me Mary.

Great, still one more mysterious unknown to have to deal with.

You'll live.

14 July

Glimpses into Other Realms and a Haunted House

I just got back from another trip to the bookstore. I'm not sure why, but I felt moved to go there again, something to do with books about the afterlife, but I'm not sure. I've got a pretty good library on that kind of stuff, but something is missing—something Mary and Annie are leading me to. I can't quite grasp it, but it all seems to come back to the True Faith. The more I study the subject, the more convinced I am that there is great wisdom to be found there.

And this Strong Weet Society—what the heck am I supposed to do with that? How the heck am I supposed to find these people? They could be anywhere. I can't afford to buy plane tickets to Ireland or Scotland or France or India or wherever just to look these people up. How the heck am I going to find them? Eight, counting me? Is that what she said? Mary said there are still seven others out there somewhere, I think. Heck, this thing is speeding by so fast I don't know what's going on. All I know is that I feel the importance of it. I understand that this really means something, and it isn't just a game or an illusion. Something big is up. Something significant is going to happen—or not, depending on how I do whatever it is that I'm supposed to do. What the heck is that? I'm so confused.

The phone will ring in ten seconds.
Mary! I—

Thirty Minutes Later

The phone call was from a woman named Danette. She told me that she had heard about my health class from a friend she ran into at the market. The odd thing was that she talked for a very long time about everything but health. She had a pleasant voice, kind of soothing, but something about our conversation was unsettling. I hung up on her.

Mary, what the heck was that all about?

You have passed the first test. If you are to recognize the True Weet of the Strong Weet Society, you must first identify the false. There will be many who will profess to be what you are seeking, but you must not believe them.

So, this Danette was a phony?

She was. She was not interested in taking your class; she was attempting to sell you a subscription to a health magazine before you terminated her call. Listen to me very carefully, Din. There are those within your current sphere of interaction who can connect in a limited way with what we are about to do. They will try hard to convince you that they are True Weet, but, of course, they are not. Remember, the power of others is limited to the power you give them.

You mean that if I ignore them, they'll go away?

Yes. First, though, you must be able to recognize them for who they are. That is not always easy as some of them are very clever. When the word gets out that you have become active in this world, there will be many who will try to convince you that they are Strong Weet. Just remember that there are only seven more besides you still out there and waiting to be Awakened.

Two questions: What do you mean by "when the word gets out," and does that seven include you and Annie?

The seven does not include us. These are seven direct, ancestral descendants of Strong Weet from the First Incarnation.

What the heck is a "First Incarnation?"

The First Incarnation is the original set of Strong Weet placed on Earth many eons ago. You and I and Annie are among those. There were only ten in total. Seven are in physical human form here on Earth and remain to be Awakened. When it becomes known that the Strong Weet Society is once again active, two things will happen. First, there will be many who will flock to you, claiming to be Strong Weet solely for their own self-gratification. Second, all of the Spirits who oppose us will be alerted, and we will have to use our powers to control them. They must be controlled, or else we will not succeed.

Good grief, Mary, I don't feel like I have any power, I just feel like a regular guy. Will these powers just kick in at some time and turn me into Superman? What if all these opposing Spirits gang up on me? I'm just an artist; what the heck am I supposed to do here? I think I'm getting scared.

There is no reason to be afraid, Dear One. We have been through this before. These Spirits are the same ones that have attempted on many occasions to destroy this beautiful world. They have always failed because we were stronger, and we remain stronger because we have Mother H watching over us and supporting us, even though we cannot always see her. Also, there is one other little secret that you will learn in time. You must trust me on this.

I trust you with my life, and I know I need to continue to trust you. But you have to understand that, to me, all of this is incredibly fantastic. I know it's true, but it's so far beyond what anyone on this planet is used to —

It does not matter what they are used to. Something of great importance is at stake here.

I know that, and I'm an imbecile, I suppose. You say Mother H is here?

She is always with us.

And Annie?

She has been with us forever, and she will be with us forever.

Then let's go. Let's do this!

Dearest One, you have the power to do what needs to be done, and together with the power wielded by me, Annie, and the Strong Weet, we will complete the task.

But exactly who are these guys we are trying to defeat? I'm still really confused about that. Are they rebel Angels? Demons from hell?

They are evil entities that have done much damage to the culture of the human race. Adolph Hitler was among their most significant leaders. Idi Amin was another, and there are many more. There are humans alive today possessed by these entities. Some hold positions of power in governments all over Earth, even here in America at the highest levels. It is upon these we must work our Energies.

So, what do we do? What do I do? I don't know what my role is here. You and Annie are used to this kind of stuff, but I'm just a guy.

You are not "just a guy." You are an incredible Being of Truth, Love, and Justice. You have no idea how powerful you are because you have not yet received insights regarding your power. But believe me. Stop whimpering, Din. Remember who you are!

I'm humbled by all this. I've never felt this way in my life. Confusion is the keyword here. I just don't feel this Power you say I—Whoa!

Seconds Later

There is your power!

Holey Moley!

Stop swearing. I had to do that.

What was that?

It was the heat and energy of a thousand suns coursing through your body.

And I survived!?

This is nothing new to you. You just haven't experienced it in a while.

Why wasn't I fried?

You were not fried because you became a part of the energy as it passed through you.

What?

Strong Weet have control over such things. Whenever negative or positive energy approaches you, you merely merge with it and become a part of it until it is gone.

You mean I became one with those suns as they passed through me?

That's precisely what I mean. You have learned the ultimate power, the power to control the elements. And you are the Strongest Weet of all.

Holy—

Annie.

Sorry, Annie. I wish I could talk to Annie.

But you can, Din.

What?

You can talk to her any time you want.

How?

Just do it.

Annie?

ANNIE: *Father, I love you.*

I can hear you in my mind, Annie. It's like your mind is sending your thoughts to my mind.

It is. I am.

There is so much I wish to say to you, but I'm still having trouble trying to figure out our connection.

I have missed you so much.

Are you crying, Annie? I can sense … something. I feel like you're crying.

I am crying because I am so happy to be reunited with you. I have missed you so much. It has taken so long for you to awaken. If that ball lightning hadn't appeared when it did, I don't know what I would have done.

Annie, I don't know what to say. I am so confused about all this, and yet I know it's true. And I have seen your sweet image. But it's all so new to me.

It isn't new, Father. We've been through this many times before. For some reason, you are having a difficult time waking up to the immediacy of this moment. I will try to help you. Mother, will you help me here?

MARY: *I will, my child.*

My God, What was that?

It was your wakeup call from your daughter, Annie.

What a jolt.

And what did you experience?

Everything. I saw my entire life—and lives I've inter-acted with—pass by me. I saw everything. I know who I am now, I think. I'm still a bit cloudy on some things, but I know who you are, and I know who Annie is and I know what I need to do with the Strong Weet Society. I can feel the power. And … I know where I have experi-enced Annie before.

And where is that?

The Boonville Paranormal Investigation. I wrote an article about this for my website, but I never made the connection. Now I do.

Can you explain the Boonville Investigation for the read-ers of this book?

It's all in the article I wrote for my website. I titled it—oh, dear Lord—I titled it, "A Tribute to Annie."

Yet another sign of your Awakening even more.

Keep writing.

Not too long after the ball lightning hit me and made me aware of your presence, I began to study incessantly, and continue to do so. Prompted by what I was learning, I brought together a little group of people who seemed to be thinking along the same lines as I was. I had read several books that were written by people professing to be intuitives. They said that it was of value to start or join what they called a Development Circle, to develop one's intuitive skills. Since there weren't any of those here in town that I know of, I decided to start one. We've been meeting for several weeks now, and it's evolved into a reasonably talented little group. It's been a lot of fun. We've even investigated a couple of supposedly haunted houses. But you know all this because you're up there in my mind.

I know this, but you need to relate this information to the readers.

Well, a few months ago, I took my DC on an Investigation. We toured an old house built in the 1800s over in Boonville, Missouri. The folks who owned this house had had some pretty strange experiences there and asked us to come and check it out. We did, and it proved to be quite an experience.

You know, Mary, this is a long story.

We have all night.

Well, okay then.

During the investigation, we took hundreds of photographs. Wait a minute, I have a journal entry that tells about this. Hold on ... here it is, the entire transcript of the investigation. I'll just copy the part about my Annie experience word for word.

The Haunted Boonville House Investigation

In the course of the investigation, orbs — believed by some to be Spirit Beings visiting from another dimension — were photographed in several areas of the house. Also, another B-PI investigator, Sheila, and I had strong intuitive reactions multiple times. We spoke very little during the investigation so as not to influence each other, and we each recorded our impressions separately and privately in our own notebooks. After the investigation, Sheila and I sat before the video recorder to discuss and compare our findings. Our interpretations were identical. We also reviewed the digital photographs and discovered that the appearance of the orbs corresponded to the sites where we received the strongest intuitive "hits."

Here is my impression of the Spirit encounter I had:

A young woman in her teens or early twenties, dressed in a long, cotton nightshirt. She was distressed. I received a vivid impression of her face. Her nose and mouth appeared to be covered by a mucous-like substance. She looked confused and worried. She was pretty — very pretty — with light reddish-brown hair pulled back in a loose ponytail. She had large reddish-brown eyes and freckles on her nose.

I received an impression of her name as Ann or Annie.

Sheila thought she received Amelia.

It would not surprise me to learn that a young girl with her name starting with an A had died in the house many years ago. Sheila received nothing concerning the girl's health problems, only a sense of oppression and heaviness. I received a suggestion that she died of pneumonia.

The girl — I'll call her Annie — looked directly into my eyes and seemed to be appealing to me in confusion — or with love. We are making an appointment to return to the Boonville house this coming Saturday. There are feelings associated with this place that I have never felt before.

The Next Saturday at the Boonville Haunted House

We learned from the homeowners that at least one Annie had, indeed, lived in the house in the late 1800s. We visited the house two more times, and Annie seemed to follow me around each time. The strongest interaction was during the last visit. It took place in the upstairs bathroom, which used to be a nursery. Annie entered—I can think of no other way to put it—into me. I shivered from head to foot as I felt her merging with me, but I could feel that this was a loving act. We concluded the investigation by doing a Crossing Over ceremony for Annie that was intended to set her off on her way to Heaven. It felt odd, though, because I sensed that Annie didn't really need to be Crossed Over, but rather that she was trying to communicate with me.

End of transcript

ANNIE: *Yes, Father, it was I in that house. I was trying to awaken your memory.*

You were so ... a part of me. Sweet Annie, I can hardly say your name.

It has always been this way, Father.

That investigation was a major turning point in my life.

And you have seen my Orb in photos many times since then because I am always with you. To return to what Mother H said earlier concerning your task when this book is released. There will be many who will come claiming to be one of us. Remember, though, that there are only seven others besides ourselves. They will not be easy to identify, but the evil ones will be obvious.

I know that, Annie. I'm starting to remember the faces of the True Strong Weet, so I think I'll know them when

I see them.

Just remember that they may look quite different now in this incarnation.

But surely I will be able to sense them.

You will. And remember, too, that we will be with you always.

Mary, Are you still here?

MARY: *I am.*

My mind is still pretty fuzzy. Things are coming back to me, but this is going to take some time."

Yes, it will, Din.

But I do wonder how in the world these seven other Strong Weet are going to find me. Or is it up to me to go out hunting for them? And if that's the case, where do I start?

Four of them are already here.

In town?

Yes. Two you already know of, but you have not been able to sense their identities. You will soon. The others will be drawn near to you when it is time.

Who are the two that I already know?

I cannot reveal them to you. You need to sense their identities on your own. That is what forms the bond of power between you.

And the other three that aren't here?

The publication of this book will Awaken the minds and partial memories of all seven. They will feel motivated to seek you out when they read this book, even if they do not understand why.

As will several hundred more.

Again, the fraudulent, self-professed witches will be obvious to you. Now you have a job to do. You must paint portraits of Annie and of me.

What?

That will be one way to recognize the Strong Weet. They will be drawn to the portraits and will be able to identify us in them.

Una problema here, Mary.

Why do you speak Spanish to me?

I don't know. Just being silly. I took Spanish in high school, and I love the Latino culture and—

That is as it should be.

What?

One day you will remember having lived a life as a Mexican. You have already sensed this life because one night, you did an intuitive writing of the times you spent with your Mexican wife and daughter.

That's right, I did! I'm working on an article about that for my website journal. Don't tell me—my Mexican wife and daughter were you and Annie?

They were. We were all Mexican in that life, and we all lived that wonderful time together. It was one of our favorite times.

Good grief. You can never understand how confusing all of this is. I know that I've Awakened somewhat, but I can tell that I'm not all the way back to where I should be. I don't know if I can keep all the life interactions straight.

You don't have to keep them straight, dear husband. All you must do is follow the dreams and visions you have and remember who you are.

In that vision I had about Maria, who was my wife, and Anna, my daughter, the implication was that Anna eventually had several daughters, grand-daughters, and great grand-daughters, one of whom is still alive. In fact, I feel that she is living somewhere around here. Does this make sense?

It does. There is a young Mexican woman who lives near you who is your great-granddaughter by several generations.

Fantastic.

All of this will come to you one day, my Love, but, for now, you must concentrate on the moment. You mentioned that there was a problem with the portraits.

I was going to say that the problem is that the minute anyone reads this book, they will know that the big secret to being identified as a Strong Weet is to simply say, "Yep, that's Mary on the left and Annie on the right."

As you paint the portraits, you will place within them two glaring flaws. If they cannot point out the flaws, they are not Strong Weet.

There's only one problem I have with this painting thing. How do I paint portraits of two women I've never seen clearly in detail?

You have seen us a few times. You know us both intimately, and as you paint the portraits, you will receive crystal clear visions of our images. Because of your great love for and devotion to us, you will have no difficulty in reproducing these.

It will be nice to have portraits of you both hanging on the wall.

Let us begin.

In the Studio a Few Minutes Later

I'm perched on the four-legged stool planted in the middle of my studio. There's a large blank canvas on my easel board, and my paints and brushes are prepared and ready for action.

I'm just waiting for Mary, or Annie, or both to tell me what to do. I've had glimpses of both of their lovely faces, but not enough to paint an accurate portrait. And man, if I ever wanted to paint accurately in my entire career, it would be now.

They've both lived lives in several different periods. Where do I go with this? What style of hair should I portray? What fashion of clothing?

I would like to paint Mary the way I saw her in my first vision of her. She was stunning. I think I can capture her face, but, again, her clothing — I need another view of that.

I remember Annie's sweet face as if her features were burned into my brain. The first time she placed her memories into my mind was during the investigation of the house in Boonville, Missouri. But then she had been projecting the experience of the illness that took her life in that particular incarnation, so that wasn't very flattering.

The vision I had of her today was in much greater detail. Any father on earth would be proud to have such an incredibly lovely daughter. I will paint her as I saw her today, complete with the cute trademark ponytail she has worn in every vision she has blessed me with.

ANNIE: *I've had a ponytail in all of my life interactions, Father.*

Annie?

You were the first and only father to place my hair in a ponytail. You told me that I must be part pony because I had such beautiful legs, so I also needed a tail. You tied my hair up with a piece of string, and we both laughed when I asked you, quite seriously, if you thought I looked like a horse. You said, "You're the prettiest horse in the world." I wasn't sure that was a compliment, but I hugged you and kissed you on the cheek anyway.

I can almost remember that, Sweetie.

You always called me Sweetie.

And I was your first father?

You are what is called my Spirit Father. I was formed from a part of your own dear Spirit.

You've probably had dozens of fathers in dozens of lives since then.

I have, but they only borrowed me for one life so that they could work out their own tests and trials. You are the only father I am eternally joined with, and I am so glad because I love you with all my heart.

And Mary?

She is my Spirit Mother. We are a True Family, and we have been close throughout all of eternity. We frequently appear in each other's lives as Helpers to make the physical dimension easier to bear. Memories of these times will awaken within you soon. And Father?

Yes, Sweetie?

When you lie down on your living room couch in the afternoon to take a nap, do you ever feel a little tickle or pressure on your cheek?

Yes, all the time. Just when I'm getting ready to drift off, and I usually need to scratch my cheek because of a little tickle. How do you know about that?

Because that's me. Every afternoon when you start to go to sleep, I come over and kiss you on your cheek. Just like I did when you used to tie my ponytail.

I love you so much. I don't know what to say. It's starting to come back to me, but you're going to have to have patience. I can feel you, I can feel the love I have for you, and I know that it is more precious than anything I have ever felt.

I love you even more from this side, Daddy.

I love it when you call me, Daddy.

And Daddy.

Yes, Dearest?

You need to start capitalizing the words Father, Daughter, and Mother from here on when you refer to any of the three of us in Mom's Diary.

Okay, but you have to understand I'm writing as fast as I can to keep up with everything you and your Mother

are dumping into my head and—
You can handle it.
But—
And she's outta here.

26 July

A Birthday Picnic
and Reflections On My Life

Today is my birthday—in this life, anyway. I never used to believe in reincarnation, but I have come to believe in this life interaction stuff without any question. Once a person has experience with some sort of beyond-normal phenomenon, there is no way to deny it. And I have had experience—times ten.

I was born in a wheat field in Kansas, and to this day, I love wheat fields. I also love sunflowers, which are the state flower of Kansas. I remember several things about my childhood that may or may not be relevant to this book, but I will relate them here just in case they are.

I may have mentioned earlier this book that I had an imaginary friend I called Marty the Martian when I was about five years old. Not a very original name, I know, but he was special to me. He started out as a hand puppet, but then, for some reason, he became real to me. It must have been the latent power within me that manifested his reality from puppet to … whatever he was. Or perhaps it was that other vibrational realm of existence sending a real Spirit person over to be with me as a Helper. Who knows?

Marty came around every night when I went to sleep, but he never really appeared as a Martian—no silver suit and all that. He looked like an ordinary guy in a leisure suit. I could see him in my mind's eye as plain as day.

He brought comfort to me every night. I don't know how or why, but he did. I can still recall the image of what he looked like—not like the guy on that old TV show, *My Favorite Martian*. He was tall and had a sincere, weather-beaten face, kind of like an American farmer.

He would be right there, by the side of my bed every night, smiling down at me. He would wink at me, and then I knew it was time to go to sleep. It never failed. Every time he winked, I dozed right off. I told my mother about Marty the Martian. She just smiled and told me to wink back at him.

My mother told me many stories about her own life, several of them having to do with occurrences of an intuitive nature. One story that really stuck in my head was when she predicted that a tornado was about to hit Kansas. She called the radio station and gave a complete description of the devastation, and the announcer actually interviewed her and broadcast her warning. The tornado hit precisely when and where she predicted, and the result was exactly as she described.

These are just a couple of examples of my own intuitive legacy. I have so many things working for me, and I know it's going to take time to perfect what is growing inside me. Maybe that's not the right thing to say. It's not really growing, it's been there for eons as part of my family line. Most of my ancestors seem to have manifested at least a few bits and pieces of it.

I wonder if my father had any intuitive abilities? I never really knew my real father. He didn't abuse my mother or my brother and me in any way, but he was a heavy drinker. Apparently, my mother felt that she couldn't depend on him, so she left, taking my brother and me with her.

Despite all that, Mother has always spoken highly of him to me, especially lately. Recently though, she has been going through the various stages of dementia. Her mind and memory are failing, and she spends more time dwelling on the past. Still, it makes me think that he might have been her real true love. Actually, I'm sure of it. Last Christmas she had tree ornaments made for the entire family, including one for my father, she hung his ornament next to hers on her Christmas tree. She didn't have an ornament made for her second husband, the man I called Dad while I was growing up, which is a shame because my stepdad was probably a much better man than my real dad.

Geez, why am I in such a pensive mood? It's mid-afternoon, and I'm outside in the back garden. I see a bluebird up in the Redbud tree, there is a gentle breeze blowing against my face, and the air is filled with butterflies. It's a picture-perfect day, so why do I feel so down?

I'm going to sit here for a while and write about ... what? Is Mary trying to teach me something that I'm not understanding? Is Annie doing something? I don't know what's going on anymore. Then there's the physical world — it's a mess. Cultures and countries are at each other's throats. Our own government is filled with evil, and people just go along with it without batting an eye ...

You must learn to think with your Spirit and not with your brain, Din.

Mary!

You are still thinking like a human, my dear.

Well, duh. Go figure.

You must remember that the sum total of such thoughts as you were just thinking are only the thoughts of others. Your mundane, of-the-world thoughts have crept into your mind from the newspaper, the television, and whoever and whatever else you interact with. You must ignore them and listen only to the thoughts you receive from the Higher Realm. Those thoughts will never lead you astray, and they will never lie to you.

But how is it possible to ignore the thoughts of the world? I'm bombarded by them every day.

You can listen to them, but you must not take them to heart.

"Live in the world, but not of the world." Very little of what you hear today is Truth. Remember, everyone who speaks has a hidden human agenda, and this situation will only get worse as time goes forward. You must believe everything I tell you, and you must act upon it. If you do this, success is assured.

I do believe everything you tell me, Mary, and from this moment forward, I will do everything you ask me to do. I assume that Annie is to be treated the same.

She is, but just remember that you are her Father, and she respects you very much, so she will also do whatever you ask of her.

I know this sounds silly, but that really humbles me. To think that beautiful young girl loves me.

She has always worshiped you, Din, and in all of your life interactions, you have never let her down. You have never let me down, either.

So what do we do now? Where do we go from here?

There is more for you to learn before you can finish this Diary. When the Diary is published, it will awaken the seven other Strong Weet.

I'm writing as fast as I can. I can only write what I hear from you. In those off moments when you're quiet, I just kind of ramble a bunch of nonsense.

Nothing you write is nonsense, it all has a purpose. Now it is time for another lesson. We are going to take a journey together.

I love road trips.

This journey does not involve a road. I am going to take you into my vibrational plane for a few moments so that you may travel to where you will return one day for good.

You're kidding!

No, I am not. You will only be gone from this world for a few moments, and you will spend a full day back Home.

Here we go again. You're blowing my mind.
All you need to do is close your eyes. I will do the rest.
And when are we going to do this?
Now.

I promised that I would believe you and do everything you asked me to do, but this seems impossible. You're telling me that all I have to do is close my eyes like this and—

Five Minutes Later

Wow. All I can write is Wow. Notice I'm not putting exclamation marks by the wows. These are muted wows—wows of respect because I just had the most amazing *I don't think we're in Kansas anymore* experience ever. I have just spent an entire day—a full twelve hours, Earth time—in Heaven, and only five minutes have passed in this realm.

Actually, they don't call it Heaven there. They sometimes refer to it as the "Other Side" because that is the term commonly used on Earth to mean Heaven, as in the Other Side of the veil that separates the vibrational realms. But that's just poetic terminology since there really isn't any sort of veil separating anything. It's just a romantic phrase to describe the way a person moves from one vibrational frequency to another to travel across the Galaxy and has nothing to do with dimensions. It's really all just physics. They also have a real name for Heaven, but Mary said I couldn't know what that was just yet. She told me to just call it Home.

Now I'm supposed to put the experiences I just had into words. I don't know if I'm up to the task, but I will try. Apparently, it's important for this stuff to be included in the book. Mary says that everything I write is for the purpose of Awakening the other seven members of the

Strong Weet Society. She says that each lesson I relate will affect every Weet differently. One Weet may remember one little tidbit of information, while another will recall a different one. I'm not sure how this all works, but I will do as she asks because I believe in her.

I felt my Spirit leave my physical body the moment I closed my eyes. The best way I can describe this is that it was kind of like all those near-death experiences I've read about. I lifted out of my body and zoomed upward at a speed that defied logic, which is typical of everything Mary does. There was, of course, the obligatory White Light that pulled me toward it like a strong magnet would pull a carpet tack. I actually felt the pressure of the energy as I was sucked into the light, and I heard Mary say, "*We are now jumping from this Earth world to another World far away.*"

Even though the White Light was the most brilliant light I have ever seen, it wasn't warm; it was fresh like a mountain breeze on a June morning. When my Being came into contact with the outer edge of the light, I could feel that it had real substance, unlike ordinary light that has none, at least not that we can perceive. This light felt like tiny droplets of mist, but it wasn't because it didn't make me wet.

I know this isn't making much sense. It doesn't have to because it was all beyond physical perception. When I left my body, I left those senses behind. I became pure Spirit Energy without the cumbersome baggage of physical sensitivities and feelings to weigh me down.

The cool mist of tiny droplets of pure, crystalline energy, felt like liquid light. It soothed my Spirit as I moved with incredible speed toward the other World. The most amazing thing about the light was the color. It wasn't white at all. Every single droplet of the light-mist was like a tiny prism that reflected all the colors of the rainbow. It was the most beautiful thing I have ever seen, and the experience brought about incredible healing, inconceivable in this world, and beyond anything that can ever be dreamed. When I passed through the light shower, I felt like … an Angel. I felt like I had been purified, healed, and transformed into something I never knew existed. I felt whole, and I felt cleansed. I had experienced something like this once before during my own near-death experience as a child — but Mary has asked me not to record that experience here.

I was somewhat dazed as I floated out of the light. I became aware of a vast green meadow filled with millions of the most beautiful flowers of all different colors. It seems that Mary gave me an overdose of what color is like in her dimension. There were colors in that meadow that I had never seen before, and flowers that are nonexistent on Earth.

In the distance to the right of the meadow, I could see an enormous building — not just enormous, but massive! I had expected everything in Heaven to look sort of futuristic, but this building resembled something out of the Renaissance. Actually, it looked kind of like Chartres Cathedral in France, but, like so many things on this other World, it was made out of pure crystal. It glistened like a giant diamond set in the middle of a sun, shooting rays of rainbow colors out in every direction. But there was no sun. The sky was a bright robin's-egg blue, and every other color was crisp and clear, but there was no sun in the sky. The entire landscape seemed to be lit by a powerful light that came from nowhere. Then Mary appeared to me.

She was there, right in front of me. I could see her as clearly as I could see any person in my own dimension. She was even more beautiful than in my visions of her.

I swear I have never seen a woman as beautiful as Mary appeared to me during this enchanted visit to her own realm of existence.

Mary told me that although her World had two giant suns, there was no need for an ordinary star to light the sky because the Light of THE ALL illuminated the entire World. In fact, I didn't see the two suns at first because the Light from THE ALL was so bright. Night was nonexistent, unless, of course, a Spirit Person wished to experience what Mary called, the romance of the night. In that case, all one had to do was to wish it so, and there it was. For all of Heaven, it remained day, but for that one person doing the wishing, it became night. How is that possible? It is because the understanding of the laws of physics on Mary's world is far in advance of Earth science.

I told Mary that I couldn't imagine a place where I couldn't go outside at night and stare up at the stars. She assured me that all I had to do was ask, and it would happen instantly.

I asked Mary about a second giant crystal building that I could see in the distance, not far from the massive Temple structure.

"That will be our second stop on this journey. It is the library that contains the Life Scripts of every person ever born on Earth throughout all of time," she told me. "You could go inside and review your entire life in a matter of moments, birth to death, which is exactly what those who die do when they reach this place. I will not be reviewing your Life Script, Dear Din, because you are not dead. Aside from that, you are a Being of such complexity that your eternal future could never be scripted."

"That's hard to believe," I said. Then I laughed, partly at Mary's answer and partly with the delight of actually conversing with her and not just hearing her inside my head.

"When you Awaken completely to your True Identity, you will understand just how complex you are, and how impossible it would be to script anything for you, let alone a plan of eternal life," Mary replied. "Before we visit the library, I want to show you something extraordinary."

Mary guided me to the left—there is no north, south, east, or west on this world—of the giant crystal building where we came to the top of a cliff overlooking an ocean. The scene from there could never be painted by even the most gifted artist. I have never seen a sight more beautiful, and I apologize in advance for the repetition of that phrase during this narrative.

What I am endeavoring to describe in words cannot be described in any Earth language. This is an entirely different World, and nothing about it resembles anything we know in the three dimensions of Earth. I think the operative phrase for this experience is "it's really intense." I mean, *really intense!* Yes, there are colors just like there are on Earth, but they are brighter and more vivid, and there are more of them. Yes, there are mountains and oceans, and the like, but they are far more "mountainy"and "oceany" than we experience here. I know those aren't words, but there are no words.

Mary smiled and said, "Watch this." Then she said, "Sunset."

Immediately, the timeless scene before us shifted to that of a spectacular Sunset over the ocean. I have never seen such oranges and reds and yellows. And that bright blue—it was beyond glorious.

Again, Mary spoke, "Autumn Forest," and the scene shifted once more. This time to an ancient forest of gigantic trees in full autumnal color. There was even that special *feeling* that accompanies the Fall season. The air was cool;

the leaves rustled softly in the breeze as they fell to create a carpet of ruby and gold; a family of deer walked by us as if they expected us to be there.

I was about to wander off down one of the trails leading deep into the woods when Mary's voice drew me back. "This is a small part of what you can do here," she said. "These are merely the physical representations that you can use for your personal enjoyment. The real Gift is something I cannot reveal to you at this time."

It didn't matter at all to me that I didn't know what she meant. I was perfectly content with what I was being allowed to see. I'm sure that few if any, human beings have ever seen such wonders as these and returned to life to tell about them. Even in a Near Death Experience, it seems that the person barely reaches the Other Side before being asked to return. Only a brief glimpse is allowed. I, however, was given the grand tour, beginning with the ocean and the forest. When Mary said, "library," we were instantly transported to the entrance of the Crystal Library.

No Hollywood producer on Earth could ever conceive of a set like this. The building was huge — and I do mean *huge*. It appeared to be cut from a single, flawless crystal. There were no seams or chisel marks or anything to even suggest that it was anything but one big block.

I could see all the way through it. I saw the Energy Spirit People working inside. They all had a glow about them, and they sparkled like they were covered with glitter. The brilliant blue sky which gave the entire building a glassy blue aura could be seen behind them, and even through them.

We didn't need to go inside since I wasn't going to be viewing my Life Script, so we took a tour around the parks that surrounded the Crystal Library. Once again, I am wordless. I'd like to say that they looked like the Hanging Gardens of Babylon, or the Japanese Gardens back on Earth, but they didn't. They didn't look like any gardens I had ever been in before, and I've been in a lot of gardens.

One thing I did notice was the abundance of roses. There were millions — billions — of roses of every color, including all those colors that are indistinguishable in the normal vibrational plane of Earth. One color, in particular, caught my eye.

It was a pink rose color that seemed to be the most predominant. It wasn't an ordinary pink, though; it had a kind of gold glow about it. Imagine a color that's both pink and gold at the same time. I swear that's what it was and it was beautiful. Mary told me that it was a color found only in one place in my world, a large island that no longer exists. That island was destroyed thousands of years ago, and, along with the island, the color vanished from the earth.

"That color is called Orichalcum," Mary said.

I felt the need to reply, but all I could come up with was, "That's Greek to me."

"Yes, it is," she replied without humor, "but the Greeks borrowed the word for this exotic color from the people of that lost island nation, who had borrowed the word from somewhere else far, far away."

"And where is this Far, Far Away? I asked her.

She just smiled and told me that she would withhold that information for a while.

We had spent an hour or two in the park outside this marvelous library that I was itching to explore on the inside when Mary told me that there was someone she wanted me to visit with.

"This person is of great significance to you," she said.

Curious, I told her to lead the way.

She spoke one word, causing my heart to pound and bringing tears to my eyes. She said, "Annie," and in an instant, I found myself standing beneath a giant Oak tree in the middle of another glorious meadow filled with flowers. The ground at the foot of the Oak tree was spread with a red and white checkered cloth laid with all of my favorite summertime foods; fried chicken, potato salad, baked beans, apple pie—the whole works.

Then I heard a little giggle coming from behind the giant Oak. I recognized that laugh. Annie stepped out from behind the tree and rushed over to me. She threw her arms around me and hugged me for all she was worth.

My little girl! Thank you, God! My little girl! I recognized everything about her. I even knew the way she smelled. It's as if I had been asleep for a hundred years, then suddenly I wake up and know who I am, and Annie is there. Annie, the Jewel of my life. The breath of my own lungs. My existence.

I held her to me as tightly as I could and wept. I know, I cry a lot, but never have I felt this kind of love in my own Earthly existence. Never.

She laughed again and said, "Daddy, I'm with you all the time! Now you remember what I look like. Do you think you can paint my portrait?"

"You bet I can," I replied.

We sat down and had the most wonderful meal anyone can ever imagine. I had never tasted such flavors before. Every item of food still tasted like it would have on Earth, only enhanced. The fried chicken was beyond comparison. I've had a lot of fried chicken in my life, but this was Heavenly. Literally.

Annie poured wine from an old ceramic jar—like something from Biblical times—that seemed to be bottomless. We drank glass after glass, but the jug remained full. Yes, we got a little tipsy, but it was such a happy and elated feeling, and there were no after-effects. No Hangovers!

It was a wonderful Family reunion. In addition to Mary, and my beautiful, perfect Daughter, Annie, there was another surprise guest, my little dog, Skeeter, who was killed when he was hit by a car only two weeks after I got him when I was nine years old. I couldn't believe my eyes when I saw him running toward us across the meadow, barking his little head off. He jumped into my lap and licked my face while I petted him and told him how happy I was to see him. And I could hear his thoughts! They were simple thoughts, all about love and loyalty and companionship, and that was the cherry on top for the entire experience.

We finished eating, then Mary said, "Annie and I have another special place to show you."

"I feel like I'm getting the fifty-cent tour of Heaven," I said, and they both laughed. I realized then that it was the first time I had seen them laugh. I wish I could have recorded the sound of their laughter to bring back to my dimension. No composition by Mozart, Beethoven, Chopin, or any of the great musicians can ever compare with that sound.

"This is not the all of Heaven Daddy," Annie said. "It is merely an other-vibrational representation of a small part of Heaven."

"Are you ready?" Mary asked.

"Ready for what?" I replied.

"This."

***

Once again, we were instantly transported to an extraordinary place. I couldn't believe my eyes. We were in outer space—without a space ship! We were floating out there in deep space, with stars and planets and constellations and nebulae all around us. I was amazed to find that space isn't black like it is in the movies. It's light blue with tinges of the color I had seen earlier, Orichalcum.

I felt like I was at Disneyland. It was beautiful! I realized that every constellation has its own color and its own personality and that every feature of deep space is alive and sentient. Every planet, and every moon, and every particle of dust floating about in space is living. Even the so-called Dark Matter has personality. But Dark Matter isn't what scientists in this dimension think it is. As we floated among the colorful realms of space, the true nature of Dark Matter became apparent. It is really the echo emanating from — I hesitate to say this, but I know it to be true — several vibrational frequencies that are unknown to Earth science, as well as from another substance that Mary said she would inform me of later. The revelation of that substance could forever change the way humans think of science.

I know that what I just wrote is far out, but I also know it to be true. The scientists of Earth can prove it. They haven't discovered how to do that yet because they are thinking along the wrong track. They are still thinking in limited terms of conventional logic and theory, but, believe me, there is no logic or theory for this. This knowledge is far beyond anything any astronomer or physicist could ever imagine. The good thing is that astronomers and physicists are different from other scientists. They are open to the wonders and possibilities of … everything. Those guys will figure this out, and I may help them do it.

Mary gave me a vision containing the details of how to locate other universes that adjoin our own, and how to travel in milliseconds from galaxy to galaxy until reaching the border of our universe. From there, we could, if we wished, jump into another universe. It's all so simple. I couldn't believe it, and I know the scientists of Earth would all think I'm a kook for proposing these thoughts. I'll keep them to myself for now, but these kooky ideas can become a reality for Earth if humans agree to change their ways. More on that later.

We traveled the entire span of the Milky Way Galaxy in less than a second, and yet I experienced everybit of it. I "felt" every planet and every sun. I saw the Earth from a million miles in space — that Tiny Blue Dot that Carl Sagan spoke of. It stood out from everything else in the galaxy and had a special glow about it — an aura of its very own, just like people have auras. But I couldn't see any auras around any of the other planets anywhere we went.

Mary told me the reason for this is that Earth is the favored planet of THE ALL. Out of all the trillions of inhabited worlds, Earth is the most beloved planet of all to the Great Creator. I asked why because I knew Earth has always been a mess in terms of its history, and it seems to be getting worse. In fact, its state today is most depressing. I have been watching the news nearly every day over the past several years, and I have found it to be terribly unnerving. Even my own great country, the United States of America, seems to be falling apart now. Mary informed me that even so, the US is the key to the future of this planet. Apparently, Mother H has been blessing our country for many years, as directed by THE ALL. She is quite upset by what it has become. Many Earth humans will be eternally punished for how they gave their aid to the attempts to destroy America.

Mary gave me a little hope, at least. She told me that the people of America are going through a confusing stage at this moment in their history, but a thorough cleansing having nothing to do with politics or world events is on the horizon. This cleansing will be initiated by the Strong Weet Society, and, if the Strong Weet succeed with their endeavors, Earth will be back in the good graces of THE ALL. If not, though... She did not elaborate.

I realized then that we had returned to the meadow where I had first set foot in this realm.

"Mary, can you tell me about the crystal building on the hill that overlooks the Crystal Library?" I asked. "The library is big, but the building on the hill makes it look like a suburban tract house compared to the Biltmore Estate."

"That information is more than you can handle right now, so I will save that for later, Din. I will tell you that the large building is the main Temple here in our Home world. It is where God visits us. It is where all decisions are made for all universes. It is truly the Heart of Creation. The grandeur and glory of the interior are beyond the human imagination. You have been inside many times in the past, and you will be able to revisit the Temple soon at any time you wish. Now it is time to return you to your Garden.

I closed my eyes and felt the same sensations as I had on my first journey earlier that day, only in reverse. When I opened my eyes, I found myself back in my garden, where I was surprised to find that almost no time had passed even though I could recall every moment spent in that other place.

Later that Same Afternoon

It's late afternoon, and I've moved out to my favorite place on this little planet—my back garden.

A few days ago, I cleared and leveled a section in the middle of the garden. I placed one-foot square red concrete paving blocks over an area three feet wide by six feet long, with the long sides oriented east to west. I then set a rock on each of the corners. These rocks may appear to be ordinary, but they are not. Each one resonates with me in some unique and mysterious way.

The stone I placed on the northeast corner is a beautiful one. I can't remember where I found it, but it has a section of plain basalt on one side, and a large quartz crystal fused to the other side. The southeast corner holds a chunk of red lava — I don't know where I got that, either. I set a heavy piece of hematite on the northwest corner and a chunk of white conglomerate containing coral and shells on the southwest corner. I set a small block of ordinary granite in the center square. What makes this rock unique is the deep, wedge-shaped groove across the middle of one side. It's directly over this wedged Stone that I place my chair whenever I come outside to commune with Nature, as I am doing now.

Some of my fondest memories of my childhood are of attending church and church-related events accompanied by my parents and grandparents. As I look back through the years, though, I find that most of my pleasant memories are centered not on religion as such, but on Nature. I have memories of parks and trees and skies, along with other odd things that I can't put my finger on, from places I know I've never been to in this life. Mainly, I remember the colors. The sky was always a perfect shade of creamy blue. The trees were always bright shades of green and brown. The flowers were always vivid and perfect. In every memory, the sensations I am most aware of are in the air around me. When I travel to these memories in my mind, I can feel the warmth of a summer breeze — really *feel* it. I can feel the crisp air of a dew-fresh morning. It's as if I'm right there, wherever "there" is.

I am convinced that those who are closer to Nature

are those who are closer to God. The hikers and hill walkers; the bird watchers; the gentle gardeners tending their gardens every day, talking to the flowers, and maybe even to the Faeries inhabiting that mystical space; the people who shun computers and sports and rock music and bars and who live quiet, inward lives of peace and contentment — these are the meek who will inherit the Earth. They are the ones who are truly protective of the Earth and of God, and because of that, they have His blessing. These are the ones the Apostle Paul referred to when he wrote:

> Do not conform any longer to the pattern of the world, but be transformed by the renewing of your mind.

— *the world* meaning the shallow society of our time, not the created Earth with all its pure, natural beauty.

I know I'm rambling here, but I don't know what else to do. I haven't heard a peep out of Mary or Annie since I returned from our little journey. I don't even know why I'm sitting out here in the garden. I guess it's just because I enjoy sitting here, and after that incredible ride, I need to slow down and relax for a little while.

Whenever I come out here to the garden, though, my mind seems to wander. I think just the act of sitting in a garden makes me focus on Nature and memories of Nature. Now, for instance, I recall sitting on my great-grandmother's lap when I was about five years old. She would hold me while she rocked in her chair and listened to the radio. I have no idea what programs she listened to — this was back in the mid-fifties — but I remember feeling comfortable on her lap. I also remember her or my grandmother, Nana, popping popcorn in the evening. They had one of those old poppers with the crank on top. It eventually wound up in my kitchen. I still have it. Even when I was sitting inside their house, though, I was surrounded by the scents and sounds of Nature that came in through the windows that were always open to the world outside.

I was born in Kansas, but my family moved from there to Oklahoma when I was still just a toddler, so I have practically no memories of the Sunflower State. I have plenty from Oklahoma, though. When I was a kid growing up there, I watched Roy Rogers movies all the time. I loved those old things—still do, actually—especially the big rocks the cowboys climbed all over, and the spectacular desert settings where the movies were filmed.

There's something magical about the desert. When a person first visits the desert, all they can see is sand and cactus. But when one spends time there and begins to pay attention, one discovers that the desert is a place teeming with life of all kinds.

I'm not going to go into any great detail about the desert here. For that, I recommend *The Desert*, by John C. Van Dyke. It was first published in 1902, but it is the best, most romantic description of desert life I have ever read.

Speaking of Roy Rogers, I wanted to grow up to be just like him. I wasn't sure though if I wanted to really be a cowboy, or just look like Roy Rogers. He had those squinty eyes and that crooked smile. I thought that was pretty neat, and that's the way I wanted to look. I have a terrible school photo of me—fifth grade, I think—where I tried to look like Roy Rogers. I squinted up my eyes, and I put on a silly grin. I felt sure that I looked just like him. It turned out to be the most embarrassing photo I ever took in school. People are still speechless when they see it. They usually wind up stammering some sort of apology and making some sympathetic remark about how ill I must have been.

I actually thought that cowboys faced a bit of an evolutionary challenge back in those days because all they did was shoot each other in the hands and kiss their horses. Even as a child, I knew the difference between a horse and a girl. Had I ever been allowed to kiss anything back then, I would have chosen a girl over a horse.

I also got a charge out of the old Rin Tin Tin shows. Now there was a dog—he could do anything! When my dad told us that we were going to move from Oklahoma to California, the only thing I could think of was that I might get the opportunity to meet Rusty and Rinny. Those of my readers who are as old as I am will recognize those names. My dream was to invite Rusty and Rinny to my birthday party. Man, oh, man, that would have been IT for me! But it never happened.

I did get to meet Roy Rogers, though. Years later, I took Nana up to Apple Valley, California, to visit his museum. That was a great experience. The place was deserted when we got there except for one lone figure leaning up against a counter by the museum office, sipping coffee. You guessed it—it was Roy, all by himself in that big museum, and he hadn't changed a bit. He still had the same old squinty eyes and the same old crooked smile. He ended up taking us on a personal tour. He showed us everything, including his horse, Trigger. He had loved that horse like a best friend, so when Trigger died, Roy had a taxidermist preserve him. He also had Dale's horse, Buttermilk, their dog, Bullet, and Pat's Jeep, Nellybelle, on display.

Throughout my life, I've had my share of interaction with animals, both as pets and in the wild. Three of those experiences stand out in my mind as distressing, if not traumatic — one involved a bird, one a lizard, and one a fish. I don't know what the significance is of these experiences, but I feel compelled to relate them here.

For Christmas in 1958, my parents bought me a pellet rifle. I thought that was just about the coolest thing ever, and I also thought it would be pretty cool to go outside and shoot at birds. I don't know why boys like to do that, but they do.

I took my new rifle out into our back yard in Riverside, California, where I spotted a little bird sitting at the top of a tree. I drew a bead on him — or her — and carefully pulled the trigger. It was a decent shot, but nothing special. I winged the bird just enough to bring the poor thing to the ground.

Excited, I ran over to where the bird had fallen. The adrenaline rushed through me like it surely must rush through any young boy when such a deed as this is done. *Oh boy!* I thought. *I just killed a bird!*

When I came to where the bird lay, I saw that it wasn't dead. I had only wounded the poor creature. The poor little thing sat there, one wing pulled in close to its side, the other bent awkwardly away from its body. There was a spot of bright red blood on one of its feathers.

The bird stared up at me, shaking. The poor thing had no idea what had just happened to it. It didn't even know that I was the one who shot it. It just sat there in shock and pain, staring up at the new threat that hovered over it — me.

Tears welled up in my eyes. I felt terrible about what I had done. I was only ten years old, and this hit me pretty hard. I reached down and cupped the little bird gently in my hands. I rushed him into the house to see what I could do to ease its pain. How in the world could I repair that sweet little wing?

I dug around in my closet and found an empty shoebox. I tore strips from an old bed sheet and put them inside the box. I gently placed the delicate little bird in the nest, vowing to take care of it for as long as needed. I kept that bird in the shoebox for over a week, doctoring it, feeding it, petting and loving it. I even dabbed mercurochrome on its little wing to aid in the healing process.

As the bird got better, it began to hop around and chirp and do all of the things that healthy birds do. I decided it was time to let the little thing go, to release it back into the wild, so I did.

I watched the bird make its way to the shelter of the trees. I could tell that it was never going to be able to fly very well again. It mostly hopped, but occasionally took to the air for short glides. Regardless, I was elated by the success of my efforts to return it to health. As I walked back into the house, I swore too that I would never again shoot a bird. The experience had been far too traumatic to go through again any time soon.

But guess what? Less than a week later, I decided that it was just the natural thing for a man to shoot birds, darn it! I loaded my pellet rifle and went back out to give it one more try. I think I must have been feeling my "man oats" or something. Looking back on this from my current state of being, I realize this was a terrible thing to do, but I was a kid, and kids just don't think.

I carefully approached the row of trees where I had shot my first bird. My heart was pounding. My blood was rushing. I was ready to kill.

It didn't take long before I spotted a likely target. I looked up into the trees, and there it was—a little bird singing his heart out halfway up the tree. This was it! I bit my lower lip, drew my rifle up to my shoulder, took very careful aim, and...the bird hopped to a higher limb!

I was disappointed, but I followed that little fellow with my rifle sight. He hopped again! He did this several times. I was surprised that he didn't fly away because he knew that I was getting closer to him. Stupid bird. He just kept hopping, and every time he hopped, I would find him again and aim my rifle. I was the master hunter on safari!

One last hop, and POW, I got him! I watched him as he fell to the ground. What a clean shot! The little sucker had to be dead before he hit the ground! I ran over to check it out.

Sure enough, the little bird lay absolutely still. I was so proud! Then I stooped down to examine my prey, and my heart sank. There, just under its right wing, was a mercurochrome stain. I'd shot the same bird that I had so lovingly cared for and released.

I cried all night and I swore — really SWORE — that I would never shoot birds again. And I never have since that day. This is one of the most traumatic experiences of my life.

The second animal-related traumatic experience was with a lizard — yes, a lizard — when I was about eleven years old. My family was good friends with another family, and we all had gone camping in the mountains of Southern California. Our two families were good friends and we did this a lot. The other family had three kids in the same age range as my brother, Jim, and me. While the four adults were doing adult stuff, we kids were free to do pretty much whatever we wanted.

That morning, my brother had gone off with the oldest boy of the other family. They were the same age and were best friends. The middle child, Barbara, was a beautiful girl about my age. I had recently decided that I was madly in love with her and was determined to spend as much time in her presence as possible. Unfortunately, that also meant spending time with her other brother, a squirrelly kid a year younger than me. He could be really annoying. He was in Little League and bragged constantly about what a great pitcher he was. I was never in Little League — in fact, I wasn't very athletic at all — but I was sick of this creepy kid carrying on about himself. I wanted to do something that would impress his sister, and bring him down a notch in the process. I soon got my chance.

While our older brothers were off doing their thing, the three of us decided to do some exploring on our own. We were following a trail that wound between tall pine trees and giant boulders when I spotted a lizard warming himself in the sun. I picked up a pretty substantial rock, turned to Little Brother, and said, "See that lizard over there? Bet I can hit him with this rock."

He laughed, and said predictably, "You can't, but I can."

Now, that lizard was pretty far away, and I knew that I didn't stand a chance of coming anywhere near it, let alone of hitting it. As I tried to gauge the distance and realized the problem I had set for myself, I thought, *What a jerk! What am I doing telling this guy I can hit that stupid lizard. I'm gonna look like a real idiot now.*

Well, I took a stance, wound up like a Yankee pitcher, and hurled that rock through the air as fast and as hard as I could. I didn't look. I couldn't look. Even though my eyes were closed tight as I threw it, I *knew* when that rock made contact, square on the lizard's head, and sent the poor little thing flying. I killed it good.

I did it! My sweet love, Barbara, was impressed, and Little Brother was speechless. Then something terrible began to well up within me. I tried to hide my tears by acting cool and swaggering away from the scene of the crime, but when I was out of sight, I sat behind a boulder and cried. The full reality of what I had done hit me hard. I now know that it was you, Mary, who led me to the knowledge that I had taken the life of a precious Being just to impress some stupid kid. I was devastated.

I was an adult by the time of the third incident, and it happened while I was fishing on the Gasconade River near Vienna, Missouri. My grandfather used to take me fishing when I was a kid, but beyond that, I've never felt one way or the other about the sport of fishing. I mean, all you do is throw a little metal hook into a puddle of water and wait for a fish to come along and bump into it. I didn't even know why I was there. I think it was just a good excuse to sit under a tree by the river and do nothing.

I sat there for a while, and eventually, I caught a fish. Usually, when I catch a fish, I release it back into the water. That's what I planned to do with this slimy little guy, but something terrible happened. The poor little thing had swallowed the hook so deeply that I was having a difficult time getting it out. I tried to be as gentle as possible, but I was afraid I was going to kill it before I could get it back into the water.

This is where it gets weird. I was holding the fish in my left hand and tugging at the hook with my right when I heard the fish scream! I swear that fish made a sound that I can only describe as a scream. It wasn't very loud, but it was audible. And it *was* a scream. It really made me take notice of what I was doing.

I finally got the hook out and threw the fish back into the water. I don't know if he survived or not, but I didn't fish any more that day. In fact, I didn't go fishing for a couple of years after that happened. I've been fishing since then, but not very often, and to this day, whenever I catch a fish, I always think of that little guy back in the Gasconade River, and I hear that scream all over again.

I swear to you that all three of these stories are true.

They happened just as I am relating them to this Diary.

I sometimes wonder if God permits things like this to happen to people—sins like this. Perhaps they are allowed as opportunities to learn valuable lessons about the sanctity of life so that in the future, we won't commit even larger sins against Nature. Just how wide—or narrow—is the gap between the senseless slaughter of a defenseless bird and the murder of an unborn human child? Between the killing of a lizard and the killing of a man?

Interesting questions to ponder, but perhaps the better question to ask is, "How can we justify/rationalize any of these sins—if they be sin? Because our society, indeed, allows for them all.

***

Mary?

My, oh, my, how your writing does ramble.

I knew I felt you popping in. I've just been sitting here killing time because I didn't know what else to do. Answer me a question.

Yes, Dear Din?

Are you "here" now? Or are you just speaking through my mind? I mean, when you come to me on these visits, is your Spirit Form standing by me, or are you just doing this with some sort of mental manipulation?

I am here with you. I am actually standing to the right of you, and I am projecting telepathic thoughts into your mind. Regrettably, you are not able to see me, but someday you will be able not only to see me but to touch me as well.

So what's the holdup? What's this "someday" stuff? Why can't I just do it now?

It is very complicated, Din. You must first reach a state of Being that is close to mine. You are working on that, and one day you shall achieve it, but we must be patient. Much depends on the ability of the Strong Weet Society to set things right in this world.

Baloney.

Take heart. I believe that will occur in the not-too-distant future. There is a great deal at stake here, so we do not want to rush things. All must be done carefully and thoughtfully.

I suppose I can't see Annie, either.

It is possible that since you have formed such a tight bond with her, she will be able to "pop in and out" as you say, and you might even be able to hug her. Our Daughter's power is great. She is, in fact, the key to all of this. I believe that it will be her power combined with yours that will accomplish what must be done. Never forget that you and I are each a mighty Being, and Annie is the fruit of the two of us. She has twice the power. As I have told you, you are the strongest Weet in the Strong Weet Society, because Annie has chosen to remain less than fully developed. When she is complete, she will be stronger than the two of us combined. There will be no force in any universe that will be able to stand against her.

Holy cow. I'm glad she likes me.

She adores you, and she always will. THE ALL recognizes her love for you and favors her highly because of it.

Wow. You know, sometimes I feel like a real dolt. I've reread some of the Diary entries, and all I seem to be able to say is "wow" and "holy cow" and "gee whiz" and stupid stuff like that. I'm related to the two most incredibly powerful Beings in all universes, and my Daughter is "favored highly by THE ALL," and all I can say is "Gosh golly gee wow." This is really blowing my mind.

As well it should because you must realize the combined power that is contained within the three of us. You must acknowledge the power that the ten Strong Weet can let loose upon this planet. It will start out slowly and subtly. A thing will happen here, and a thing will happen there, then all of the world will wonder. But in the end, we will unleash what we must, and those humans who are in control of the evil of this world will fear for their lives.

I really don't want to say "Wow" here, but that's what I'm feeling.

Good will triumph over evil, Din. Evil will be destroyed, and those who have brought it forth will suffer terribly for having done so. They believe they are immune to eternal punishment, but they will experience it in full. We simply must wait until the energy is right to do what we must do.

You know, I just thought of something last night that blew my mind, Mary. Years ago, when I was confirmed in my Catholic Church experience, I chose as my confirmation name, Joseph.

I really didn't know why I chose that name. I thought about it before I was confirmed. I thought about it a lot, and several names popped into my head, like John, after St. John of the Cross, one of the most mystical of all the Catholic saints. He influenced just about every other saint that came after him. I also considered Thomas, just so I could be called Tom, after Thomas Merton, my idol at the time, and one of the biggest influences in my life. And there were also the four Apostles who wrote the synoptic Gospels, Matthew, Mark, Luke, and John. Or how about St. Paul?

But for some reason, the name, Joseph, kept coming up, and I couldn't figure it out. I looked him up in a few books and found that besides being the husband of the Virgin Mary—as if that wasn't enough—he was the patron saint of families and a few other things that didn't have anything to do with me, my current life, or my interests for the future. I don't have any kids—at least not then—so his being patron of families didn't make sense for me. Even so, just as the bishop was getting ready to make the sign of the cross on my forehead and anoint me with the oil, he asked me who I had chosen as my confirmation saint. The name, Joseph, burst forcefully out of my mouth. It was beyond my control. After the confirmation ceremony, I thought, *Great, now I'm stuck with that name for eternity.*

I realize now that it had been my name before—when I was your husband, Joseph. It may be my original Spirit name as well. I don't know about that, but it would explain a lot.

You are starting to think like a Strong Weet, Din.

You mean I'm on the right track?

You are on the only track. Who you are is who you are. These memories and experiences will be coming to you more often now that you are Awakening to your Spirit identity. But aren't you forgetting something, Dear One?

Am I?

Today is your birthday!

I did forget. We've been so busy that it just kind of slipped my mind. No big deal. I forget my birthday every year.

You must never forget your birthday. I have something extraordinary to tell you. Your birthday and mine are the same. In our Spirit Forms, we were both born on July 26, in terms of Earth dates.

You're kidding!

I am not. But that is not all. Annie was, as well.

But how is that possible? She's our Daughter.

I'm not speaking of the year we were born but of the day and month. All three of us were born on the 26th of July.

You mean we're all Leo's?

We are. One day I must explain to you about the Earth pastime called astrology. It is not as it has been taught on this planet in the past many years.

What do you mean?

For humans on Earth, it has become a pseudo-science. Some think it to be useful in determining certain things about human nature, but one key element has been left out of the current teachings.

Can you tell me what that is?

Astrology is ineffective and irrelevant to our duties within the Strong Weet Society, so I will tell you the only part you need to know. The innate power of a Strong Weet far sur-passes any imagined astrological influences invented by some people. A Weet's power is a Gift that has its genesis in God, Who created all of the bodies of the universe those amateur astrologers like to fiddle around with.

Go on.

Astrology is ineffective because it is simply not True. In a word, it does not work. A dependence upon astrology is only necessary for those who have not risen above such simplistic, fashionable influences. They are mired in the superficiality of the mundane culture that is responsible for feeding such nonsense into those human minds that allow it. When a person reaches a particular state of Being, one in which he or she has been Truly Awakened to the Higher Laws that come not from this universe but from God, faddish beliefs such as Astrology are no longer relevant. At that point in one's life, the Higher Laws take over, and the mundane laws must subside.

You, for instance, are being given a large sum of knowledge from Heaven itself. That knowledge is leading you to redis-cover the power within you. To advance above the world, a person must leave the world's laws. They must learn and observe the Higher Laws, many of which have been explained over the years by great teachers who were human beings, but who had been given insight into the more profound principles that create and sustain all universes.

You're talkin' Buddha, Krishna, St. Francis, and all the

great masters and avatars, and the like.

No, I am not. Some of those people you just mentioned never even existed. Their entire life-stories were fabricated, manufactured in the minds of humans. I am speaking of those few humans who have truly understood this excellent knowledge for what it is. Many of their names are not recognized or honored in any way.

You mean I probably haven't even heard of them?

That is what I mean. These few Spirits are the greatest of the great among the human species, for they were Truly enlightened. Many wrote volumes that have been read and discussed down through the centuries. Their work, however, has often been dismissed as either too mystical to understand or as the writings of madmen. The first appraisal is more accurate, as none of these men were mad. These enlightened ones have jumped into this plane of existence at various times throughout history, including the present day. Two of the Strong Weet that you must find are among this group.

So the Weet are really like avatars.

No Dear, there are no avatars. Avatars came from the minds of humans, not from God. Just one more complication to the religious chaos found in this world.

So … okay … now I'm confused.

There is nothing to worry about. All will be clear in a short time. But always remember that nearly everything taught in this world in terms of religion or eternity is inaccurate. Yes, human hearts may have been in the right place when they invented such things, but their inventions only served to confuse things rather than to add Truth to what they were attempting to understand.

Anyway, I can't wait to meet some of the Strong Weet jumpers.

It will happen in time, but remember, even they do not really know who they are as yet and must be reminded by the reading of this Book. When that happens, everything else will come together quickly, and the powerful frequency that will either save or destroy this world will be released.

And now I have a birthday gift for you, Din.

Oh, yeah. My birthday. I hope you didn't buy me a tie; I don't wear those things anymore. But of course, you didn't. You—meaning *you,* as in *who you really are*—can't just walk into Walmart and buy a tie. Ha! You'd scare the heck out of them if you did!

Your gift is on your altar inside.

You mean, in my office?

I do.

Can I go check it out?

Of course, you can. That is what I wish.

Ten Minutes Later

The altar in my office was pretty much as I had previously described, but with a few changes. I've added a little dish filled with water and sea salt that I use for blessing certain ceremonies, and I've added an element or two and removed a couple of others. The altar as a whole seems to be developing a Nature-based theme. I don't have a clue where all of this is coming from, but I suppose it has something to do with my being a Strong Weet. If you had asked me three years ago about the Weet and the goings-on in some other Heavenly realm, I would have said something profound like, "I'll look into it,"—which I would have. Then, maybe, I would have been off on another path that may or may not have brought me back around to Mary. All I can say now is, thank THE ALL for the ball lightning that opened up a short cut to get us back together.

Every day that Mary is with me, I feel the closeness growing between us. I know this is strange and almost unbelievable, but I am beginning to understand what is happening. The Great Plan of All Life set into play eons ago by THE ALL, and the temporary sharing of bodies fit together somehow. I don't have a grasp on all the details yet, but maybe in time, I will.

Anyway, I'm standing here looking at my altar, and I can't for the life of me figure out why Mary sent me in here. I'm looking for some sort of gift she has given me for my birthday, but I don't see it. Everything looks pretty much the same as usual, except … except for that one little rock there, in front of the Christmas tree. Where did that come from? I didn't put that there. You mean that's it? My birthday present is a rock?

It is a very special little rock, Din. Annie is giving it to you.

It's from Annie?

Yes, and with my good wishes added to hers.

Then it doesn't matter that it's just a little rock. I will cherish it as the best birthday present I ever received.

But it is not just an ordinary little rock.

I don't understand.

Look at it carefully.

Yes, this is a little different. What is it, jasper? And look at that. What is that? It looks like a drawing of an eye — sort of like that Eye of Horus symbol the ancient Egyptians came up with.

It does, but that is not what is special. It is not the Eye of Horus, but the Eye of THE ALL, who watches over you day and night all the days of your existence. And the rock does not come from here.

You mean from my back yard?

I mean from this world. This rock is from Home. Annie was able to transform and rearrange its molecular structure in such a way that she could transport it from our world to yours, and then return it to its original shape. What you hold in your hand is a rock from Heaven.

Oh, my God! I'm sorry, I shouldn't have said that. Do you know how much this rock must be worth? Think about it! Remember those rocks they brought back from the moon? They are literally priceless because there are so few of them, and now they are impossible to obtain. Think about what a rock from Heaven would bring!

And you would sell this?

Of course not, I'm just trying to keep my sanity. This is incredible. I'm just trying to make a comparison—I don't know what the heck I'm doing. My Daughter, Annie, gives me a rock that came from Heaven. How am I supposed to react?

I understand, Din, but there is something else you must know about this rock—something you already know deep within you but have not yet remembered. The Eye that is engraved upon it represents the Eye of God, etched upon the surface of the rock by Mother H, herself at the expressed desire of God. This little rock holds power within it that can be used in many ways to further the cause of the Strong Weet. Guard this rock with your life. It must not fall into the hands of the evil energy that is being generated upon this planet.

Oh, my, what the heck does that mean? Is this like the Ark of the Covenant scene in Raiders of the Lost Ark? What is this evil energy thing? What is going on here? You're telling me that Mother H carved an eye symbol on this rock, and it contains some sort of incredible power?

I am. It contains more power than this world has ever seen. It must be used only for good. "Evil energy" is the description that best describes those persons or things that oppose the Strong Weet Society, which, of course, represents the energy of goodness and righteousness.

You mean the Hitler types.

That is precisely what I mean, only worse, and you must be careful. Do you not remember that Hitler was an exceptionally charismatic man who wooed his supporters through his speeches and his false promises to change the world for the better? You can hear the same false promises coming from world leaders in this present age, and they are far more dangerous today than Hitler was then, and there is more at stake.

But what kind of power is inside this rock? And how do I activate it?

The power is beyond your comprehension as yet. You will understand how to activate it when it is time for you to do so. The rock will tell you.

You mean the rock can talk?

Every living thing is a sentient Being and can communicate. The rock will begin to glow and feel hot in your hand. Telepathic images will appear in your mind, and you will know what to do. There will be no confusion or misunderstanding.

I think I'm getting a headache.

I'm sorry, Din. Can I help you in any way?

I don't mean that literally. I'm just boggled by all this. I guess it's because I don't understand how all this works. These incredible rocks and all those universal laws and principles—what are those, anyway? You mention them all the time. They seem to be the key to everything.

They are. They have been called many things, but on Earth, they are referred to most often as the Laws of Hermes, or the Hermetic Principles. The person, Hermes, never existed. The Laws were actually revealed by One far greater than humans can imagine for their mythologies. It was that Greater Being Who gave the Laws to humanity in the spoken fashion. Men wrote them down as best they could, but all that remains today after passing through the minds of humans for so many centuries is a mere shadow of their totality.

Wow! So there was no Hermes? I'm starting to wonder just how many of the so-called greats that have popped up throughout the years even existed at all! Holy—

Careful what you say, Din. Annie is here.

Golly, Annie, I'm sorry. I don't mean to cuss around you.

ANNIE: *It's okay. I don't care. I know the real you on the inside. Besides, your cuss words are pretty mild compared to some I have heard. Mother is a little harsh with you on that subject. Mother, really, "heck" is not a cuss word, and "Holy Moley"…come on.*

Wow, Annie, I want to thank you for this incredibly wonderful birthday present. I just don't know what to say.

Just tell me you love me as I love you.

Oh, I do, Annie. I love you with everything I have.

That is all I would ever ask.

But Annie, this little rock with the eye, it seems so harmless—

Father, never think that! Remember that all you see in this world is not as it appears. The Rock of The Eye has more power within it than a hundred trillion of your hydrogen bombs. I will teach you how to use this power.

That sounds dangerous.

It will only be dangerous if it is allowed to be used by the evil energy. That must never happen.

How do we stop that from happening? What am I supposed to do with this rock? How can I protect it?

You will keep it on your altar for now. It will be safe there. If an intruder breaks into your house and touches the Rock in any way, they will be instantly killed.

Good grief.

It is the way of Truth. Those who would be destroyed belong to the evil energy, and they would have been dissipated later had the rock not killed them sooner.

It all sounds so brutal.

It is not. It is wrong to kill a human being who still has his or her Spirit Being inside, but those who would try to steal the Rock of The Eye do not have Spirits. They are evil and without Spirit — pure evil energy. The Rock is not really killing anything or anyone. It is merely taking the evil energy and transporting it to a different place.

So, Annie, can I ask you a question?

Of course.

When you were growing up in any of your life interactions, were you … did you ever want to be anything … I mean … do you know what I mean? Were you ever a cheerleader, or were you ever on the debate team at a university, or did you ever play with dolls or anything like that?

Do you mean, was I ever normal? I did not have the time. I have known who I am in all of my incarnations. I knew that I had a task to perform — two tasks. One was the Strong Weet Society and the saving of this world. The other, the more difficult, was to always keep in step with my precious Father. For some reason, your mind and your memory are much harder to manipulate than they should be, especially in this current life you have chosen.

What's so different about this life?

You have so many complications in your life. You must identify them and resolve them before you can progress farther. You will soon come face to face with more complications of even greater consequence. You will meet —

MARY: *That can wait, Annie. First, I am going to give your Father some all-important instruction. He must learn the Hermetic Principles so that he will understand how we do the things we do here on this world, and how we will be able to destroy the evil energy that has somehow taken hold without the aid or permission of THE ALL. THE ALL has been aware of its growth since its inception many ages ago. Why or how this dark energy was allowed to flourish on Earth is a secret known only to THE ALL. THE ALL tells us only that it is a part of The Great Plan, and that someday we will understand.*

That's it, Mary? That's the job? We're here to destroy the evil energy?

I'm sorry. I thought I had made that clear. The task of the Strong Weet Society is to destroy the evil energy once and for all. Remember, Din, the concept of evil is a human notion that never was, and can never be accepted by God. It is not something that He created — that would be impossible. Evil is a human invention that can never truly exist in the Presence of God. What humans regard as evil is merely an experiment that was devised by rebellious minds and has gone astray. The repetition of so-called evil acts among the populace has allowed the energy of evil to accumulate and coalesce into a powerful force for darkness, whose name will be revealed to you soon. Again, THE ALL remains silent for now as to why and how this terrible energy is being tolerated. When the Strong Weet destroy it, the Earth will enter into its final incarnation.

You mean, even the Earth reincarnates?

Not reincarnation but renewal. Throughout time the Earth has seen wisdom and knowledge ebb and flow like the tides. It has reached a level now that is so low that it can only continue into the depths of destruction. We, the Strong Weet, can provide the infusion of energy to reverse the flow and guide the Earth toward a new era of enlightenment, but only if we take action and do what we must do.

And what, exactly, is that?

You will learn that later, but Mother H has directed me to instruct you in the Hermetic Principles before we proceed any further. You need to understand these Laws and apply them to your own life if you are to Awaken and fulfill your duties as a Strong Weet.

You mean I have to take a class?

Yes, but this will be the most engaging class you will have had in many years. I know that because I am inside your mind.

Thanks for reminding me of that. Is Annie going to help you teach the class? Is she still around?

You love her very much, don't you? And no, Annie had to leave us for a while.

I can't explain it, Mary. There's something about both of you. I guess I know what it is—I think. I love you both with all my heart, and Annie is the most precious thing to me. Every time she brings the image of her face into my mind, my heart melts.

That is the way a father should feel about his daughter, and that is why we both love you and always have. You are crying.

So, when does this class start?

Tomorrow.

Let's do it.

27 July

The Lessons on the Universal Laws Begin and Another Memory Returns

Tomorrow is here, and I'm sitting on the couch in my living room awaiting the arrival of Mary and my first lessons on the Universal Laws, aka the Hermetic Principles. I remember reading about these a few months ago in some book or another about deep-thought stuff. I only vaguely remember anything about them, but I wasn't in the same frame of mind I'm in now, so I could not have understood them like I would today. I wonder how is Mary going to do this?

Are you ready to begin, Din?

You mean, right now?

Now is always the best time, Father of my Daughter — who is standing at your right side as I speak.

Mary, Annie, I wish I could hug you both.

ANNIE: *I'm hugging you now, Father. Can you feel me?*

Yes, I think I can — a brief, soft, warm pressure. And was that a feather on my cheek?

You know what that was. I just kissed you!

Yes, Annie, I know. Thank you. I wish I could kiss you back. I think that's the most frustrating thing in my life right now.

Don't worry, Father. It will happen one day. I will make sure of that.

You have that kind of power?

I do.

I do long for that day. Please hurry it along for me.

I will do my best; everything is according to the Will of THE ALL. You need to pay attention to Mother for now. She is going to guide you through the Principles gifted to this world by one of the Great Ones. I hope you have plenty of paper and ink.

I do. Let's go.

MARY: *Din, I want you to relax and to open your mind and your memory. I am going to take you through the seven Hermetic Principles, which I will now refer to as the Universal Laws, since that title, while not entirely accurate, is closer to being right. This information is of the utmost importance to your readers as well as to you. These words should stimulate the Awakening of your readers and lead them to our cause. They will then be able to work with us and to help us defeat the evil energy by using these great Principles given to humanity by God.*

Among the readers to be awakened will be the Weet. The words you record will have the wisdom of the ages behind them and will contain a code. As those who are of our family read those passages, changes will occur within the chemistry of their brains, and they will see visions of sunsets and storms and beautiful colors, recalling ancient memories to their conscious minds. Then they will come forth. These words are a catalyst for them. Are you ready?

Go for it. I have a ream of paper and a brand new box of Bic pens. To be honest, though, I hate this kind of thing. I hope it doesn't bore the readers.

I will try to be concise. This vital information must be delivered to the remaining Strong Weet, and to all those who would join with us. Their power will be added to ours so that the darkness that has risen among them may be defeated.

It is said that the seven Laws of Hermes were postulated by Hermes Trismegistus. That was not his real name, but it means "Thrice Great." He was considered at the time to be among the most significant philosophers, priests, and kings in the world. His origin was not of this plane, but he made his debut in ancient Egypt. He was referred to initially as a sage or magi, but at some point in his existence among the ancient Egyptians, he acquired godlike status. He then became known as Thoth. You can find references to him in the Pyramid Texts from that time.

This "Great One" has been linked by some to the Roman god, Mercury, but this is incorrect. Mercury was a representation of a physical energy force, while the One who was given the name Hermes was a real Being.

People of Earth credit Hermes with having written dozens of books. It is from these books, which include THE EMERALD TABLET, THE DIVINE PYMANDER, *and the* BOOK OF THOTH *that the seven Laws of Hermes are derived. We who are watching this world's progress agree that the Eternal Universal Laws of THE ALL are best represented by these laws.*

The seven Laws of Hermes were regarded as magic or witchcraft for centuries, but modern science and physics have shown them to be grounded in fact. What is more, they are all in perfect correspondence with the mystical teachings of the Judeo-Christian Bible. Nothing in the Hermetic Laws is contrary to or contradicted by the teachings of Christ. In fact, these very principles are taught by Jesus in His sermons and parables. At that time, the message was understood by only a few, the twelve Apostles, among them. There were many, however, who did not understand. It was their misconceptions that became the foundations for many of the religions existing today.

Can I stop you here for a second, Mary?

Yes, Dear.

Are you saying that the Christian Church of today is not doing what Jesus taught?

Yes, isn't it obvious? But I am not singling out the Christian Church alone. All organized religions are incorrect in their doctrine, for they have all been manipulated for millennia by humans with self-serving motives. Today, of them all, Christianity is closest to the Truth, but if Jesus were to walk again upon this world, He would not recognize His Church. A careful study of the Bible will show that the modern church is far different from what He taught. This is an important matter, but we can discuss and clarify it at a later time. You must first understand the fundamental principles of the Universal Laws.

Sorry.

These Laws define the transcendental relationships between the mind, body, and spirit, and God, and Nature. All are related and share various attributes. The sacred writings of all religions are filled with these laws. Some admit to it, and others do not. The Bible is especially instructive in that it gives great detail to the underlying mysteries that churches do not teach today. If they did, this planet might have a chance to become what it was truly meant to be.

Like the laws of physical science, the Universal Laws comprise their own science, or system, to be studied and put into practice by anyone. If your readers simply learn from what is presented on these pages, they will be able to conquer many things in their lives, and, more importantly, they will be able to aid us in our battle to defeat the darkness.

Every secret society and mystery religion has taught these Principles. Eleusian Mysteries, Dionysian Mysteries, Egyptian Mysteries, Builders of the Adytum, the Rosicrucians, the Freemasons — all of these have either been directly involved with these great Truths or claim to trace the beginnings of their groups back to them. However, most of these organizations are now outdated and terribly misguided, even to the point of absurdity. Still, there remains a secure link to a rich legacy that can be activated and put to use by those who have the knowledge.

The writings of that delightful Hindu mystic, also one of

the Great Ones, Paramhansa Yogananda, are based on the Hermetic Laws. Principles such as positive affirmation and negative denial, the power of positive thinking, and faith healing are commonly found in New Age or New Thought groups, based on these, although they have never taken those concepts beyond their most basic tenets. The New Age groups have not advanced beyond simple visualization exercises. They largely ignore the fact that it is God Who is doing the work, not humans. Thus their efforts are futile.

These Laws are central to the definition, accomplishments, and existence of humanity. The mathematical and astronomical principles the ancient Egyptians used when building their pyramids are derived from these Laws. The miracles and mystical events told of in the Bible flow from the workings of these Laws which God gave to this world for that purpose. All scientific, physical, and spiritual knowledge grows out of these Principles and is supported by them.

Even so-called witchcraft finds its genesis in these Principles that are as old as the beginning of time. What is lacking from witchcraft as it is practiced today is the acknowledgment of God. God must be included in the act, or it just does not work; that is a principle Law on this world. If God is not a part of it, then it is probably rooted in evil and will never work.

These lessons will provide you with an outline or overview of each of the Hermetic Laws. My thoughts will become yours, and you will write them down as I reveal them to your mind. An in-depth study would take much more paper than you have and many more Bic pens. Besides, your knowledge of them will expand as you put them into practice.

Remember, these Laws and Principles are not magic, nor are they witchcraft. They have nothing to do with any of the various New Age groups that claim them for their own. The Laws are a matter of physics and can be analyzed and proven *by science. They were introduced to this world not by human philosophers or metaphysicians, but by God, Himself, who set apart specific individuals for the sole purpose of revealing the Laws to the Earth humans.*

***

This is me, Din, speaking directly to you, The Reader. I expect these lessons will be long and tedious, but interesting. According to Mary, this knowledge is of the utmost importance in the grand scheme of all things. Listen with your hearts, as well as with your heads—something may change inside of you. I don't know where this is all going yet, but I do know that Mary and Annie are the *real deal*. I know, too, that there are Strong Weet—angels from God, for lack of a better description—in this world who need to be Awakened. This ain't Harry Potter, folks. This is the real thing. This is *not* a book of fiction; it's an instruction manual. Take it seriously. Mary is anxious to get started, so I'll turn this back to her, and maybe Annie. Enjoy.

The Law of Mentalism

MARY: *The first Universal Principle is the LAW OF MENTALISM. Briefly stated, the universe was created from and is sustained by the Mind of God.*

The opening chapters of the Book of Genesis and the Gospel of John describe the process. That sweet man, Paramhansa Yogananda, expressed the concept beautifully when he wrote:

"The factory behind creation is beyond imagination, the whole universe is a single thought in the mind of God! So simple, yet the galaxies are guided by mathematics inconceivable by man. Everything runs in perfect order. What tremendous intelligence is manifested in creation! The Infinite is working in everything. All the different eddies of motion called life are controlled by that Cosmic Intelligence."

I recognize that quote. I have that book.

Paramhansa Yogananda had more to say about the Spirit and its relationship to science than any other human spiritual teacher.

I'm happy to hear that. I knew he was special, but I had no idea that he was "one of them."

He was, indeed. His life was dedicated to living by the highest spiritual motivation. As a youth, he sought the oldest and purist teachings of Hinduism and yoga. When he came to America, he applied the same dedication to understanding the spiritual truths of the original teachings of Jesus and how they were in harmony with the higher principles of Hinduism and yoga. You, Dear Din, and I both knew him very well. One day that memory will come back to you.

Mary, I just realized that you've been calling him "Paramhansa." I always thought it was "Paramahansa."

It is not his name, it is a title given to one who is Awakened and has attained the highest level of spiritual development. Paramhansa is a transcription from the ancient Sanskrit language of India. Historically, it was not spelled with the additional "a." That was added later by a few of his students here in the United States.

Interesting. I wonder why?

No one really knows. It was probably just a simple mis-understanding, but it seems to have been picked up and used by some of his followers to distinguish themselves from his other followers — a sort of childish family squabble of no real importance.

Wait a minute, Mary, I think it's time to queue up the *X-Files* theme. I'm starting to remember this guy in a different sort of way. You know that back in the 70s, I lived in a place called Cabot's Old Indian Pueblo and Museum — after all, you've been in my head forever. It's a fantastic adobe structure in Desert Hot Springs,

California, built by a fellow named Cabot Yerxa. He constructed it to look like an Indian pueblo. It has something like forty-eight rooms and over a hundred windows, and each one is different. I was out there one day and met Cole, the owner of the place, and we hit it off—actually, we became good friends. He was having trouble with vandals at the time, and he asked me if I could move in and help keep an eye on the place, especially at night, when he wasn't there. What an experience that was. That place sure has an atmosphere.

But back to Yogananda. Cabot Yerxa had left boxes and stacks of papers, magazines, and pamphlets stashed away in various closets and cupboards throughout the Pueblo, and I had the opportunity to sort through them. One day, in particular, sticks in my memory. I was sorting through a stack of magazines from the Theosophical Society—Cabot's wife was into that—and at the bottom, I found a little pamphlet with a picture on the cover of a doe-eyed Indian guru named Paramhansa Yogananda. It was from an organization called the Self Realization Fellowship. What's really amazing is that more than twenty years later, I found myself living on an ashram in California that had been founded by followers of Yogananda.

Yes, Din, I was with you then, and I loved every moment of it, especially the gracious folks who worked there. You will describe your experiences at the ashram later, but for now, we must stick to the lesson.

You have had a long acquaintance with Yogananda, and it has helped to prepare you for these lessons. You do understand, do you not, that those words written by him are basically a definition of the Law of Mentalism.

Yes, I do. He was a brilliant man.

Everything—all knowledge and wisdom, the atomic structure of the planets and the suns, all magic, wishing and hoping, dreams and desires — exists in the mind of God. By way of His Eternal Spirit, God shares a part of His mind with us. The Bible, in the book of James, tells humans that if they lack wisdom, they should ask of God, and He will provide it. With the asking, a human mind touches the Mind of God, Whose Mind then moves the human conscience when He answers. Therein lies the human connection to God. Does this make humans little gods? Does this mean that a human shares divinity with God? Of course not, only a simpleton would believe that to be the case. What it does mean, is that a human can have a relationship with God that far transcends even the best relationships humans have with each other, which are shallow indeed by comparison.

How does the Spirit of God do His Work? When prayers are asked and answered, energy flows like an electrical current back and forth between the human mind and the Mind of God. The difficulty is that it is not a process that people can feel. The people of this culture have been taught to "feel" everything, and that if a thing or a process cannot be felt, then it can be denied — it is not real. There is much a human being may learn or understand through the senses and emotions, but the feelings encouraged by this culture are superficial and misleading. They do not come from the inner spirit of a human, nor do they come from God. Do you want to take a break, Din?

No. Go on. I think I'm following this.

This, then, is the Law of Mentalism. Since most of those reading this book have their roots in Judeo-Christian culture, I will draw another example from the Bible. Consider the Book of Genesis, chapter 1, wherein God both thought and spoke things into existence. Couple that with a passage from the New Testament, Hebrews 11:1-3, which implies that faith is a real substance. Just like a rock, or a pearl, or a carrot are substantial, so is faith, and this substance, faith, creates and sustains everything in the Universe. I will reveal to you now that faith is thought, and that thought is vibration, and that vibration is pure energy. Energy has substance, and God uses the substance of mental energy to produce everything in all universes. Do you understand what I am teaching?

I am. These ideas are fantastic, but I understand what you're telling me. I think.

I am going to make this simple for both you and the readers. I could go into great detail, but that would only result in your confusion. This is not magic, but rather, pure physics. This knowledge is the key to power when it is combined with the Gifts provided by the Eternal Spirit of God to those who are obedient to His Will. As you have said, Din, this is not a work of fiction, it is a dangerous course in the mysteries of God. This information could be devastating in the wrong hands, so please, take this seriously. Life is not as it seems. Soon the order of this world will be overturned. The stage is set, and the days and seasons of humanity are being played out. The End Times are upon this world.

The Law of Correspondence

There is a familiar saying that illustrates the second Law quite nicely:

As above, so below. As below, so above.

The Truth described by this Law is that we live in two worlds, the physical and the spiritual. Most humans accept what they see as the apparent reality of the physical world, which they experience as their life on Earth. The spiritual world, which includes the realm of Heaven, is not so widely acknowledged even though it is every bit as real. Everything you do in this plane of existence is repeated in the realm where God resides, and everything God does in the spiritual plane becomes a reality in the physical. Energy is the same in both worlds, and the energy produced in one directly and equally affects the other.

The Apostle Paul tells you that you walk by faith and not by sight. You are also advised that faith gives you the knowledge of things that are otherwise impossible to believe in. Sight is limited to what a person can see directly in the physical realm. If one looks only with the physical eyes and does not use spiritual sight, then one will never be able to understand that this earthly plane is a microcosm of the Heavenly realm, which is a macrocosmic template for all of life.

The Law of Correspondence is reflected in our own plane of existence by many scriptural concepts. For Christians, the Golden Rule tells them, "In everything, do unto others what you would have them to do unto you." Likewise, Hindus and Buddhists are guided by the Law of Karma, which implies that everything a person does for good or for evil will come back to them in like manner. Even science has a similar code. One of your great thinkers, Sir Isaac Newton, observed this principle at work in the physical world and described it as one of the laws governing the motion of objects:

> *For every action, there is an equal and opposite reaction.*

Consider as well what is called "The Lord's Prayer" wherein Jesus instructs His followers:

> *This then is how you should pray, 'Our Father who art in Heaven (our Home), hallowed be thy name, thy kingdom come, thy will be done, on Earth as it is in Heaven.*

Or

> *As above, so below. As below, so above.*

There are many more references to the Law of Correspondence to be found in the Bible, such as:

Whatever you bind on earth shall be bound in Heaven. Matthew 16:9;

and

He which soweth sparingly shall also reap sparingly. Corinthians 9:6.

Even those followers of modern pagan religions recognize what is called the Threefold Law, which states that whatever you do, be it good or bad, will be returned to you three times.

These are all statements of the Law of Correspondence, which predates them by millions of years.

The Law of Correspondence is what lends credence to the practices of positive affirmation, faith healing, and prosperity gospel. It functions in tandem with the Law of Mentalism — thoughts are things — so that when a thought is spoken, the essence of that thought is activated in the realm of God, allowing the thought to become reality. Prayers from your plane — Earth — manifest actions in my own plane — Heaven — which, in turn, affect yours. This will only happen if God is not just a part of, but is foremost in the equation. New Age thought removes God, and followers of the prosperity gospel are motivated by greed and ego. Therefore the results of mere positive thinking or affirmations are insubstantial or nonexistent. Nothing works without God.

Are you still understanding this, Din?

I think so, but I'll bet it's much harder to teach this stuff than to be a student of it.

I am sure that it is. It is not easy to explain the mysteries of this universe, but they are not difficult if the mind is open and ready to see the larger picture of life. Shall we move on to the next Law?

Shoot. We're just movin' right through these puppies, and that's probably a good thing.

The Law of Vibration

Light is energy in motion, and that motion takes the form of vibration. The Law of Vibration describes how light affects everything in the universe. The light that is perceptible to human eyes is carried by waves with a narrow range of frequencies, each color corresponding to a vibrational frequency. These colors do not exist in purity like lines drawn with crayons but blend continuously from one to the other along the spectrum of frequency—from fast to slow, violet to red. This can be observed in the rainbow where it is impossible to tell where one color stops and the next begins. Just as there are no boundaries between the colors, there are no boundaries between visible light and other manifestations of energy; it is all light, and it vibrates at all frequencies from unimaginably fast to infinitely slow. All life depends on light, and everything is made up of and is connected to it in some way. Everything produces light—even thoughts formed within the brain—because everything vibrates. Numerous studies have been published in which scientists describe how they have detected and recorded measurable vibratory essence as thoughts are formed and emanate from the human brain. In effect, brain waves have weight. Not only do they have weight—or rather, mass—it is a mass that is in a constant state of motion. Motion and energy and light are all related.

This knowledge opens up many topics for discussion, but they all begin with the idea that every being is made of the same thing. Every being and every thing is made of the spinning particles of light—pure light energy. And humans send out messages and information continuously with the energy they produce. This explains many things such as déjà vu, clairvoyance, intuition, faith healing, ESP, body language, and on and on. Every single person or thing has a vibratory signature that is much like a fingerprint — no two are the same.

No event is ever lost in this wonderful universe. The vibration produced by each event or experience is retained forever as an imprint or a residue. Energy is never destroyed. All of the programs produced since the invention of television continue to speed out into deep space on waves of light energy.

I've heard that story. They say the Martians are watching *I Love Lucy* on Mars and thinking that's what's going on right now on Earth.

In a manner of speaking. The vibratory essences of those old programs are now decades out into space, and they will continue to travel into eternity. Thousands, even millions of years from now, the beings on planets in distant galaxies will be receiving the I LOVE LUCY *signals, and it will be a significant event for them, perhaps even a "First Contact" of sorts for some. It must be stated, however, that the energy frequencies of a TV show will dissipate and degrade according to the distance they travel. The energy itself will never die, but the pattern of the TV program does not remain intact. The alien Beings may not be watching Lucy, but they will be receiving an unmistakable, sentient life-based signal from a neighboring planet.*

I'm sorry, I must sound like a dolt, but I'm really flabbergasted. You're telling me stuff that I've never heard or read anywhere, and I've read a whole heck of a lot.

You are not a dolt, my Dear, whatever that is. I will be glad when you become fully aware of WHO you are and quit berating yourself like that.

Regarding vibrations, Yogananda had this to say:

Everything in the universe is composed of energy or vibration. The vibration of words is, by extension, a grosser expression of the vibration of thoughts. The thoughts of all men are vibrating in the ether ... when you are near and dear to someone, you can feel the thoughts of that person; but you are probably not able to do this with anyone as far away as India unless you have developed range. Those of you who practice the Self Realization Fellowship Lessons on concentration and meditation, and are very calm, will be able to feel the thoughts of others, even from a distance. Your mind will become more sensitive.

We are all human radios: you receive the thought messages of others through your heart, the center of feeling, and broadcast your own thought messages through the Spiritual Eye, the center of concentration and will.

Are you putting in a plug for the Self Realization Fellowship?

I am not. It does not teach the full Truth of God. I do, however, believe it to be a wonderful organization. Mr. Yogananda spoke those words back in 1938. I was there. And so were you.

Okay, wait a minute. I'm both baffled and honored to think that I might have known Yogananda personally—I love the guy. I think I mentioned before that he and Thomas Merton were two of the biggest influences on my life. But to have known either one of them—in a past life interaction, I'm assuming—would be amazing. I don't think I've written much in this Diary about Thomas Merton.

And I have mentioned that you did, indeed, know Mr. Yogananda in one of your past life interactions. You were a student of his in the early years of his American ministry. You were like a son to him, and for a brief time, he was grooming you to be his successor.

No.

He was. Yogananda was and still is a wonderful Being. The organization he created here on Earth is a reflection of his own Spirit and his knowledge. Although his Fellowship has experienced a few bumps along the path of its own existence, it still teaches many things of relevance to the Universal Principles. The combination of religion and science, as taught by Yogananda was far ahead of his time, and accurate relative to the times in which he taught. If it lacks in detail, it is because there was no one alive at the time able to understand it. Even today, his Fellowship is missing many key elements in Universal Science, but that does not affect their own work, which is more of an individualized spiritual development.

I don't know what to say.

Perhaps it is time for you to say nothing, Dear One. I love you with all my heart, but you must be quiet if I am ever to finish this lesson.

ANNIE: *You need to listen, Daddy. She knows what she's doing.*

I'm sorry, Annie.

You're just not fully tuned in yet. It will happen soon, and then you will understand. Do what you need to do to understand everything Mother teaches you.

Okay, I'll shut up. Where were we?

MARY: *We are discussing the Law of Vibration. I was getting ready to explain that this is the Law that rules many things in human life, mainly sensitivities such as geographical power spots, power stones, earthquake faults, ley lines, and vortices.*

You are familiar with the Bermuda Triangle. This law explains why that place is so mysterious. The vibrations of places and people can affect the minds and the bodies of others, and influence situations. Humans send messages and information by the emanation of the energies they produce. Clairvoyance, clairaudience, clairsentience, and claircognizance — the four "clairs" of intuitive people — can be explained thus.

Scientific studies in parapsychology will eventually show that the basis of all forms of telepathy is this transfer, or movement, of energy from mind to mind along invisible, web-like light waves.

As with the previous Laws, the Law of Vibration plays a role in the symbolism of all scriptures. Consider the ever-present halo around the head of Jesus and the saints who came after him. This is the vibrational effect known as an "aura." We know now that an aura is a simple heat signature that emanates from all human bodies. Its qualities are dependent on the power within a being. Jesus, being the Son of God and God Himself in human form, contained power within Him more intense than any human and had an aura of corresponding intensity. Remember, too, that a person's aura is not the same thing as a person's Glow.

The Law of vibration is further illustrated in sacred scripture. I have chosen to use the Bible since the culture we find ourselves in is primarily Judeo-Christian, but these things are also spoken of in the scriptures of every other religion of this world.

First of all, Genesis 1:27 tells us that God created mankind in His own image, and in 1 John 1:5, we are told that God IS light. The Apostle Paul, in 1 Timothy 6:16, also tells us that God lives in unapproachable light. Finally, according to John 8:12, Jesus tells us that He is the light of the world.

Looking beyond the Judeo-Christian tradition, one finds the words of the Great One who was mistaken for Hermes to be most enlightening:

*... the Father of all things consists of light and
life, whereof man is made. If therefore, a man
shall learn and understand the nature of life
and light, then he shall pass into the eternity of
life and light.*

*That is the reason I am teaching you these things — so
that all of those who join with us will, indeed, pass into the
eternity of life and light. These are among the more profound
Mysteries taught by Jesus but suppressed or corrupted by
evil despots throughout history, the very reason the so-called
secret societies and the mystery schools were kept secret. As
people discovered a few of these Truths, they were viewed
as threats by the communities in which they lived and were
forced to remain silent if they were to live unmolested. Today
they are free to share their knowledge without repercussions,
although many of these organizations retain the appearance
and tradition of secrecy. The knowledge held by the secret
societies is superficial at best when compared to what we
seek to teach this world. You, Din, are learning the Higher
Truths as you record them in the pages of this Book.*

*That being said, all that is taught by the so-called secret
societies, and even by the Self Realization Fellowship, pale in
comparison to what is found in the first chapter of the Gospel
of John. That single, short chapter offers more wisdom for
study than do all of the religions and secret societies combined.*

*The knowledge I have next to impart is challenging to
explain in the language of this plane, so please pay close
attention. The significance of this information will become
apparent to you as you attain your full potential as an
Awakened Being. I am about to disclose a description of the
substance of God. It is unlike any you or the readers of this
book have ever heard. I will try to be concise.*

God, The One Creator of All, is the sentient, organized

matter, light, and energy of everything in all universes, seen or unseen, including the combined consciousness of every cell and atom of all things in all universes, past, present, and future. He is the intelligent, conscious, Creator God who is above everything because He Created everything. He is more than just a "universal mind," as is taught in many New Age groups, He is the First Personality, ever. Even though His physical substance can be given definition, His Spirit Being cannot. The Bible is clear on the fact that God is a Mystery. No human has ever known the depths of God, and no human ever will, but any human will benefit from knowing that definition and understanding the principles behind it.

God requires worship, but True worship is not what has been practiced by the religions of this planet. Jesus taught His followers to, "Love the Lord your God with all your heart and with all your soul and with all your mind," and to "Love your neighbor as you love yourself." That is True worship. It is as simple as that. Every great spiritual teacher in the history of Earth has taught the same thing, but the essence of the teaching has been largely ignored. Over the years, humankind has, through ignorance and ego, insisted on adding disciplinary doctrine to this wonderfully sweet and simple message from God. But the dogma and the discipline are not Truth; only the Truth is the Truth. It can be no other way.

Because we are all made in the Image of God—which is light and vibration, or Spirit—we can, in our own limited capacity, create. Such is the essence of the Arts. Humans cannot create anything out of nothing, as God can, but they can be creative with their thoughts, and that process can bring about results for either good or ill.

Hang on a second here. Let me see if I'm following you. Do you mean that while I can think with my one mind only, God taps into all of us simultaneously, and uses our combined minds for His thoughts, right? I guess that could explain omniscience.

That is not entirely accurate, Din. God has His own Great Mind, totally separate from all of His creation, and He does not need to utilize human minds for anything, but He does know the thoughts of every being—human or otherwise—before that being even thinks them. This means that God can ensure that the experiences of one individual do not interfere with the experiences of others long before humans create situations and circumstances in their own lives. In effect, He coordinates all thoughts everywhere. This in no way diminishes the free will of a human, it merely brings order to what would otherwise be a chaotic state of affairs.

That makes sense to me. Man, I love this stuff!

Shall we go on, then?

Sure. By the way, where's Annie?

ANNIE: *I'm right here. I do so wish you could see me.*

I'm sorry. You mean everything to me now, Annie. Every day I experience memories of you and me and your mother together, but they're all jumbled up. Just yesterday, I saw a vivid scene in my mind's eye. I was just falling into one of those hypnogogic dreams with the faces coming at me—

What faces do you see?

I don't know. I don't know who any of them are. They're just faces, and they just keep coming through, one on top of the other. Dozens of them. They come and go fast, and I don't recognize any of them. Most of them just look like regular people, but some of them look evil, like monsters out of a Stephen King movie. I've grown accustomed to them, so they don't bother me too much. I just pick and choose; I sort out the good from the bad.

But yesterday I saw you, Annie. You were so beautiful and so innocent looking, We were somewhere on a hilltop.

A warm wind was blowing, and the pine trees around us were making that sound that only pine trees can make in the wind. I love that sound. You were putting sticks onto a fire that I had started earlier. We must have been on a camping trip of some sort somewhere. We must have been talking, but I don't know about what. I was happy, and you were giggling in that cute little way that you have. Then you stopped what you were doing and pointed up. You said, "There you go, Daddy, look at you!" I looked up to see a beautiful hawk swooping over our camping spot. Then I awoke with a start, and I couldn't explain what I had envisioned.

Don't you remember? I am going to touch your forehead just for a moment, and it will help you to remember.

Aren't we getting away from the Hermetic thingies?

Mary: *It does not matter, Din. We will get back to them. Let Annie do what she must do, for you are Awakening to another part of your Higher Self.*

Annie: *Father, I love you with every fiber of my Being, and I will always be with you, and I will always protect you, so do not be afraid of the experiences I bring you.*

I won't, Sweetie. You can do whatever you want, and I'll just sit back and enjoy the ride.

Mom? Do you mind?

Mary: *No, Dear. The lesson can wait for this.*

Annie: Just close your eyes while I touch you here —

Ten Minutes Later

Wow! What the heck was that, Annie?

Annie: *It was the day after my confirmation into the Catholic Church. You had taken me up into the hills to reward me. I loved to go camping. I particularly loved to sit out under the night sky and watch the stars.*

The Catholic Church?

Yes. You are having the remembrance of a past life inter-action. Do you remember Mom talking to you about a life in Mexico with Maria and Anna?

Oh, yeah.

You are having a flashback to that time. Every time you have a vision of a previous incarnation, I can see what you see. This vision was one of the times we had in that particular life together. You need to enter it into this Diary.

Can I just copy this memory out of my own journal? It's right over here on my desk. Wow, it's about you and your Mom, isn't it?

Yes, it is. I am familiar with your journal entry. It tells the story well, so please copy it for the sake of our readers.

Okay. Here is the entry from my journal:

> I mentioned before that I must have lived in Old Mexico, although it may have been Southern California, Arizona, or New Mexico. I've never really believed in past lives, so I don't know what to think about it. The vision contained a mixture of images, but mainly of desert ... and hot wind ... and some Mexican-styled buildings that appeared to be made of adobe and painted with whitewash.

What the heck does this have to do with your lesson, Mary?

MARY: *You must relate this. It will be significant one day.*

Okay. Here I go.

> The dream-scene took place by or near the ocean. What follows is, to my best recollection, a description of what I saw: Waves rolling in on light sands. Intense Sun and hot wind. The heat and the tropical feel of

the dream reminded me of the movie, *The Night of the Iguana*, starring Richard Burton and Ava Gardner, except other than a small amount of lush greenery near the water's edge, there was more desert and beach than the Mexican forest that dominated the scenery of the movie — and it was much hotter. I was shirtless in my vision, and the intense heat felt wonderful on my upper body.

A small village sat atop a barren, rocky hill overlooking the beach on one side and one of the hottest, most forsaken landscapes I had ever seen on the other. A couple of palm trees and perhaps a half dozen palo verde trees were the only signs of greenery in the entire village. Everything else was sun and sand, with more sun than sand. It must have been around noon because I noticed no shadows.

The settlement wasn't much more than a cluster of small one or two-rooms huts and a few larger villas. They were all made of white-washed adobe, and most were chipped and in need of repair. The exception was the large square building in the center of the village with *Cantina* freshly painted on the gleaming white wall facing the single dusty street that ran through the center of town.

People were moving throughout the scene. Back and forth they went, almost in slow motion. Some women stopped to lower buckets down into a well at the edge of town; children ran around carelessly, laughing and paying no attention to the heat. Several men stood or sat on porches, taking advantage of the sparse shade offered by crude wooden awnings. Most of the adults were quiet. The occasional conversations were spoken softly, punctuated by soft laughter from one of the women, or by a good-natured shout of caution to the children from one of the men. All appeared to be content and happy. It was not a depressing place, despite the bleak landscape. In fact, the place and its people exuded an energy of joy. It was rather delightful.

My impression was that I was an invisible observer of the scene, but then I saw a young girl run away from my apparent position. She stopped dead in her tracks, turned on her heels, and looked directly at me. I was unnerved at first, but as I studied her, she began to look familiar to me. Then it came to me — this girl is my daughter, and her name is Anna. The knowledge flashed in my mind like a neon sign.

Anna ran toward me and leaped up at me so that I had to catch her in mid-flight to keep the two of us from falling over backward. As we laughed together, I heard a shout from across the road, "Jose!" I was suddenly but briefly drawn back from this dream and into my conscious mind. I remembered that my Catholic confirmation name in this present life was Joseph, or in Spanish, Jose. For some reason, this "knowing of my name" seemed significant, and I made a note of it.

When I returned to my vision, it was to the exact moment I had left it. I was standing across the road from where the men were sitting, but now I could feel a pair of arms wrapping around my chest, pulling me backward. A woman behind me was laughing and hugging me tightly in front of her. I wiggled my body around to see who it was. Our eyes met, and I knew immediately that the woman was Maria, and that she was my wife.

The lucidity of this dream was startling. I could feel the strength of the family bond I had with Maria and Anna. I even sensed that the porch I was standing on belonged to our house and that I was the village brick maker. Images sped through my mind. Maria was a dressmaker; nearly every woman in the village wore one of her dresses. Anna was a beautiful little thing who played and giggled and talked to Angels wherever she went. We had a dog named Pingo and a pet lizard that Anna called Francisco.

The vision ended, but I continue to remember my life with Maria and Anna as fleeting visions. I have learned that Maria and Anna lived reasonably long lives for the time in which they lived, but my life was cut short by an accident that occurred while building a villa for a wealthy man.

Now it gets complicated. I believe this entire life experience took place in the 1870s. Maria died in 1897, and Anna died shortly after that. Anna had married a man named Miguel, and together they had several children. One of their daughters had a daughter who bore another daughter who gave birth to another daughter—I think I have the right number of daughters here. I have sensed this many times, and it all comes out the same. That last daughter is still alive today, and, depending on the exact life spans of the mother and the grandmother, she could be anywhere from twenty to sixty years old. I know this is a broad time-span, but it's the best I can do based on the dreams. But the fact is, if I could locate the last daughter, I could substantiate the truth of the existence of past lives.

I can't prove any of this, but somewhere out there, I may have a Mexican granddaughter—plus a few "greats." I don't know her name or where she lives, but I believe that she exists. I also think that I would be able to recognize her if I saw her because I am assuming that she will look like a mixture of Maria and Anna, whose faces are burned forever into my mind.

***

Wow, I can see it all now, even the names! Mary and Maria, Anna and Annie, Jose and Joseph—

MARY: *We have shared many lives together, my dear Din, but it is always the present life that is the most enjoyable.*

And do I have a granddaughter out there somewhere, Mary? Because if I do—how wonderful would that be to have a living relative who carries both your genes and Annie's.

Although your dates are a bit off, you do have a granddaughter. The energies of THE ALL have prompted her to locate her home not far from where you reside.

When can I meet her?

When the time is right. You must understand that there

is a purpose behind all of this synchronicity. Everything must occur precisely if the task of the Strong Weet Society is to reach a successful conclusion. You must also know that you have several children in the world at this present time. Most importantly, you have another extraordinary daughter living not far from your home. You will recognize her as well. She looks very much like Annie. Her name is Katie.

Good grief. I have a Wife and a Grandmother and a Daughter—who has been my Daughter many different times—and now a Mexican granddaughter—and another living daughter, and I can't see, feel or touch any of them!

I know this is very difficult for you, Din. But you will one day see that it was necessary. I promise you this: it will not be long before it all comes together.

And just how long is that?

I cannot say. God is in control of this.

Well, I guess if I've waited this long, I can wait a little longer. Anyway, thank you, Annie, for that vision. But I still have one question that you should be able to answer for me.

ANNIE: *Yes?*

The hawk. When we were on that camping trip when you were Anna, and we saw the big hawk flying over, you looked up and said, "There you go, Daddy, look at you!" What in the world did you mean by that?

Every human being has an energy spirit animal that accompanies them throughout all of their lives.

You mean like a Heavenly Helper, only it's an animal?

That is exactly right. The hawk we saw that day was your helper making an appearance in the Earth realm just to let you know he was still around. You created his essence out of your own spirit. Back then, you were able to sense this, and after I pointed up to the hawk, you recognized who he was.

How incredible is that?

Not so incredible. Once you remember just how inter-connected the vibrational realms are, you will see how this is possible.

So I can create energy spirit animals, and they can pop in and out of the realms with ease?

Most of them can. Animals do not fear the extraordinary like humans do. It is merely a part of their existence.

I knew it! Sometimes I see my little poodle, Natalie, do the darnedest things. I mean, besides the other day when you and Mary tossed around the tennis ball with Natalie. I have a lot of friends that tell me the same thing—how they observed their dog or cat staring out into space, seemingly at nothing. Or how their pet walked up to a bare wall and started pawing and making noises like something, or someone was there. I've seen Natalie do that many times. Just the other day, I watched her play with another dog—that wasn't there. I know that's what she was doing.

The dog was there. It was Skeeter, who has visited your home often since he left Earth many years ago.

You're kidding. Skeeter comes around here?

He does. You had him for only a brief time, but in that time, he sensed your devotion to him so strongly that he swore to never jump into another physical life but to become your Helper and protector.

That's wonderful! Skeeter! Here, boy!

You don't have to call him like that. All you need to do is speak his name in your mind, and he will be at your side in an instant.

Skeeter, you were such a sweet dog. I did love you so much, and it was wonderful to see you back Home with Mary and Annie the other day. And I feel really silly talking like this to thin air.

But you are talking to Skeeter. He's standing right at

your feet.

Skeeter? But this is so hard, Sweetie. If I could just see him or feel—ugh! What the heck was that?

You felt him, didn't you? Skeeter just jumped into your lap.

Wow. Skeeter boy!

MARY: *Dear One?*

Mary?

We must return now to our lessons on the Universal Principles. These are very important to the outcome of our mission.

Can Skeeter sit on my lap while we do this?

That is up to you. He is your dear friend, and he will stay as long as you like.

How cool is that?

Can we get started now?

We're ready—Skeeter and me.

The Law of Polarity

This is the Law of walking the middle path. This Universal Law deals with direct opposites that exist and function together in the same space and time. Think of a car battery with the two poles of positive and negative. Each pole is the direct opposite of the other, and yet they must work together in the same space to accomplish their task of starting a car engine and sustaining its power. They are opposites, and neither is of use in and of itself. They must function together at the same time and in the same space. Think of the two ends of a magnet.

I never thought of that before.

Polarity is a primary component of the power of the Universal Laws. It is what God has used to create and sustain all of the universes. If a being can comprehend this power and learn how to control even a small part of it, then the power of God will be behind everything that being does.

Real Power — Power that is substantiated and backed by the Truth of God — must have the blessing of God, and if that blessing is not present, then the being can never make use of the power of the Hermetic Principles. God will only grant the gift of True Power to those who will use it properly.

But how does this True Power come out of two things that are exact opposites?

It does not come out of the individual components of the pair of opposites. It arises from the agreement of the two opposites working together at the same time and in the same space. This can be an inter-realm agreement as well, but that is difficult to explain at this time. In fact, all of this is difficult to explain. Try to explain the concept of "Now," which contains within itself both future and past. Or electrons, which can be present in two places simultaneously, "here" and "there," with "here" being the opposite of "there."

The difficulty of this concept is yet another reason why human beings should "Walk by faith and not by sight," as the Apostle Paul instructed in his second letter to the Corinthian Church. When a person relies on physical eyes alone for guidance, only the obvious and mundane superficial realities can be seen. Remember, though, nothing material is as it appears to be. We live in a universe that is ruled not only by the laws of physical science but by the laws of supernatural science as well. On Earth, human beings are subject to the ordinary laws that govern the simple, everyday occurrences of life. Most people are not aware that a realm exists beyond what is seen, and that is controlled by Heaven, which also has its way in the affairs of the physical world — remember the Law of Correspondence. That is the difference between laws and Laws.

At first, one might say that this is not fair. Who are they to interfere with our ways here on Earth? The answer to that question is simple. If those beings in the Heavenly realm did not interfere with man's activities on Earth, mankind would have destroyed the Earth a long time ago — long before The Great Plan of God was meant to be resolved. The laws that are being "forced" upon you from Heaven are necessary for the good of humanity.

I don't have a problem with that. Every day I get up and watch the news, and I follow the latest political silliness. I realize that we just aren't bright enough to do this on our own. I believe that's why humans began searching for God in the first place. They knew from somewhere deep inside that they just couldn't do this without a Higher Being helping them through the rough spots. It appears, though, that there really is a God, and He is THE ALL of Everything. I like it. I like the whole plan. Can God do something about the demons we have in our government that are really screwing up our country right now?

It is all a part of The Plan, Din. Those who are in power in the governments of all nations and have their own private agendas counter to The Great Plan of God, will be taken care of. The paramount Law above all others is that whatever or whoever opposes The Great Plan will be removed by THE ALL

I love that! When can we see this removal begin to happen?

Soon, Din, but let us continue with the Law of Polarity. This is really a very simple principle that can be summed up in the thought that the universe cannot, in and of itself, tolerate any form of imbalance. Imbalance brings disharmony in opposition to the Great Plan. The paramount Law is invoked, and the perpetrators of discord are removed by THE ALL. When two opposites come together in the same time and space, the result will be the release of energy, often with the destruction of the opposites, and therein lies the power. Two opposites cannot reside in the same space and time without resulting in significant consequences. If the opposites are equal and balanced, the end result will be constructive and useful. If they are unequal and unbalanced, the effect will be destructive and harmful. That is how the simultaneous application of the positive and negative charges in a battery results in a useful flow of energy. This is a power of rejection. Both are rejecting each other equally.

Let me give you some examples. Some of the more common polarities known to your dimension are the following: right and left, man and woman, black and white, empty and full, negative and positive, good and bad, weak and strong. None of these opposites can exist together in the same space and at the same time. If this happens, the opposites are changed.

My personal favorite illustration of this Law can be observed in the horse. A large horse can be both meek and mighty at the same time. Horses can be gentle enough for any child to lead them, feed them, and ride them. Yet they are strong enough to pull wagons, and they can wield tremendous force with their hooves. They can easily crush a man to death should the horse be threatened or abused. This quality is known as strength under control, and it demonstrates the Law of Polarity in action. The power of this Law comes from the control of opposites.

Jesus illustrated the Law of Polarity when he said, "The first shall be the last." He also said, "It is only in losing your life that you shall find it," which is of similar significance.

Again, this Law is well known beyond the confines of Judeo-Christian thought. Lao Tzu, The Chinese mystic and originator of Taoism, wrote:

> Be bent, and you will remain straight.
> Be vacant, and you will remain full.
> Be worn, and you will remain new.

This, too, is a platitude which, in and of itself, means nothing. When fully explained, however, it reveals to perfection the Law of Polarity.

In summary, this Law is all about the harmony and balance of all that exists in the physical world. Life's energy streams on a continuum between the poles of opposites. You are never stuck in any one spot in the continuum — you are just like an electron. You can be in many different places at the same time, whether you are speaking of mental revelations or physical experiences.

One of the goals set for themselves by those who practice yoga is to achieve balance in life, which can be described as maintaining a life free of dominance from any one factor or extreme. To live within the boundaries of the Law of Polarity without causing disruption to one's life, one must walk the middle, or moderate, path of self-control in all things, including food, drink, sports, music, television, opinion, politics, religion, attitude — the list is infinite. This is vital to everyone, not just the Weet. When one oversteps the boundaries of this Principle, the reaction could possibly destroy that person.

Guidance for the application of the Law of Polarity can be found in ancient proverbs such as, "In the middle is Truth." Slipping to one side or the other may cause you to lose sight of the Truth. In John 8:32, Jesus makes clear just how vital the Truth is to all of us by saying:

> *You shall know the Truth and the Truth will make you free.*

If you walk in the Universal Laws — which are Truth — you will be made free. You will become what you are meant to be because the universe makes way for Truth. This is the secret to success in life.

True spirituality requires adherence to the middle path because it contains both extremes, and that is the most secure position to be in. To refrain from harsh reactions to one extreme or another is the healthiest way to be. Great power results when the opposites come together at the same time and in the same space. Sometimes that power is overwhelming, but there is a higher spiritual power to be found when one learns to not overreact by going to one extreme or the other. Walking the middle path is the way to experience the oneness of all things. Jesus taught this over and over again.

I'm not sure I totally understand this, but I think I get the main points. There are those pairs of opposites, which can be any number of things. There is also an extraordinary, even destructive power that is released when the two opposites try to mix it up together in the same place at the same time because a pair of opposites can't exist in the same time and space. Left cannot be right, and right cannot be left. Empty cannot be full, full cannot be empty. A man cannot be a woman, a woman cannot be a man. Good cannot be bad, bad cannot be good. To claim these things can become their opposites goes against not just the Universal Law of God, but physics itself, and to attempt such a thing can only result in grievous damage to the pair and the eternal annihilation of their energy frequencies, as well. It is not a matter of cultural desire, or even of morality, it is a matter of Universal Law.

That is correct.

So the True power of a Strong Weet lies in learning how to go just to the edge of that boundary where opposites meet and blow the world into outer space. Then somehow — let me think this through — somehow tap into that potential power just as it is becoming an actual power, and channeling that energy into doing the Will of God.

Bingo!

Ha! Where the heck did you learn that word?

From playing inside your head for decades.

Oh, that. So, can the Strong Weet do this? Have they learned how to go to that edge and capture the power just before it blows up the world?

Yes, they have in their True Energy Forms, but they must Awaken first, and it will take the combined effort of all ten, and especially the three of us to do what must be done when it is time to do so.

And I take it Annie is the key?

Annie is the key to everything, my love. Everything.

I'm beat.

I know you are, Din. Let us end this session. We can begin again when you are rested.

I think that's a good idea. I've been feeling under the weather for the past day or two, kinda like I'm catching something.

What do you intend to catch, Sweet Din?

I think I'm catching a cold, Mary. Or the flu, or something like that. I've got this sore throat, and I feel kind of achy. That ain't good.

ANNIE: *You mean, you are getting sick? I will not allow that!*

WOW! What the heck was that?

I'm sorry. Do you feel better?

Good grief! What the ... I do feel better. My throat isn't hurting, and all of the aches are gone. I thought I was getting a fever there for a while, but I feel cool as a cucumber now. What the heck did you do, Annie?

God healed you through me.

Wait a minute. You healed me? You, my Daughter from the Other Side, came to this side — and I don't know what I'm talking about here — and you completely cured me of the common cold? How did you do that?

God and I both love you. That's how we did that.

I'm not sure what that means, but if we could bottle it, we'd make a fortune.

You should never make money on love.

I know that, Princess. It's just a silly Earth saying.

Princess? You called me, Princess?

Yep. I did.

More of your memories are returning.

What am I remembering? Help me out here, because I don't know what the heck you're talking about.

Daddy, do you have to use such profanity?

I'm sorry, Annie. I forget you're just a fifteen-year-old kid, and you're so ...

I was just kidding, Daddy. That's what Mom does to you all the time.

Great.

You see me now as a fifteen-year-old because that is how I choose to appear in this incarnation. In reality, I am many years old ... billions.

I know that, but don't burst my bubble. I want you to be my fifteen-year-old Daughter. I don't want you to suddenly appear to me as a 900-billion-year-old lady with grey hair and no teeth.

You are so cute. I will forever be for you the way I am now. I will forever be fifteen. I remember what you said to me many years ago while I was that age, so this is my favorite age to be.

I'm sorry, Annie. I don't know what I said ten minutes ago, let alone many years ago.

It was the same time you spoke to me about my ponytail. You said many things that day, but the most endearing thing you said was, "Sweetie, I love you so much. You are so perfect in every way. I don't want you to ever change." I took you seriously, so I have remained this way for centuries.

I … I don't know what to say. I guess that just goes to show you how much influence we parents have on our kids.

MARY: *It is true, Dear Din. Annie practically worships you and she will do whatever you tell her to do. She will be whatever you wish her to be. That is why you must be mindful when you speak with her.*

ANNIE: *Oh, Mother. I just love my Dad. I love you, too.*

MARY: *I know that, Honey. But you know how you are.*

ANNIE: *I'm just me. It's just that it has been so long since I have seen my Father that I am confused about how I should relate to him. I am so tired of this! All of these different lives going on. One ends, and another begins, then it starts all over again. I never know from this life to the next what I will find or where I will be able to locate you or my Father. And, yes, I love him more than I love my own life, but that is because … even you don't know Mother.*

MARY: *Annie, it is time for your Father to rest. We can continue this tomorrow. There is much to be done, as you know.*

ANNIE: *I know, Mother, but it has been so long since I have seen him that I take every opportunity to be with him.*

MARY: *That's okay, Dear. You will have plenty of opportunities.*

Don't I get a say here?

MARY: *Of course, Din.*

I don't know … this is just coming from my gut, but heck — sorry — I just wish we could be a family again. I don't know what I'm saying, but I just wish … I just want … wish … but that isn't possible. You guys can't do what I want you to do. I want you to materialize in front of me and become *real*. I want to hug you both. I want to kiss you.

MARY: *One day, Din. One day. But there is so much work to do. You must trust us.*

I just want to chuck it all, get drunk, and play Yahtzee.

MARY: *Do not be discouraged, Din. Just know that we love you and that all things will work out in the end. It has to be. And you do not even drink.*

After hanging around you two, I've been thinking about taking it up ...

ANNIE: *And please know that I will be at your side through all of this. Nothing will harm you because I will not allow it.*

Annie, when I called you Princess, you told me that I was starting to remember. What, exactly, am I remembering? Because I don't think I'm tuned into that yet.

ANNIE: *Daddy, we have lived many lives together, but in every one of them, I was always your Daughter, and you were always my Father. In one of those lives, I was indeed a princess, and you were the king.*

What?

ANNIE: *I prefer not to answer this at this time. It has little relevance to our mission.*

Will you tell me about it sometime?

ANNIE: *I will. But not now.*

So now what? Another Universal Law?

MARY: *No, not now. It is time for you to rest for a while. I think you sometimes forget that Annie and I are eternal. We have no need for rest. You must be tired.*

I am tired. I think I need to stop for a while and cogitate on these Universal Laws. My inner voice is telling me that they are important, but my physical mind is hoping that the readers of this book aren't bored to tears by all of them.

MARY: *They will not be bored, Din. Those who are of the Strong Weet Society will be awakened when they read these words.*

I'll take your word for it, Mary.

MARY: *When you are rested, we will begin again. Before*

we approach the next Law, though, I would like you to work for a while on the portraits. These are very important, for they will identify the members of the Strong Weet Society. Annie and I are going to return to our realm while you rest.

When will I hear from you again?

MARY: *Soon. Later, when you are rested, we have an assignment for you that should prove to be interesting. It is time for you to exercise your intuitive gifts, and to meet others of a like mind.*

You mean other Weet?

MARY: *Possibly. There may be Weet among them, but they probably do not know that is what they are. They are, however, intriguing, and they have intuitive gifts that you will help them to release.*

Now I'm curious. What is this assignment?

MARY: *I will tell you when you have rested for two days.*

Two days! You mean I have to wait that long?

MARY: *It's for your own good, Din. You're starting to develop bags under your eyes.*

But—

ANNIE: *Please.*

All right. I'll do it for you, but I'm angry with your Mother.

ANNIE: *No, you're not.*

You're right. I'm not.

ANNIE: *Bye-bye then.*

MARY: *The time will pass quickly, Dear.*

29 July

Speculations About the Weather and Instructions for the Development Circle

It's a gorgeous early Sunday morning. I love summertime. The winters here are cold and damp, and they seem to drag on forever. I was made for summer, the flowers, and the birds, sitting in the back garden sipping iced tea, watching the tomatoes grow. Can't beat it.

Today is that kind of day. It's hot already and going to get hotter. I'm guessing around a hundred degrees. Everything is really dry, too. Actually, it's been pretty dry all summer. The grass has withered into a kind of brittle, dark brown mat of … short spaghetti? That's kind of what it looks like. I can hear it crack and break when I walk on it in my bare feet.

The poor trees have had a hard time, too. I've been giving them extra water to try to keep them from feeling the pain of this drought we seem to be having. This spot here in the middle of Missouri is a funny place. It can be pouring rain just a mile or so to the north of where I live—maybe two or three inches in twenty minutes—and my yard will be dry. Or a storm might come around from the south and dump water on the folks just a half-mile away but, again, not a drop in my neck of the woods. I've actually driven through torrential downpours in town one block at a time. At the end of the block, I'd drive out of the rain onto bone-dry pavement. Another block or two along, and I would be in the rain again.

I do love the thunderstorms and the wild spring rains that come through here every year. It can be a bit frightening, though, if a whirling funnel is spotted up in the clouds. That can only mean one thing: tornados. I guess

237

those tornados are what scare me most about living here. You just don't know when or where they're going to touch down. It's funny; one of the reasons I didn't mind leaving California was the increased frequency of earthquakes in the area where I lived. Instead, I end up here where the tornados are much more threatening—and much more frequent! I suppose that's the doing of Mother H. She seems to be the one in charge of such things. I guess she knows what she's doing.

Weather can be very confusing to me. I feel the dramatic weather changes deep in my "inner me," so to speak, but the mechanics of the whole thing don't make sense. This whole global warming deal is a big question mark as far as I'm concerned. I wonder what Mary thinks of it? I've spent quite a bit of time in the past several months researching it, and I haven't come up with any evidence that it's really happening the way the media are portraying it. Earth's climate goes through cycles that last centuries and even eons, and what we are experiencing may be only a part of the cycle we are in. It seems that these changes may be more related to solar fluctuations rather than earthly ones because the other planets in the solar system are affected as well. I think everyone should stop calling it global warming and start calling it climate change because that seems to be what is really happening. I think it has very little to do with humans, and more to do with Nature.

Guess we'll just have to see what happens as time goes by. I wonder, though, just how much time is left to this planet—not because of global warming, but because of The Great Plan. Given the chaotic state of politics, terrorism, and tensions between the nations today, cyclical weather patterns may be a moot point in just a few years.

I wonder what Mary has planned for me. I've been

working on the portraits, and it's been two days since I talked with her. Hmm ... before I go any further, maybe I ought to clarify what I mean when I say I "talk" to Mary. I have some time on my hands, so I'll give it a try.

When either Mary or Annie make their appearance, it is not in any physical sense at all. They are not standing right there in front of me. First, I hear their voices, as clearly as I can hear someone next to me. Then I begin to get pictures in my mind, like a movie. Even if my eyes are open and I'm aware of everything else around, I can still see this movie of Mary and Annie running in my head. It's almost as if they really are right there.

Not only do I hear and see Mary and Annie, but I can feel their presence and smell anything they have with them. It's a complete, sensual experience. While they are with me, I could swear they are really with me! That's why it's so frustrating that I can't hug or touch them in any way. So near and yet so far.

ANNIE: *One day soon, we will be able to touch each other, Daddy.*

Annie! I'm so glad to hear your voice.

I missed you, too.

Ever since you guys came into it, my life hasn't been the same. I suppose that's the understatement of the year.

Don't worry. Things will begin to sort themselves out.

Where do you go and what do you do when you aren't hanging out with me?

We return to our realm, where we live within our own eternal lives.

But what's that like? I mean on an average day? I only saw that brief glimpse of a tiny part of it when you guys took me there, but what do you ... do there?

Well, we spend a lot of time worrying about you.

Thanks a lot. Besides that.

It's a most wonderful life. You've been there many times, only you don't remember. You live there when you aren't here. Mother created an exact replica of the little cottage you shared in Massachusetts, the one that you and she built not too long before you died in that life, and that's where we live, in that replica cottage. It sits on a hill overlooking a large lake just behind the Great Temple back Home and is used as our family Temple. It looks small on the outside, but the basement of the cottage is the size of Texas. Like the Crystal Library, even though the vault is underground, the views from the windows can be anything we wish them to be.

I know I've had dreams of that place before. Is that where the circle of different trees is? And the flower garden beside the cottage?

It is. Both here on Earth and back Home, the cottages and the surrounding gardens are identical. We will clarify that later in the Diary.

Aha! That's always been a mystery to me, those trees. What the heck is that all about?

The circle of trees was planted to give honor to sweet Grandma H, who loves us all very much. It was she who made it possible for Mom to be acquitted during her trials. She changed the heart and the mind of the local magistrate. After that, he would not threaten Mom again.

What did your Grandma H do?

She appeared to him in a most frightening way and told him that if he continued to persecute her Daughter or her Daughter's Family, she would destroy him and his family and erase all memory of them for all time.

Good grief. But I thought Joseph — that is, I — bought her freedom.

That was the tale told for the history books to remove any evidence of the appearance of Grandma H during that time.

Wait a minute. You said something about your Mom being the Daughter of your Grandma H? What the heck is that all about?

It is about Truth. Mother is —

MARY: *Annie.*

ANNIE: *Mother?*

Mary?

MARY: *There is no need to speak of such things at this time.*

ANNIE: *I'm sorry, Mother.*

But wait a minute —

MARY: *Din, I need to prepare you for an important task. You must treat this seriously.*

Come on, Mary. I've got a ton of questions.

MARY: *Thanks to Annie.*

ANNIE: *I'm sorry, Mother.*

Come on, you two. I'm the one in the dark here.

MARY: *You will not be in the dark much longer. That is why this assignment is so important to you.*

All right. What hoop do I have to jump through now?

MARY: *There are no hoops, Sweet One, but you are expected to assume a great responsibility. The Intuitive Development Circle that you have been leading over the past few months is about to become something truly exceptional.*

Annie will explain the details as she is the one who will be helping you the most with this assignment.

ANNIE: *You will love this, Daddy. You're going to turn your DC into a beacon for attracting the Strong Weet Society to your door. You're already doing a great job raising the mental and spiritual awareness of everyone attending your meetings, including yourself. As you continue to teach this class to the others, you'll begin to Awaken more rapidly to your own true self. This class is a catalyst that will stimulate the recovery of your memories of your true nature and what you are capable of achieving. It also provides an opportunity for the Strong Weet to locate you. After they read this book and their Higher Selves have been tweaked by its words, they will seek out the Development Circle when they hear that it is nearby. This is most probably where many of you will be brought back together.*

Some of your current members will soon be dropping out. When that happens, Mother and I will help to bring several new students to you. These are the ones that we know to have high intuitive power hidden just beneath the surface of their consciousness. You'll be able to carefully observe the development of each of these newcomers as you teach the exercises. You'll also be able to determine which among them are Strong Weet. Not all will be of that level, but there will be a few.

The heat is on.

There is no heat. This will be fun for all of us.

All of us?

Yes. I'll be with you at every meeting, just as I've always been. Mother will pop in as often as she can. At the end of every session, you'll continue to lead what you are now calling your group quiet time. You'll find that it will become much more active.

You're going to have to give me detailed instructions if I'm to pull this off, and you're going to have to be with me every step of the way. I'm just a novice at this intuitive stuff, and I'm not sure what you mean when you say, "active."

I will. By "active," I mean that you'll be aware of a higher rate of spirit contact, as well as much more photographic evidence. You'll be taking pictures of some pretty exciting stuff.

I can't get used to you using words like "stuff."

I learned it —

From me. Yeah, I know. And you promise you'll be with me at these meetings?

I will still visit you in your mind as I always do.

So, when do I get started?

Your next meeting will be this coming Saturday at 6:00 p.m., and this is when the changes will occur.

What kind of changes are we talking about?

You'll bring more organization to your meetings. In the past, the sessions have been a bit haphazard. It's now crucial that you emphasize to your students the importance of the Circle. They will not fully understand what you're referring to, because they know nothing of the Strong Weet Society, nor of the dire future of this planet if our mission is unsuccessful. They will sense something unusual and compelling about the meetings, and even those who are not Strong Weet will become allies to the cause.

So, I have to organize this thing a bit. I thought I was doing a pretty good job with it.

You've been doing an excellent job. Perhaps "organization" wasn't the most appropriate word. "Focus" is a better one. You must bring the focus of the meetings around to the quiet time because that's where you'll find strong support from our realm. You'll need all you can get when the time comes.

I think you need to clarify what you mean exactly by "support from our realm." Some of the readers are going to think we're talking about ghosts and the like, and we're not.

No, we are not. Your support does not come from wandering ghosts and specters, but from those who are set aside to be your angelic helpers — we talked about those before — and from any other beings that God sends your way to convey relevant information to the DC group.

More Angels.

Perhaps. But others as well. Do you not remember when you followed the Catholic faith, and you sometimes prayed for guidance and wisdom from the saints? Catholics and many Protestants, as well, pray to the saints or talk to relatives who have preceded them into Heaven. It is all the same thing. In the case of the quiet time, you need only to ask, to receive all the help you need.

And some people are going to be leaving the circle?

They are, but you will not miss them. There is one particular individual in your group at this time who has a very negative spirit. It will be to your benefit when she leaves. Two others have chaotic hearts and minds and are much too confused to be of any good to the group.

Are we talking about the same people?

Trust me. You have three in your midst who should not be there. They must be removed, and that will happen at the next meeting. After Saturday night, the Circle will be left with only five members, and you will need to recruit three more. It will take some trial and error, adding and subtracting members until you find the ones who will remain with you. Not all will be Strong or Secondary Weet, but, again, all will be faithful allies in the end.

So, after these three negative folks leave, who do I invite? I don't have that many friends. Let's see … I can't think of a single guy who would be suitable.

I am afraid you will be working only with women. The men in this geographical region are not known for their spiritual maturity in these matters.

Well, all I can think of are my history students. There's Kris. She seems to be pretty aware of things. And there's Katie. She looks a lot like you, Annie. Wait a minute! Is she my—I know, don't go there yet. You know everything, don't you, Annie?

I know what I know.

So, are these two okay so far? Good grief, Katie has to be okay.

You must choose according to your own intuition.

Yada yada.

I'm sorry?

Forget it. Okay. There's Kris, and there's Katie. Who else? I need eight total? Why eight?

Eight is the traditional number for a development circle. It is big enough to be effective and small enough to manage easily. Also, the number is even so that you can pair off to do specific exercises.

I can't wait to find out what those are.

You will enjoy them. Everyone in your group will.

I can think of a few others to add, just off the top of my head. Besides Kris and Katie, there's another woman in my history class, Mary. I think she is someone who is ... special. And another girl that I think the world of, Kristen, but she's living in Hawaii right now.

She could still be a part of the circle. You can use her for intuitive messaging and remote viewing. Just keep in mind that not all those you are mentioning will be the correct ones who will remain with you, and not all of those you start with will be the ones you will finish with. Several will drop out; others may join. This is a selection process. Only TRUE Secondary and Strong Weet will be left in the end, and they may not all come from your development circle, either.

I just can't think of anyone else. I can't help but think that a whole lot rides on whom I choose or don't choose. I don't want to make the wrong decisions. What if these people are wrong? What if I leave somebody out?

You won't. All will work out just as it should.

You know, Annie, I'm noticing some differences between you and your Mother. For instance, she still uses archaic lingo from some time back in history, and you're a little more modern in your chitchat with me. I mean, you don't use contractions all the time, but you do mix 'em in here and there. Your Mother, though — geez.

There's a reason for that, Daddy. I've used human forms

many times throughout eternity, and I've picked up the language and the slang from all those life experiences, whereas Mother has not. When you were living in your role as Joseph, the two of you were very close. After you died, even though she was a Strong Weet and knew that she could return for many life experiences, she chose to come back only a few times after that. She was trying to arrange conditions that would allow her to awaken within you at a specific time. That time came when the ball lightning struck in front of your house.

So, she has only taken a few life forms since being married to Joseph?

That's right. One time was when she came back as Maria, the mother of Anna. She only did that because you were animating Jose. And just a couple more. You guys were so close that she didn't want to mess with any other men.

How sweet is that? I think … and, Annie, I, too, feel that closeness with your Mom. I just wish that I could have her here in this physical world. I'm repeating myself, but …

You will be able to see us both soon. There will be more visits Home where you can have that experience, and we are working on a plan that will let us appear before you in a physical form in this realm.

You mean you would be solid and three-dimensional, and I could touch and feel both of you?

That's what I mean. It's a matter of physics. It won't be long before we can become as real to you as you are to yourself.

I so long for that.

Have patience. Trust us, and enjoy what is to come.

If you say so.

I do.

So, what now?

You have much to do. What I would like you to do now is to lie back on your living room couch and try to go to sleep. I will place you into a hypnagogic state that will be restful and allow your mind to receive, process, and retain instruction from me.

But what about the Universal Laws?

We'll finish those soon, in the time we have allotted.

So let's get started. What now?

I want you to go into our house and lie down on the couch.

You mean I have to leave this beautiful garden?

No, I guess you don't. This is a fine place to do what must be done. You are reclining comfortably on the chaise lounge. You are also completely exposed to the sun, which is not a bad thing. Because of who you are, the sun is a large part of your being and of your spiritual essence.

I'm not even going to ask what that means.

It only means that — no, I will tell you later. Just lie back in your chair and close your eyes.

Okay. Here I—

Five Minutes Later

You know, it's tough to tell the difference between these visionary states Mary and Annie put me in and so-called reality. I am aware of the passage of time, and I can remember what went on, but I only know for sure that I have been in one of these states when I look at my watch and see that only five minutes have passed since Annie put me under when I have memories that span hours. I wonder if this is what it feels like to be abducted by aliens? I can't help but wonder if there are any others out there going through what I am going through.

While I was in this odd state of altered consciousness, Annie instructed me in how I am to lead the Development Circle in general and gave me specific details regarding the exercises for Saturday's meeting.

Here is what Annie fed into my brain:

You will be explaining many things to your students on Saturday, but there are two points of primary importance. The first is that they must attend every meeting. The helpers in the other realm need to become accustomed to the presence of the participants—get to know them, so to speak. The Helpers need to lower their natural vibrational frequency just as the DC members need to raise theirs for you all to meet at a frequency range, which lies somewhere in between. It is all about energy. I will repeat that. It is all about energy. This is pure physics, not paranormal hocus-pocus. All of you must concentrate on helper contact.

The second thing your students must know and pay close attention to is that everything you will be receiving from THE ALL during the DC meetings will be positive and loving. Nothing harmful or depressing will come from THE ALL; negative feelings arise from emotion and ego. If one of your members is experiencing negative images of death and trauma, or anything like that, it means they are manufacturing such things in their minds, and they have barely begun the beginning stages of spiritual development. They have much to learn, and it would be best to ask them to leave the circle and to find a replacement for them. You do not have time to train novices from the ground up. You must find the secondary and Strong Weet as quickly as possible.

Annie went on to explain how a development circle is conducted with everyone sitting in the same assigned position from week to week so that the helpers can identify and communicate with specific people.

The DC session generally lasts about two and a half hours and should follow a specific agenda—which I haven't really been doing. The meetings will begin with each participant briefly sharing any intuitive experiences they may have had the previous week. This is to be followed by what Annie calls a psychometry exercise, during which an old object, piece of jewelry, item of clothing, et cetera, is passed around to be handled and examined by each person in turn, gaining intuitive impressions from the object. Apparently, physical objects—especially metals—that have been owned by people for a long time have some sort of personal energy imprint on them that doesn't go away. An aware person can pick up on that imprint and glean images from the owner's lifetime.

The main lesson of the night follows the psychometry exercise. These can be activities as specific as training to see human heat auras, or of broader focus such as what I call a wisdom search, which is the presentation of a single problem of a spiritual nature followed by the discussion of possible solutions, and determining the wisest course of action. I'm really looking forward to that.

The session will conclude with an hour-long quiet time during which everyone concentrates on making contact in some way with a helper. Annie has instructed me to take dozens of digital photos during the Quiet Time to detect orbs, light streaks, shadows, and any other anomalies that might occur. The photographs serve to validate what the DC members perceive from the other realm. I've taken some photos at past meetings, but Annie tells me I need to take as many as two hundred per night! Geez! I'll do what she says because I can't argue with this perfect Being who has apparently been around almost since the beginning of time.

The hypnagogic state Annie placed me in was a pleasant experience. I felt as if I was asleep, and yet I knew I wasn't. I readily understood every word she spoke to me and logged it all away in my memory in perfect detail. When I woke up, it was as if I had known it all for my entire life. I felt like I'd been leading development circle sessions for years. It was a total hypnotic transformation.

Annie also gave me two names to consider as replacements for members that will be leaving the circle. Neither of them was among those I had mentioned to her earlier. I was a bit taken aback as both of these women attend the little church I lead on Sunday mornings. That is something I haven't really gone into because I didn't think it would ever be relevant for this Diary, but I guess it is.

I am the pastor of an independent Christian Church that meets not too far from where I live. It's a small group, but we have a good time together. We base all of our beliefs on the teachings of Christ, as found in the Bible. I believe the Christian Churches are way off base with much of what is being taught today, but I believe that what Jesus taught is Truth. He said that He is "… the way and the truth and the life," and that seems like it might be a pretty good thing to say. If you look at the way people's lives have been changed by reading His teachings on love and truth in the Bible, it just makes sense.

I lead a small group of spiritually-concerned individuals. They are dissatisfied and burned out by the current mega-church scene and its variety-show atmosphere of rock bands and pop-inspired music, not to mention all the dogma and doctrinal nonsense that has been added to the original Truth. As an alternative, we have come together to do our own thing. I deliver sermons in a relaxed style that are more like lessons. They are mostly about the pressing issues of the world today and the Truths that Christ gave to humanity so that humans would be able to confront those issues. I'm also not afraid to dump the politically correct rhetoric that other pastors seem to think they need to adhere to, which makes me kind of an odd-ball as a pastor. It's kind of an odd church altogether, come to think of it. If any one of us were to walk into a "normal" Christian church, we'd probably walk right out again, if we didn't get thrown out first.

So, back to Annie. It's obvious to me why she named Nora and Sheila as possible replacements—they both seem to have the unconscious intuitive leanings shared by many who are sincere in their church activities.

Could these two ladies be Strong Weet? When I think about it, I have a gut feeling that Sheila just might be. She has become my right-hand at the Church meetings, and she already has the characteristics of a highly advanced intuitive. With the instruction I've been getting from Annie and Mary, and my own increasing awareness, I'm more knowledgeable about what to watch for. I don't know Nora as well as I do Sheila, so it may take a few sessions to figure her out. Nora and Sheila are both excellent people with strong and compelling characters. Saturday night should tell me what I need to know.

That's all I have time to write this morning. I don't want to be late for church—I am the preacher, after all.

4 August

More About the Nature of the Family, and the Fifth Universal Law is Explained

Everything went smoothly at the Saturday night Development Circle, just as Annie planned it. We even got some contacts from the other realm. I won't share any of the details because those communications are personal and private between the person in the DC and the spirit being making the contact. I still don't fully understand just how people and things get moved back and forth from one realm to the other across vast distances in a matter of moments. I know it isn't a non-physical, other-dimensional thing. The domain that Mary and Annie call Home and Heaven is a real, three-dimensional place that exists somewhere "out there" in deep space. Anyway, it was an active session—more so than any previous DC meetings, which tells me that Mary and Annie are now running the show, and that's a good thing.

Just to be clear, even though most of the DC members also attend the little church that I lead, the church is not one of those spiritualist congregations filled with psychics and mediums conducting séances and the like—that is NOT what we do. We simply give any of our loved ones who have passed on the opportunity to contact us, should they need or desire to do so. We don't pray to our aunts and uncles or hold séances to force them into our presence, and nobody goes into a trance. We just send them our love, and if they wish to send us some loving thoughts in return, we are happy to receive them. It's really more of a prayer circle or quiet time. We send love, we receive love. No hocus-pocus involved. A couple of years ago, several of our church members suffered bereavements and were having a difficult time dealing with the loss. I suggested that we start a prayer circle where members of the Church who have had these experiences can get together as a church family and say goodbye to their loved ones. Everybody thought it was a good idea, so we did, and it stuck.

As per Annie's instructions, I took a lot of photographs during the evening's quiet time—about two hundred of them. It's almost midnight, and I'm beat, but I got the pictures loaded onto my computer and have looked at every one of them. I am pleased to say that I caught some really good stuff. I was excited to see that a number of the photos contained orbs, sometimes only one or two, and sometimes a half dozen or more. The really neat thing, though, is that as I was looking at them on the screen, one orb, in particular, stood out from all the rest. I knew it was Annie. I got out the photos from the Boonville investigation, where we first discovered Annie's orbs, and sure enough, they were the same. Orbs are like fingerprints; no two are alike. If you find two that are the same in every way, you have two photos of the same spirit being.

Annie's orb is the most beautiful of all I have photographed. It usually shows up large and bright with a purple glow around it that is almost always stronger on one side than on the other. In all the photos I have taken of her, the orb has the same interior pattern, as well.

ANNIE: *That's me, all right.*

Annie!

I'll be present at all of your meetings, and you will always capture my orb there. You realize, of course, that the orbs aren't actually the people themselves, but are only an indicator that someone is present for you to communicate with. Each being can create his own distinctive orb to use to identify himself every time he comes around.

Yes, I figured that out already. So, how did I do tonight?

You did very well, and many loved ones were allowed to come through. What's more important, though, is how did you feel about those in attendance?

They're wonderful. I liked them before this evening, but after spending several hours with them and getting to know them better, I really love them. They are special, and I think they all have the potential to develop their intuitive skills to high levels.

I'm glad you feel that way. They are all good people, and you'll be spending a lot of time with them.

I'm looking forward to it. I just hope these meetings bear fruit. I want to meet the other Strong Weet.

You will after this book is published. Then the real work will begin.

What if nobody wants to publish the book?

It will be published, although the first publisher will not be of our same mind and will remove some of what you will have written, thus altering or diluting the truth presented on those pages. It may be necessary to republish the books so that the truths that may be removed during the first publishing can be restored.

You're really serious about this doomsday stuff, aren't you? You really believe that the world is going to come to an end if the Strong Weet Society fails to intervene?

It is a fact. Don't forget, where we reside, we are granted access to the Truth. We know exactly what will happen, and we know when. It can be changed, but only through the efforts of the Strong Weet Society. When the ten Strong Weet get together, enormous power will be released that will alter the course of history.

That reminds me of the TV show, *Charmed*—the power of three and all that.

I used to watch that show with you.

You're kidding!

It was very entertaining. And you're right, it is similar to what people call the power of three, but the power of the Strong Weet Society is infinitely more so. We — Mary, you, and I — are the Three.

You really watched *Charmed* with me. How cool is that?

We must also discuss the dreams that you'll be having in the coming weeks. Mother and I will be guiding and direct- ing them. They will clarify much for you. At the end of this dream cycle, you will have all the information you need to help prevent the coming disaster. When the book is published, and the Strong Weet have come forward, we must act fast. It may take some time for the remaining seven to be revealed, but when they are, there will be very little time left.

So now what? The DC is over. It was great fun, and I really loved it, but I'm feeling just a little unfulfilled. I guess I was expecting some sort of magic to occur, but it didn't. I thought maybe I'd be able to pick up something from one of the ladies in the group. I thought I'd be able to identify at least one Strong Weet. Shouldn't I be able to do that? Aren't my powers getting strong enough to make that possible?

You will be able to do that soon, but Grandma H is very protective of The Great Plan. To reveal the Strong Weet to you before the proper time might prove disastrous. The primary purpose for this meeting was to get you used to the fact that Mother and I will now be with you at every meeting, and that many otherworldly experiences will occur from here on out. Your past meetings were not so successful. All we are trying to do is build your confidence in the other realm so that you will know you can rely on it one hundred per- cent. Remember, these DC meetings are not the paranormal nonsense you see on TV. The portrayal of the paranormal by those shows is incorrect, and often contrary to the truth. The meetings of the development circle are training venues for the Weet and will be discontinued when the members have advanced sufficiently.

I kind of gathered that was what you were doing. Speaking of Mary, where is your Mother? She hasn't popped in for a while.

Isn't that what Darren Stevens used to ask on BEWITCHED*?*

Did you watch that show with me, too?

I did.

You little stinker. Why didn't you make yourself known to me back then? That might have changed my life, taken me into a totally different direction, and—I guess I just answered my own question, didn't I?

You did. Everything that occurs on this planet is a part of The Great Plan of THE ALL. It was not time for me to introduce myself to you, and Mother couldn't, either, because the ball lightning hadn't occurred yet.

I get it. You know something?

What?

You're starting to talk like a modern girl.

What do you mean?

It's something that just started a few pages back. You're starting to speak with even more contractions than when I first "met" you.

I don't know what you mean. You keep mentioning these "contraptions."

Didn't they teach you anything back whenever it was you went to school? You're using words like "isn't," instead of "is not," and "hadn't," instead of "had not."

I had not noticed that.

Now you're playing with me.

Ha! But I really didn't notice until now. I suppose I'm merely becoming attuned to this current era. It is not as easy as you might think it would be.

There is no way that I can understand what you do, let alone how you do anything you do. I certainly don't believe any of it is easy. But I like the change. That old ancient talk was getting tiresome. I do appreciate that you've been around a bit so you can go back and forth between the archaic and modern, but you still need to see if you can get your mother out of that nonsense.

Mother is of her own mind and will.

She is a brilliant and beautiful woman—not to mention powerful—but she needs to blend in more with the times.

It will happen slowly, but surely.

Anyway, I like the way you're changing. I guess I'll have to buy you a smartphone and a red sports car now.

I don't need a smartphone, I'm far smarter than any technology on this little planet. I don't need a car, either. I can simply enter a person's mind when I wish to communicate, and I can be anywhere in the universe in a flash.

I know that. I was just trying to be funny.

You're funny a lot, Daddy.

So, now what do we do?

It's time for Mother to take you through the remainder of the Universal Laws.

Oh, that. Are you sure the readers aren't going to space out on that stuff? It can be kind of boring to a person who isn't into all this otherworldly whatever. I'm even kind of bored with it.

That's because your memories are returning, and your true identity—who you really are—is being restored. Those who are inclined to purchase a book like this in the first place are those who are interested in what you call otherworldly whatever, especially the intuitives among them and those who believe themselves to be one of us. The Strong Weet—whether they know themselves to be, or not—will read these Universal Laws, and will resonate with them.

Their genetic memories will be quickened, and they'll begin to dream dreams. They'll Awaken and make themselves known."

So, where has your Mother been?

She's been with Grandma H.

Really.

Yes. Mother is the coordinator of much of what is to occur when the Strong Weet are revealed, and everything must go off like clockwork. A challenging task.

But she told me that you are the main power behind The Plan.

I am, but Mother is infinitely more powerful than any other power known. She has trained directly under Grandma H for all of her life. She's not The Chosen One, but she is Grandma's chosen one. That's what I meant when I said that she is the Daughter of Grandma H. Grandma H selected Mother to be her Daughter millions of years ago. They are very close.

Holy Moly! And that's why you call her Grandma H.

Daddy, you really need to know that you, Mom, and I are so very powerful that we are feared everywhere we go. We've been set apart by THE ALL to be the Messengers of Justice to this and countless other worlds.

You're losing me here, Annie. You're going off into a dozen different directions. Other worlds? I've been to other worlds? Messengers of Justice?

I wish I could just slap you and tell you to wake up. You'll remember all of this soon, but I was hoping you would remember before this. That was the reason we sped you off through the galaxy a few days ago. You really must try. You really must awaken to who you are and to what your relationship to THE ALL is.

Is this plot getting complicated, or what?

There is no plot. Everything is Truth. We can only wish that when the readers read this, they'll believe it and will do whatever they can to help us.

Let me get this straight. It seems like such a long time ago when I first heard your Mom's voice in my bedroom. Scared the heck out of my poodle! Then there was the time she spun me around in my office chair, and when the back garden exploded into light and color and fairies and whatever. And now this! *Messengers of Justice?* What does that mean? *For this and countless worlds?* Just what the heck are we? I'm thinking of Arnold here — The Terminator — is that what we are?

Don't worry, only God will permanently annihilate any being. Your role will be to carry out physical terminations only. At this point in time, though, our primary function is to place thoughts into the minds of beings that will lead them to proper actions that will bring about the fulfillment of The Great Plan. We are also charged to disrupt the lives of those who are not willing to cooperate with The Great Plan.

What do you mean by disrupt?

We can place obstacles in their path. We can teach them lessons in a variety of ways, and we can cause them more grief than they have ever known. If they do not learn from us, we will refer them to Grandma H, who then presents the situation to THE ALL.

And THE ALL fries their butts.

I wouldn't put it that way, but that's what happens. Depending on the severity of their lack of cooperation, the final resolution can range from removing only their spirits from their bodies —

Killing them.

— to removing their entire family, as well as anyone who associates with them in a supportive fashion. In the most egregious cases, they would be spiritually annihilated, and all memory of their existence would be removed.

And that is justice?

It sounds cruel, but it is necessary. There are those who are just plain evil and need to be removed for the greater good.

Hitler, Stalin, Mussolini, Amin—

They have all been removed.

I've got to ask you this, Pumpkin. Both you and your Mother have this absolute, beyond all imagination, infinite, atomic power that can explode worlds with a thought. Am I right so far?

You are.

And you're saying I have this, too?

Daddy, you are our equal in every way. The three of us have different gifts and different skills. I am more skilled in some ways than you, and you are more skilled in other ways than I. Some, you use more powerfully than I.

Two things here, kid. First of all, I just don't feel it. I can't sense the power in me like you're talking about. I mean, every once in a while, I get this little pinch of a memory, but when is it gonna hit me full force so that I know what the heck I'm doing here? And second, your Mom told me that you are much more powerful than she and I put together.

When you awaken to your power, believe me, you'll know it. And it will be soon. What Mother was referring to was one of my many gifts, which are different from yours.

Can you give me an example?

One is the gift of fear.

What does that mean?

It means that I can place terrible fear into the hearts and minds of those who oppose The Great Plan. And even though it is not my duty to take lives, that will often be the result when I place that fear within them.

Holy Moly! But you do more than just make people afraid. Your Mother told me that you can destroy entire solar systems!

Galaxies, actually. Well, universes actually, all of them if I want.

And all of the people in those galaxies and universes!

You can do that too, Father, but it is seldom that we take such measures. Now, entire planets, or solar systems—

For cryin' out loud.

You must remember that you are familiar with all of this. The three of us are a team. You must also realize that what we do is necessary.

So here's my problem with that. For years I've been teaching my little church that the opposite of love is fear. That means that if love is of God, then fear—fear must be from the Devil! Is my Daughter the Devil?

Don't be silly. Shaitan is the only devil. Misguided church leaders have used him to threaten and coerce their congregations for many years. Many people go to church and pay their tithe without question only because they are afraid not to. I am not the silly little devil, nor am I his messenger, but I do place a necessary thought of fear into the minds of mortals so that they will be able to correct their errors and be successful in their lives. That is the real purpose of fear.

To get mankind back on the old "straight and narrow."

That's correct. It's just that some people are so caught up in their own egos and illusions that they have become irrevocably evil. They must be dealt with before they harm the work of the higher beings.

Here we go again. Who exactly are these higher beings?

The Children of God. Those few whom God has chosen to move forward into eternity.

So you don't just go around randomly killing evil dictators and despots?

I usually only plant the life-changing thought of fear into their minds, and that thought pretty much does the trick.

And you can do this with anyone?

I can.

But you seem so sweet.

I am sweet. And it's my job to be protective of other sweet Beings. It's my job to be protective of this planet. Occasionally some beings will take on physical form for the purpose of placing a shadow on all of humanity. I cannot allow that to happen. Both good and evil, or at least the potential for them, exist on this and all other worlds. We have sent out many lesser messengers of justice to maintain order in this particular part of the creation. Evil interactions are rare in the universe — Earth being the exception — but shaitan is continuously seeking to influence other worlds. Shaitan is pretty much a defeated devil, but evil is a reality that is fabricated in and flows from the minds of men. It must be dealt with because, in the physical realm, evil can be more potent than love. Without the lesser messengers, evil could spread outward from Earth. When you awaken, you will realize this. You will also remember your own primary gift, and you will begin to use it.

Can't you just tell me what my stupid little gift is? I know, The Great Plan—

You have a most marvelous gift. You will be so thrilled when you remember.

So, let's get this show on the road. Get your Mother down here so we can finish these Universal Law thingies and get this book published.

MARY: *I am here, Din.*

I kinda sorta sensed my last statement would bring you here, but you've been here for a while, haven't you?

I have.

So you've heard everything we've said?

Do you not remember that I am present in your mind every moment of every day? I hear all your thoughts.

Well, we've been talking about you, now, haven't we?

I do not mind. I know that everything that comes from both you and Annie is out of love. However, the discussion regarding contractions was troubling.

I'm sorry. It's just that sometimes I find your "pilgrim accent" a little distracting.

It is just my habit. I will try to change.

I didn't mean anything by it, Mary. You don't have to change the way you talk just for me.

I don't mind.

You did it! A contraction comes forth!

I did. But I can't promise I won't be going back and forth a bit.

ANNIE: *That's okay. I do it, too.*

MARY: *Perhaps it is … it's … a good idea for us to become more acclimated to our surroundings. It might even increase our power.*

ANNIE: *I think you're right.*

Okay, yadda yadda, what about those Universal Laws? We need to get them down so we can get this book off to a publisher, where it will, no doubt, be refused and mailed back.

ANNIE: *A-hem.*

I know. Positive thinking and all that ca-ca.

MARY: *Must you swear so much in front of your Daughter?*

You mean in front of my Daughter who can destroy this planet with a single thought?

MARY: *You're being sarcastic.*

I am.

MARY: *I like that. You're sounding more like your old self. I guess that's one quality you haven't lost through the eons.*

Now there's a phrase you don't hear very often in this contemporary mortal world.

ANNIE: *I have to go. Mother will stay and work with you on the remaining Universal Laws.*

Do you have to go, Annie? Where are you going?

ANNIE: *I'm gonna go to the mall and do some shopping.*

Sarcasm — what have I created? I'm assuming I'm the one who "created" you.

ANNIE: *With Mom's help.*

Of course. And I'll bet that was quite a night.

MARY: *We will talk about that later. But first, we must finish the Universal Laws.*

Yeah, right.

Now please get serious here, Din. We have only three of the laws left. These can be difficult to explain, so it is imperative that you interpret them correctly.

I'll do my best, Mary.

The Law of Rhythm.

The operation of this Law is best observed in the work of Mother Nature. The seasons, night and day, and the tides are all subject to the Law of Rhythm.

Recall that the fourth law, the Law of Polarity, describes the power contained in the function of the pairs of direct opposites that exist in all things. The fifth law, the Law of Rhythm, describes the power inherent in the shifting of focus between the extremes of polarity. The period of movement between one extreme and the other — the ancient Druids called it "the in-between time" — has been recognized by many so-called primitive cultures as a portal giving access to great magic or power. The movement between the poles is constant and regular, and the pattern is unique to each and every individual. Everyone and everything is a sentient being, and all sentient beings have measurable, rhythmic signatures of frequency, amplitude, and direction that sets them apart from everyone and everything else.

Does this have anything to with what people call bio-rhythms? That it was a big fad a few years ago. Some people wouldn't even get of bed before calculating whether or not it was going to be a good day for them.

The biorhythm fad of the 70s came about when a few individuals recognized some of the workings of the Law of Rhythm. What they saw, though, was only a small part — the tip of the iceberg, as you might say. All of the formulas, calculators, workshops, and seminars were just attempts to profit from a gullible public by convincing them that they have the ability and understanding to predict and manipulate the Powers of the Universe. Rhythmic signatures are, indeed, influenced by many things such as time of day, weather changes, and moon phases, to name a few, including the biorhythms of other sentient beings. Still, it is beyond humankind's understanding of mathematics to comprehend.

Things don't travel in straight lines only, they move back and forth, and they ebb and flow like the waves of the sea. They turn round and round like the energy centers in the spine. They rotate like wheels and spirals, up and down, left and right. Everything, including the molecules of your body, is in a state of constant change that sometimes seems a bit chaotic but is in perfect order. You're never going to be "who you are" for long because you are in a constant state of change — ever going forward. Even when you die, your life has not really ended; it has merely changed into another Energy Form. In death, the Spirit moves on to its Eternal Home, and the physical body begins to turn to gas and liquid. Energy — which is what all Beings are — never really dies or disappears, it merely changes.

Rhythm is like the changing of the seasons. It's a circular motion that has no beginning and no end. It is a process of flowing in and flowing out, one season into the next, never-ending, the same as breathing. The Law of Rhythm deals with the breathing process of all of Nature.

The Bible says, "God breathed the breath of life into matter and into man, and so began life." This statement is not a metaphor. It is a principle of physics. God—THE ALL—is the Conscious, Intelligent Mind that creates and sustains the universe. God does this by breathing—which is to say God activates the electric energy necessary to get the job done. The result is what we call "matter," and even "man."

I will give you a simplified definition of Rhythm: You're born, you die, and the rhythm is the life in between. Every system in our body is controlled by this Rhythm of Life. Everything—the circulatory system, the nervous system, the respiratory system, every cell, and every atom—is controlled by this law.

Astrophysicists are now talking about the expansion and the contraction of the universe. It is as if the cosmos is breathing! As if it has lungs. How wonderful is that? And how wonderful is it that human scientists are finally discovering what we have known forever?

Mary, do you think it's only a matter of time before scientists and spiritual people come together in some sort of agreement?

If humans can remain in existence throughout the turmoil they bring upon themselves, I do. As long as there are Beings who ask questions, the human race will be moving toward a grand merger of science and religion. One of the main obstacles is the theory of evolution. That theory is incorrect, and the proof of that is in the fact that it just does not answer the more complex questions of life. Where did life come from? Why are we not knee-deep in fossilized evidence supporting this theory? What was existent before the Big Bang to cause a Big Bang?. Everything points to a Creator Being, and that Being is God.

Everything is governed by the Law of Rhythm. Think about it. Night flows into day. Chaotic storms flow into sunny skies. Spring flows into summer. The ceaseless passage of life from birth, through growth, decay, death, and rebirth, is governed by this great Law. This never-ending natural rhythm is one of the main things that continuously sustains the order of the cosmos. Without the Law of Rhythm, there would be nothing but chaos in this and all universes, and life as we know it could never exist.

Rhythm is the motion between the extremes, the life we live between the birth and death polarities. What gives us most of our problems is that we spend far too much time focused on the extremes — the exultant highs of the good times and the despondent lows of the bad times. We tend to ignore the ordinary, in-between times.

It is unfortunate, but most people of this current society have decided to live in what I have heard you, Din, refer to as a "Soap Opera World."

You have indeed.

This culture, defined and supported by popular entertainment, informational media, and the current system of inadequate, radically falsified and distorted public education, instructs, advocates, and perpetuates this shallow way of life. Many humans are what you have referred to as drama queens and crybabies — personalities that suck energy from the positive momentum of the rhythm and into the mania and depression of the extremes.

The more these folks feed on this negative energy, the more it pulls them down the spiritual ladder. People fighting this Law show certain signs, such as anger, over-reaction, mood swings, narrow-mindedness, lack of respect for Truth, habitual lying, hatred for God, or Jesus. These signs need to be recognized for what they are. The root of the behavior must be dealt with and eliminated. To dwell on those issues will only feed them and cause reversals on the Path of Life.

More than anything, when speaking of the Law of Rhythm, I must remind you of the need for self-control.

This goes back to the Law of Polarity—follow the middle path—practice self-control or moderation in all things. Almost all religions on this planet have a clause or a verse in their scripture echoing this concept. For example:

> TAOISM: *He who possesses self-control is lasting and enduring.*

> CONFUCIANISM: *Commit no excess; do nothing injurious ... pleasures should not be carried to excess.*

> HINDUISM: *He who avoids extremes in eating and fasting, in sleep and waking, and work and play, wins balance, peace, and joy.*

> CHRISTIANITY: *Let your moderation be known unto all men.*

> SHINTOISM: *If a man oversteps the limits of moderation and self-control, he pollutes his body and mind.*

Hold on a second, Mary. Here's my beef with that line of logic. Organized religion can be terribly wrong, so how are these verses of any value?

They are of value because they do not represent organized religion. Those verses describe the thread of Truth that runs through all religions. They show that all people everywhere, at one time in their history believed, and continue to believe in certain things that make the world a better place to live.

It all comes down to three things:

> *One, learn to listen to the rhythm in your own life. Listen to your intuition, that still, small voice inside you. Make sure your decisions are made on solid judgment, common sense, and Truth, and not swayed by the opinions of others or by lies fabricated by the media.*

> *Two, study Nature and learn from what you ob-*

serve. There currently exists a gross imbalance be-tween humans and Nature, and that must change.

And Three, don't let yourself be turned into a charac-ter in the soap opera that society is trying to produce. Above all, don't allow others to bring you down to their level by swaying you from the Truth. Once you find Truth, hang onto it.

And that's it?

That's it for the fifth Universal Law, the Law of Rhythm. The sixth is the Law of Gender.

That sounds interesting, but can we take a break here?

Are you tired?

No, just boggled. I need to cogitate on this stuff so that I can understand it.

We can take a break. Would you like to take a day or two to rest yourself?

I'm not sure. Maybe.

I think this is a wise decision. And I have a suggestion for you.

Dare I ask?

This will be simple. I wish for you to record on the pages of My Diary—

Oh, it's your Diary now, is it?

It always has been.

Yeah, okay. What do you want me to write?

I want you to sit out in the back garden for the next few hours and write about your spiritual past.

What?

You have had quite a varied life, Din.

I'm not sure I know what you mean. And why would I want to write about that anyway?

Many will read this book who have had journeys sim-ilar to yours. If you can tell of the many things you have experienced, perhaps, it will make it easier for them to find their own way.

You gotta be kidding.

I am not. You have had a quite colorful past, and the lessons you have learned will be of great benefit to the true seeker.

Okay, I'll write. But where do you want me to start? What do I write about? I've had all kinds of experiences.

You will start with your childhood when you first learned that the prayers you prayed were answered by God.

What? Wait a minute. I didn't even really know all the subtle nuances about God 'til you popped into my head.

Yes, you did, Din. You knew about God. You have always known about God. Do you not remember that morning in June when you were standing out in your backyard in Tulsa, Oklahoma in 1955? You wanted to play with the little girl next door. You didn't think her parents would let her come over to play, so you went over to the back of your house where you couldn't be seen, out by the fence, and you bowed your head. You put your little hands in the prayer position, and you prayed to God, "Please, God, tell Sally's parents to let her come over and play."

I remember that! I've remembered that all my life. Sally was my best friend back then, and we had such good fun when she came over. She told me that her parents were cross with her and that she probably wouldn't be able to come over to play, but right after I prayed that prayer — like five minutes later — there she was. She said, "It's a miracle! Mommy didn't care at all. She likes you."

And what is there not to like? You were a good child, Din, and you have always been a good man. You have a wonderful story to tell to those who read these pages.

So, you mean, God answered my prayer?

You prayed to God, and God is God. And since you are a favored child, God answered your prayer.

Favored what?

I will explain that later, Joseph.

You just called me Joseph.

I'm sorry, Din. After all of the lives we've been through together, I get mixed up once in a while.

I understand. And I really want to ask you how many lives we have been through together, but I'm going to hold off.

I am glad because I do not wish for you to discuss past life interactions, only your current life so that others might identify with your journey and benefit from it.

Okay, Mary. So, we just did the child prayer thing. Now what? Where do I go from there?

I would suggest you begin with your first baptism into the Christian Church and move forward from there. Touch on all the spiritual highlights from that point to where you find yourself today.

I just hope I can remember that stuff.

I'm sure you will. You can always refer to the journal you have been keeping since 1966 as it is an accurate record of your spiritual journey. One day the contents of that journal will be the source and inspiration for many books that you will write.

It is kinda like a personal testimony, but I'm not sure how "spiritual" it is. There's more than a few worldly, lusty, and bizzare things thrown in.

No one can live in this world without experiencing those worldly, lustful, and bizarre things, Din. Those who say they can are liars. I will leave you for now as I have things I must do.

Where are you going?

That is for me to know.

And for me to find out.

It would be wonderful if you did find out, as it would

mean that you have all of your memory back.

Don't tell me—you're going to go visit Mother H.

You are correct! Perhaps your memory is coming back already.

I think it was just a lucky guess.

In any case, I am leaving now. Happy writing.

Thanks.

And poof, she's gone again.

4 August, Continued

My Spiritual Quest

I'm left here with Bic pen in hand, wondering what the heck I'm supposed to say. I'm also trying to figure out why she wants me to write about my sordid past. I'm guessing it's because I'm just a regular kind of guy who has gone through many things during his life. I've had my ups and downs and experienced my own dark night of the soul more than once.

One thing I have learned is not to question Mary or Annie when they ask me to do something. Well, maybe I do question it—a lot—but I go ahead and do what they ask.

So here I go. After the prayer incident with Sally, I went on to be sort of an ordinary child. Well, not really. I guess I was always interested in the spiritual aspects of things. While other boys were doing whatever they were doing—playing baseball outside or whatever—I was inside reading books about Greek mythology, ancient Egypt, and a bunch of the classics. I think I already mentioned that I had asthma and that I never was able to do the physical things the other boys my age did, like play sports and such.

Heck, I can't even remember what I've written in this book. Most of it is a blur because it's all been a kind of guided writing with Mary and Annie doing the real stuff in the background.

ANNIE: *Father?*

Annie?

Mother gave you an assignment, and you have to know that it's imperative. You have to stop wandering around with your thoughts and do what she asked.

I'm sorry, Sweetie. That's just the way my head goes

these days. It ain't every guy in the world that lives his life with his—

Dead family?

Yeah, that would be it.

But we aren't dead. We're merely communing with you in our True Form—that of Spirit. All of the physical bodies we have ever had are long gone, but our Spirit Forms are eternal, as is yours.

I know that. I think your Mother gave me that lecture.

Then listen to her and listen to me. You are not who you appear to be when you look in the mirror when you get up in the morning.

Thank Heaven for that!

You are an eternal Being of Energy. You are a child of God, and God loves you very much. You must believe me. And you must write what Mother asked you to write. It's a good thing for many of those who will be reading this book.

Okay, Cupcake. I'll do it. Go do whatever it is you do, and I'll crank this out.

I will leave you now for a little while. Just remember that I love you with all my heart.

I know you do, Annie.

***

Annie is gone, and I'm left to my task. Let's try to get serious here. I'll start with my baptism into the Christian Church when I was nine years old. That was a long time ago, but for some reason, I remember it now as if it were yesterday. I guess that's what Mary and Annie are doing to my mind because, on any ordinary day, I can't remember where I put my car keys.

I even remember the date. It was June 4, 1957. I was nine years old. My family was attending a church in Oklahoma, called the Cincinnati Avenue Christian

Church. This was what they referred to as an Independent Christian Church, in that it was not affiliated with any particular denomination. The Independent Christian Church group, plan, structure—whatever you want to call it—was begun by a Presbyterian minister named Thomas Campbell. He was an Irishman who came to America in April of 1807. It just so happened that his move took place during what came to be called the Second Great Awakening in America, a period of Christian revival that saw thousands of people come to Christ. Thomas settled in western Pennsylvania, where he began to express disagreement with some particular points of Presbyterian doctrine. He ended up leaving the Presbyterian Church and starting his own movement, which eventually became known as the Restoration Movement. The goal was to "restore" the practice of Christianity to the simplicity of the patterns outlined in the New Testament and to stick strictly to what the Bible says, nothing more, nothing less. One of the more well-known mottoes of the Movement is "Where Scripture speaks, we speak, and where Scripture is silent, we're silent." Thomas's son, Alexander, eventually joined with him. What has become known as the Independent Christian Churches got their start in the Restoration Movement, and has grown substantially in size and number. There is more to it than this, of course, but this brief history is adequate for this assignment. The point I want to make is that the Independent Christian Church is probably the best church on the planet when it comes to teaching and preaching what Jesus initially taught. It doesn't really have an organized denominational structure like, for instance, the Baptists, the Catholics, the Lutherans, or the Methodists. Instead, each church is independent of all the other Independent Christian Churches. The only leadership comes from the pastor and elders within each congregation. Each Church relies on itself and its own leaders for everything. They go to the Bible for guidance and try to do things the way they were done in the days of Jesus, the Apostles, and the early church. It's pretty neat, really.

So, this is where my story begins. My brother was getting baptized, and I decided that I wanted to get baptized, too. I hate to admit it, but envy might have played more than a small part in my decision. I had witnessed many baptisms, and had observed how the baptizee—yes, I just made that up—was at the center of attention and was showered with praise and approval. Now that my older brother was going to be in that position, I thought that I might like a piece of the action, as well. To be fair, that wasn't my entire motivation. My brother was older than me by more than a year and was considered to be mature for his age, while I was seen as being every bit the child that I was—still innocent and not yet of the age of accountability. Even so, I had paid attention to the sermons and lessons, and I knew that if you wanted to call yourself a Christian, you had to be baptized in water, as the Bible clearly states. I was also fully aware of the fate that awaits those who are not baptized, and frankly, it scared the hell out of me.

Looking back through time after having had years to think about things, I'm glad I went ahead and did it. I no longer fear hell because I have come to realize that it's reserved only for those who refuse to believe in God, and who demonstrate that disbelief with their words and deeds. Unfortunately, if what the Bible teaches is accurate, it appears that the majority of humans on planet Earth when time runs out in the not so distant future will fall into that category.

Funny thing, though, I did feel *different* when I came up

out of the baptismal water. I felt like a new kid. Was it the power of suggestion? I don't know, but I felt really good.

The moment I came out of the water back in 1957, I believed that life would be different. I already knew that I had been altered in some way. I had been reading lots of that mythology stuff in grade school, and I was attempting to identify with the gods I was reading about. As a kid, I found it much more enticing to believe in make-believe cartoon-type gods than in the REAL GOD. But *something* happened at my baptism. I felt empowered in a way that I had not been before. Something got switched on. I can't explain it, but after my baptism, I left the cartoons and the myths behind, and I began, in my own innocent way, to worship God. I even read the Bible from cover to cover and then went back and began to study it in earnest.

Even as a kid, I knew that I was more than just flesh and blood. I believed somewhere down deep in my heart that I was connected to God in some dynamic way. I wasn't sure what that connection was, but I had a firm belief as well as a personal, innate feeling that God does exist. To this day, the best explanation I have received for His existence is the one Mary has given me:

> *God is simply the form of THE ALL — the One Spirit Who created everything, and Who contin- ues to sustain the life of even the tiniest Gnat.*

I'm rambling. So, what came after my baptism? In 1958 my family moved from Oklahoma to the west coast and joined another Independent Christian Church. I'm not sure that I really understood everything the preacher said during the hundreds of sermons that I experienced while sitting in the pew next to my family. To be honest, my brother, Jim, and I occasionally brought toys to church to play with while the preacher rattled on. Even so, my curious mind managed to pick up enough of what he was saying so that I learned to distinguish right from wrong. I credit those sermons with helping me to develop a positive and moralistic outlook on life, and that's something a lot of people in this increasingly atheistic culture can't or won't claim these days. Since the Bible is the main focus of the Independent Christian Church, I was encouraged to memorize hundreds of verses of scripture. I remember them all to this day, which is handy given the fact that I am now one of those Pastors, with my own little Independent Church. Being able to pull verses out of my hat, so to speak, helps to illustrate sermons, turning them into learning experiences relevant to the needs of the congregation at that moment and make them more memorable than just words heard on a Sunday morning.

I won't drag this on, so I'll just say that I attended a lot of Christian Churches, and while they weren't perfect, those times were filled with happiness and fond memories. There is nothing like having a close-knit church family to share your life with — and the potluck lunches are out of this world.

In 1970, I moved to a tiny desert town in California. It was really out in the middle of nowhere, and the nearest Independent Christian Church was many miles away.

I was a bit dismayed when I discovered that "my kind of Church" did not exist in that desert wasteland, so I began to shop around. I decided since I didn't have much choice in the matter, I would take whatever I could find so that I could make some friends and start a new church family.

Well, the only choice within fifteen miles of where I was living was a Catholic Church, Saint Theresa of Lisieux, so I decided I'd give it a try. I attended a few Sunday Masses. Although the people weren't as friendly and family-like as my old church, I stuck it out and began to take a catechism class under the direction of a priest named Father Brown, who wore cowboy boots and smoked like a Russian sailor. Fr. Brown had an intellectual bent. He didn't just stick to the rules and regulations found in the church manual. His mind tended to wander off into areas which, I suppose, he would have been disciplined for had some higher-up priest or Bishop caught him doing it. He definitely had an independent streak to him.

My time with Father Brown turned out to be a milestone in my life. One of his directives to me was to go out and buy all the books I could find on the Catholic faith. He told me to study them as if I were preparing for a final exam in a university class. I did and found myself reading books by saints such as St. John of the Cross and Teresa d'Avila. I was blown away. These folks were profound, mystical thinkers on the great journey of life. This is also when I first read a copy of the autobiography of St. Therese, *The Story of a Soul*. It was wonderful. What a sweet human she must have been. My reading also included the works of Thomas Merton. Wow! I won't go into details here because if I get started, I'll never shut up.

It wasn't long before I was baptized again, this time in the beautiful Saint Theresa Catholic Church in Palm Springs.

I've gone through so much in my life, I really don't know what Mary and Annie want me to write here. I've got mixed feelings ... I'm both Protestant and Catholic, and neither of the two. But wait! There's more! A little later on — after the Catholic bit — I almost joined an Americanized Hindu-based cult called Radha Soami Sant Mat Satsang. I don't know if it still exists, but it was an interesting group at the time. I was beginning to get a little concerned about some of the details of the Catholic catechism, and I needed to take a breather from it. Having received serious Bible study experience in the Independent Christian Church, I knew that a whole lot of the Catholic catechism was not in the Bible, and I just couldn't agree with, or see the point in much of it. Those things are not found anywhere among the red-lettered words of Jesus in the Gospels of Matthew, Mark, Luke, and John.

Anyway, "Radha Soami" or "Radahsoami" means "Lord of the Soul," "Sant Mat" means something like the "Teachings or Path of the Saints," and a Satsang is a gathering of truth-seekers. The members of the cult just called it, RS. I was introduced to the basic teachings and practices of RS by an acquaintance who said that it had literally saved his life. The underlying philosophy is quite straight forward and, in many ways, not too different from what I had learned in the Independent Christian Church. Some of the practices, though, especially meditation while chanting a mantra, definitely raise Christian eyebrows. Another difference is that RS teaches that a person must be initiated by a living guru or his directly appointed delegate if he is to have any hope of achieving spiritual enlightenment.

I began attending the local gatherings, or Satsangs, with my friend. Occasionally, the regional guru would be in attendance. Even though the teachings of the cult were big on equality and did not confer any formal distinction on him, the members tended to treat him like the Pope, or at least, a cardinal. I certainly didn't get any vibes from him that made me want to venerate him like they did. I also knew that God doesn't really need any middlemen here on this planet to interpret His Teachings for Him. So, to me, the RS guru was just an ordinary man with a beard and a rather well-practiced smile.

There was a three-month waiting period before a person

was actually deemed worthy of initiation. During those three months, you had to adhere to a strict vegetarian diet, abstain from sex, and meditate several times a day, literally for hours. Well, guess what, I had a hard time with all that—especially the vegetarian thing. I was driving home from a cult meeting just three days before my initiation when I caught a whiff of barbecued chicken. That was it for me. I got home and immediately lit some charcoal and threw three chickens on the grill. I ate them all in one sitting. I had been a vegetarian for almost three months, but I always felt hungry. The whole process of eating had become a chore, and it just wasn't fun anymore. Needless to say, the chicken was delicious, and I said goodbye to RS forever.

So, now what? Not long after I gave up on RS, I was approached by a couple of Mormon missionaries, and I was intrigued by what they had to say. I read through the Book of Mormon and began attending the Mormon Church. When I went back to really *study* the Book of Mormon and the other Mormon scriptures, the Doctrine and Covenants and the Pearl of Great Price—which contains among other things, the Book of Moses and the Book of Abraham—everything fell apart for me. They were so infantile. These books, along with the King James Bible, are the primary scriptures of the Mormon faith. While they study the Bible and believe it to be the Word of God, Mormons also believe that it is incomplete and flawed in its currently available form. They look to the other three texts, and to the words of their modern prophets and apostles, for clarification. Instead of being deeply profound, as they should be, I found these books to be the most absurd, disjointed, and poorly written things I think I have ever read. I learned later from credible scholars that Joseph Smith had plagiarized the manuscripts of other people and even the Bible itself to write the Book of Mormon.

The Book of Abraham is Smith's "translation" of hieroglyphs found on Egyptian papyri purchased from a traveling mummy exhibition. Smith claimed that they were written by Abraham, himself, and described the patriarch's early life and travels, and his vision of creation and the universe. More recent examination and translation of fragments of these papyri has shown them to be Egyptian funerary texts included in the "Book of the Dead," and have nothing to do with Abraham and his revelations.

We have to remember that while there had been considerable interest in ancient Egypt for a couple of centuries, the ability to read ancient hieroglyphs was a relatively recent development at the time Smith was working on his book. There were very few scholars around who were up to it, so it would have been easy for Smith to pull the wool over the eyes of his followers.

In my eagerness and desire to be part of some sort of Church Family, I did the Mormon baptism as soon as I finished my first quick reading of the Mormon scriptures, but unlike my baptism in the Independent Christian Church, I didn't feel a thing. My initial enthusiasm waned as I studied the books more closely over the next few months, and it wasn't long before I moved on. A couple of years later, after I had moved to a new city, I decided to go back and give the Mormons another try, just in case I had missed something the first time. I hadn't.

So, Mary, what do you want from me on this? I've been a Protestant, a Catholic, a cult member (almost), a Mormon. I even did a Jewish thing for a while. I love Jewish people, but it takes a lot of work to become one. There are detailed rituals to perform and rules to follow, and page after page of convoluted rabbinical teachings to memorize. Not to mention that if you don't know Hebrew, you're going to miss out on a lot of stuff along the way. It's very complicated. I envy those who were born Jewish. If you grow up hearing all the teachings during your early years, it gets ingrained within you. As an adult, however, it takes a lot of work to learn to be a proper Jew. So, I reluctantly crossed the Jewish religion off my list.

***

I'm getting a signal in my head from Mary. She wants me to continue to talk about my spiritual life, but to focus on more recent experiences.

Where do I start?

Psst... Daddy? Mom wants you to start with Ananda.

Annie! Thank Heaven you're here. I feel like I'm spinning my wheels.

No, you're doing very well.

I hope so. I just don't want to disappoint either one of you.

Don't worry, Daddy, that will never happen. Now, take some time and write aout how you found Ananda Village and your experiences there.

I'll give it a shot, Sweetie, but it won't be easy. Ananda is different from anything I've talked about so far.

You'll do just fine, and I'll poof back anytime you need me.

Thanks. You can "poof" outta here if you want.

Soooo ... Ananda Village. It has to be one of the most enjoyable memories I have.

I was living in Missouri, in 1998, when I traveled out to Nevada to visit with my mother. I had only been there a week or two when, for some reason, the thought entered my mind that I should join a yoga class. So, I did.

The class was taught by an incredibly lovely woman

named Deborah. I mean, she was not only beautiful on the outside, but she was also even more beautiful on the inside. I fell in love with her the moment I saw her. But she had a boyfriend named Tom, who was a very nice person as well. They were quite happy together, so we just became good yoga friends.

The three of us ended up doing many things together, including attending a gathering of Yogis in Lake Tahoe. What an experience that was. Deborah and Tom belonged to a group led by another one of those "guru" guys, Sri Sri Ravi Shankar. (There must be millions of these gurus running around.) As one would expect, this Sri Sri was a lovely person too, and surely a holy-type-sort-of-fellow and a great teacher, just not the one for me. He did give a good party, though. This gathering included musicians playing sitars and tablas, Indian women dressed in saris, and even movie stars. I got to have my picture taken with one — Juliet Mills! It was quite a night.

After the festivities, a few of us were invited to visit with the guru in a private home a few blocks away. I was asked because I was a friend of Deborah and Tom. Don't get me wrong — Sri Sri Ravi Shankar is a decent man, and I'm sure he is providing some deeply appreciated service to those who follow him. But the operative word is "man." He's just a man. And these folks were going absolutely ga-ga over him whenever he walked into a room. I just didn't get that. To me, he was just another one of those Indian guys with long hair and a cute smile. He has to unzip when he pees. And most of his teachings are merely overused platitudes with no real depth of meaning. There is no ... magic in them, unlike Yogananda's writings.

I guess I'm just tired of all the organized religion stuff. It doesn't matter how you package it — Buddhist, Hindu, Christian — it all comes out the same. It's all ritual and dogma. God doesn't work that way. God works in the heat of the noonday sun, and in the storms that crash and tumble across the Earth. Not in beads and bangles and bells and gaudy prayer wheels.

Anyway, back to the Ananda experience. Most of the last two paragraphs were to illustrate where my head was at that time. A few days after returning to my mother's house from the Lake Tahoe guru thing, I decided to visit a nearby bookstore. Despite my reservations about cults, I still wanted to get into the yoga stuff. I was also sensing something I had never felt before. I was feeling a growing desire to become a yoga teacher! What a surprise! I had practiced yoga for many years and had even led classes from time to time, but I had never dreamed of making a career of teaching yoga. This urge was so strong that I decided to check out the details. And this is where the story gets a bit spooky.

I had driven into Carson City for lunch. When I left the restaurant, I decided to check out the bookstore next door to see what they had in the way of yoga books. Back in the New Age section, I found one shelf that was completely bare except for a single copy of one book. I picked it up and looked at the cover. The book was *Autobiography of a Yogi* by Paramhansa Yogananda. In addition to the title, there was a picture of the yogi on the cover. I knew that face! It was the same as the one on the pamphlet that I had discovered in the Pueblo out in Desert Hot Springs, over twenty years before. I felt a shiver go up and down my spine.

The store had a well-stocked New Age section. I looked through all of the other books, but I couldn't find another single one on yoga. I was convinced that I was meant to buy this book and take it home. Which I did—like a cherished treasure.

I read through Yogananda's book in less than two days. I was spellbound by it. It was a charming mix of spirituality and the daily experiences of this odd little man who began life as an ordinary Indian but became an extraordinary individual. By the time I had finished reading the book, I had made the determination to become a Yogi.

I was in the market the next day, browsing through the magazines. I thought I might run across something a little different in the way of inspirational or motivational reading that I could relate to. I was thumbing through one likely publication when another magazine slipped off the rack and fell open at my feet. When I stooped down to pick it up, I couldn't believe what I saw. There on the exposed page was an advertisement for a yoga ashram/ retreat in Nevada City, California, called Ananda Village. I tossed the magazine into my grocery cart and checked out.

Back at home, I reread the advertisement carefully, and I discovered that Ananda Village offered a program for training yoga teachers. As soon as I read that part, I called the number listed in the ad and enrolled in the next course, even though I had no idea how I was going to pay for it.

After completing the details of my enrollment, the woman I was speaking with began to fill me in on what to expect. I could hardly believe it when she told me that it was highly recommended that the participants read *Autobiography of a Yogi*, by Paramhansa Yogananda. I couldn't believe it! I explained that I had found that book just a couple of days before, and described how the magazine had jumped off the rack at me. We agreed that it was more than just coincidence and that "Someone Up There" wanted me to become a yoga teacher.

That was probably one of the best decisions I have ever made in my life. The teacher-training program at Ananda was perhaps the most comprehensive yoga training course in the United States. The instructors were exceptional, and the camaraderie was something I had been looking for. Everyone there was so friendly—not just the staff, but the other students, as well, and they came from every walk of life, including nurses, doctors, two Catholic nuns, and even a Baptist minister. Those five weeks at Ananda were a blast, and I count those thirty-five days as some of the most enjoyable of my entire life.

When I had completed the training, I left Ananda Village with mixed emotions. I didn't really want to leave the beautiful environment and the wonderful people who had changed me—from the way I used to be, to this new person who now had a direction in life. On the other hand, I was excited to discover what my new life had in store for me.

I think the point that Mary wants me to make here is that, next to my baptism, my time at Ananda was the most profound spiritual change of my life up to that time. My transcendental beliefs about life and the world, in general, come from a broad range of study, observation, and experience, but have been strongly influenced by the lives and work of two people in particular, Yogananda and Thomas Merton. I consider them to be mentors, of a sort, like several Christian ministers whom I have known and who took me under their wing. I've learned a lot of different, good things from a lot of different, good people in my life, and it has made me who I am today: a good person, but very different.

I think it is this odd mix of religious training that Mary wants me to present. Here I am, an ordained Christian minister, influenced by a Hindu mystic and a rebel Catholic priest. If the world were to look at just the surface of that, I would no doubt be judged a kook. But to make an accurate judgment, one would have to know all of the details that went into my finding myself in that scenario. Why would a Christian Minister even consider living at a yoga retreat? Or read any books by a Hindu mystic? And being a Protestant minister, why would he ever study the works of a maverick Catholic monk?

For starters, Yogananda wasn't just a Hindu mystic, he loved Jesus, and he interlaced the Teachings of Jesus throughout all of his books. Some of my most profound insights into Jesus came from reading a few of Yogananda's books. Some people, including the Baptist minister I met at Ananda, even like to call Yogananda the "Thirteenth Apostle," because he seemed to spend more time talking about Jesus than anything else. Quite frankly, from my studies of that gentle, incredibly bright little man, he was a far better Christian than most of the Christians I have known.

Thomas Merton, for all of his faults and mental wanderings into religions other than Catholicism, remained firm as a devout lover of Christ. He was an explorer who liked to discover new things and to learn about the experiences of others. Through it all though, Merton remained faithful to Jesus and to his Church. He was not a rebel. If anything, he was an example of how an ordinary man, who felt commonplace emotions, and who had thoughts shared by many but, unlike many, he was not afraid to share those thoughts. He was able to devote his life to Christ and even after all the questions, ponderings, and whims of human life slammed him right between the eyes daily, he could still make it work. He was an open, honest, everyday kind of guy who, despite himself and his Church, risked becoming a saint. Isn't that what it's all about for everyone? What better example of a spiritual seeker can there possibly be?

As for how a Christian can be involved in yoga — that heathen, Hindu worship of many strange gods and goddesses — the answer is simple. Yoga is not Hinduism; it predates it by hundreds of years. If you were to attend my yoga classes (which I no longer teach), you would not find the slightest mention of Hinduism; it's all about the postures. As a child, I was not the healthiest kid on the block. I was born with severe chronic bronchial asthma. When I was nine, I died of double pneumonia, and miraculously came back after an impressive experience in a Heavenly place. I was also born missing a rib, which caused all kinds of problems in my spine and with my breathing. Because of all that, I spent a lot of time reading instead of playing outside like the other kids. Long before I had ever heard of Yogananda or Hinduism, or even before a doctor who was also a Christian minister told me that yoga would help me, I came across a book by a guy named Richard Hittleman. I won't go into all the details, but I will say that yoga changed my life. Not only did it help with my asthma, but I also gained strength that I never had before, my breathing was better, my spinal problems improved, and not once did I ever have the urge to leave my Christian faith to become a Hindu. So, if anyone has a problem with all of that, then the problem is not with me, but with them.

I came home from Ananda, a happy yoga teacher. I taught classes at a local health spa for quite some time, but when the health spa went out of business, I packed up my things and headed back to Columbia, Missouri. I also had the privilege and opportunity to teach a few classes for Deborah when she was not able because of scheduling conflicts. That was a great honor for me. As I write these words many years later, I still feel a tremendous fondness for Deborah. I do hope she has the best in life.

After resettling in Columbia, I landed a couple of spots teaching yoga that were very successful. That's also when I started the little Independent Christian Church, which I currently pastor. I guess I forgot to mention that I had been ordained as a minister in the Independent Christian Church back in 1991, long before I went to Ananda Village.

I have to admit that even though I am now pastoring an Independent Church, I still enjoy some of the Catholic literature and ritual. It might be possible to get me to move back in that direction, except for the fact that I have unanswered questions about parts of the Catechism. When I was attending the Catholic Church, the Monsignor of my local parish called me a "Lone Ranger." He didn't mean it in a bad way—he just thinks that I'm an odd duck who knows exactly what's going on, but who refuses to toe the line. Even though he was a little upset that I left the Catholic Church, he told me that he holds out hope that one day I will return to his way of looking at things. Who knows? But at this time in my life, if I am to be totally honest, I just don't sense that any religion on Earth today is what it was truly meant to be. I feel the need to steer clear of the organizational parts of all denominations and to concentrate on the necessities that God gave to the inhabitants of this world so that they can become the Beings they were truly meant to be. I also have a hard time with added rituals, traditions, and dogma that Jesus never mentioned in the Bible, like loud musical productions during Church "worship" services and the theatrical costumes worn by some clergy. The TRUTH is more profound than the variety-show Christianity we have today, and it's undoubtedly much more uncomplicated.

The life Jesus led is described in the Bible as one of quiet worship. When He wanted to pray, He walked off into the wilderness and chatted alone with God. In fact, He told people:

> When you pray, don't be like the hypocrites who love to pray publicly on street corners and in the synagogues where everyone can see them. (Matthew 6:5)

Be alone with God. Your relationship with God is nobody's business but your own. That's why the Independent Church is a good fit for now.

I really don't know what Mary and Annie want me to write here; I've gone through so much during my life in this world. My feelings are mixed—how do I sort them all out? I've been in and out of a bunch of things. I've been both Protestant and Catholic, yet I am neither of the two. And I feel like this is becoming my autobiography more than Mary's. What the heck are you looking for, Mary? And what does this have to do with the Strong Weet Society?

MARY: *Everything, Din.*

Mary, thank THE ALL you're here. Hallelujah!

You are being sarcastic.

You bet I am. I'm just trying to figure out what this is all about.

I have given you a simple assignment, and you have done it well. The purpose of the task was to accustom you to taking action as an Energy Spirit. You have been caught up in the physical for so long that it has impeded your spiritual outlook.

Okay, what the heck does that mean?

It means that you must leave the physical behind and concentrate on your spiritual development from this moment forward. Don't you see that you have lived an incredibly varied life while learning many deeper truths about things of which you were unaware? Do you not see that others might

still be going through what you have already experienced?
Your words here can perhaps help them make serious decisions
for their own lives.

I suppose so … yes … I know so.

Do you not see that your life is not only a bit unusual, but
that a Higher Being has been leading you along?

I guess you're right, Mary. I don't know anyone who
has gone through all the …

Training?

That's it. I know a lot of people, and none of them give
much of a hoot about religion or God. They just watch
their TVs and play on their computers and life goes by
for them. They never even think about religion. I seem
to have been almost tormented by it.

Tormented is not accurate. Guided is the word you
must use.

Sometimes guidance seems like torment.

The great saints experienced the same feelings.

I'm not a saint.

You have your moments of sainthood. You are a Strong Weet.

You know, it's tough for me to see myself as anything
like a saint.

It's irrelevant how you see yourself at this point in time
because you do not see yourself correctly! When you're fully
Awakened, you'll realize the Truth. You're much more than
an earthly saint.

Thanks for the contractions.

You're welcome

Before we go any further, I do have a couple of things
that have been bothering me throughout this entire Last
Days scenario we've been discussing.

Yes, Dear?

I've been a Christian pastor for many years, and some
of the things we've been talking about just don't mesh

with a lot of what I learned from the Bible and what I now teach in my little Church.

Go on.

Important things, like salvation, the rapture of the Church in the End Times ...

What is your conflict?

I just want to know how those things relate to the stuff you've been telling me. What about salvation? The Bible says that salvation is found only in Jesus, and when a person dies, if he's saved, he goes to Heaven, and if not, he goes to Hell. This End Times disaster business we're explaining in your Diary doesn't really fit with the Bible explanation. I'm having a hard time with it because, as a preacher, it's my duty to preach the Truth.

But there is no conflict.

Isn't there?

Of course not. How can Truth conflict with Truth? The Bible was written by men who were chosen by Jesus and inspired by the Holy Spirit. Of course, the Bible is True. It is rightly called "God's Word," but the Truths it contains are often expressed in metaphors and parables that can be difficult to understand. The Book of Revelation, for example, is written in an ancient code by the Apostle John to make it less visible to those who opposed the followers of Jesus, but not be so complicated that those followers would not be able to understand the code. In a way, our Books are similar. A careful and open-minded reading of this Diary will reveal that they contain nothing contradictory to any of the Teachings found in the Bible. Most of what is seen here is disguised in symbols and metaphors so that those who would oppose the message will disregard the Diary before they even read it, while those who would support it will be attracted to it and understand.

What about salvation? It sounds like all humans are

going to be annihilated at the very end of the Last Days. Kiss their butts goodbye and adios to any thought of Heaven. What about the "confess Jesus" message in the Bible? Do they get saved? Are they raptured away before all of the dangerous and deadly stuff starts to happen?

There is no way I can hope to explain it all in greater detail on the few pages of our Book. Suffice it to say, all those confessing Jesus and doing the Will of God will, indeed, be saved, and all those who do not confess Him, will not be saved. That is what Jesus said, and that is what the Bible Truly teaches. Regarding the rapture of the Church, remember that it is a subject of great controversy, even within Christianity. Some believe it will occur, and some do not — the Bible does not speak of it directly. That being said, remember what Jesus, Himself taught about Salvation, and believe His words above every human conjecture you may have heard.

In chapter seven of Matthew, Jesus says:

> *Enter through the narrow gate. For wide is the gate and broad is the road that leads to destruction, and many enter through it. But small is the gate, and narrow is the road that leads to life, and only a few find it.*

What do you think He means by those words, Din?

He's saying that the majority of people in this world are going to take the broad road to destruction, and very few will take the narrow path that leads to life, which is another word for salvation in the Bible. Lots of people are going to hell, and very few will make it into Heaven. But according to statistics, there are billions of believing Christians on this planet. Is this scripture implying that the majority of them won't be making it to Heaven?

You will find the answer to that a little further along in the same chapter. Listen to the words of Jesus:

> *Not everyone who says to me, "Lord, Lord," will enter into the kingdom of heaven, but ONLY the one who does the will of my Father who is in Heaven.*

Do you think that all of those "confessed" Christians will make it to Heaven simply because they say they believe in Jesus? Because if you do, you are implying that they are all doing the Will of God. Don't you think that if all those billions of Christians were actually doing the Will of God, the world would be a much better place than it is today?

I'll give you one more verse, and then we will move on:

> *If we claim to have fellowship with Him and yet walk in the darkness, we lie and do not live out the Truth. (1 John 1:6)*

Wow. You know your Bible, don't you, Mary. Basically, that verse is saying that if you aren't doing what Jesus wants you to do, and you call yourself a Christian, then you're a liar. Jesus is saying, "Don't claim to be saved if you aren't doing what I ask you do." Like anybody else, Jesus doesn't want somebody representing Him if they're not fit to do it.

You will find that the majority of those on this Earth who call themselves Christians are liars. The Bible is very clear about this. Both the New Testament and the Old contain the message that there will always be Godly Believers in this world, but there will only be a few. The Bible says there will always be a remnant, and that is all. A remnant is a small surviving trace. Jesus supports that claim in all of His Teachings.

Those verses are pretty clear.

Yes, they are.

So, now what?

We will get back to your spiritual story later, but for now, I have two more Universal Principles to relate.

Ugh.

You must believe me that there are those with a Higher Awareness who will read these principles and not merely enjoy them, but will resonate with them. I have told you this before. This is one of the keys to bringing memories back to the seven unrevealed Strong Weet.

I get it. Let's get started.

Not just yet.

Now what?

Now we have something else that must be done. You must lead some of your Development Circle members into a lesson they will not soon forget.

What are you getting at?

You cannot take all of your members on this journey; only three will be able to go, and what they experience will be life-altering.

And what exactly is this journey?

It will be revealed to you tomorrow.

But I have my Church thingie tomorrow.

It will be after Church.

Can I have a clue as to what this might be?

You cannot. It must come from your own Spirit.

I'm not so sure I've evolved to the point that—Mary? Mary, are you there?

I have a feeling that Mary has left the building—poofed out on me. I can feel it now whenever she does that. Darn. What am I supposed to do with this little tidbit she's just given me? Darn.

5 August

A Discovery in the Cemetery

What a day. The entire church group went out for lunch after our meeting to a local Mexican restaurant—I love the chili verde there. The drive home took me past the cemetery, where something compelled me to turn into the tree-lined drive. It was a beautiful day, and the sky was a shade of blue I have never seen before. I'd never been to this cemetery because there had never been a reason. None of my family is buried there.

As I drove slowly along the paved road through the cemetery, I wondered what the heck I was doing there. Then I remembered; Mary had told me that something would be revealed to me today. There was something here that I was supposed to see. The road ended at the back of the cemetery. I pulled over, got out of the car, and looked around. Then I saw it. Right in front of me was a family monument. It was rather plain in an elegant sort of way, and it was big. The only adornment on the face of the gray granite was the name, BLISS, chiseled out in large capital letters. What?

I stepped over to the Bliss family plot and found several smaller stones with names of individuals engraved on them, one of which was Mary Elizabeth. I knew it couldn't be *my* Mary, because my Mary was buried back in Massachusetts—sort of.

I knew instantly what Mary wanted me to do. She wanted me to line up a few of the DC members to investigate this spot. Who knows what we might find? I believed in my heart that the folks buried in the Bliss plot were relatives of mine—distant yes, but real kin—but I wasn't sure what the lesson for me and the DC members was to be.

ANNIE: *Daddy?*

Help me, Annie. What's your Mother up to this time?

You need to contact our DC members and arrange for them to do an investigation of this plot next Saturday. Mom is going to be present as an Orb on the large stone. Two of your DC members will capture her Orb on their digital cameras.

Cool! This is a sure thing?

Money in the bank.

Ha! You are getting to be a contemporary child.

I'm not a child.

Spoken like an actual teenager. I know you aren't a child. I just like to think of you like that.

You're very sweet.

Now, what do I do?

Call the members and tell them to meet you at the cemetery at 3:00 pm next Saturday, then take it from there.

And what does that mean?

Just like any other investigation. You take a lot of pictures. Don't worry about audio records this time because it's not time for us to speak with the DC members. We will reveal ourselves to them in that way at a later time.

That will be a real eye-opener.

But only for those within your group who are Strong Weet.

So, not everyone will be able to hear your voices on a recorder?

If you recorded our voices on your digital recorder, everyone would be able to hear, but only the Strong Weet would understand who we are and what it means for their lives. But you will not be recording in the cemetery. And remember, you are to take only three DC members.

Okay, next Saturday it is. Are you going to poof out now?

Not without kissing you on your cheek.

She did. That has to be the sweetest thing any Father can ever experience. If I can feel it from her realm of existence over into my own, how much more enjoyable must it be for a human father and a human daughter? I love her so much.

11 August

The Nature of Ghosts, the Sixth Law, and a Revelation

I took three of the DC members to the cemetery as instructed by Mary and Annie. We each had a camera, and everyone was snapping away like crazy. At home afterward, I emptied the photos into my computer and studied them carefully. Out of the hundreds we took, a single Orb was revealed in just two pictures. Two of the members had caught Mary in her Orb form right where she said she would be on that stone. Not one Orb could be found anywhere else. I don't know if that's because Mary chased the other ghosts away, or what.

MARY: *I did not chase the ghosts away.*

So, Mary, what was this really all about?

This experience was not for you, Din. It was for the others. When they see the photos of the Orbs, they will be impressed, and it will change their lives. They will realize for the first time that things such as this exist, and it will give them faith to carry on with the DC meetings. It will also increase their interest to learn more about the unknown, the place where Annie and I — and even you — reside.

But why weren't there hundreds of Orbs all over the place? It's a cemetery. Dead people ought to be roaming around every stone.

This is not the case, Din. When a person dies, he or she is taken into the Great Light, the mechanism used by God to enable a person to Cross Over into the other realm of their heritage. The ghosts you refer to are unfortunate souls who may have died more recently and not yet Crossed Over. They do haunt various places, but seldom do they haunt their own burial plot because most of them do not know they are dead

303

yet. Those poor souls return to the homes where they grew up, or to other places they loved. The thought of haunting a cemetery never crosses their mind. Other Spirit People who have already Crossed Over have no reason to return to their gravesite. They, too, will come back to visit where their loved ones reside because their only wish is to be with them. Do not forget that most ghosts are not ghosts at all, but a bit of residual energy pattern left behind for a while by humans who have already Crossed Over.

Since you brought it up, can you give me a little more info on that "bright white light" some people go through when they die? I know a couple of people who have had near-death experiences, and I've heard them tell their stories. I had my own NDE when I died of pneumonia as a kid, but my experience was a bit different from most. I did meet an Angel—in fact, I think I met two—and I went through a colorful mist-like shower, but I didn't really see a tunnel of light like others claim to have seen. What, exactly, is it that the light does?

The Great Light is the mechanism that transforms a Spirit that has just left the physical realm and still holds onto a large amount of physical energy, into the original Higher Spirit they used to be.

It's kind of like a big, bright shower, isn't it?

It's a shower of highly focused and specific Energy, just like the colored mist you went through when you died. It cleanses away every physical element that may have attached to the Higher Spirit. At the same time, it also raises the vibration of the Spirit back to the frequency it previously held. Lower frequencies cannot enter into our realm.

Wow! I just had a thought. The Bible talks about the transfiguration of Jesus on the Mount of Olives. It describes Him as glowing like the sun, so brightly that the disciples at the bottom of the mountain couldn't even look at Him. He was so bright that it would have blinded them all if they'd looked directly at Him. Is that what we're talking about here? Was Jesus raising His vibration so that He could communicate with Elijah and Moses because they were already in Spirit form?

That is correct. Jesus transformed the molecular structure of His Body to meet with the vibrations of Moses and Elijah. For a moment, He, Himself, became a Sun. The same power that allowed Him to do that is what is found in the Great Light. Your colored mist shower was quite different from the tunnel of light that other humans must go through, but I do not want to get into the reasons for that just yet.

Okay, most of this stuff is starting to make sense to me, but still …

It is all Law. Are you not learning anything from the Universal Principles?

I am, but some of this stuff is incredible!

As you Awaken more of your True Self, you will not be so confused.

Mary, how can I speed this up? How can I Awaken more quickly?

Your next step is to simply relate the sixth Universal Principle, The Law of Gender. You see, you are much like the other Strong Weet we seek to Awaken. You are many steps ahead of them because of your experiences with Annie and with me, but you are still not entirely … with us. You will speed the process as you record the Universal Principles in this Diary.

Let's do it. I'm really anxious to become everything I'm supposed to be.

Everything you already are. We just have to chip away the stone.

I beg your pardon?

Here is a little story for you. The great artist, Michelangelo, had just finished his famous statue called The Pieta, a beautiful marble statue depicting the Virgin Mary holding the lifeless body of Jesus on Her lap. It is one of the most beautiful sculptures in human history. Just after Michelangelo laid down his chisel and hammer, a nobleman walked into his studio and exclaimed, "My Heavens! You have outdone yourself, great artist. This is the most beautiful statue I have ever seen." Michelangelo replied, "I have done nothing. The shape was buried within the rock. All I did was chisel away the excess rock to reveal the beautiful figure within."

Wow.

That's what many humans are, Din. They are beautiful figures within. They must chip away the excess stone of the culture that has enslaved them if they are to achieve their True state of perfection.

And the Universal Principles will speed this along?

They will.

Then let's get started.

I will leave you now, and Annie will return to —

Where is Annie? I mean, right now.

She has just finished teaching a class in the Hall of Change, and she is nearly here.

What is a Hall of Change?

It is where the newly gathered Spirits first learn about their life back in their Home of origin.

Annie's a teacher?

It is one of her talents. She has been teaching this class for centuries.

She's quite something, isn't she? I'm so proud of her.

You will be more and more proud of her as time passes. Now, let us continue with the Universal Principles. There are only two remaining, and when they are recorded, we can begin to close the Diary and seek a publisher.

Let's get this done. What is this one called?

The Law of Gender. Annie will be instructing you because I must leave.

And where are you going?

I am called to be with Mother H.

Your Mom.

That is correct, but Annie can give you the words just as well as I can. She is an excellent teacher.

Annie? Are you here?

ANNIE: *I'm here. Bye, Mom!*

Let's get started.

First of all, the Law of Gender isn't really about male and female — or sexuality.

I'm really glad to hear that. I don't want you to be doing any of that kind of stuff at your age.

I'm millions of years old, Father.

I don't care! You're still my little girl.

I know, but don't get upset; you'll understand as we go along.

Maybe. Okay, go for it.

The Law of Gender

The Law of Gender has to do with duality, which is not the same as polarity. Polarity deals with direct opposites like positive and negative, while Gender deals with complements — two parts of the same thing that come together as a whole.

This sounds really complicated.

It's probably the most complicated of all the laws. Let me give you some examples. Yin and yang are always together. Male and female are always together. These are dualities that always exist together and complement each other and do not repel. But they are also opposite. To a certain extent, it really does deal with sexuality — male and female.

Watch it.

Don't worry. Let me go on.

Go carefully.

There is so much to tell here. I'm not sure I can do the job as well as Mom could.

But you're a teacher, and Mary tells me you're the best!

That's very kind of her.

So just do what it is you came to do. Let's get on with this so we can find the other Strong Weet.

You're right. Here we go. In Genesis, the first book of the Bible, God is referred to as "Elohim" or "Elokim." What the general reader may not realize is that the prefix of those words, "Eloh," is feminine and is attached to terms used referring to women. The suffix, "im," is masculine. Obviously, when you combine the two, you create a name for a Higher Being who can relate to both males and females. Even the ancient Hebrews recognized that God is neither male nor female, but is a Spirit above and beyond all genders and labels—the Creator Who invented all those things but Who resides above them all.

All of this talk about Creation and the proper order of things makes me long to get back completely to whatever it is I'm supposed to be. It's aggravating to me to be in this state of … whatever it is.

Relax Father. I'm excited because Mother tells me you are just about to have a breakthrough.

I am?

She tells me that something good is about to happen that will help to restore your memory and that you will Awaken to almost everything. Much was left out the first time we informed you of your true nature so that you would not be confused. You learned a lot then, but there is much more. You will know everything soon.

I hope so. You gave me that one vision, but it left me wanting to know more. I'm so frustrated with this stuff.

Cheer up. I promise you that within the next few days something will happen and you will know more. You will also become aware that you have many of the same powers that we have to manipulate energy. After that, there will be no limits as to what we can do as a team.

The same powers? You mean I'll be able to move back and forth from this realm to yours any time I wish?

Because you are still in the physical form, you will need our help with that, but many of your powers will be equal to ours.

So, we're talking spell casting, and cauldron boiling, and—

Please, don't be silly. You know what I mean. Whatever you manipulate in this realm will follow the Law of Correspondence and be created in our domain, and then be given back to you in completed form. Every blessing you give, every curse you invoke, will be realized. You are not playing at being a witch like many in your community.

This town is filled with what I call "wannabe witches." They wear all the stuff, and they dance around and try to act all witchified.

Don't be too hard on them. Even though they are confused and behave awkwardly, our influence will one day lead many of them away from what this world refers to as "witchcraft," out of their confusion, and closer to Truth. But that is a choice they must make for themselves.

They're just so corny.

I know they are, but some of the more evolved of them are at least open to Truth.

I never thought of that. I guess you're right. I know several of these ladies, and, to be honest, I like them. I just can't get into all the drama-witch-queen stuff. It just seems so silly to me.

It is, but that shouldn't concern you. You have nothing to do with that. You are an extremely powerful Being—far more powerful than any so-called witch who has ever lived. Only Mom and I are your equals. You must understand this.

All right, Cupcake. I can't wait to see what Mary has in store for me. I don't know how she's gonna "Awaken" me, but I'm ready for anything now. No man can go through what I've gone through in the past few weeks and still be concerned about a simple little thing like having his eternal memory being restored by his long-dead great-grandmother and his precious Daughter. A Being who, by the way, has the power to destroy the universe at the drop of a hat.

You're being sarcastic again.

So let's get on with it. Are you through with this Law of Gender?

Not yet, you butted in.

Sorry.

Let me give you another example. This Law isn't about the contrasting or opposite attributes of black and white, it's about the complementary qualities of black and white. This is where the idea that a man and woman uniting to become one comes from. The essence of the Law of Gender tells us how the black relates to white, the male to the female. We need to be aware that the receptive feminine and protective masculine aspects exist within all things, including human beings. It is a matter of science, and nothing can change it. It is written in Genesis that

> *God said, Let Us make man in our own image...*
> *So God created man in His own image, in the*
> *image of God created He him; male and female*
> *created He them.*

This goes back to that word, Elohim. There is much to

understand here.

So, a man is a man, and a woman is a woman, and no amount of cultural experimentation can ever change that?

That is correct. The efforts to change the Laws of both God and science go far beyond political desires and whims, they have drastic consequences.

I'm getting it. But there's so much political correctness out there.

The world must get rid of political correctness and return to Truth. If it doesn't, not only will America fall, but the planet Earth will be destroyed as well. This, too, goes beyond political affiliations. This is serious.

That is true, Annie. I've felt it for a long time. But every time I talk to anybody about it, I get yelled at.

That's because God is only active in the Spirits of those who love Him. Those of a different persuasion or who are poisoned by politics and social pressure, experience only confusion and immaturity.

I don't know if I want to get into this here. This has been a major frustration in my life. It just seems like the whole world is going mad like someone put something in the water supply, and it's screwing up people's heads. Common sense doesn't exist anymore in many parts of human society.

You are correct. The darkness creates deception in the minds of those who would condemn what is right and just.

I know we have to go on with the Universal Law thing, but is there something that can be done to change all this absolute nonsense?

That's in the hands of God. It is all a part of The Great Plan, and that Plan may include the destruction of this planet. It will undoubtedly include the utter annihilation of all those who perpetuate the nonsense.

Oh, great, back to the Doomsday stuff.

It's a reality. Unless the leaders of Earth shed their egos and their greed and come to their senses, God will have no choice but to destroy this planet.

Are you telling me that there will not be a nuclear war, but that God Himself is going to fry their fannies from His realm?

I don't know precisely how God will do it. I only know that it will be done. I remind our readers that, although it may seem frivolous at times, the contents of this book are True and prophetic, depicting things and events the way they are destined to be. You must help us turn this around… if it is not too late.

Great. What now?

There is so much to be learned from history. It all applies to this great Law of Gender. Think of all the false gods and goddesses who have been worshiped throughout the centuries on this planet. They really weren't physical people; they were characterizations of Energy Forces, much like cartoons. Isis and Osiris are a perfect example. They were Energy Forces in opposition to each other, but they were unified in their relationship. Venus and Adonis are another example, and there are countless more. One reason there are so many sexual problems in society today is that the people of this time don't understand the concept of gender in its purest form. Gender problems arise from an incorrect imbalance of energy.

Huh?

Being what your current culture refers to as a "super macho guy" is not the model for what a human male is intended to be.

That's a good thing for me.

Real human nature is a balance of all things. Men are at one end of the continuum, and women are at the other end. That is the way things are. They are different. Not only do they complement each other in their difference, but they also cannot live without the other. A male–male relation-ship cannot produce offspring. A female–female relationship cannot produce offspring. This is simple logic. And this gender aspect can vary or fluctuate with the Law of Rhythm. It can change; it can adapt to meet specific needs. That's why some men are able to mature into more balanced men — in a spiritual light. They can leave the macho image, which is superficial and physical, and correct the imbalance. The man can put on any persona he wishes, but his gender will never change. He will always be male. To try to alter that fact is to willfully distort a perfect creation of God. It is also a frivolous attempt to change the laws of science.

The movie star and war hero, James Stewart, is an excel-lent example. There is no doubt that he was a masculine person. In his real life, beyond his Hollywood persona, he was a very balanced man. He was sensitive and intelligent. He was careful and thoughtful with his words. He was liked and respected by both men and women. He was actually more attractive to women than was even John Wayne, one of the most famous movie stars of all time. Men who develop these characteristics are healthier as a result.

That's also why some women mature into more bal-anced women at a faster rate than men. They can leave the ultra-feminine image, which is superficial at best, and correct the imbalance.

An excellent example of this is another one of your human crushes, the character of Samantha Carter, from the television series, Star Gate SG-1.

I get it. There's no doubt Colonel Carter is brilliant. In fact, she's the smartest person in that series. But she's also a beautiful woman.

I know you are in love with her, too, but we can't spend too much time with this, or we will never finish the book.

You've gotta understand, I've been in this incarnation

for some years, and until recently I didn't have a clue
about you or your Mom. Besides, most of this stuff about
Amanda Tapping and —

*And Doris Day ... and Carey Mulligan ... and Jennifer
Love Hewitt ... and Anne Francis ... and Helen Shapiro ...
and Jennifer Lien ... and Joanne Kelly ... and Jenna
Coleman ... and Marilyn Monroe ...*

Alright, but I fell in love with Marilyn a long time ago.

*I get it, Daddy. But you have to concentrate on The Great
Plan now so we can generate our power together. Do you
realize some of those women left this world years ago?*

You forgot Anna M. Plowman and Melissa
Sue Anderson.

May I continue?

Go ahead.

*Humans are not locked into a static gender role. Some
men do like quiche. Some men do cry at movies. Some men
do not like sports. And this does not make these men strange
in any way, nor can it change their gender.*

*Some women don't like quiche. Some women don't cry at
movies. Some women do like sports, and some women can
change the oil in a Dodge pickup, but that doesn't make them
strange, either.*

*It means they are managing to balance themselves, often
on a subconscious level. They are still clearly men and women
on the outside, but their behaviors and their likes and dislikes
vary in normal and healthy ways.*

But what about spirituality? How does this relate to
male and female?

*This is the reason why women are sometimes more open-
minded to spiritual growth than men. Men are very much
involved in the pragmatic world, or the worlds of business
and sports, while women see the larger picture. Neither is
wrong or right. It is just a part of who they are. Both genders*

are exhibiting behaviors that are natural to them.

And that's why more women attend church than men.

That's right. This culture has instilled into the minds of men that it is unmanly to go to church — that's for women and children. It's better for a man to stay home and read the newspaper or to watch a football game on TV than to sit in a building singing songs and praying prayers. Women, since they are more in tune with the influence of polarity, will support the things of Spirit over the stuff of culture.

You sound like a feminist.

I'm not. I have no superficial political leanings. I just speak what I know to be Truth. That's the biggest obstacle facing the Strong Weet. Weet owe their Being to Truth, and this culture owes theirs to fad and fashion. The politicians and the feminists and everyone else with egoistic agendas must wake up soon, or time will cease to exist for everyone.

This whole thing really bothers me. Why do we have to have Republicans and Democrats, and feminists and macho dudes, and blacks and whites and —

They are all subject to the Universal Principles. Unfortunately, these labels represent the very beginning, very primitive stages of spiritual growth. Remember, the immaturity of humans has given rise to these cultural and racial categories here on Earth. They do not exist anywhere else in the universe; they are anathema to God, and God will eventually destroy them since cultural and racial divisions are contrary to the process of enlightenment. What will remain will be those Beings of Higher Awareness who have gone beyond the simplistic, and into the realms of Truth.

How soon will that be? I am so afraid that these PC groups are going to destroy us, and there seems little that I, or the average Joe, can do to stop it.

Daddy, you are not an "average Joe." At this time, being in the physical, there is little that you can do yourself, but after your full Awakening, your strength will be combined with Ours and together, We will do what must be done on this world. For now, leave it to God to sort those who resonate with evil from those who resonate with Truth. God is watching over us as we prepare to do His Will.

But you and I are not quite finished with the Law of Gender. We must continue. Just be comforted in the fact that God has The Great Plan laid out, and the Plan will unfold in perfection and in its own time. This will be soon, and no one human or one group of humans can stop it.

I'm not so sure that sounds very good.

It all depends on how the world accepts the Strong Weet.

What? You mean the rest of the world is going to know about us?

They have to know about us. And they will. After this book is published, we will have many supporters for what we teach. If the Book is believed and its teachings are put into practice, there could be a global shift toward Truth. The evil energy could be destroyed forever, and there could be pure peace upon this earth for thousands of years.

And if they do not practice what the Book teaches?

The chaos you now see on your daily news will soon play itself out. It will get worse at first, but then God will activate the more stringent aspects of The Great Plan, which cannot fail.

What exactly does that mean?

Only two solutions exist for what is occurring on the Earth today, and both are part of The Great Plan, and operate according to the Universal Laws of Correspondence, Polarity, and Rhythm. The people of today must realize that a law is a law and will do what it must in every situation. In this case, one of two things will occur. Either good will triumph over evil — meaning that the Strong Weet Society will have successfully completed its task — or evil will triumph over good.

Wait a minute, Sweetie. If the Strong Weet are the most powerful forces on this planet, how in the world can anything stand against them?

Weet strength is in the total accumulation of the love that others have for them. Don't forget that God is the Spirit of love. If the majority of the people on this planet do not understand what True love is, if they do not comprehend what is really going on in society, then few may support The Great Plan, and all will be for naught. However, Mother H informs us that with the proper instruction by the Strong Weet Society, large numbers may join with us to fight and defeat the darkness. If enough devotion to God is produced, if enough love is generated, this planet will be safe for at least another ten thousand years. If not, it will be destroyed within a short time.

I'm afraid we are going to be repeating this warning often throughout the remaining pages of this book, and many of our readers may get tired of hearing it. Just be aware that each and every repeated warning contains an encoded message to the Strong Weet. We are not redundant or repetitious for no reason. Every word of this book is carefully and deliberately placed upon these pages. These encoded messages fit together like a jigsaw puzzle to cause the awakening of the Weet. Some of you readers who are not Strong Weet may be able to decipher at least a part of the encoded messages, and we will be interested to learn just who among you out there has that kind of energy buried within you.

Okay, you've talked about this before — this Doomsday scenario. I don't know what that involves, but I can see the logic behind everything you've said.

It's all up to the readers. Either they will support us and stand behind us and do what we ask them of them — which will be simple — or they will treat this book as a fictitious, fun read, and will realize their mistake when it is too late.

I repeat, only a short time will remain after the publication of this book, then Earth will be no more.

So, how is God going to destroy the Earth, if it goes that far?

There are many options, some engineered as acts of Nature, and some allowed to arise from cultural or governmental entities. At this very moment, an astronomical object is speeding toward the Earth at an incredible speed. If God chooses, this object can either hit the Earth or be diverted. If it hits the Earth, it will cause global destruction. The axis of the Earth will be shifted, leading to the death of possibly every living thing on Earth. The massive dust cloud that will be raised upon impact will hide the Sun for over twelve hundred years, also destroying all life. The shock waves of the collision, which will be near Washington, DC, will be more destructive than any earthquake this world has ever experienced. Within seconds, most of North America will be destroyed. Tidal waves will speed across the Atlantic, engulfing Europe within a few hours. All of Europe will be destroyed entirely. Nothing will remain except the sea. And, of course, the dust which will do the rest.

This will be the end of the Earth. It's all part of The Great Plan. The collision will trigger a chain of events that cannot be reversed. The shock waves will trigger the command codes of every nuclear facility on Earth. The missiles will be armed, but electrical interference and physical damage will prevent their launch, and they will explode in their silos. Every country will be devastated.

Good grief.

The atmosphere will be filled with the dust of Earth, much of it metallic, all of it compounding the effects of the massive collision. Every human on Earth will be gone in a matter of days.

What a lovely picture you paint.

It's a fact. It will happen if we don't get support.

Is this the way it has to play out?

It is only one of the possible means. Only The Great Plan of THE ALL matters.

Annie, you've gotta understand that all of this information about the destruction of the world is a bit unsettling. I mean, what's the point? If we're all gonna die anyway, either by some sort of monster impact or by any of the other options THE ALL might have up His sleeve — good grief, I don't even want to know what those options are.

Don't worry. The other options are even more terrible than the one I just described. Understand, though, that all of the actions leading to destruction are merely the natural way of things. The Strong Weet have control over Nature. If we are successful, the Earth will survive.

You gonna tell me — what is that astronomical object, Dear Daughter?

Of Course not, Dear Father.

Thanks. Okay, so what now? Did we finish that Hermetic Gender thing?

We did.

So, let's get on with the next Law.

Not yet. Mom wants to talk with you.

That doesn't sound good.

She's got something stuck in her craw.

What did you just say?

I said she has something stuck in her craw.

Ha!

Did I say something funny?

No, Dear, it's just out of character for you. It's not something I would expect you to say.

Did I say something wrong?

No, Sweetie.

Well, I'm sorry if I did. I really don't know what a "craw" is anyway. It's just something I heard you say once.

Mom's coming now, and I'm returning to Home for a while. I have to teach a class in just a few moments.

Annie, I've gotta tell you, you look just like this—

—girl named Katie. I know that. You already told me.

The resemblance is uncanny.

I will tell you only this, and then I must leave. Katie is related to you.

I know … I think I know. She's my daughter, isn't she?

I can't tell you that now.

I'm getting so tired of that line.

I can't help it. Mom is here.

***

Mary! What the heck is going on with this Katie stuff?

MARY: *That is not what I wish to address at this time, Din. I need to instruct you on a matter of great importance.*

And what might that be? The destruction scenario again?

No.

And I have to ask you about something totally unrelated to anything we've been talking about here.

What is that, Dear One?

This name, Cloth Twill, that keeps coming into my mind in my dreams at night. Do you know anything about it?

It's nonsense. I could tell you that it's the name of the King of the Faeries, and I'd have you believing it. It's nothing, but it does bring to mind a topic that I wish to correct you on—unless you feel that I correct you too much.

I don't mind correction from you, Mary. I don't really look at it as a correction. You're teaching me things I could never learn in books.

I wish to mention something about names.

Shoot.

Shoot what? I have nothing to shoot with.

Good grief, Mary, you've been in my head for years. Don't you know any slang?

I'm sorry. It just takes me a while to sort out the slang from correct communication. You wish for me to "shoot" my concern to you. Am I correct?

Close enough, babe.

Babe? That's the first time you've called me anything but Mary.

I guess it just slipped out. I'm sorry.

No. It's okay. Perhaps you are Awakening to more of your history.

Well, maybe I am, but I'm pretty confused right now. Sometimes I think I'm going to wake up from a dream, and all of this Mary and Annie stuff will just *poof* away like you guys do.

Dear Din, that will never happen. We are inseparable. We have millions of memories that we have made together.

But here's something that's been bothering me. The recorded history of mankind only goes back four or five thousand years! How could we have possibly been linked for millions of years?

Very simple. What has been recorded as the history of mankind is wrong. The history books only take civilization back to the time of the ancient Hebrews, or to the ancient Egyptians or Babylon. But there were vast civilizations existent long before those cultures. In fact, those cultures were created by the cultures that came before them.

How is this possible? Are you talking about civilizations that were thriving on Earth more than five thousand years ago?

Earth has gone through many stages, Din. There have been dozens of significant civilizations long before Ancient Egypt and the Hebraic culture. Long before the

Mesopotamian culture.

You're kidding me!

Not this time. I know you have knowledge of the civilization called Atlantis.

Yeah, but that's a myth, isn't it?

It is not. Atlantis was a very real and special place. But what modern scholars have not yet discovered is that there were civilizations even higher than Atlantis, predating it by thousands of years. The Earth is, indeed, billions of years old, and during that time, many civilizations have come and gone. Ancient Rome was one of those. Atlantis was another. Lemuria was also a high culture, although modern humans haven't a clue as to where it was or what it was about. Even the names you know them by were made up by humans and are not the real names of those lost cultures. Millions of years before all of those, however, there existed a truly amazing civilization. If only the New Age writers of this era knew about this—

Hold on. What are you talking about? I've read Plato's ramblings about Atlantis, and I see no reason to doubt what he wrote. What the heck? Why couldn't there be a really cool civilization like that way back then? I know, the New Age people have taken the idea and run with it. They've got Atlantis being controlled by giant crystals, and they've got all this stuff about Atlantean "healers" running around today laying hands on people and claiming to work miracles just like Jesus—

And some of that is true, Din. Atlantis was an extraordinary place with grand temples, healers, and much, much more. But there are no Atlantean healers alive today working miracles of any type, nor was Atlantis filled with technologies far in advance of those of today. Those New Age myths are simply not true. Atlantis was more in line with the Egyptian way of life, as portrayed during the Amarna era. However,

millions of years before Atlantis, there was another incred-
ible civilization that stood out from the rest and was far in
advance of today's culture. When the scientists of this time
discover that civilization, it will rock this world.

What did you just say?

You wish for me to repeat everything I just said?

Just the "rock this world" part.

I simply meant that—

It doesn't matter, Mary. I'm just happy that you're
coming out of your shell.

And what does that mean?

Forget it. We have a lot of loose ends to tie up here.
Tell me about Atlantis.

Atlantis is a minor civilization in the scope of all time.
There have been many Atlantean-styled civilizations
throughout Earth's history, but one, ANNICA, surpassed
them all. Annica was so exceptional that it was given the
same name that is used for the other realm. One day soon, a
thought will pop into your mind, and you will know that the
other realm, Home, is actually called Annica, not Heaven.
The human word, Heaven, is rooted in another location a
few hundred light-years from Earth, but that location is
not the same as Annica.

Okay, this is a new one. Annica? Heaven? Space?

Annica is the greatest civilization in the history of this
planet. In fact, it is the greatest civilization ever produced
in the entire universe.

When did it happen, and what makes it so great?

Annica was an artificial community that was planted
by Annie.

What?

Three million, two hundred seventy-five thousand and
twenty-three years ago, Annie seeded life onto this planet.

Oh … my …

Don't be worried, Din. Annie is not God.

I don't think "worried" is the right word here.

We have been around for millions of years. You will remember this very soon.

That's what you keep telling me!

It's true. You will soon have an experience that will clarify everything.

I can't wait. But what's this beef you have with me, whatever it is that stuck in your craw?

Very well, but we must return to the subject of Annica after I set you straight on this. You'll get it. Totally.

You sound like a Valley Girl.

Just listen. It's all about names. I've heard you call your little dog Poodle, even though her name is Natalie.

Yeah, I named her after a very special person in my life. So, what's the big deal?

Names mean little to humans, but to our animal relatives, names are significant. All animals value the names they are given by humans. They wear their names like badges of honor. They are proud of the fact that they are so important to such a powerful species as mankind that we would gift them with a special name. When you refer to Natalie as Poodle, it's belittling to her.

You're kidding.

I'm not kidding.

Well, I'm sorry. I didn't know I was hurting her feelings.

Very little hurts the feelings of an animal. But their name is important to them.

I guess I'll stop calling her Poodle. It was meant as a term of endearment. I really love the little thing.

I know you do. And she loves you unconditionally. But please treat her well, because soon she will be Crossing Over into my plane.

No! Don't take Natalie away from me.

No one is taking her away from you. It's just her time — but not quite yet. She will not leave you for a while. Just remember that she will never die. Natalie will just be changing back into her pure Energy Spirit Being, and she will be waiting for you when you leave this planet.

I'll really miss her, though.

Of course you will, Din, but not for long. A few years of separation is nothing to the eternity you will have with Natalie and everyone else when you return to your True Home.

Mary, I guess I'm sort of afraid of dying. I've seen a lot of tragic deaths in my time. It doesn't look like a lot of fun, but I'd love to get back to you and Annie. If I thought it would speed things up, I'd blow my brains out.

You must never do that, Din. It would destroy The Great Plan.

I'd never actually do it, but I'm beginning to feel the bond between all of us. You're both becoming more familiar to me, and I realize that we have been together for a very long time. It seems so natural to me.

Your memories are returning as your Awakening progresses. Annie and I promised you another event that would reveal them all to you. Again, it will be soon, but first I want to tell you about Annica and the life we lived there.

We? You mean I was there with you and Annie in this Annica place? By the way, where was Annica? Was it an island like Atlantis?

You were not only with us, Din, but you also helped seed the Annica community.

I think I need to sit down for this one.

You are sitting down.

I know, but I had to say something. This is boggling my mind.

I will give you some background. You and I and Annie were, and still are, a family. We have been for millions of years. But we are a very special family. We originated on a planet many light-years from the earth in a section of the galaxy that Earth scientists call the Pleiades.

The Seven Sisters!

Correct.

Wow, that's really strange. I've always been fascinated by the Pleiades. Every night when I take Natalie out for her "business," I always make it a point to look for the Seven Sisters.

You do that because that is our original Home as sentient Beings. Somewhere deep inside, you have been aware of this. Notice the seven plastic glow-in-the-dark stars you put on the ceiling over your Altar in your office. Examine the pattern, and you will find that you have duplicated the relative positions of the stars of the Pleiades as seen from Earth.

Wow. I had no idea.

This is why we are Strong Weet, and there is more. We have been in existence far longer than anyone on Earth. We come from a society that many millions of years ago was far in advance of that of this planet today. Just think of what it must be like today. What I am telling you now only hints at the reality.

I can't think like that. For years, though, I have had a gut feeling that all of the technology of Earth—computers, space shuttles, hybrid cars, all of that stuff—was, well, primitive. I've often thought that we should be speeding across the galaxy in split seconds by using mind power alone. I don't know where I got that, but it's what I feel.

It is fact. That is precisely what this culture should be capable of, but its progress has been detoured and delayed so many times that the technological advancement of this planet has been held back by over two thousand years.

So, where does Annica come in?

Many eons ago, you and I and Annie were created by God

as prototype Beings as the first of a new and unique species.

Holy cow.

For the first three thousand years of our lives, we lived in harmony on our own planet in the Pleiades. Our Home planet was and is still called Hectarus — of course, that's as close as I can get to sounding out the real name in the language we use. It was named after Mother H, and it is from there that she has her origin. God established her as the supreme Energy Being over the Pleiades and the rest of the universe — hence her title, the Mother of Humankind, much more than just Mother Nature. Mother H created us shortly after that. All three of us, in our Highest Being, are her Children, and most of the pantheon groupings on Earth reflect this. The ancient Greeks, Romans, Egyptians, and even the Atlanteans, all find their genesis in Mother H. She was responsible for sustaining life all over Earth, so she was elevated by humans as the primary goddess of Earth. She hates that because goddesses don't exist — but what can you do? Humans can't seem to function without manufactured gods and goddesses. THE ALL thinks it's absurd as well, but He tolerates it.

Chalking it up to human immaturity?

Indeed.

Of course. No wonder I devoured all those books on mythology when I was younger.

I know this is hard to grasp, Din, but this information will lead you to a more complete Awakening. After three thousand years of learning nearly everything there is to know in the universes, the three of us were sent to the Earth to establish a community of enlightened individuals. Earth was to be a model colony — filled with superior Beings gathered from the entire Pleiadean complex, which includes not just the seven stars visible from Earth, but hundreds more, all with inhabited worlds attached. Only the greatest Minds were transported to Earth to develop a center from which they could direct the progress of the entire galaxy. THE ALL gave oversight of this project to Mother H, who allowed you and me and Annie to govern the Minds — that is what they were called, just "the Minds" — and to guide them into becoming the ruling class.

So, what went wrong? Earth's culture is a mess. There sure aren't any great "Minds" running around today.

Annica thrived for centuries until the Minds fell under the influence of darker worlds and became too big for their britches. They believed that they had become more important than Mother H, or even THE ALL — and they rebelled. They tried to alter The Great Plan and turn Annica into a colony only of those who would worship them as gods. It was not long, though, before they found out just how powerful Mother H is. They underestimated her power. They felt she was a mere figurehead designed by THE ALL to keep order in the land. Even though the Minds knew from the beginning that Mother H was an Energy Being of tremendous power, they began to believe the lie that she was a mere goddess. Deep inside, they knew they could not defeat the TRUE Mother H, but a simple little goddess would be easy. Mother H showed them the Truth.

Within moments of the Minds' first attempt to convert Annica, Mother H produced a power unlike anything ever experienced in this Galaxy, and she did it with the complete approval of THE ALL. Annica was rendered lifeless in an instant and covered over with granite, grass, and trees. Only the three of us survived because we were given advanced warning. We watched the destruction of Annica from far above the Earth.

You mean Mother H just fried all the people in Annica?

That is exactly what she did. And let us hope that this is a lesson for the people of today who are living under the delusion that they are superior to God. Within a heartbeat, the entire Earth can be annihilated. God does not need to use a mere asteroid.

I'm assuming that this Annica was an island like Atlantis.

No, it wasn't an island. Although the geographical features of the Earth have changed a lot over nearly three-and-a-half million years since the creation of Annica, the original location is right here.

Here?

Why else do you think you were brought here in 1989?

My parents retired here, and I came back to be with them. You know that already.

No, you didn't. Annie tweaked your memory, and you felt compelled to move here. She did the same for your parents. They were the lure to get you back to Annica.

I don't believe this! I was expecting Annica to be this supernatural place where orange trees grew all year round and where the people laid out in the sun all day long, soaking up the rays and getting a tan. But it's cold here. It rains all the time … and the tornadoes! And the snow in winter!

It wasn't always this way. When the civilization of Annica thrived, this state you now call home was located in a tropical region. There were orange trees, and avocados, and golden sunlight every day.

So, you're telling me that underneath this plot of land, there is a tropical Eden that was once the most powerful civilization that ever existed?

I am. Edin, not Eden, was the name of the Gardens that surrounded the main outdoor Altar. If geologists were to dig down into the ground beneath your backyard today, they would find fabulous things.

My backyard? What the —

Your backyard is the Power Center of this Galaxy.

What? I mean ... *what?*

Your backyard is the Power Center —

I heard you the first time. But what's so special about my backyard?

There is one small section of your backyard where you planted an apple tree that has recently died. That section is located directly over the spot where the Annican Temple rites were performed. And the little red block area you have sectioned off in your garden is where you and Annie and I stood — not always in physical form — to watch over the rituals. The center of the red blocks is the most sacred spot in the Galaxy. The large, ornate marble bench that the three of us sat upon as we led those rites still exists several hundred feet beneath it. There are many who continue to visit Earth regularly and hover over your red blocks so that they may acquire healing power from what lies below.

You mean aliens!

They are not really aliens, Dear, they are from the Pleiades. Some are even related to us.

You mean my garden is like a shrine to these guys? Like Lourdes or Fatima?

I do, in a universal manner of speaking.

Wow.

One thing you don't know is that one of the rocks you have placed on your red bricks is a powerful stone that was brought here from our far away Home. It is called the Memory Stone of THE ALL. When you bring it close to the Rock of The Eye, the most amazing things will occur.

The Rock of The Eye? We talked about that earlier. That's the little rock on my office altar that kind of looks like an eye. Annie said it has a lot of power attached to it.

It does. It is the key to everything. When it comes into contact with the Memory Stone of THE ALL, anything you ask will be granted. Anything.

So, if I want a Cadillac?
Think bigger than that, Din.
So, if I want to destroy the world?
It will occur.
Wow.
Just be aware, this may have to happen. We may have to do this.

I don't get it. How can a couple of rocks have such power?

It has nothing to do with the fact that they are mere rocks. It has to do with the fact that God has breathed His Great Plan into them. He has programmed them for what they must do. It is the essence of His Mind that manipulates the proper frequencies within the rocks.

So which rock is it? I mean, the one besides the Rock of The Eye.

It's still light outside. Go out into your garden and see if you can feel its Presence.

In the Garden Ten Minutes Later

Okay, Mary, what am I supposed to do? I'm standing right in the middle of the red bricks and—Good grief! I can feel something.

Hold on, here you go!
WHOA!

The Awakening Increases

I have just come to my senses to find myself lying on my back on the red bricks in the center of the garden, and I can barely hold this pen to write what I just experienced. I have just Awakened to most of my memory, and I know who I am. I am Din.

When I stood in the center of the red brick altar in the garden, a sensation came over me that I had never felt before in this incarnation. I felt a white-hot heat, like something from the sun, fill my body. I looked down and saw the small, plain stone with the wedge cut out of it, and my eyes filled with tears. I knew that rock was a piece of my Homeland. Then my Spirit rose from the Earth and sped out into space a million times faster than the speed of light.

Within seconds I was standing on the sacred ground of my home world, Hectarus, Mary, and my precious Annie by my side, and most of my memory restored.

I am Din, he who brings Justice.

ANNIE: *Daddy?*

Yes, Sweetie?

Do you know who you are?

I remember almost everything, Annie.

Mary?

MARY: *Din. You are back.*

I am.

And you remember everything now?

I remember most. It is flooding back into me. There's much to do before we make the decision whether to aid the planet Earth or to destroy it.

ANNIE: *I've missed you, Father.*

I've missed you, too, Princess. And, Mary. I'll never do this again. I will never jump into human form again. It's no longer necessary. We must now band together as Three and return to Earth to seek out the other seven Strong Weet. I now know that they are of our kind. The seven are from Hectarus, and they are Family.

Back on Earth

MARY: *Our priority is to locate the seven Strong Weet.*

I can feel them, but not all are close by. This Book must be published soon to draw them in. Very soon.

ANNIE: *The Book is almost finished. Soon there will be other Books building on the lessons of this one. Soon too, Father, you will write your own Book of instruction, not too long before the end of this world.*

There's much to tell, and we must do it quickly. There isn't much time left. There's a great deal of political turmoil in the world today that will do our work for us if we don't stop it.

MARY: *The humans are on a course of destruction, Din.*

I'm well aware of that. It's time to take full action.

ANNIE: *Can we hold off on the Rock of The Eye?*

We will not destroy Earth unless we have to. But if we must, then we will use the Rock of The Eye and the Memory Stone as they are intended. It's as simple as that.

ANNIE: *I know. I just wish ... I have a bad feeling about this. I think this world hasn't long to live.*

That will be a decision for the humans of this world. It's our responsibility to carry out The Great Plan. There's nothing that can stop The Great Plan, regardless of what we do.

MARY: *Din?*

Yes, Mary?

MARY: *You're back. There's no doubt. I can hear it in your voice and your words. But you seem a bit tense.*

I'm sorry. I've been held captive in this body for so long that I've forgotten how to act.

MARY: *I think I liked parts of you better as a human.*

So, what do I do?

MARY: *Just relax.*

ANNIE: *Yeah. Just relax.*

Annie? Why are you talking like that?

ANNIE: *Because you taught me how to talk like this.*

I'm sorry. I've been out of touch for a long time.

MARY: *You'll get it back, Dear. Just concentrate and take*

some of the new with some of the old, I'll help you. I sort of like these contractions.

12 August

The Seventh Universal Law and What Comes Next

The Law of Cause and Effect

ANNIE: *Daddy, there is still one more Universal Principle to explain.*

I know, The Law of Cause and Effect, which speaks to the interconnectedness of all things. It's the most important Law of all, and when the Strong Weet read it, they will know exactly what to do.

MARY: *Annie, this is your field of expertise, so I would like for you to handle this one.*

ANNIE: *Yes, Mother. This is all about the "Web of Life." On Earth, there's a science called quantum physics, and this science tells us that there's a chain of causality in all of life. This Law of Cause and Effect ties all of the other Laws together.*

We live in a universe governed by energy. All things, down to the smallest sub-atomic particles, are bound together by energy, and the energy of each thing is in contact with and interacts with the energy of every other thing. The energy of the air molecules touches the energy of a person's skin molecules, causing a person to feel cold or hot.

You have probably heard of the Butterfly Effect: A butterfly flapping its wings in the Amazon can cause a hurricane in the Atlantic. It is an illustration of how minute actions or changes in one area can lead to profound events in another. It is also a perfect description of the workings of the Law of Cause and Effect. This can also be seen in the way throwing a stone into a pond causes rings of little waves to emanate from the point of impact, eventually to reach the shore where they may cause dirt, sand, and pebbles to fall into the water. The "snowball effect" is similar in that it illustrates how energy can build once things are put into motion.

The message of this great Law is that there is nothing a person can do that does not have some effect on the entire universe — great or small. Even our thoughts and emotions are pure energy that radiates out to interact with the rest of the cosmos.

Some scientists believe we live in what they call a holographic universe. That topic is too complicated for this discussion. Put briefly, it means that every particle is imprinted with the pattern of every other particle in existence, past, present, and future. Everything "knows" everything about everything else. These scientists think that this is the answer to everything, but they are only partially correct. There is so much more to it.

Things are happening right now on the other side of this globe that people on this side have no idea about. The rippling effect of those events will change all human lives five or ten years from now, or maybe sooner, and not for the better.

Think about your favorite TV show, Daddy, STARGATE SG-1, or the old STAR TREK series. Several of the plots involved time travel. When they went back in time, the crew members were cautioned not to change anything, and when they returned from some future time, they would not share what they found. They took those precautions to keep the effect of their activities from rippling through time and changing their present or altering the future.

Consider the assassination of Abraham Lincoln. It might have been prevented had a time traveler used his or her powers, but how would that have affected future events on this little planet?

Some things are beyond the control of humans. Once the Law of Cause and Effect is started, it doesn't stop. Like rust, once it takes hold, there is no stopping it. That's why everyone on Earth needs to consider the ramifications before taking *action. To yell "fire" in a crowded room when there is no fire is a terrible thing.*

The Earth concept of karma is explained by this Principle. The Butterfly Effect sends energy in all directions at once, eventually returning to the butterfly. Good energy returns positive effects, and bad energy returns adverse effects. It is not the behavior that determines the outcome, but rather the frequency of the energy expended.

Remember the Law of Vibration? You know that when a sound is made, its energy frequency travels out into space and goes on forever, in all directions at once. The planets in the Orion System and the constellation of Leo are now receiving the energy frequencies of Stargate SG-1.

Everything done on this Earth, every penny dropped on any sidewalk, all actions by anyone affect everyone everywhere. They affect our uncertain future and our ultimate existence or destruction.

The Apostle Paul presents a perfect illustration of this Law in 2 Corinthians 9:6:

> *But this I say, he which soweth sparingly shall reap also sparingly; and he which soweth bountifully shall reap also bountifully.*

In what has become known as the Sermon on the Mount (Matthew 5, 6, and 7), Jesus told His disciples that they should not present their gifts before the altar — that is, worship — without first seeking reconciliation — forgiveness — with their brothers and sisters. He also warned that one should not "judge lest you be judged." Forgiveness transforms the negative energy of hate and resentment into positive energy and returns it to the individual. This is what karma really is, and the Apostle Paul explains it further in Romans 12:20 when he says,

If your enemy is hungry, feed him; if your enemy is thirsty, give him something to drink. In doing this, you will heap burning coals on his head.

I'm using a lot of Biblical illustrations because most of the readers will be familiar with them, having been raised in a primarily Judeo-Christian culture. As the Law of Cause and Effect is key to the success of our assignment, they must understand clearly what we are giving them.

You're doing fine, Annie.

Thanks, Daddy. I'm almost done.

Jesus wraps up His Sermon on the Mount by saying, "Do unto others as you would have them do unto you," which is a perfect statement of The Law of Cause and Effect. Our readers will recognize this principle as the Golden Rule. It is central not just to Christianity, but to nearly all major religions. Here are some examples:

JUDAISM: *What is hurtful to yourself do not do to your fellow man. That is the whole of the Torah, and the remainder is but commentary.*

BUDDHISM: *Hurt not others with that which pains yourself.*

HINDUISM: *This is the sum of all true righteousness — treat others, as thou wouldst thyself be treated. Do nothing to thy neighbor which hereafter thou wouldst not have thy neighbor do to thee.*

SIKHISM: *Treat others as thou wouldst be treated thyself.*

JAINISM: *A man should wander about treating all creatures as he himself would be treated.*

TAOISM: *Regard your neighbor's gain as your gain; and regard your neighbor's loss as your own loss, even as though you were in their place.*

SIOUX: *Do not condemn a person until you have walked in their moccasins.*

There's no question that this is the most important Law of all, as it is found in most of the religions on Earth. Even the ancient Druid culture had a similar Law, as did the ancient Egyptians. Those who follow any spiritual path must take this Golden Rule seriously. It is the key to everything.

Thank you, Annie. You did an excellent job. Why don't you give us a brief summary of the Laws' central theme when taken as a whole, then we can put this to rest and proceed with our primary task.

It's quite straightforward. First, if you are attempting to transform your life, you must be absolutely sure about what you are doing and why you are doing it. This is very important. Build a picture in your mind of the end you wish to achieve. That is your intent. If the change is to be effective, the intention must be clear.

When the intent is clear, make sure that your attitudes, opinions, actions, and thoughts are pure and properly motivated. That is, they must be in accordance with The Great Plan of God and not prompted by a selfish ego. This is not as difficult as it might seem. The Great Plan of God deals only with love, and Its fulfillment is the establishment of what is right and good for all life. Just use your imagination. Don't pollute the air or the water system. Don't hurt each other. Make sure that what you think, say, and do doesn't harm anyone or anything in Nature, intentionally or otherwise.

Finally, when you decide to do something, give it everything you've got. Build the image of your idea and your goal in your mind, think about it every day, then direct your physical energy and your conscious will toward getting the job done.

Perfect, Sweetie. I couldn't have said it any better.

Thanks. Do you think it will be enough to draw the other seven Strong Weet to us?

Yes, I do. I think that all of this is now pretty much inevitable. What has to happen will happen, and what the rest of the world does is irrelevant. The Great Plan will go forward, on one of only two paths—the path to survival, or the path to destruction.

Annie, would you describe what the rewards will be if The Strong Weet Society is successful?

The result will be thousands or even millions of years of peaceful life on this planet if we succeed. The United States of America will become what it was always meant to become, a center of perfection and prosperity, a new Atlantis, and even better, a revival of Annica.

The Strong Weet will reveal the ancient civilization of Annica, and you and I will personally direct the excavation of an archaeological site that will baffle the minds of everyone on Earth. Discoveries at this site will bring about a renaissance in all of the arts—painting, sculpture, music, poetry, and the like. The United States will no longer need to be an agent of correction using threats to maintain peace but will be a center of cultural awareness. In fact, it will be given its original name, New Annica. A great civilization will arise that will encompass the globe, and all countries will become one country. There will be no Third World. Everything will be hunky-dory.

Hunky-dory?

Everything on this world will be wonderful.

You are very special, Annie.

I know, Daddy.

***

Mary? Are you here?

MARY: *I am.*

Here's what we need to do now that The Universal Principles have been explained. It's time to concentrate on how we want to finish your Diary so that it has the most significant impact on the readers. If we can't draw in their cooperative support, all will be in vain.

MARY: *Yes, Dear Din. Let's hope it doesn't come to that. First, though, I have some information directly from Mother H.*

I felt you had something important to tell me.

Mother H has informed me that the key to what we are doing lies in an essential altar that must be constructed in the back garden. It's already been started, but something more must be added.

The Apple tree.

You are definitely back! Yes. It's the little Apple tree you planted that died just a few weeks ago. Mother H allowed it to die for a reason.

It must have something to do with the fact that its location is so close to the spiritual center of the universe.

Exactly. There is a ritual to be performed with the little Apple tree that will begin the salvation of the planet ... if all goes well.

Yes, I understand. Since the Apple tree is standing directly over the original Annican Temple, not only is that spot sacred, but the tree itself, as well.

We must carefully and gently pull the little tree from the Earth—

And cut it into small pieces—

Then burn the pieces of this Sacred One and spread the ashes over the red blocks in the center of the garden.

That's where you and Annie and I conducted the rituals back in the time of Annica's greatness.

When the ashes of the little tree fall upon the Memory

Stone of The One, its powers will be activated, and the final phase of The Great Plan will be set into motion. The Memory Stone must be removed to a safe place. Should the Rock of The Eye come in contact with it at this early stage, the entire galaxy will be destroyed.

I know exactly where to keep both stones.

We must work quickly, so let's get started. If anyone on this planet learns of this, they will try to steal these stones.

You know that would be impossible, Mary. Our Power can overcome anyone who might come against us. Anyway, they could not activate them without the —

But there is one who would try.

I know.

Shaitan.

That imbecile has followed me for eons.

Even in this life, he's given you a difficult time,

The stories I could tell!

I think you should.

What do you mean?

The readers must have as much information as we can give them. You ought to —

Not in this Book, Mary.

ANNIE: *He's right, Mom. It isn't time yet.*

MARY: *Whatever you wish. But these Truths must be revealed someday.*

Shaitan is a dolt.

ANNIE: *But you do need to say a little about Shaitan so that the readers will understand who he is. Just a brief explanation.*

Shaitan is the name given to the personification of the evil energy that has risen on this planet independently from the desires of God. As mentioned before, there is no doubt that this has something to do with The Great Plan. God has allowed this dark form to manifest over the centuries, and now the "it" has become a "he." As it is, Shaitan's power has been diminishing in the past few years.

Even though his power is failing, Shaitan can still complicate The Great Plan. In fact, his last remaining energy is being directed solely toward doing just that. He knows this is his last stand. If he fails to defeat The Strong Weet Society, he fails forever, and forever his energy will be dissipated among the stars.

However, if he succeeds, this planet will descend into a chaotic state, the likes of which you have never seen. Geological catastrophes will be felt all around the globe. They will start small, such as minor earthquakes. Then volcanoes that have been dormant for centuries will begin erupting. This will be followed by diseases and plagues, cultural and religious persecution, food shortages and world unrest that will develop into terrible wars both hot and cold between many nations. Russia and China will use many dangerous and devious methods to disrupt and destroy America. The Middle East and Israel will, of course, play major roles in the destabilization of the world. In fact, violence and terrorism will erupt in that region at a level that will be difficult to mitigate — due primarily to a weak, incompetent and illogically anti-American, anti-God faction of the American political establishment. America will be corrupted by false leaders at the very top.

ANNIE: *That sounds like some of the prophecies in the Bible.*

It does. Jesus knew this was going to happen, so He tried to give humanity a clue before He left this plane of existence. The Apostle John also wrote about it in the Book of Revelation. Other scriptures from other religions also allude to some sort of End Times scenario. They all speak to the existence of two forces, the good and the evil, in the forms we now refer to as God and Shaitan. They never knew how these forces actually operated, and that is where the human personification of Shaitan came from. He has many names, but Christians know him as Satan.

The fact is, there is a choice. The world does not have to end. The energy of Shaitan can be defeated! It's all in the hands of the Strong Weet Society and the readers of this Book. It's as simple as that.

ANNIE: *And the key is the Altar in the back garden.*

That's right.

ANNIE: *Is it time to construct the Altar?*

Not just yet. First, we need to ask the permission of Mother H.

MARY: *She will give it, Din.*

I know that, but it is a formality that I insist on.

MARY: *You are such a good man.*

Mother H, hear my plea. We stand at the crossroads of the End of Time. You know us well. Mary is your Daughter, Annie is your Granddaughter, and I am your High Priest as well as your Son. Every age has been overseen by the three of us, your children. Now, as The Great Plan is about to reach its zenith, Mary, Annie, and I are in command of what is to come. We ask for your permission to build an Altar in the back garden of our home upon the sacred ground of Annica. This Altar shall become the central focus of all power for the preservation or destruction of this planet.

Five Minutes Later

As I spoke the last word, the sky darkened, a strong wind blasted through the area, and bolts of lightning shot everywhere. It was clear that the Mother of Humankind had approved our request to build the Altar. Natural outbursts such as these are her signature.

Moments after Mother H's display, a vision came into my mind of the exact details for building the Altar.

Appen, the dead Apple tree, must be removed from the ground with the greatest of care, and only by me, as I have the High Priest status. The precious tree will then be cut into small parts and placed in the fire ring where it will be burned. A small portion of the ashes shall be taken from the fire ring and poured onto the sacred square of red blocks, directly over the Memory Stone. A cold cinder of the tree will be used to bless the Rock of The Eye, then both the Rock and the cinder will be placed in a guarded container kept inside the house.

When this is done, the memories of some of the Strong Weet Society will be Awakened. Wherever the other seven are, they will suddenly know they are something extraordinary. They will not quite know their true identity as Strong Weet, but the process of Awakening to complete knowledge will have been begun.

Let me make this point very clear. This ceremony is not some sort of New Age ritual or magic rite. As in the days of the Old Testament ceremonies, every action releases energy of a specific frequency that speeds upward, joins with the outer layer of the Earth's Atmosphere, and then encompasses the entire globe. This specific frequency will penetrate the Glow of each and every one of the seven Strong Weet. Like turning on a light switch, the energy will activate the exact neural pathways necessary to stimulate the early stages of their Awakening.

As soon as this Book is published, the Strong Weet will feel compelled to read it. When they do, the final application of knowledge will begin, and they will be off on their search for the Annican Family Triad of Mary, Annie, and Din, the children of The Mother of Humankind.

The altar where the Apple tree has stood will be carefully tended. Three blocks of stone will be set where the tree was pulled out of the ground—two blocks standing

on end, with the third across the top, bridging the two.
A piece of Hectaran Crystal will be placed on top of the
bridge, and a solar light will be set behind it. I already
have the Crystal that will be used.

Seven natural stones will be arranged in a circle around
the stone bridge, leaving space for a plaque that will read
"Appen," which is the name of the Apple tree that lives
on via this Altar. The Energy Spirit of Appen will forever
protect this sacred Altar.

Outside the Altar ring, seven solar lights will be placed,
leaving a space of two feet by one foot. In that space is to
be placed a section of green moss. At the time of each
new moon, the Annican Triad will kneel there to show
respect to God as the sun rises in the east. And any time a
member of the Annican Triad passes by the Altar, they will
bow in reverence to God, and to the memory of Annica.
This act does nothing for the Family Triad, for they do
not need it, but the action will attract and strengthen
specific forms of energy that will feed the cause of The
Strong Weet Society.

The color blue is significant in the design of the Altar.
Eventually, a mosaic design will be placed at the center
of the Altar to hold the precious stone containing the Life
Force of Appen and the Central Radiation of Annica.

MARY: *Din, may I interrupt here?*

Yes, Mary.

*Since we are using terms and images that are not common
to this plane of existence, or to this planet, a few added details
might be useful for our readers.*

You're right, Mary.

May I?

Please.

*I want to clarify two things, Din. The first is about the
color Blue. Blue is the most sacred color in the Annican*

culture. A deep Blue, known as Navy Blue to current Earth culture, is the color Mother H surrounds herself with as she performs her work with Nature. If ever you witness a dark storm with powerful lightning and thunder, this is the color she will be using.

A light Blue — Robin's Egg, or Turquoise — is the color of the mosaic tile work that made up the floor in the main sanctuary of the Annican Temple. It was so beautiful, and it's still there! One day modern archaeologists will unearth this magnificent place, and the entire world will be struck with awe. They will find a tiled floor with an exquisite design depicting the images of every animal living at that time in Earth's existence. Many of these creatures would surprise the people on Earth because they are so different from the animals living today. Only four are related to modern species — the dolphin, the dog, the eagle, and the hummingbird. All the others are totally different.

The scenes on the mosaic floor, which extends several hundreds of feet in all directions, are interconnected with this beautiful light Blue color. Upon entering the Temple, an Annican could immediately feel the energy emanating from the tile floor. It was a sensation of incredible peace and tranquility. Blue, in any form, is the color of peace. But another thing that was different back then is that Annicans treated colors as living, sentient Beings. Just as a person living today caresses their dog and speaks sweet words to him, Annicans of that era approached a tree and treated the tree as not only a tree Being but a color Being, as well. I will attest that color is alive and that each color's unique frequency contributes to the health and well-being of this planet. Blue, in any shade or hue, is the most healing of all the colors.

I also want to explain the Central Radiation of Annica. The Central Radiation was the energy hub for the culture of Annica. It wasn't the actual source, because that came from

God, but it was what we referred to as the transformer for the power of God.

The Central Radiation was a small Stone, similar to the Rock of The Eye, that focused the energy God gifted to us. In those days, we didn't have to worry about oil and gas and fuels of any type. All of our needs were met by the gifts of God, which were given daily in many forms. Perhaps in the next book, we will be able to reveal these energy gifts to those living in this age. If God allows that, you will never have to worry about such things as gas and oil. I believe God has it in The Great Plan to divulge those details soon — depending upon the state of the world, of course. However, God will not give out such information if humanity continues to wallow in its own evil mud. He will begin the first stage of the removal of humanity from this world if humans continue to support evil leaders and initiators of corrupt laws and regulations that are contrary to the sacred Laws given by the Founders. We are not very optimistic at this point, but that can change.

The Central Radiation Stone wasn't a quartz crystal like those misused by New Age practitioners for just about everything under the Sun. Crystals can be used today for many reasons, but they are not the most powerful stone for controlling energy or for healing. The most powerful stone for healing and for energy transmission is common desert jasper of which the Central Radiation Stone was made.

The Rock of The Eye is also comprised of jasper. Because of its particular crystalline makeup, it can focus and direct the incredible energy flows of God, much like a laser beam is condensed and directed, only with greater efficiency.

When God directed energy into The Central Radiation Stone, the Stone trapped it, amplifying it and raising its frequency. This is even beyond my reasoning. The Stone also contained some sort of mechanism or programing that controlled the release and direction of the energy. The result was that every home, building, and business in Annica was provided with endless energy for whatever was needed. All devices requiring energy received the exact amount needed for their use. Of course, on Annica, and back Home on Hectarus, very little energy is used as we do not employ the same forms of technologies as used by humans here on Earth.

The Central Radiation Stone provided everything we needed. Unlike today, we never even thought about the price of gas or the rising fuel costs. All Power came from God, via the CRS. That Stone is still existent, but it is not under the Annican Temple. Just before Annica was destroyed, we, the Family Triad, removed the stone from its Altar and hid it in a secret place. It remains there to this day. It can be reactivated by us should it be necessary.

According to The Great Plan of THE ALL, it is not in the best interest of humanity to reveal the location of the CRS at this time. No country on this world today is capable of being the custodian for such power. It would be foolhardy to allow any current Earth government to possess this Stone. The power would no doubt be used for all the wrong reasons. This is yet another incentive for your culture. The CRS is the answer to all of your energy needs. If it is used, there will never be a concern over energy again on the face of this planet.

ANNIE: *Time is getting short. This Book is nearly finished, but there are still several topics yet to be discussed.*

I know, Cupcake. Like war and politics and disease.

ANNIE: *Yes, Daddy. When we send this Book out to the people of this planet, we must give them a few instructions.*

MARY: *Words of wisdom.*

ANNIE: *Yes.*

I really don't want to pontificate.

ANNIE: *This isn't pontificating. This is necessary for the survival of the human species. Time is short, and I must go into action soon. Grandma H told me just yesterday that she wants me to step into my role the moment it is meant to begin.*

I know. So, what do you want to discuss?

ANNIE: *We can't cover everything in this Book. War and political intrigue are far too complex to just gloss over in a few sentences. Instead, let's share some hope, such as the elimination of all diseases and the healing of all those who currently suffer from them.*

Yes, that is one reason we are here. The cures for all diseases known to mankind will be revealed in due time. An Energy of a frequency never before known on Earth will be released, and in that instant, every person suffering from disease or illness will be cured. Regardless of the cause, the new frequency will rearrange the molecules in every person's physical body so that illness cannot be tolerated. It's a simple process, really. I'm surprised Earth doctors haven't come up with it yet.

ANNIE: *May I interrupt?*

Of course, Annie.

It has to do with the Rock of The Eye. The energy of The Family Triad, which is directed by God, is transmitted into the Rock of The Eye, and the Rock of The Eye transforms it and sends it out with the frequency that will heal every human being on Earth. There will be no more disease.

Of course, one might think that if there's no disease, then everyone will live forever, and pretty soon this planet will be overrun with people, all of our energy sources will be depleted, and we'll have a heck of a mess!

Not so. The Great Plan will compensate for all of those concerns. We will explain how that works, but not yet. Keep in mind that when The Great Plan wraps up—even for the good—most humans will not make the final cut. Most will be permanently removed. Others may choose to be transported back to their place of origin. The population of Earth will be enormously reduced.

MARY: *Very good, Din.*

We've talked about energy. If things go according to The Great Plan—and I have no doubt that they will—energy will not be a problem. The Mother of Humankind can provide power for an eternity.

Politics, however, is another story. Free Will is both the greatest gift and the deadliest curse to this planet. Everyone alive has been given Free Will, including the world leaders, many of whom are corrupt or downright evil. Those humans who cannot tell the difference between the good and the evil suffer from seriously distorted thinking and will be judged along with world leaders.

ANNIE: *Be gentle.*

I will. I am so tired of the nonsense and the immaturity found in every corner of this insignificant little globe. We are about to unleash a terrible fate upon the entire Earth! Surely the inhabitants can sense that all is not right with their world. But this is the only warning they will get.

MARY: *We must share the Book quickly.*

We will, Mary.

MARY: *What you say is true, Din. If they only knew.*

And if they only believe.

MARY: *Let's hope so.*

13 August

Reflections On What Has Transpired and On What Is To Come

I just needed to come out here to the back garden for a few moments to clear my head. Mary, Annie, and I will soon be making the greatest of decisions. The night is pitch black, except for the trillions of stars overhead blessing me with their presence.

When I was a young man in this incarnation — about nineteen or so and living in Mira Loma, California — I used to go outside and stare up at the night sky as I am doing right now, just to ponder the universe. I would imagine myself as being in a giant Crystal bottle staring up through the neck of the bottle into some unknown and wonderful world outside the confines of the Crystal.

I don't know why I thought the bottle was made of Crystal and not glass, it just came to me that way. At that time, I thought I was just an ordinary kid. I didn't have a clue about Crystals and Atlantis and all the New Age stuff and nonsense that would be all the rage some twenty years later. All I knew then was that there is a great big, black sky up there, filled with stars and constellations and galaxies and who knows what. I remember saying out loud to no one in particular, "Jeez Louise, if I could only be a part of it all."

I saw a UFO once in Riverside, California, sometime back in the sixties. It made the local news the next day. I wasn't the only one to see it swoop in and hover over the football field at Rubidoux High School. Hundreds witnessed the oblong-shaped, metallic object cruise deliberately over the field and then disappear over the low hills behind the school. I was captivated, as was everyone else who saw this mysterious craft. I felt no fear in my heart when I saw it, but there were some in the crowd who screamed in fright at the foreign object in the sky. One woman shook like a leaf and nearly fainted when the UFO passed overhead. Not me, though. I wondered what the heck it was, who was in it, and I couldn't help but wish they had come for me. I kid you not. I was "different," and I knew it, even in my human form.

I had no clue as to who I really was. I knew nothing of the Strong Weet Society, or The Annican Triad, or Shaitan, or The Great Plan of God. I was just me. There are times when I think it would be better to have that kind of innocence again. Now that I have full remembrance, and now that I know just what is in store for this beautiful Earth, I will be saddened if we do not succeed. This is such a lovely planet. Just think for a moment about all of the lovely national parks—Yellowstone, the Petrified Forest, the Everglades, to name a few—how beautiful they are, each one arousing a different and distinct emotion within the hearts of humans.

These days everyone is so concerned about pollution, but you all need to understand the Truth. Pollution is indeed damaging the planet, and mankind's activities are the source. Even so, it will take three hundred and twenty-seven years for the current worldwide output of pollutants to sufficiently contaminate this planet to make any real difference. However, Earth doesn't have three hundred and twenty-seven years left.

The reality is that The Great Plan makes these issues irrelevant. Regardless of the environmental state of the Earth, there are only, at most, a handful of years remaining before God "removes" all problems. Politicians, scientists, and theologians MUST realize this, and focus on doing the Spiritual Will of God, instead of directing all of their attention toward the physical state of the planet. If they do not, then we, the Annica Triad, must do what we must do. There is no alternative.

That is why I came out tonight to escape for a few moments from what I know is our duty. I have learned that when I touch the sky with my mind, it brings about a deep meditative state.

***

Early on in this book, I described the Pepper tree I used to sit in as a child in California and see the faces of the Leaf People. I loved that tree. I also used to sit up in that tree and dream of traveling to the stars. The stars spoke to me.

Every night—just like tonight—I would go outside and climb the Pepper tree. I'd look up into the night sky, sensing none of the terror of darkness like some kids my age might have, but only the vast universe before me, teeming with life. I knew there were other Beings on millions of planets out there—I sensed it in my Spirit—and I often wondered if any of those bright lights were UFOs coming toward the earth at a speed far beyond the speed of light.

I also wondered about the types of people that might be found on other planets. What were they like? Maybe they were just microbes. I tried to imagine what it would be like to be a microbe, and that brought me to the conclusion that that's exactly what I was—sort of. I was, after all, just a tiny speck on a little planet among the zillions of other planets and stars in the scope of this vast universe.

MARY: *Din?*

Mary?

Are you okay?

I'm fine. I just had to get away for a while, and this is how I do it.

I know. It's a lovely night.

Yes, it is. Mary?

Yes, dear Din.

Now that I'm nearly back to my True Self, is there any reason we can't ... become real ... become physical forms?

There's no reason why we can't. All we have to do is touch our Spirits together and recite the words our Mother gave us. Do you remember those words?

I do. And I remember when she sent us off into this life to live among these humans. Even Mother cries. I saw her mist up as we went through the transition.

She loves us very much.

I know that. I also know how much I love her, and you and Annie, and our Home, and all of those who are dear to us. I look forward to the time when all of our Weet have Awakened so we can commune with them.

Let us recite those words now. I want us to be close this night under these stars.

But I will never put our Mother's words in this Diary.

I agree. But say them quickly to yourself now. I don't want to waste this beautiful night.

14 August

The Role of the Triad is Revealed

I am still awestruck when I think back to when Mary first made her presence known to me that night after the ball lightning. I still recall my confusion and, yes, fear when I woke up in my bed wondering who that voice belonged to and where it was coming from.

It seems as though much time has passed since then, but it's only been about three months. Now I know it's time to immerse ourselves in the execution of The Plan, and I am ready for it. This world is a mess, and the only hope is for the Strong Weet Society to band together and do what they were sent here to do. That is exactly what we will do once we all get back together. The only way that will happen is to get this, Mary's Diary, published, so I'll concentrate on that for now.

Daddy.

Annie, my Sweet!

Daddy, there is evil in the air. I can feel it.

What are you feeling, Sweetie?

It's close … I'm not sure … but …

Sweet Daughter, I know how sensitive you are. If you say some sort of evil is hanging around, I believe it. I'm just surprised that I don't feel it. I always sense the presence of evil when it comes by,

It's Shaitan. He's cloaked his evil because he is coming for you. He knows how powerful you are.

It's okay, Annie. I feel his presence now.

What is he after?

He knows that time is short. He's going to do everything possible to destroy The Great Plan.

But he wants you, Daddy. I can feel it.

I know he does. This is not the first time.

357

I can feel what he's doing. He's manipulating time and space to get to you. He's so angry with you.

He's angry because I've removed him hundreds of times over the centuries.

But he thinks he can get rid of you now because of what is happening in America today. I can read his evil mind. He believes that if he can eliminate you now, he can gain a stronger foothold than he already has because of the corruption in the American political structure.

And I understand Shaitan's mind.

I'm so worried about you.

Precious Cupcake of mine, you are one of the three most powerful Beings in every universe that God has conceived. Just what is it that you have to fear?

There's only one thing I have ever feared in all of time, Daddy, and that is losing you, my precious Father.

You won't lose me to this simplistic creature, Sweetie. I have tricks up my sleeve that even you don't know about.

As do I, Daddy.

What do you mean, Annie?

Do you remember when Mom was talking to you about me, and she mentioned that I was the Greatest Power of all?

Yes.

Well, she didn't go into details, but here's the scoop. One thing she did say was that I would have the combined powers that you each have because I am the child of the two of you. She was correct, but she didn't tell you everything.

Annie, I'm not following you.

I'm not just as powerful as you and Mom combined, I'm magnitudes more powerful.

Does your Mom know this?

I'm sorry, Daddy. She tried to give you a hint way back in the way back.

So, what the heck does that make you?

Daddy... I am the Great All–Powerful One who brings all things to an end in the End Times.

The Great and Powerful Oz? My Daughter? Why didn't I know this? After all these eons. Why didn't your Grandma tell me about this?

It's The Great Plan. That's just the way it is. Who's Oz?

Mary: Listen to her Din, she is in charge now. You have to trust her.

What a thing to learn about my own Daughter. Why didn't you tell me this, Mary?

Mary: Mother H made that decision. She was just trying to avoid a problem.

Mother! What is this really all about!

You are my son, Din, and everything is in accordance with The Plan. You must defer to Annie now. Shaitan will be no more, but only if you do as Annie instructs. Her words are not her own, but mine. I love you all, my sweet children.

Mother? Forgive me, Mother. I will do what you ask. It has to be the right thing, but I'm still a little concerned for my Sweet Annie.

Fear not, my son. No harm will come to her.

Daddy, you have nothing to be afraid of. I've already defeated Shaitan in my mind, and that's all that matters.

What do you mean by that?

You are still a bit confused, Daddy. You know what I mean — it is The Law of Mentalism. I have destroyed Shaitan in my mind. I've planned out exactly how it will happen and precisely when it will happen, in accordance to the Will of God's Son, Who, of course, will be the One to destroy Shaitan forever.

I know the Law, Cupcake, but does Shaitan?

He ignores the Law. He believes he will be able to work his evil against us. I will allow him to do so but only in a small way and only for a little while. I have set limits on his abilities, and when we arrive at my set time, he will be obliterated for all time.

But why are you letting him have any time at all?

Because I am using him to our benefit. Much of the evil he is producing will eventually be turned around and backfire on him. I will use that moment as a catalyst for the final moments of The Great Plan.

Annie, I'm your Father and a member of the Family Triad. I know that I have the power to destroy this world with my own mind if I so desire. I know that your Grandma tells me to let you handle everything, and I can tell by talking to you that my wisdom can't hold a candle to yours. No intelligence in a thousand universes can approach the gift you have been given. You are The Chosen One of Great Powers.

I am, Daddy, but you are still my Father, and I respect you infinitely. My wisdom is far greater than anything any sentient Being has ever known. It cannot be either explained or imagined because I have been chosen by God to be who and what I am. Time and space mean nothing to me. Solid, liquid, gas — they mean nothing to me. I am the chosen child of you and Mother and of THE ALL. With one whisper, I can bring all creation to a halt, and with another, I can create whatever I want to replace it. All is within me.

Annie... I'm humbled.

Daddy, please, don't be so human. I'm not God, nor am I His Holy Spirit. I am merely His instrument, and believe it or not, I'm still your Kid. I will continue to seek your counsel as we go through this process.

You don't need my advice. That seems kind of silly. You're above all counsel. You're even … above your Grandma. How does that work? As smart as I am, this is really confusing to me.

There is much in this Diary that doesn't make sense, but it all works, and it all comes together eventually. Grandma is your Mother, and she is my Grandmother, but that is only because of The Great Plan. It all has to do with the way we have "Jumped" from one life to another to bring The Plan to its current state. All that has been done and every life we have lived has been necessary to get us here now.

I can understand part of that, Cupcake. Ha, listen to me! I'm calling The Chosen Great Power "Cupcake."

I am your Cupcake, Daddy.

But how can you be my Kid—Mary's Kid, the Granddaughter of Mother H—and still be The Chosen Great Power?

Sit down, Daddy, and I will answer your question. First, though, I need to clarify this for the readers because they have no idea who The Chosen Great Power is. I have been around since the beginning of time. I was the original Creative Energy that God's Holy Spirit used to produce life everywhere. Like Grandma, I, too, am an ancient and sentient Energy Being who can take human form at will. I am pure LIGHT. *I am not the Holy Spirit, nor can I do the wondrous things the Holy Spirit does. The Holy Spirit is responsible for the wonders and miracles found on the pages of the Bible. No Being ever in all of history can do what the Holy Spirit can, for the Holy Spirit is God—one-third of the Trinity. I am only a tool, a mere spark from the Mind of God, to be used to create and sustain the universe. I am intense Power. The Holy Spirit molds me and focuses me as needed, and I obey. I've had to take human form many times, hundreds of times throughout history.*

I can read your mind, Daddy. You're thinking, "But I thought you were my Daughter!"

That's exactly what I was thinking. I remember you telling me that Mary and I were your real Parents.

I didn't lie to you, Daddy. When I became personified, THE ALL allowed me to select one set of exceptional Spirit People to be physically born to and to keep as my very own. It's a one-time deal. I have been in existence for millions of years. I could have chosen to be born to the Queen of England, a President of the United States, or even a great leader of an alien world, but out of all the multitude of options I had, I chose you and Mom. You were and are precious to THE ALL, and even though God is my Creator, you guys are my Mom and Dad, and I will protect you both with all the power I own. I will destroy anyone or anything that seeks to harm you. No exceptions. Immediately! It is THE ALL that tells me that is the way it should be.

I still don't get this. Why in the world do you need parents if God is your real Parent?

It has to do with only one thing. When I first explored your mind, I fell in love with you. I knew that you would be the best Father ever, and I felt the same about Mom. I have never regretted that decision. I would die for either of you.

But you can't die!

That's true, but you know what I mean. I will always protect you. Even Shaitan will feel my wrath, and my wrath is mighty!

So, what does this guy have in store for me?

He's going to try to destroy the Altar of Annica out in our back yard.

How does he think he's gonna do that? Send fire bolts, or some of the other childish nonsense he's tried in the past? I remember that time in —

He will use more subtle means than that. He knows you

too well, and he is afraid of you, but the one thing he doesn't know is me. He has no inkling of The Chosen One of Great Power. It has been kept from him."

Explain something to me, Annie. What's the big deal? What's the purpose of The Great Plan? You can fry this guy in a heartbeat! We all can. You don't need all this Great Plan stuff. Just get rid of him.

The Great Plan is an intricate web of possibilities where each action is dependent on the implementation and outcome of previous efforts. The Plan is ultimately more important for the humans than it is for us. It is complicated, but you must trust me. Everything will transpire as it must.

Do your Mom and I have roles in any of this, or are you just carrying us along with you?

You have a vital role, Daddy. You must listen to me and take my words seriously. According to The Great Plan, I can never take necessary action without the help of The Annican Family Triad—"Family" being the operative word. You and Mom and I are a team. That is the way God set it up. Family relationships are KEY to God's Plan. Humans must understand and take that seriously. Yes, I can destroy the entire universe with a single nod of my head, but this assignment is more subtle than that. If this planet is to survive, it will take our combined powers to pull it off because God is waiting to see what the humans do. And God watches everything.

I guess I'm not fully Awakened after all. I still don't get it. If you are the One of Great Power, then nothing—absolutely nothing—can get in your way.

Nothing except The Great Plan that was set into motion by God millions of years ago. For some reason, even I am unable to change that. Only God and the Holy Spirit can change it. Only they know particular details and time frames. We must have faith and trust them, and do exactly as they tell us when they tell us. That is as it should be, for God knows all, and we know very little.

So, what now?

We must confuse Shaitan.

Confuse him? Let's just remove him again.

Not yet, Daddy. But he must be confused to draw his attention away from you.

I can handle him, Annie.

Yes, you can, but we must keep him around long enough to use him as we advance The Great Plan.

I still don't get why all of this had to be kept from me.

We know how hot your temper can get. There are some things that God felt it best to keep from you. We were all afraid that if you had this information, it would somehow cloud your judgment and, possibly, harm The Great Plan.

You're right. I can be a little impulsive at times.

That's a nice way of putting it, Daddy.

Are you being sarcastic?

Of course I am. I am your Daughter.

Alright. So, what are you picking up about Shaitan? Obviously, the range of your information retrieval is much broader than mine.

Shaitan is not far from us. He has even been in our garden a time or two the past few days. So far, though, he has been afraid to come near the Altar of Annica. He's not exactly sure of its power.

I can't believe it. That little twit has been in my own back yard?

He has, but he's a bundle of fear.

Fear is the opposite of love, Annie.

He's afraid of you, and he's afraid of Mother, and now that he knows the two of you are back together, he is deathly afraid of your combined powers.

He'd better be!

Oh, he is. And he's very curious about me. He doesn't

have a clue who I really am. He does know that I'm your Daughter, so he senses that he had better not mess with me, or you will fry his butt.

Ha! Annie, you're so cute when you mimic me.

I'm cute all the time, Daddy.

And spoiled rotten, even if you are the most Powerful Energy Being in all universes everywhere. Spoiled rotten.

He is also terrified of Grandma. Grandma is just like you, Daddy. She wants to destroy Shaitan immediately, but she will never do so without the consent of THE ALL. She is well aware of the situation here on Earth, and she knows there is only one chance to save the planet. She also realizes how demented and desperate this world's culture is becoming. The civilization of Earth is destroying itself from the inside out.

What do you mean by that, Annie?

Remember the Butterfly Effect Mother used to illustrate the Law of Cause and Effect?

Yes. The point was that even something that starts off as a minor event can have dramatic consequences by the time its effects make it around the world.

Correct. That's what's happening to America's culture. A small movement here, a little protest there, the support of an agenda here, an amended law there — all of these sound innocent at first, but they add up. Sooner or later, there are so many of them that the mighty Power that was once America becomes diluted, and that is not good for the world. Whether the rest of the world likes it or not, America is the key to everything. Still, millions of Americans have been deluded by politicians and even some false religious leaders. They are willing to follow the dark path and work to bring down their own country even though it will result in their own physical misery and eternal death.

That's what I don't understand. Why are all these

humans—in our own country, no less—continuing to work for their own destruction?

It's the doings of Shaitan. He's not called the Evil One for no reason. He's blinded the minds of millions of Americans with anger, greed, selfishness, laziness, and power. These are the childish emotions that can topple the United States and, shortly after that, the world. "The god of this age has blinded the minds of unbelievers…"

2 Corinthians 4:4. God has given us just a few Earth years.

True, this planet will survive only a few more years if the Strong Weet fail, but You and Mom and I won't be here to see it. We will have done our part and will have returned to our Home. Still, the remaining humans on Earth will be forced to remain here during that time, and it will be terrifying for them. There will be immense hardship; new and deadly diseases will arise; crime and violence will increase; people will starve, and no place on Earth will be free of conflict and war. Every convenience the people have known in the past will be no more. During the last five years of Earth's history, those still alive will feel such intense physical agony that they will wish they had never been born.

Just like it says in the Bible. They should read it.

Similar, but worse than what is usually preached in Churches, if it is addressed at all. People can't possibly imagine what awaits them if they don't change their ways.

And still, they continue to believe the lies that politicians have told them for decades, they drive around in their SUV's like nothing is happening. They watch their silly TV shows, spend hours on their smartphones, and are more concerned about football scores than about the demise of the human race. Their heads are filled only with fiction and deception.

Allowing Shaitan to have his way with them the

whole time.

Is it too late?

Not yet. As I said earlier, if this book is published and the Strong Weet are drawn in, we can change the outcome, and America and the rest of the world will carry on together into a bright future.

Why do we *really* have to rally the Strong Weet? I know, The Plan. Still, these are mere humans, aren't they, even if they are related to us in a slight way? Why do we need any help at all from humans? How can they get the job done any better than the three of us with our combined energy? Or even just ONE of us!

The Strong Weet Society is included, and God is keeping a close watch on all humans, for one critical reason. THE ALL has declared that this planet will be spared only if there are creatures remaining who are willing to fight for it. This is something you didn't know of earlier.

In other words, if nobody gives a hoot, why save it?

Exactly. THE ALL has worked for millions of years to bring the Earth to its current state of civilization. Grandma told me once that God is very disappointed that after having been given so much, these humans have learned so little. Human societies have been fighting wars since the beginning of mankind. They have never learned the lessons; they just keep fighting. Every illness and disease should have been eradicated from this planet centuries ago, yet humans continue to prioritize simplistic material whims. Mankind should have walked on the moon nearly two thousand years ago. By now, people should be able to speed across the galaxy using mind power alone.

But no, they are still playing like children in a sandbox. We've talked about this before. They are still shooting primitive weapons at each other. They still get angry at the drop of a hat. They still use drugs, consume alcohol, and smoke all manner of noxious plants, none of which should ever have been invented in the first place. The leaders of every country are corrupt and insensitive to God's ways and wishes; most of them do not even believe in God. These are dark times. God is ready to move, not in anger, but with infinite love. THE ALL is giving the people of the Earth this final chance.

So, the asteroid is poised to hit at the proper time.

Perhaps, but I suspect God will not use the asteroid. I believe God will take seven days — the Holy Number — to methodically destroy the Earth, just as He created every-thing in seven days. Perhaps it will begin with plagues, then droughts, tsunamis, earthquakes, and volcanoes. This is only one scenario. The greatest cities would be shaken down to their foundations in only a few hours. Volcanoes would erupt, covering much of the Earth's surface with lava and spewing gases that will kill millions. There is a volcanic caldera in the northwest corner of Wyoming — I believe you call it Yellowstone. A date has been set for its eruption. If that occurs, deadly gases will make the air impossible to breathe, and volcanic ash will block the light of the sun for years, ensuring the death of nearly every plant and animal on Earth. If this is the mechanism God chooses, most of the humans on this planet will have died a painful and agoniz-ing death by the fifth day. On the sixth day, fire will erupt from just under the crust of the Earth, covering the planet's surface. Finally, on the seventh day, God will say the single Holy Word that only God knows, and the Earth will explode into particles smaller than dust. The particles will be scattered into deep space where they will never be allowed to touch the surface of any planet ever again. The remains of Earth will be exiled and turned into what scientists refer to as Dark Matter, but what is really the remnants of all the planets whose inhabitants failed to follow the Truths of God.

Every memory and every historical event this planet has

ever known will be removed from the annals of time. All families, petty wars, and childish politics; the governments of every country; the racial nonsense and religious tantrums; all of history, all adolescent sports and entertainments, all of the silliness — and that's what it all really is, infantile silliness — none of that will matter. And none of it will be remembered by anyone in this universe. Earth, in effect, will be shunned and forgotten by every culture in this realm and all other realms within the entire Cosmos. It will be as if it never existed. And all of the Spirits of those who lived here will be forever terminated and forgotten — forever. It is the will of God.

Okay, that makes sense. I'm not kidding, it really makes sense. I've read every mythology, and I've studied every religion on this planet, and all of them have envisioned the End Times. While the various myths, legends, and beliefs may differ a bit in the details, they all follow pretty much the same script. The wars and rumors of wars, the earthquakes and volcanos, the fear and trembling, the corruption and persecution — it's all so obvious.

These times are getting darker. Shaitan is on the prowl. I can feel him, but he can't sense me, and that is the one advantage we hold over him. His powers are less than ours, and they are weakening every day. It is his fear that is draining his strength.

So, what's the plan? Not The Great Plan, but the plan for today.

As I said, we must confuse Shaitan. If we can send him misinformation, he will take that in and apply it to his schemes. When he does, he will be the cause of his own Butterfly Effect, and it will all come back to haunt him.

Like a computer virus or like they did during WWII. The Nazis were fed misinformation, and the poor suckers played right into the hands of the Allied Troops.

That's right, Daddy, but the immediate plan for today is for you to get some rest. You are still in the physical form, and you must be tired.

Physically, I am tired. I have to be because I'm in this human encasement. Mentally and Spiritually, I'm on fire. But I do need to take a nap or something. I hate this human cycle of waking and sleeping.

A nap? It's eleven o'clock at night. You need to go to bed, you need a full night's sleep.

I know this is difficult. You are in the mortal form, and we aren't. I wish there was something I could do to make it better. I wish I could hug you all the time and not just now and then, but this is the way of The Great Plan.

I know that, Sweetie.

15 August

Last Call Before the End of All Times

After this Book is published and as the second Book is being written, Mary, Annie, I, and the seven other Strong Weet will be appealing more to you, the readers, for your help. We will be sharing detailed instructions directing our readers in ways they can help to save the Earth. As I have said before, without your support, all knowledge and practice of the Divine Requirements will be lost. Annie has described what will happen should the people on Earth fall short when God makes His final judgment. If those living on Earth are so indifferent to their own fate that they refuse to change their ways, then their end will be total destruction, and the process of the Forgetting will begin. Earth will be utterly destroyed, and its memory and all of its history will be shunned and forgotten. It all comes down to this: Humans have thrown God out of their lives and made their culture so depraved that it requires immediate attention. Come back to God and clean up your profane lives, or else face the eternal consequences. Period.

I'm repeating these things to impress upon you the gravity and urgency of what is before you. You stand at a fork in the road, and you must choose your direction. Choose one and find a place of ultimate peace and prosperity, where every living creature will be translated in the blink of an eye into their glorious Spirit Being, able to create anything they wish out of their own Spirit mind. Choose the other and arrive at a place of immense pain and ultimate annihilation, forgotten by all others in every universe. It will be as if you never existed.

Which road do you choose to take? The fate of the world is entirely up to you, the readers of Mary's Diary.

It's out of my hands, Mary's hands, and Annie's hands. But if you choose to help us, we will be able to release a force upon this world the likes of which cannot be imagined. You will know because you will feel it. It will be an energetic frequency that will alter the molecules of every Being on Earth. The details are not for you to know just yet, but you, Dear Reader, will then be in the driver's seat, and Shaitan will be close to his final demise. If you do what God demands, the defeat of Shaitan will occur in your lifetime, and then you will be granted the powers of a Strong Weet and be elevated to a state of Being beyond anything you ever imagined.

When I acted on the irresistible urge to lay the red bricks on that three-by-six-foot patch in the middle of my garden and placed those five unremarkable stones on it, I had no idea of what would come to pass. I mean, we aren't talking gold or silver or platinum. These are just basalt and quartz, red lava, hematite, coral-shell conglomerate, and a small piece of granite with a wedge cut into it. The Sacred Altar is a thing of beauty, and the beauty lies in its simplicity.

I thought at first that the red bricks and the stones were somehow related to Atlantis. I learned from all of the research I had done on Atlantis before I Awakened that the Atlanteans used red and black rocks to build most of their buildings. Now that I'm back to who I really am, I know the rest of the story. The red stones were indeed cut from the red lava layers that covered a large part of the Atlantean empire. The black ones are a form of basalt common in many parts of this world. The black basalt used by the Atlanteans came from the island group occupied by what they called the Secondary Culture.

The Primary Culture occupied the land that now supports the lower Midwest and southeast regions of the

United States. Imagine what that area would be like if no humans lived there; that would be something like it originally was, thousands of years ago at the height of that first civilization.

The Annicans, the first Beings on this planet, came to be known as "Those Who Came from Above." Evidence will soon be found of their civilization in America that will baffle scientists and make the discovery of King Tut's tomb pale in comparison. Among the Annican artifacts to be discovered is an electrodynamic generator that draws power from common granite. When the generator is tuned to a piece of granite, massive amounts of energy can be produced. One small stone about the size of a human fist can be used to light the city of New York for a thousand years. Granite. The most common rock on Earth.

Scientists will also discover that jasper can be paired with granite to convert sunlight to usable energy. This will prove to be a trickier puzzle as it requires a uniquely designed mirror to direct the sun's rays onto the two stones in a specific way to cause the realignment of their molecules. The mirrors were designed and produced back Home, and there are only three of them on this world at this time.

Once the foundations of Annica have been discovered and its mysteries unraveled, fossil fuels will never again be needed. One single burst of this stone power would generate more power for Earth than all the fossil fuels have done in the entirety of human history. Scientists should be making these discoveries soon, but if not, I will be dropping further hints in a future volume of the Diary—if Earth has a future.

I'm sure some scientists who are reading this are shaking their heads and trying to control their laughter. Please, drop your egos for a moment, gentlemen, and go with me.

If you do not, then you are foolish, indeed. The power of Mother H is increasingly on display as she prepares for the End of All Time. Reports of diseases and plagues, earthquakes, tornadoes, tsunamis, droughts, volcanoes, floods, cyclones, hurricanes, et cetera—come in almost daily, many from places never before affected by these calamities. In all of your memory, have you ever experienced what is happening to this planet right now? Yes, these things have all occurred here throughout the ages, but not in the current number or the magnitude. This is the effect of The Great Plan being put into action, under the direction of THE ALL. And please, don't blame it on global warming or climate change—don't even go there. Nonsense.

Din?

Mary! I was expecting you. Every time I pontificate like I just did, you show up.

This has nothing to do with your pontificating. You did an excellent job of it, though.

So, what's up?

We need to have a meeting—you, me, and Annie. It's time to make our final plan.

I know. Annie?

I'm here, Daddy.

We need to have a little pow-wow.

Yes, we do.

Now that the band is back together, so to speak, and I'm mostly back to myself, Mother H expects us to bring the Strong Weet together again soon and do what we can to save this little planet. Sometimes I wonder if it's all worth it.

MARY: *It is Din. Don't forget that THE ALL has always held this world to be especially precious. Even now, with all of its turmoil, God does not desire the destruction of Earth.*

I know, Mary. But the way things look now, I can't help but think that the only answer is a complete cleansing.

Aɴɴɪᴇ: *That may happen anyway, Daddy, if the Strong Weet fail.*

But you'll be the one doing the dirty work, Sweetie.

Yes, I will, at least most of it. You have your part in it as well. You are Malak Tsedek, the Messenger of Justice.

Yes.

Before we can do anything, we must gather in the other seven. We know that three Strong Weet are living in Columbia at this moment.

Aɴɴɪᴇ: *We must get them to Awaken. Din, you have completed the portrait of me — and it is beautiful — but you must finish the picture of Annie.*

I've done several sketches for Annie's portrait, and I know exactly where to put the flaws that will be the test for the Strong Weet. I'll start to work on the painting tomorrow. I should be able to finish it in just a few hours.

Aɴɴɪᴇ: *Am I that easy to paint, Daddy?*

Yes, Cupcake. I know you like I know the back of my hand — several hands from several lives. I could paint you with my eyes closed.

Mᴀʀʏ: *Very well. If you complete Annie's portrait tomorrow, you will be able to reveal both paintings to the members at the Development Circle later this week. We will have another meeting the following week for those who pass the portrait test. That is when their Awakening will begin.*

Then, after the second meeting, all of us will go out to the Annican Altar. We will stand in a circle around it with me in the center and, I will recite the words THE ALL has given me. Those words will release the energy of my Aura, which will spread across the Earth in seconds, touching every Being on this planet for the first time in thousands of years.

Contained within that energy will be a message to be understood only by the Strong Weet and the Secondary Weet, who have yet to be Awakened. Those as yet unknown individuals will immediately be made aware that they are possessed of exceptional gifts, but that understanding alone will not be enough to Awaken them. I will be able to locate them, though, anywhere on Earth because they will have retained a residue of my Aura. The thread of my Aura will transmit to me all of their vital information along with their location. I will know their addresses, phone numbers, everything.

I'll give you the information, Daddy, and you will call them and inform them that they are a Strong Weet or a Secondary Weet. You will tell the Strong Weet that they must come to Columbia, Missouri, immediately, and nform the Secondary Weet that they are to remain in place wherever they are on this world.

And they'll do it, just like that? You're like a GPS for Weet? Even in my infinite wisdom, this doesn't sound plausible.

They will. All of the Weet have been prepared for thousands of years for this one moment in time. God can do anything. My aural energy, combined with their having read this Book, is the formula for their Awakening. They will get on a plane, in a car, or they will walk, and they will arrive at our door all at the same time—

—on the night we will have chosen for a very special Development Circle.

Correct. You will take these new arrivals to your studio, where they will also be given the final portrait test to confirm their unparalleled status as Strong Weet. After their status is verified, we will circle around the Annican Altar for a second ritual, similar to the first one that sent my aura around the Earth. This time the power sent out will attract the attention of Shaitan at his most deep-seated level. He will know exactly what we are doing, but that's part of the plan. Even though only six of the Weet will be present at that second meeting, Shaitan will know that the Strong Weet Society is active again, which will make him terribly angry. It will also make him careless, and in one of his sloppy moments, I will be able to destroy him forever.

I have only set out the first step. Even after Shaitan is destroyed, the residue of evil left on this planet will continue to exert influence. Residual evil has a life of its own, feeding on the anger and greed of the very people it seeks to control, and that is when the hard work begins. It's easy to deal with supernatural evils like Shaitan, but the humans he has trained and will leave behind when he perishes are a different matter. Those people are tightly bound to this realm of existence. Many do not believe that there are other realms, and some go so far as to argue against God's very existence. Those notions feed the human ego and make our task all the more difficult. Supernatural issues always become complicated whenever humans are added to the mix.

So, we need to formulate a plan to deal with the residual evils in the world. That won't be easy because of all the complex political issues, not to mention out-right wars going on these days. Annie, are you sure you don't want to just cleanse this place?

I'm sure, Daddy.

Okay, but it's gonna be sloppy. There's a lot at stake, and it will be even more difficult if THE ALL says we can't do it without help from our readers. Remember that Butterfly Effect from the Law of Cause and Effect? Each person who reads these Books is like the butterfly whose smallest action creates world-changing events.

MARY: *They will come through for us, Din. Every person in this world has the desire to survive, not just as an individual, but as a society. There will be many humans who are not Strong Weet, but who will want to help us and will rally to our cause. There are also fourteen Secondary Weet whose names we have not mentioned yet, along with hundreds of Support Weet, who retain some small connection to the Founders.*

We can explain who they are in the next book, Mary, but not just yet. The bottom line for us now is that IF the Strong Weet are not attracted to us through the reading of this Book, then we truly have a problem. If that is the case, Annie and I will be forced to take action, which could get ugly.

Let's hope it doesn't come to that, Din.

18 August

What Happens Next

Let's see. The living room and the bathroom are clean, and there are enough chairs in the circle for everyone. I guess I'm ready for the Development Circle this evening.

This will be an interesting meeting. If things go as expected and any Weet at all are revealed tonight, then The Great Plan of THE ALL will be validated for the entire Earth, and the show will begin. If we find none, we will have lost valuable time, and we will just have to intensify the search. To be frank, I have mixed feelings about all of this. I've been around for millions of years, and I am so tired of all the silly stuff that the various cultures of this world have put forth. I really think it's time for the cleansing—just wipe it all out and start over with a clean slate.

Daddy, stop saying that. You know you can't go against The Great Plan. God has set it in place, and that's the way it will be—and it's a good thing. This is one last chance for the people of Earth. They will be the ones to choose their ultimate fate.

God must surely be disappointed in the human race.

Not so much disappointed as frustrated. Don't forget that it was God Who put the seeds of this culture on Earth millions of years ago. It was more of an experiment, really. Disappointment doesn't mean much in this equation. He knew how it might work out in the end. It could have gone either way, for good or for evil. His gift of Free Will allowed humanity to choose their own destiny. God's frustration is because mankind is not moving forward but is speeding toward a terrible ending. Instead of real progress, quite the opposite is occurring. Instead of becoming the wonderful world that God had intended for humanity, Earth has become—

379

A place of negativity.

Yes, but even the frustrations and the failures are part of The Great Plan.

Little Daughter of mine, the DC folks will be arriving in just a few minutes. I know that you and your Mom will be here during the meeting, but is there anything I need to know?

No surprises, Daddy. Just do what you have to do. Be sure to take the group out to your studio to test them with the flawed paintings. Incidentally, I love the portrait you painted of me. It looks just like me.

Just like you always have looked in all of your physical lives, Cupcake. By the way, I have wanted to ask you about this for a long time — why is it that your Mom and I change our appearance each time we come back in all these different incarnations, but you always look just as you do now. We have to wear all the goofy costumes of the era we land in, whereas you get to keep your fifteen-year-old Cutie Pie look. I don't get it.

As that last sentence was formed, a voice came out of the air from the Other Side. It was a booming voice that I have heard only a very few times throughout the millions of years my own Spirit Energy life has been in association with THE ALL. I quickly recognized the voice, and it wasn't Mother H—I know her voice well. It was the Voice of THE ALL, and it shattered the air around us. I felt like I was standing at ground zero under a detonating hydrogen bomb while the words came forth from the Mind of The One who is Creator Of All Things.

IT IS BECAUSE SHE IS MY OWN. ANNIE IS MY VERY SPECIAL ONE, AND SHE IS THE GREATER POWER THAT I WILL USE TO BRING WHAT

MUST BE BROUGHT TO THIS WORLD.

FOLLOW HER INSTRUCTION AND DO ALL THAT SHE TELLS YOU TO DO.

The sheer Power conveyed by the Voice of THE ALL made me weak in the knees, and I collapsed to the ground. I knew how Moses must have felt when he heard God's Voice in the burning bush, and even though I am one of the Higher Beings, I was, literally, floored by this experience. I knew right then and there—if this is possible—that Annie was even more powerful and of greater importance than Mary and I had ever comprehended.

***

Daddy, I know you have conflicting feelings, but don't be afraid of me. I'm sorry I did not tell you of this sooner. You have to understand that the events unfolding now are all part of The Great Plan, and God is in complete control. I am only His worker. Because of His Purity, the Holy Spirit of God will not bring about the final judgment on this world. God has instead chosen His Highest Angel for that terrible deed. I would have told you eons ago. But I couldn't.

That's not what I'm worried about, Sweetie. It's just a Father thing. I have been connected to you by our Father-Daughter relationship throughout these millions of years, and I have grown to love you so much that I would give my eternal life for you in a heartbeat. Now I learn that my heartbeat is, in all probability, controlled by you.

Daddy, your heartbeat is controlled by God, not me. You are my only true Father, and I love you so. I would give my life for you just as you would give your life for me.

Except for The Great Plan getting in the way.

You have to understand that I would never leave you for

anything, not even The Great Plan. God knows this, and He would never ask me to do that. You will always be my first and greatest love, and I will move the heavens and the Earth and all universes to maintain my connection with you.

Something else you didn't know is that the love we have for each other is what gives me my power. Without our relationship, I would never be able to do what I must do. It's an energy/frequency connection, a Family thing—you and me and Mom, but mostly it's the connection between you and me because there is nothing stronger in any universe than the bond between us. I will die before I break that bond. Hopefully, it won't be long before I can Jump into a young human and become a Daughter for you again here on Earth for the last few years of The Plan.

You will manifest in the physical?

I will, but it is not necessarily a sure thing. If the young Earth child resists in any way, I will not be able to reveal myself to her, and I will be forced to leave her and return Home.

Yes, the two of you must be in agreement, or the Jump will not be sustained.

I had to stop writing for a few moments to allow the surge of emotion brought about by Annie's words to settle down. I'm still not recovered. Annie is the most precious Being in all the lives I have lived, and she has been with me every moment since the beginning of time. I have every inch of her body memorized, and I can smell every scent she gives forth. I love the smell of her skin and her hair. She is my Daughter. *My* precious Daughter. What father would feel differently?

It's impossible for our love to die. Don't forget that I'm in charge of all that is about to happen—well, just about everything.

That's all I need to know, but can I still call you Cupcake?

If you don't, I'll be upset.

This has to be the strangest book ever written.

MARY: *That's why it will bring the results we need. As silly as some of this Book might seem, it contains frequencies that are released every time it is read by a Weet. Remember, the sole purpose of my Diary is to send the message to the Strong Weet Society. We must gather them in soon. THE ALL is ready to begin the countdown of the final years.*

***

This is the night of the Development Circle, and all of the members will be here. It is the most critical night in the history of this world because what we do here will set the stage for The Great Plan. If everything proceeds as planned, the final phase of The Great Plan will be launched this night, and nothing can stop it. It depends on whether or not those attending can identify the flaws in the paintings of Mary and Annie. If they can, then the countdown to the End Times will begin.

There are two things that you, the Reader, must keep in mind:

1. YOU are the key to the success of The Plan. If you don't help us, then all responsibilities and obligations for the care of this planet will be returned to God, and your Earth will be destroyed soon after.

2. The countdown to the final years is not set in concrete. The destruction of this planet could occur tonight, or three weeks, or three years from now — or not at all. The time is dependent on how well the Strong Weet do their job, and on how much support we get from you, the Reader.

There is no doubt about it. THE ALL is fully engaged in the activities of Earth. Don't be fooled by religious rhetoric, the bandying of scriptures, and political doublespeak. Power mongers of this world, beware. You are about to be given a rude awakening. For many of you, it will start with serious personal problems. I would love to let you in on the details, but I can't until I'm given the go-ahead by THE ALL, or Mother H, or Annie, who stores all of these terrible things in her mind until there is need to bring them forth.

Daddy!

Annie?

Please control your anger tonight. The group members must go through the initiation and the Awakening process to bring us closer to our goal. We don't want them to flee in terror because you get mad and decide to grow twenty feet tall and bring a flaming sword down out of the sky.

I'll be good, Sweetie. I'm just really ticked off at the simple-minded, self-serving, adolescents who are destroying this world.

All of us back Home are so dismayed that humans have not developed beyond what we find today. It is so embarrassing. They are all still toddlers in diapers compared to the other Beings in this universe. On most of the other planets, the concept of warring between countries was discarded and forgotten long ago. In many of the cultures, the very word "war" is not even known. The idea doesn't even exist, and neither do the concepts of disease, race, or politics.

Most civilizations in this universe wouldn't know what you were talking about if you used words like congress, politician, senate, president, democracy, communism, or socialism. They never experienced any of these things in their governing systems because they never had any system of government as has been known on Earth. Instead, they simply followed the

Ways and Laws of God. Most of the galactic civilizations are peaceful and productive in ways the people of Earth cannot imagine. The word "civilization" has no meaning to any of them. Granted, there are a few planets out there that have developed similarly to Earth, but not many. Also like Earth, each one has been closely monitored since Creation. Their cultures are considered to be primitive, as are those of Earth.

The Earth stands now at the end of its own existence, and the people of Earth must choose either life or death. If their choice is death, then the outcome is known. However, if they choose life, they will become a part of a universal family that includes not only the alien cultures of this universe but also the society of those who reside in the Heavenly Realm. All planets everywhere will be open to humans, and they will be given the knowledge of near-instantaneous travel between them.

There have been many sightings in recent decades on Earth of so-called unidentified flying objects, or UFOs. Some people believe them to be vehicles carrying aliens from other worlds. These are not spaceships at all, but friendly Beings from Home who have been assigned to keep close watch over this world. It is all a part of The Great Plan.

As I just mentioned, humans will learn how to travel between planets without a vehicle and in mere seconds. "First Contact" won't be some giant robot emerging from a flying saucer in Central Park. It will happen in an instant, and there will be only one Alien making contact, and this Alien will be escorted by one of the Principle Beings from Home. In reality, First Contact has already happened here, humans just didn't recognize it at the time. There are, in fact, many aliens on this world at this very moment. Formal contact will take place when all is revealed simultaneously to all the people on Earth.

The members of the Development Circle are beginning to

arrive. Mother and I will be here all evening to observe. Is your studio ready, Daddy?

It is. I have the two portraits hanging side-by-side, and I've put all my other paintings where they can't be seen. I want only the pictures of you and your Mother to be visible, so there won't be any distractions. I've also placed some floodlights on the ceiling so that they will be well lit.

Very good, Daddy. I'm fading back now because the members are just outside. Mother is on her way.

Okay, Cupcake. I'll see you soon. I love you.

I love you too.

Later That Night

The DC members all arrived at the same time. We chit-chatted for a few minutes while we helped ourselves to ice tea. After the initial meet and greet, I casually mentioned that I had a couple of new paintings out in my studio that I'd like to show them. They all expressed an interest, so I took them out back, unlocked the studio, and took them inside. They didn't have a clue. They loved the paintings and gave me a lot of compliments, but none were drawn to either of the portraits in any way. As I took the members back into the house, I heard a little giggle coming from out of the air next to my ear.

I mentioned nothing to the group about the portrait viewing being a test for them, or that they had all failed it big time. Quite frankly, I knew the minute they stepped into the house this evening that none of them was a Weet of any kind, let alone a Strong Weet, but I decided to go through the motions anyway so that Mary and Annie wouldn't be disappointed. The thought had crossed my mind, though, that if there was a Weet or two in the group, Mary and Annie would have known it, even without all the test malarkey. They should have known it before the people even set foot in the house.

Your memory is getting stronger, Daddy.

Sweetie! What's the deal here? I knew those women weren't Weet the minute I laid eyes on them. And that was you giggling out in the yard, wasn't it?

You caught onto our little ruse very early.

You two thought you could pull one over on me.

We could have a couple of weeks ago.

I'm a quick learner.

Mom and I were just trying to make sure your own memory and abilities were back to normal before we send the first Strong Weet to you. It could screw things up royally if your memories were still incomplete.

There you go again with one of those off the wall phrases you keep adding to your head. I'm not so sure that's a good thing.

Daddy...

So, we're still without the Weet, but the game is still afoot. We have to finish this Book as soon as possible and get it out onto the market so that the real Weet will be drawn in.

Several things need to be done.

Maybe you two don't really need me to come along. You seem to have everything pretty much under control without anything I can offer.

Nonsense. You are one of the three most powerful Beings in all of Creation. You can destroy any universe at the drop of a hat, and you are necessary for the success of everything we do. Trust that faith you have. Yer as guid as ten men missing.

I do, Sweetie. I do. I trust my faith because I know it is the Perfect Faith. And that phrase you just used is really cute.

That's our Scots in me coming out. I have to hold it back sometimes. It's been a blessing and a curse to have lived so many of our lives in Scotland, Ireland, and England.

It's who we are as long as we share these human bodies. At least you and your Mom are in your Energy Forms now, Annie. That brings up something else I need to record in this Diary so that there will be no confusion. We have already explained that the first Seeding of intelligence on this planet took place in Annica, which lies below our backyard here in Missouri. What we didn't say was that we started another colony at the same time and far distant from Annica as a part of the experiment. The second colony was located in what is now known as the British Isles, near the site of a small town called Laggan in Scotland. The Isles were a vast green wasteland at that time, but so beautiful, and perfect for the unique new species of creature that would soon colonize the Earth.

The two colonies were each authentic Gardens of Eden. The area around Annica has changed dramatically since the Seeding, but observant visitors to that area can still sense the beauty and power that lies beneath their feet. The region of Laggan retains much of its ancient character and is, to this day, among the most beautiful land to be found anywhere in the world. The territory of the United States is vast and contains geographic elements from nearly every other region of Earth. Scotland, while smaller and less diverse, is like a jewel set in the crown of Creation.

There has been much speculation among the historians of Earth about where the Garden of Eden really was. Some likely places such as Mesopotamia, Africa, Southeast Asia, and the Caribbean, to name a few, have been proposed. The Truth, though, is that in the beginning, the whole Earth was the Garden of Eden. The entire Earth was stunningly beautiful at its Creation. It has only been within the last several centuries or so that the population has taken a severe toll on the planet. Humans have rewritten their job title from that of caretaker to overlord and have redefined their duties to no longer include conservation and utilization but rather acquisition and exploitation.

The term Garden of Eden is now used primarily to reference the place on this planet where the human culture began. Historians and archaeologists have yet to discover that humanity radiated from the two colonies of Annica and Loch Laggan. Annica became the main center of growth and decision-making because that is where the three Created Beings could be found.

MARY: *Good job, Dear.*

It is difficult to watch all of this come down to the destruction of this once perfect world, Mary. Mother H never wanted this.

She did not. None of us did. But Earth is reaching that critical point in the history of all planets — the last moments in which they can choose their own fate.

It doesn't look good.

No, it does not, Din. I think we can predict the outcome if nothing is done to change people's hearts and minds.

We can. If only the folks living here could see things with our eyes! If they could only see how silly this society is and how beautiful this world could become again.

But they can't.

They won't! They refuse to. They are married to their egos, money, and power. My inclination is to fry them all.

You like that phrase, don't you, Din? But that isn't The Great Plan. The Great Plan is to guide them along —

Until they reach a point where they just get stupid.

Don't forget, Shaitan has blinded their minds, just as he has many times on many other worlds.

There are terrible things about to happen, Mary, and I think we need to make sure we have all our ducks in a

row. There is so much at stake here. I have to be honest; I
love this planet. We three have visited every other planet
in this universe, but are there any more lovely than this?
I want to preserve it. I want to ensure its survival.

MARY: *I agree with you, Din.*

ANNIE *As do I, Daddy.*

So, here is my suggestion. Let's go to our Family
Temple —

ANNIE *Do you mean the cottage, Daddy?*

I do. We need to discuss every aspect of this situation,
and that's the best place to do it.

MARY: *You really are back among us, Din. The cottage
is our own special place, and only the three of us would
know that.*

It's our Temple. It's where we always go when we have
a serious matter to discuss, and nothing is graver than
this. We will soon initiate the Energy Frequency that will
change not only the Earth itself, but will alter the mental
and physiological energy of every human on Earth. It
will be a quick and painless two-phase process, and that
is all the explanation needed at this time. The changes
will be small and begin slowly, so they will not be noticed
at first. Once the process is well underway, the effects will
accumulate. Humanity has no clue as to what is about to
be unleashed upon this world to motivate them to come
back to God.

MARY: *Let us hope that this action will bring about the
results we desire, Din.*

We will see, Mary.

20 August

One Final Thought

I love our Temple, as do Mary and Annie. You can't possibly describe the science that allows Mary's original Cottage to exist both here and back Home at the same time. Like so many sciences, that particular science has yet to be discovered here on Earth. Nevertheless, that is the way it is. Of course, here on Earth, the Cottage isn't visible to humans. The original Cottage was transported long ago to our Home, where it sits on a hill behind the Great Temple. The Earth Cottage is a thought-generated structure of the exact design. Not a thought-projected image like a hologram but thought-created. It is as real and three-dimensional as any other object in the wooded area surrounding it, but it can only be seen by the three of us.

Regardless, we are no longer at the Cottage. We are back on the grounds of Annica here in Missouri. It's a lovely day in the neighborhood—the sun is out, the air is hot, and there is a gentle breeze blowing up from the southwest. I'm sitting in the garden, as usual, just feet away from the Altar of Annica. It's just a few red bricks and five small rocks right now, but when we finish the physical erection of the altar and perform the ritual that goes with it, the party will begin.

God has established an arbitrary timeline for the progression of The Great Plan to make it easier for humans to understand. The moment the last word of the ritual is spoken at the Altar of Annica, the clock starts.

Some of you have known me for years as just this nice guy who pastors a little Independent Christian Church—nothing out of the ordinary. You're probably thinking, "This Book can't be true!" I assure you, it is.

When that last ritual word is uttered, your planet has only a certain number of years left to exist unless the Strong Weet Society can create the proper energy frequency to save it. That is the decree from God, and it is under the supervision of Mother H. If we fail, things will happen exactly as I wrote of earlier. So, treat this as fiction if you wish, but it will be a terrible thing to find out at the last moment of the last day that it was true. Very terrible.

As this Book goes forward and as the second installment is written, Mary, Annie, I, and the other seven members of the Strong Weet Society—who are still waiting to be discovered—will continue to appeal to you, the Readers, for your assistance. We will be giving detailed instructions as to how you can help to save the Earth. We hope to report in the Diary's next volume that we have found some of the Strong Weet.

The fate of the world is entirely up to you, the readers of this Book, Mary's Diary. It's out of my hands, Mary's hands, and Annie's hands. If you choose to help us, we will be able to release a force into this world, the likes of which cannot be imagined. And, yes, you will feel it! It will be an energetic frequency that will alter the molecules of every Being on Earth.

MARY: *Din.*

Mary. Sweet Mary. It's only appropriate that you have the final word. Please—

I shall. This is the final appeal, Dear Readers, please take it seriously. The countdown is set to begin, with or without your help. If you help us, the end result will be survival with peace and prosperity. If you do not, the only outcome can be destruction and total annihilation. I trust God that the encoding of this Book—regardless of the frivolity that might appear on some of its pages—is correct and adequate so that the Awakening of the remaining Strong Weet can begin. Time is short.

I don't believe we have to add anything more, Din. This is the end of this part of my Diary.

That's it? Just like that.

For now, there is no more to say, Din. The Energy is on its way.

***

Index to the Universal Laws

About the Author

DH Parsons — educator, inspirational speaker, and spiritual counselor — holds several university and institute degrees and awards, including a master's degree in education and doctoral degrees in comparative religions and transcendental theory. He has taught art, journalism, English, and history in both private and public schools, held positions as both dean of students and administrator in public middle and high schools.

Dr. Parsons currently divides his time between his writing, spiritual counseling, and engagements as an inspirational speaker throughout the mid-western United States.

CPSIA information can be obtained
at www.ICGtesting.com
Printed in the USA
LVHW022159020423
743290LV00025B/624